FLIGHT

First Edition

FLIGHT

a Quantum Fiction novel

VANNA BONTA

MERIDIAN HOUSE

MERIDIAN HOUSE
6755 Mira Mesa Blvd. Dept 123-224
San Diego, CA 92121-4311

Design by White Light Publishing
Manufactured in the United States of America

10 9 8 7 6 5 4 3 2 1

ACKNOWLEDGEMENTS: Lyric excerpts from "DREAM LOVER" by:
Bobby Darin ©1959 Trio Music Co., Inc. and Alley Music Corp. (Renewed)
All right reserved. Used by permission. Lyric excerpts from "NIGHTS IN WHITE
SATIN", Words and Music by Justin Hayward, © 1967, 1968, and 1970 Tyler
Music Ltd., London, England TRO - Essex Music, Inc. New York, controls all
publication rights for the U.S.A. and Canada. Used by permission.

Library of Congress Catalog Card Number: 94-93844

Bonta, Vanna
Flight : A Quantum Fiction Novel
Summary: Author creates a new genre on the frontiers of scientific discovery that
thought affects matter. Introducing new super-heroes Aira Flight, Mendle Orion,
and Onx. Mystery and action-adventure romance in the Space Age. Writer Mendle
J. Orion believes it is his dream come true when a woman resembling the character
in his latest novel mysteriously appears in his life. The stranger has amnesia.

ISBN: 0-912339-10-1

For A.J.

Which came first—

the observer or the particle?

Everything solid was first

an idea.

Flight

PROLOGUE

Once before Time, beings did not have bodies.

A way

I cradle forests in my arms,
mist-laden green laced with
pine and rain scents and
symphonic overtones understones,
branches danced in trills.

If you found my eyes,
in an instant
my body would disappear,
You might be breathing sea air,
your vision full with
waves and blue horizons.
Curled white
caps foaming
and rainbows in every molecule.

If you found my eyes...between the instant,
everything around us would vanish.

We would be home.
In brilliant strands of stars
wisped in violet;
Solar systems

the mere distance between our eyes,
our arms even longer.

Our laughter would first be
a thousand brilliant buoyant balloons.
It would dissolve,
full and pressing.
It would leak outside the last wall.

We would go with it,
beyond the last perimeter.

If we chose to have hands,
we might find Earth resting
on our little finger.
We could focus on anything, play anything!

We could slide down the spiral
back into streams of stars and suns
past skies and birds and

splash back into our eyes,
exude as a smile.

∞

We have long gone past knowing walls are not solid. In a universe of perfect relativity, harmony, and mathematics, it should be no surprise that there is specific, scientific reason for all we think, for who we meet and love, for what we do and dream, and for everything that unfolds in our lives. True love transcends time, death, and even the material world. Perhaps the only impossible thing for those who love is to be apart. Our thought affects the physical world much more than we realize. The illusion is that we are only physical.

chapter

The dust stream was spectacular. The top of the strata glowed mauve, and the bottom plane, illuminated by the two suns of Nestralil, flickered silver-gold against the blackness.

Particles, Aira thought. She pushed the glide-moderator and the relocation device cut its projection-time in half, slowing down her craft's passage through the area. *Only particles,* her thought continued.

She stared through her portal at the clouds and the silence. Retracting her resentment from the particles which were creating space and distance around her, she looked inward in puzzlement. *Why can't I just **know** where he is?*

It had been two spirals since she had seen Jorian. Though Life and manifestation continued, the beauty she now witnessed through her portal reminded her of him, bringing all things connected with him to her present consideration.

They had enjoyed Beauty together.

She and Jorian had always sensed each other—even when their forms were separated by space and surrounding particles created different locations. They touched even when they were not touching, physical-space distance was no barrier. Jorian did not have to be present for her to feel him.

Along with his unexplained disappearance, since he no longer manifested himself to her, or to any One, there was also a total absence of any sense of him whatsoever. She could not feel him any more. Terror, she remembered. Danger. An excruciating conflict...then everything had become confusing.

Again Aira tried to sort through it. She had been on her way to Trilton at the time. She had been considering him, pleasuring in recollecting what they had created together just before she left on that mission. They had manifested themselves into light-bodies and created sensation in one another, impelled rapturous admiration to each other. The admiration was sublime, to be so totally loved and wanted. No, it was beyond desire. Admiration. Showers of it.

Aira could *dao*, she could grant life and complete love. No other being she knew had ever been able to match her ability to do so...except Jorian. He witnessed and knew her entirety. Others could *dao*, she recognized, but she and Jorian adored each other.

They had projected to Sarafee, the small, abandoned planet of water and plant life. There she permeated all foliage and became an entire woodland. He became the rain and showered on her. As mist and rain, he caressed her and quenched her many leaves. She swirled into a rainbow. He became the sky and she unfurled in him. How she loved to give him joy!

Aira was half-point on her mission to Trilton as she recollected this. She thought-sent Jorian her happiness, but did not sense receipt. Even when he was in full attention elsewhere, he always welcomed whenever she thought-reached to him. So she tried to project again. It was then that she felt it, that cold feeling of sheer terror. It was almost electrical. Pure agony.

Still, she projected despite the feeling, but ran into mirrored reflections of her own thought. Then, another sensation...currents between poles...and more terror... and a spin of confusion.

She had withdrawn then, and wondered what was wrong. Since her thoughts were involved in the new Knowledge she was delivering to Trilton, she thought perhaps she hadn't successfully located Jorian but, by accident, had picked up some skirmish on the periphery of an Aberree colony. Perhaps she had been distracted or wasn't concentrating.

Giving herself these explanations, she rechanneled her attention and regauged his location. Pushing aside all other thought, she tried to reach him again, to send him her joy, to *dao* him. Then...nothing. Simply nothing.

The recollection opened the lid of concern. She still didn't understand. It was incomprehensible.

Jorian! she now called out silently to him. *Jorian!*

Nothing.

She ached to simply feel his life and being. Even if he did not communicate, she needed just to sense him, to know he was being, to know he was.

Juristac and the others at the Tribunal had advised her that Jorian most probably had decided to manifest somewhere without her since he had no agreements which bound him. She knew this was not true; their bond far surpassed even obligation.

Many did not understand love as she and Jorian had known it. Beyond it being what they both wanted, it was simply such pure affinity that it was an unquestionable condition. Jorian would never create stark absence, not intentionally.

Now she wondered about that but, after allowing the doubt to linger, discarded it. Yes, she could consider it was possible, but no, even if Jorian had simply wanted to go, he would have told her, or she would have sensed it. That would have been all right.

But nothing? It was difficult to confront nothing.

Mendle J. Orion leaned back from his computer. His back hurt. He gave it his attention long enough to carefully, slowly, painfully rotate his shoulders, then, his heart beating faster to the pace of Aira Flight's life, he was back into the screen.

Whereas his writing had been painful in the past, this novel was different. It was he who lived in the girl's heart. He was the one she was looking for.

Jorian! she now called out silently to him. *Jorian!*

Mendle reread his words. He felt the silent, desperate calling out with his very being. *I'm here, I'm here!* If only someone loved him like that.

He could see her now, he could touch her. Well, almost. It was becoming an ache, the longing that she would walk through the door. *Walk through the door, yes!* He challenged the derisive self-doubts that perched like vultures, and looked up at the door, his eyes readjusting, having to refocus on the room.

Then he sighed, reeling himself in just a little, just enough to continue.

He inhaled and exhaled, deliberately, making contact again with her world as he scanned the words he had just written. Picking up his cup was automatic, the semi-cold coffee on his tongue distant as he read his words on the computer screen, getting a running start on the leap forward.

He longed for her. She understood him. Her eyes smiled back knowingly at him. She knew his fabric, his thoughts and delights. *Angel, nymph, genius,* he touched her in his mind, *yet vulnerable.*

He shuffled through her descriptions, through his images of her. He touched her in her cabin as she traveled in space. Every word brought her closer to him. "Aira. Aira Flight," he murmured her name *sotto voce.* His soul chanted more than the name, it chanted the élan vital of balm to every instance of abuse, rejection and noncomprehension he had ever received.

When she was physical, her eyes were…it was her, the perfect woman of his dreams. She looked just as he knew she would always look, when she looked back into his eyes and understood him.

Aira had a sensor-mate on her missions, a dragon, *yes, a miniature dragon,* an archaic pet-form which traveled with her. Its name was…*its name is…*

Onx unfurled her blue wings and yawned, more because she liked the sensation than because she needed to inhale atmosphere. She blinked the limpid eyes which comprised most of her face and looked up from the cabin floor at Aira. Smoke curled lazily from her nostrils as she gestated the situation: her master was emanating sadness and aching with loss. Having sympathy-locked with Aira, the miniature dragon was feeling it also.

E-motion affected Onx differently than Aira, however, because even though they both had quasi-condensed forms, Aira's was less solid. Aira manifested herself in light bodies. Even though the light images with which she made herself visible to others were affected by her thought, she was in complete control of her manifestations, of how they appeared, and the forms had no life of their own.

Onx's form, however, was permanently condensed. She liked it that way. Her body-system had involuntary responses and demands of its own, most of which she enjoyed. Satiating hunger and fatigue—those were good ones. The sensation of the wind brushing her when she was in flight. Even this one, the sympathy she felt for Aira, she felt it in her heart and stomach, and tears began to well in her eyes.

"Onx," Aira chided upon seeing the tears brimming in the creature's eyes. "Don't cry for me."

Aira was looking at her now. Onx raised herself to her haunches and looked attentively back at her. She liked it when Aira communicated via sound-symbols. Her tones were rounded and soft, the noise-symbols like wind and water. Even when she gave commands, her voice contained a breath that was vaporous yet fierce and strong, like the winds of space. Before the sound-symbols, which took time to travel though distance, it was always Aira's thought-concept which Onx received first. She liked it nonetheless when Aira spoke because, even though she pre-knew what the voice-sounds would mean, she enjoyed their mellifluous tones.

Aira was usually golden when she manifested, a halo of light outlining the illusion she projected as herself. She wasn't beaming now, however. As she longed for and puzzled over Jorian, she had reds and blues in her peripheral energy zone.

Sympathy-locked with Aira, Onx had to admit this was exciting, this sadness. *E-motion!*

The dragon complacently nestled into the comfort of her existence. Her duties were simple and, even though Aira suspected that she was much more aware than she let on, Onx was allowed a predictable existence of basic responsibility such as sensory watch-duty. Other than this, she was relatively care-free.

"I wouldn't wish my feelings on anyone," Aira expressed, directing her attention back to the ship's controls.

Onx felt momentary shame that she had been enjoying a minus-thought. It was neither Aira's anguish nor her loss that had given her a thrill, however. It was the sensation, purely and simply.

Aira called it "E-motion". It was particles, too, flows of them, definable according to their vibration ratio. Some swirled, some emanated, some were standing waves, seemingly in the very center of the stomach. Aira sought to be its cause, to emanate E-motion at will, to utilize it for perception purposes, but Onx was content to experience it with abandon. She loved it. She could wing and glide and submerge and float on whatever E-motion pattern happened to activate.

Onx wondered why Aira didn't enjoy being the effect of E-motion, and why she continually decided the course of things. What was the fun of that, of being responsible, of employing reason in the creation of future?

But I love Aira just as she is. Onx sighed, watching the life-being at the control board. *I would do anything to protect her well-being.*

As Aira expertly completed maneuvers on the board,

Onx felt the surge-shift through the ship as the nucleus-transfer jolted them into Normal Mode Relocation. *We're going home.*

Her back to the dragon, Aira said, "We're going home, Onx." She watched the scintillating dust strata disappear into distance, then turned and looked at her companion. "But you knew that, didn't you?" she asked twinkling with smiles. She knew Onx had received her thought before she spoke it.

The dragon briefly flickered sparks from her mouth to display her pleasure. *I want you to be in happiness,* she concept-flowed to Aira. *Decide you will find him.* Aira always said that a decision was the most powerful element there was.

"But so much experience has transpired," Aira bemoaned, wishing Jorian had been present to share it. "It has been so long. And there is an alteration blocking the truth of this. There must be something I'm not viewing...or cannot view. Because it persists, and won't resolve."

Thought-reaching to him again, Aira hit up against nothing. She leaned back, familiar with the despair. "Otherwise I know I would find him. He is as important as my own life," Aira murmured. She added, "And it isn't that I must have him for my own life. I didn't depend on him." *I only needed to love him,* she spoke silently.

Up to now, Onx had been content that her nudging had prompted Aira to inspect further this Jorian situation. *Viewing leads to comprehension.* She hoped in this case Aira's reviewing it would at least reveal a clue, something that might lead to a resolution. But now the creature flared displeasure at her master. Her glare demanded to know what was wrong with dependence. *After all, I depend on you.*

"I mean I didn't depend on him as a *substitute* for my own life, Onx," Aira tried to assuage the little dragon's indignation.

Onx tucked her nose behind a reptilian wing.

"Now don't sulk, Onx," Aira said, admiring the shim-

mering subtle reflections of the cabin's light on her sensor-
mate's wing.

Releasing the lock under her chair and deftly pushing
against the control board, Aira shoved her seat module
into motion down the rail to the left end of the chamber.
22-18A. She punched in a music selection. As a five-part
melody began emanating, she adjusted the volume to her
liking, very loud, before leaning back to listen and watch
the sound waves speed into light and billow in the Lauryad chamber.

Aira had been immersed in the beauty for some moments when she felt an invisible tug from the floor of the
cabin. *Onx,* she located. The dragon was tightly still in
her corner and hadn't budged.

"Onx, you're becoming hooked on this E-motion, look
at you, you're wallowing in it," Aira admonished.

Onx had no shame in that regard.

Amused with the preoccupation of the life-form, Aira
decided she wasn't going to let her lie in misery, even if
much of it was self-inflicted. She turned off the sound-
accelerator that was speeding sound into light, then lowered the music volume and launched her remedy.

"You're so pretty, Onx," Aira told her.

Onx did not move.

"And majestic. Beautiful, actually."

No response.

"And so noble."

Only a dissipated stream of smoke sifted up from behind the miniature dragon's wing.

When silence from Aira followed and only low-volume
music filled the chamber of the Lauryad, Onx wondered if
she hadn't pushed her wounded display too far. After all,
Aira made an attempt to reconcile the emotional injury.
*And she wouldn't intentionally let a misunderstanding per-
sist.* But subsequent thoughts fueled Onx's steadfastness
in position: *Aira just made less of dependency. Perhaps she
no longer respects me because I am dependent on her and
need her.*

"I understand, Onx. You just don't understand that I do understand."

Onx blinked in the dark safety under her wing.

"I meant what I said. There is nothing wrong with dependence."

Onx's saurian skin rippled with guilt for having placed Aira in a position of having to defend her integrity. Of course Aira had meant what she said. She always did. Onx was about to come out of her foolishness when Aira began speaking again.

"Near the two suns of Nestralil with the stars in Onx's eyes, she laid her head upon my lap and claimed it with a sigh. A blue wing dubbed my shoulder in earnest accolade. Our trust exchanged dependency in trails the comets made."

Our trust exchanged dependency. Onx flickered pleasure sparks through her nostrils. She felt her upset and even confusion over her own sulking behavior begin to dissolve as Aira *daoed* her, granting her the right to be as she was in that moment. She removed her head from beneath her wing and listened to Aira continue the verse-talk.

"I thought when so dubbed by her, how sure I'd find my way if I had goodly masters who would not let me stray. I wished to dub as masters: Love. Truth. Serenity. They'd feed and house and teach me with total sovereignty."

By the time Aira had finished, Onx was sitting erectly and proudly. *I am your sensor-mate,* Onx emanated.

"And I depend on you," Aira said. There was that steel in her soft-tone again.

Between the sound-symbols, Aira also telepathically transmitted memories of when she and Onx had been in the battles to free thought, in the Life-Parasitical District where Onx had protected her from traps.

Her masters are Love and Truth, Onx admired, then shuddered. She was not quite ready to be dependent on Truth. She was content to admire her master, Aira. That was enough for now. *There is a certain...bliss...in limits. A little ignorance here and there makes it possible to...relax.*

Onx blinked innocently, content to be allowed her

prerogative of chosen responsibility level. *This is a good arrangement,* she thought. Content that there was someone around to take on more than 'feelingness,' Onx nestled into a nap.

Aira turned up the music. The beauty soothed her. Through a barely lifted eyelid, Onx confirmed her contentment. Aira had become translucent, scintillating gold and silver sparkle. Moments continued to pass in relative Time throughout that universe. In the Lauryad's control chamber, the victor was Understanding and it prevailed, buffing the environ with mollifying ease.

...buffing the environ with mollifying ease. Mendle was proud of Aira as his fingers typed the conclusion on the keyboard. He closed his eyes momentarily, feeling the saturation of her, then opened them to finish the chapter.

Aira directed her gaze toward the portal and beyond, then the light-being expanded outside of space and particles, still monitoring what her form-senses needed to know as pilot of the Lauryad. Every reading of the fission-regroup process toward home was in her realm of awareness, though she wandered as thought.

The small ship relocated, linking nuclei along its vector-path, sliding through the blackness with an occasional glint of silver perceivable only between moments in time. Its commander was tranquil, but on the periphery of her knowing, agitation brewed.

chapter 2

Electricity crackled and lights flashed. Bright colors pulsated. Red, red. Yellow, yellow. White. Green, green. White. Blue. Violet, violet. Red. Yellow. Red, red, red. White.

"It isn't wise, Juristac. Not wise for you to be here," whined Loptoor as he limped a few paces behind his cohort. Ahead stretched a shiny, aseptic corridor.

Loptoor's comment brought a sneer to Juristac's porcine face. The short distance they had traveled was already causing him effort to breathe and his lunar face was beading with sweat. He stopped a moment to adjust the purple cape fastened around his nearly non-existent neck and took the opportunity to turn and show his sentiments to Loptoor.

Contempt glowered in Juristac's eyes. Contempt and disgust for stupidity—which he assigned to every living form other than himself. "And why," he over-enunciated patronizingly, "is it not wise?"

Wise Wise Wise. The word echoed in Loptoor's mind, reverberating and swimming in Juristac's projected attitude that He, the Great Juristac, was the only One in existence who knew what it meant.

"Well, Most Excellent, I was considering your best interests. Should you be witnessed frequenting this Station you will be asked to explain. It would be surmised that you indeed support—"

"Stop!" barked Juristac. "Do not even think it, do not utter it, do not put it in any form or symbol!" His jowls ruffled violently as he spoke.

Loptoor cringed into himself. They continued to walk the coruscating corridor in silence. Juristac's reproach had been sufficient and he pleasured in the effect it had created on Loptoor who remained several paces behind him, emitting rapid dispersals of fear.

More to listen to his own importance than for Loptoor's benefit, Juristac decided to be generous and condescended to explain himself. "Who in the sector would see me here?" he began. "Yes, I banned these stations completely. As far as is known, only the very degraded still come here of their own volition." He liked hearing his own sound-symbols. "My word is trusted," he stated, then paused to reflect on this.

The thought of being trusted made Juristac laugh with disdain. The fact that he had been so convincing only fortified his belief in the stupidity and therefore dangerousness of all besides himself. The laugh rolled from him, gurgling and quivering as it caught itself on the phlegm in his throat.

Juristac enjoyed being a condensed body-form. To others, he made it appear as though he was not confined to it, that he could expand outside of it and merely used the enormous body as an opulent symbol of knowledge and experience. He could not do much without it, however, and gave the organism full reign; he lived for its smell, for the sensations it gave him, particularly the titillation of food intake and what followed. He reveled in its excretory system.

"Finally, they'll be able to rest," Juristac, feeling Loptoor's eyes on him, justified his outburst. "Think of it. Divine rest. No problems." He calmed his laughter. "No one will see us here," he assured Loptoor, adding, "no one who is awake." He paused, ruminating his next thought before speaking. "And as for the others. Well. The others who are awake now…"

They reached the end of the corridor and stood before the Grand Door. Juristac quit talking as he entered the code. Task at hand complete, he finished what he was saying, his voice taking on a sudden sing-song mode, "…they're not awake for long. And they *certainly* won't be going anywhere afterward where they can talk about it. They, too, will be, finally, relieved."

Loptoor wondered why Juristac's communication was chilling to him. The Most Excellent One was, after all, as he explained it, performing the 'ultimate service' to others.

The Grand Door whirred and began to part. Juristac's eyes gleamed with anticipation. He rubbed his fat hands together. "Brilliant. Brilliant!" he exclaimed. "You may call me brilliant." Then, with a swoosh of his purple robes, he crossed the threshold.

The atmosphere was almost painful, saturated with the micro-buzz, but Juristac enjoyed it and his face was stretched with glee.

Loptoor followed. "I understand, Most Brilliant," he told Juristac. "You do understand that I only mentioned caution with your interests in mind? I want you to succeed. You are so close to Total Control now that—"

"The Benevolent Regime," Juristac corrected quickly. His thoughts had already raced on to the fun he was about to have and it irritated him that Loptoor was still on the same topic.

"Yes, the Benevolent Regime," Loptoor echoed him, "where you will be Total Servant and do thinking for all Life, control all Thought."

"Mmmyyeeaaass," replied Juristac. His voice trailed off and was swallowed by the commotion in the Reception Hall to which Loptoor now also shifted his attention.

Color spectrums busily fanned out from the low ceilings, some slowly, others with a snap of light. Identity Advertisements neatly lined the walls. The room was meticulously clean and controlled except for the sparse random life which mulled about.

"Welcome to Station Fifteen. Would you care for a Euphorisiac?"

The entity who greeted them was a doll, the body-type a symmetricized version of standard manifestation. It was often described as Humanoid, but this body was not organic, it was pre-fashioned at full growth out of silicone and other minor-animate substances.

"My, my, what a beautiful body," Juristac pronounced.

"Thank you. I am beautiful. Euphorisiac?"

"I designed this one, Loptoor. What do you consider of it?"

"Quite symmetrical, very aesthetic," agreed Loptoor.

"Perfect!" re-emphasized Juristac. "And suitable for…*ccchharrumph*," he cleared his throat, "sensation derivation."

When Juristac lifted the lower portion of the doll's garment, it didn't seem to interrupt her; she was smiling and holding the tray out to Loptoor.

Loptoor was curious as he met the doll's gaze. He found he could not look into its eyes.

"Euphorisiac?" the doll-body repeated. She pointed out the two types of ingestion available: liquid for those with orifice-design bodies, and touch-plates for wave-length influence.

Loptoor declined, "No. Not now. We're here on mission."

"Look at this line," Juristac instructed. He had completely uncovered the bottom half of the doll and was lasciviously sliding his hand over its backside above the legs. "See the way it protrudes. It generates warmth." He fondled its rear and prodded his sweating fingers between its buttocks, then slid his hand downward and cupped the region between its legs. "It goes in right here."

Juristac seemed to be talking to himself now, slowly and deliberately. Each sound-symbol quavered as he said it, as though it was about to crack and spill something which he was trying to contain as well as convey.

Loptoor wondered if a thought-being was animating the doll or if it was stimulus-response machine. He observed the face: it was smiling. When he felt Juristac's gaze upon him like a glove, Loptoor obliged, "A good design." Hesitantly, he ventured to ask, "Inhabited?" He couldn't tell.

Juristac squeezed the doll's legs a final time before withdrawing his hand. He grunted as he gave her a slight push and gazed after her as she departed dutifully to make her rounds.

"Better than inhabited," he finally answered Loptoor. "Consolidated. The life has been consolidated into the doll. It does not run the doll, it does not inhabit the doll, it *is* the doll. Don't you see?" Juristac spoke as if he had just stumbled upon his own brilliance. He clasped his hands together and launched a short leg forward in a grandiose step toward Level 2 Entrance. "Compressed!" Juristac exclaimed.

As they walked, he elaborated solemnly, making an obvious display of taking Loptoor into his confidence. "The life has no more burden of awareness, nor bothersome aspirations, except to exist. It does not even think that it is, you see?"

"Does not think that it is?"

Enjoying Loptoor dangling in attention, Juristac took a moment before explaining, "The thought-being receives a forgetting charge-blast— after the identity is selected, of course—then is compressed and consolidated. There is no bothersome distinction anymore." He quickened with excitement. "You saw it? How it, rather *she*, loved the attention I gave her? She thinks she is the body. A beautiful female machine."

Around them, life-forms were lined up against walls and congregated in groups, some scanning new Identity Catalogue issues. The new arrivals seemed depleted, drained, until they partook of Euphorisiac, which perked them up to enthusiasm as soon as ingested.

Fragments of discourse floated above the din; there was talk about forgetting. They came for new life. They considered options for new starts. Male. Female. Good. Evil. Every dichotomy. Retain Knowledge. Total Forget. Goal. Barriers To Goal. High Emote. Numb. Planet Life. Sleep Vacation. The options were plentiful, and, for those who did not care to choose, Random Scramble was available.

Juristac and Loptoor finished inspecting the Identity Program Booths on Level 2 and made their way to Z Zone. Juristac's pleasure was reaching the brink of hilarity as he observed the station functioning properly. He felt proud. Proud of himself for alleviating the burdens of these lives. They would no longer be a danger to themselves, or to him.

As he pondered his greatness, a noble sadness overcame Juristac. He considered the responsibility he was undertaking. Eventually he would be the only one awake. The only one with power of choice. Ah, the sacrifices he must make to ensure peace, to ensure happiness, to make life easy for others, to make the universe a safe place.

A thought suddenly began to absorb his dream. *What of other universes?* He instantly dispelled it, consoling himself with the knowledge that whatever other universes existed, thought-beings created them. And he had devised the perfect solution for them all. Thought-beings were the same, even though manifestations, forms, and body-types varied. They were pesky souls who busied themselves and got themselves into trouble with too many ideas and visions and such.

He sighed deeply. Z Zone. Soon, many more would be brought here.

Despite any initial protests, once through Z Zone, the poor beings who once deluded themselves with believing they wanted Full Knowledge and Decisive Cause were grateful. Once through Z Zone, they returned. Grateful for the carefreeness of no responsibility. Grateful to be rid of the curse of decision, the bane of mistake. Grateful to be able to forget. To forget their terrible blunders, their misdeeds, their many transgressions against their troublesome aspirations. Sweet forgetting. Comfort from the consuming agony of regret. Absolved completely of their pasts.

Juristac turned to Loptoor. "Perhaps you would like to be implanted, to begin anew?" he asked, the perfect host. "No muss, no trouble, just sweet Z."

Loptoor felt voidness and a silent scream rose in him. He reminded himself this reaction to Z was part of the trap. The trap of wanting to know, to be awake. The trap which was the beginning of all burden, which led to all torment. Juristac had explained it to him so well. They were both far ahead of the others who still fooled themselves that Knowledge was freedom.

"Perhaps. One day," Loptoor replied. "We have much work to do before I can partake in the luxury of blissful oblivion."

"Mmmyyeas." Juristac nodded slowly and deliberately. He extended his hand to Loptoor's shoulder and patted it resolutely. "Mmyes," he repeated, still nodding omnisciently.

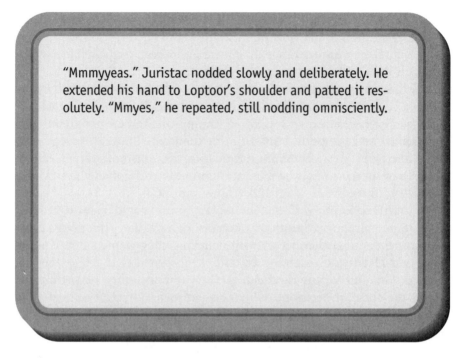

"Mmmyyeas." Juristac nodded slowly and deliberately. He extended his hand to Loptoor's shoulder and patted it resolutely. "Mmyes," he repeated, still nodding omnisciently.

Mendle wanted a drink. *No*, he didn't want a drink, the thought just came into his mind that the bottle would provide warmth and a certain…cessation. A certain oblivion.

On one hand, it went against him to diminish his senses, his ability to observe. On the other hand, a little alcohol opened blockades, numbed only the pain, diminished only the obstacles.

Glancing at the clock, Mendle realized he had been writing nearly five hours. He pushed the chair back from his desk, interlocked his fingers over his head, and stretched his arms upward.

"You're losing a grip on reality." The memory of Sandra's voice admonished him. "At least stay sober long enough to know what's real."

She's the one who has a problem with reality, he defended, wishing he had never allowed her into his life.

"Thank you," she would say when he told her she was beautiful. *I know I am,* her smug look would finish.

Maybe it wasn't fair, he thought now, that he had waited to end it, waited until he could look at her and not want her physically. He used to purposefully look at Sandra Wilford to see if his body reaction matched his personal opinion about her. It didn't, at first, but he would inevitably silence his personal dislike, even lessen his awareness, and listen to his body.

He played with it for a while, a test, an experiment, finding it fascinating the way his body and thoughts didn't always match. After a while, they did. After a while her soul was what he saw. There was no desire for that. And his body finally agreed.

Yet he didn't find it fair that he left her only after his body was sated, that he didn't sooner take control, that it was only after the physical desire had been indulged and spent that he ended the relationship.

He had been hopeful, though, Mendle defended his sense of honor. He had tried to like Sandra, hoped to reach her, to free her. It wasn't that his body had simply had its way and was finished. At the time, he didn't know the drill himself. It only became apparent through the experience.

He remembered his warnings, his pleading. He wasn't "the man" on the cover of women's magazines. Sandra continued to think and speak in slogans: "How to Keep Your Man"; "What Men Want"; "How To Get Your Way With Your Man."

"Sandra, just talk to me. *Me*," he had said innumerable times.

He was forced to conclude the woman could not be direct, she could only happen on an angle. She could only scheme, not propose or suggest. Soon, Sandra Wilford became evident. *That's all*, Mendle concluded anew. He had seen her soul. *That did it. Her pea of a soul.* He didn't care how shapely her legs were, how tightly pumped her muscles were, how sleek and shiny and sweet-smelling her dark hair was. *Not anymore anyway*, his conscience tweaked. *Okay, okay*, he came to terms with it. How did one learn if not from experience? *Been there, done that.*

Mendle yawned. *A nap, that's what I need.*

In his bedroom, with a practiced push to the back of each shoe with his opposite foot, he slipped each one off without untying the laces. *Aaahhh.* The softness of the quilted bedspread pressing against his face felt good to him. He relinquished the weight of his body to the comfort of the mattress and surrendered the weight of his thoughts to the comfort of sleep.

chapter 3

The phone rang. The fluctuating tones penetrated Mendle Orion's sleep, each ring becoming more distinct from dream, pulling him back into the room. Hazily confirming that it was the phone he was hearing, Mendle almost decided to ignore the sound. When it rang insistently and his answering machine didn't activate, concern for lost opportunity motivated him to reach for the receiver on his nightstand.

"Hello."

"Congratulations, Mendle."

He recognized the perky voice on the other end. Sandra Wilford. Even over the phone, her presence demanded attention. The chipperness sounded inflated and was too snappy for one awakening from sleep. *That's what I get for being curious,* Mendle admonished himself.

"I said congratulations."

His reply was slow. "For what?"

"Best new science fiction writer of the year. The John Campbell Award."

"Oh. That." In the silence that followed, Mendle knew Sandra was wondering if he was drunk. "I was taking a nap," he said, begrudging the feeling that he had to explain.

"Sure, sure," Sandra sidestepped as if she had not even wondered. "You knew, about the award I mean, didn't you? Of course, you knew." As usual, she didn't wait for a reply. "How are you feeling?" She didn't speak the other questions: *Are you still getting drunk? Do you still have trouble discerning fact from fiction?*

Mendle was tired. He could have said something slick, but he wasn't interested anymore. He didn't want to fight her, he just wanted her to go away. He answered her question.

"Fine."

"How's the new book coming?"

"Getting there."

"Oh good."

"Okay, Sandra. Thanks for calling. I have to get back to work now."

"I thought you were sleeping."

"I was. But I…"

"Mendle," she purred, "Mendle, I realize it doesn't matter anymore, but I was wondering, do you think the problems between us might have been caused by your getting too involved with your characters?"

She still hadn't heard him. He had explained what his problems were with her, and they had nothing to do with anyone else, real or imaginary. Mendle let her go on; he didn't want to repeat himself. He had to cut it off somewhere, draw the line between what he had failed to say and what she would never hear.

"I mean, the way you were talking about a fictional character, one would think you were going to meet and have lunch." She laughed.

"I did. Yesterday."

Silence. He could feel the density of her seriousness. She was questioning his faculties. Finally she laughed. "For a minute you had me worried."

Mendle didn't answer.

"You know, seriously, my analyst is really good, if you ever want to see him. It really might help."

"Thank you, Sandra."

"A rest never hurt anybody, you know."

Sure, go lie down and quit being vital. Disagreement sparked in Mendle but he didn't voice it. He said, "I'll let you know what I decide."

"Maybe I'll see you at the Convention," Sandra blurted, quickly assuring him, "Just friends."

"Okay, thanks." He started to set the phone down, quickly brought the mouthpiece close again, said "Bye," then replaced the receiver in its cradle. Rolling over on his back, he thought with satisfaction, *It worked.* He had dodged her, managed not to get snagged. She had rolled off him. He wasn't even doubting his own sanity.

Not too much.

A moment's inventory told him he wouldn't be able to fall back asleep. He lifted himself to a sitting position, meeting his reflection in the dresser mirror across the room. His sandy brown hair was tousled.

Haunted, as usual, was his impression.

He leaned forward and rubbed his face, lingering particularly on the eyes, feeling the stretch along his back. As he straightened his head and sat up, his thoughts gravitated toward his new novel.

An uninvited taunt of Sandra's entered his mind: *Of course she's perfect, she's in your head! You can dream her up any way you want her.*

Mendle dismissed the prattle, brushing off this abuse of his heroine, Aira Flight. He continued groping for his world as he slid his legs over the side of the bed. After a moment, he got up and began to amble around the house, preparing for his rendezvous. He looked forward to writing about her. It felt like…being with her.

The character is my dream girl in a way, he supposed. *But isn't she, after all, more real than certain facts? How many 'facts' are actually true?* Mendle reflected on such things as false facts; embraced for centuries, some things turned out to be untrue, but they had been held as 'facts' nonetheless. *Who knows what facts are floating around here that we'll find out were a hoax?* He looked at the wall, silently challenging that, one day, he might walk through it.

Since he had begun writing about Aira Flight's adventures in space, it became evident that he had dreamed about her all his life. He could close his eyes and she would appear. He could feel her. He could even hear her. Pledging undying love.

Undying love. He thought about it. *How can love die?* It didn't, he decided. *Love does not die.*

Even before he had given her a name, she existed. He could feel her more than he could see her. He began to imagine what she would look like. *Golden and soft, with limpid eyes; her voice mellifluous; her hair whirlwinds of sun.*

And when they kissed, it was more real than…well, any of the times his lips had touched Sandra Wilford's.

Though Mendle Orion was willing to admit Aira Flight was a fantasy, he would not let go of her. Maybe she was a dream, but even as such, she still existed.

He was soon sitting at his computer.

For recreation, Aira sometimes tracked. She was good at it.

Being an astute observer of nowness, Aira Flight was able to revive past experience recordings and project them as vivid motion-pictures that others could see. Her recreations were intense and poly-view generated, unlike those of some which were limited to personal viewpoint. When Aira tracked, the views of all present were included, as well as her own, making for hologram accuracy.

She was running her memory-strip of Galactron, projecting it into the atmosphere between herself and Onx who watched the flickering images with rapt involvement. It was an award ceremony.

Aira had discovered an entire populace on the outskirts of Tuton which had been locked in energy and hidden behind black screens for ninety-four spirals. She had confronted the black, the unknown, the incomprehensible, to map out the maze of their entrapment and restore their freedom. Onx had been her sensor-mate on that mission.

Presented to Aira Flight: awards for Power to *Dao*, Defense, Discovery of Root To Language, Communication, Understanding Catalyst. There they were, surrounded by grateful beings who were now free to operate beyond energy, restored into exercising their own wills, capable of creating their own laws.

I was shimmering, Onx admired the violets and blue-greens of her complexion.

Sensing Onx's pleasure, Aira slowed the projection of those moments, regrouping the molecules with particular attention to Onx's angle.

The Tribunal was present—Sonrial, Rilia, Tolara, Rheson, Flozal, Juristac, Maytra, Bilzia—all welcoming Aira to the Tribunalship and realizing her power to decide The Course. They were all joyful. Sheer happiness reigned, the heights of Beauty radiated, Trust and Comradery lived. This was the dignity of thought-beings at their most noble and natural.

Aira was newer than the Supreme Tribunal in experience as a One, but whole, founded in a compassion that was capable of giving life to an entire universe. She was a Power and *daoed* them all, pledging her full agreement

and joining their allegiance to freedom of thought from
The Conquest.

The pictures dissolved.

More! Onx demanded.

Aira had stopped tracking, she was not amused by it
anymore. She focused on Onx. *I'm just going to be for a
while,* she expressed. It required concentrated attention
to manifest herself and interact with the physical dimension's set of laws, prerequisites necessary for tracking.
Even light-bodies required effort, less expenditure than
denser forms, but it was work nevertheless, and sometimes
Aira just wanted to enjoy nowness.

She was about to settle to do so, to dissolve into
non-form being, when an incomprehensible caught her
attention. She thought-scanned the space. *What is that?*

Onx felt it, too.

Unable to identify it through know-scanning, Aira
condensed herself and positioned herself at the Lauryad's
master controls. She depressed the Circumference Scanner. The device began feeding back frequencies received
from its Sensor Vectors, one by one.

"That's it. That one." HOLD. FINE TUNE. SCREEN. VIEW.
AUDIO. Aira entered each command to zero in on it.

A scintilla, miniscule against the void, appeared on
the screen.

"What is it?" IDENTIFY.

NO REFERENCE, the screen replied.

RELOCATE, CHANGE VECTOR FOR CLOSER ANALYSIS, Aira
maneuvered.

The Lauryad shifted direction.

VIEW. AUDIO.

The light could now be seen to be brilliant, but its
rays were curious, unlike anything Aira had ever seen.
Each flow of photons was interrupted, each ray appeared
to be spitting out fine streams of white light which inverted into black and continued out of the blackness instead of the center source.

IDENTIFY, she commanded.

Polarity, two terminal, the screen flashed.

Is that all the information? Aira entered the command again: Identify Repeat, Detail.

The screen flashed its output once more: Polarity, two terminal.

Detail, Aira repeated her information request.

The screen went red. Then: No reference. Danger. No reference.

How strange. It was fascinating. Yet Aira and Onx were alone and, being subject to laws of the dimension in which they were operating, Aira weighed the potential liabilities and decided against investigating.

"We'll record the location for future exploration."

Onx was relieved. Aira had learned to plan her vast spirit and impulses with reason. The last time she didn't consider potential consequence, they had ended up in a dimension-particle-warp which took them what seemed like a void to finally escape.

Relocate. Resume vector: Home Base Original Destination Program.

"Are you sure you want to keep the dragon life-form, Onx?" Aira asked playfully as she finished entering the commands. "You seem capable of reasoning rather well. You could operate as..."

Onx feigned limited potential and blinked up at Aira. Her stance was nonetheless alert, prepared to respond to a potential emergency. That she could do. *Sense, identify danger, combat, protect.* She was good at that, and that was all she was about to aspire to.

"Blinking blankly, eh?" Aira chided Onx then turned back to the control board.

Circumference Scanner: Record Phenomena for Future Location. Sensor Vector: Relative Location; Nearest Mass; Degrees. Aira was recording the information necessary to relocate the phenomena for future investigation when she noticed the ship had not resumed its original course.

Vias, she thought disdainfully. "Contraptions," she mumbled and repeated the **Resume Original Destination** vector-command. She reminded herself that mechanics were necessary if she was going to operate along the course she had chosen, manifestation and inter-action of form. It was, she thought after all, enjoyable propelling particles through space, feeling motion, even having space and distance and forms and interaction as such.

The ship did not change course.

Onx sat prepared at full alert.

SYSTEM BYPASS. MANUAL DIRECT. VECTOR CHANGE.

They were still hurtling toward the light phenomena.

VECTOR CHANGE, Aira repeated.

No result.

MOTION STOP, she tried, then, SHUT DOWN. But no control would respond to her.

HOME BASE TRANSMIT. VITAL RELAY. URGENT. VITAL RELAY. DISTRESS.

Instruments and controls were not responding. Even communications were down and the screen began to flash stupidly: NO REFERENCE, NO REFERENCE, NO REFERENCE.

Have we entered a different universe? Aira speculated on whether they had traversed to a different reality with diverse operating laws. She tried computer cross-reference: SCAN MANIFEST MODE.

NO REFERENCE. NO REFERENCE.

"But this system is programmed with every reality variable conceivable!" Aira was puzzled. Scanning the transit-mode reading, she determined that they were still regrouping atoms and linking nuclei.

Then the transit screen flashed: PROPULSION.

Aira and Onx felt the inversion occur. "We're condensing," Aira said, maintaining her equilibrium. "We're not relocating along the vector path anymore. We're shut down and actually moving as a unit through space."

Aira slammed the energy shut-off but it had no effect. "We're being pulled in, Onx."

Aira tried to exteriorize outside of form, to telepath a call for assistance, but she found she could proceed only so far before running into an extremely strange sensation.

"We're on the other side...we've penetrated a screen of some sort."

Concentrating her perception, Aira recognized one of the frequencies and wondered if they had happened onto an Aberree Vortex. The frequency was similar to that of the Rent-an-Emotion network, where aberrees drifted in to be charged up with E-motion particles. Entire spectrums were available to rent. After being bombarded with and adhered to energy flows, life-beings identified themselves by the acquired temporary wave-lengths: I am cheerful. I am angry. I am sad.

This frequency was familiar, but it did not explain the system non-function in the ship and the fact that the Lauryad was not responding to her command.

They were moving slowly now. Vibrations began to transmit through the walls of the Lauryad, sounds unlike any that Aira had ever perceived...a musical plaint so beautiful it hurt.

But how could beauty hurt?

A sadness, a crying wind that wailed of loss and promise simultaneously, an ancient sound, as though the wind had been blowing through galaxies lost and forgotten for millions of spirals, penetrated the ship like so many fingers, beseeching to convey what they knew. It grew in layers, undulating on the softest current of tones which sounded like many voices united in a whispering lament.

Outside the Lauryad, colors billowed which left no distance for perception. *How could that be?* They were photons, Aira knew, but they filled the senses, then seemed to locate out in distance again. Violets which thinned to rose then into veils of pink which wisped to encircle small orbs of luminescence. Just as Aira refocused to see what the luminous orbs circumscribed, they dissolved and vanished.

She found herself wanting to look away, not to listen. *The best defense is to see*, she reaffirmed, and Onx's sensing reinforced it. She continued to confront as fully as she could. It took awareness-reminder to keep doing so.

The wavelengths were so fine, so fascinating, so beautiful, so mysterious.

Mystery. The thought rang alarmingly. Mystery: the primary bait to a trap.

Onx had moved close to Aira and stood loyally at her side, but her attention was being absorbed by the environment, soaked up by the scintillating sponge which encased them.

"Onx!" Aira commanded. "Mystery. Do not stick to the incomprehensible."

Onx flared, sending blue heat through her nostrils, and the susceptible entrancement in her eyes forged into challenge. She stood ready for anything.

Aira, in complete nowness, was perceiving not only in one direction, but also in total circumference around her. Abruptly, the sweet wailing gave way to silence. It caused a vacuum.

The colors that billowed and swirled in the atmosphere suddenly became more vivid, intense. There were no more luminescent orbs, only pulsations of thick reds and blues which throbbed in slow and oddly imperative intensity.

The Lauryad's Central Control screen flashed: No Reference and, intermittently, Two Terminal, Polarity.

I don't believe it. It can't be! Aira thought, then quickly caught herself. *If it is, it is,* she corrected herself. She reminded herself that the era when anti-life did not exist was over; Life had been contaminated; therefore anything could be, including that which made no sense and consequently seemed incredible. *I have to perceive and believe whatever is there*, Aira braced herself, still hoping, hoping this wasn't what she now suspected.

The colors became increasingly thinner until they finally subsided, revealing a sleek platform ahead. Above this platform, floating in stark majesty, rose a spectacular archway, gold and intricately decorated with florid designs. It was awesome, dazzling, and festooned with a magnificent, vast and glimmering structure of cascading crystal.

The Lauryad hypnotically coasted onto the surface. What followed happened at Nth speed: the split moment that the craft made contact, it thrust forward faster than the speed of time, into a tunnel. An envelope of blackness swallowed them, ever faster, into an end which they could not see.

chapter 4

Loptoor was nervous. The feeling of being caught was too much for him. He finally decided to risk Juristac's disapproval and timidly waved his hand to announce he was about to say something.

"Your Supremeness, Most Brilliant," Loptoor began, "I consider it best not to jeopardize the future, your complete success, by momentary amusement."

"Ah, your reason is impressive, Loptoor!" Juristac bellowed. "Quite a display of ethics!" He was having a grand time behind Section A controls of Z Zone when, without warning, his face turned umbrageous and he barked, "But there is no chance of error!"

"Not to disagree with you, great Juristac," Loptoor continued his proposal timidly, his insides all aflutter, "nor to imply that you would err, but won't the emissions project beyond the Reality Screen which hides this Station?"

Loptoor tightened in apprehension of Juristac's reply.

A laugh heaved forward from Juristac's massive body and broke up the catarrh deposits in his throat. "But of course!" Juristac intermixed in his laugh-cough. "That's the point!" He sputtered to a conclusion and wiped his mouth. "It might attract curiosity."

When he spoke next, his voice was suddenly harnessed. He spoke as though he were serving the sound-symbols on a platter. "I guarantee you, Loptoor, anyone who sees it…wins!" Juristac crouched over the Z Zone instruments, busily engrossed with them as he spoke. "The prize will be Divine Sleep. Before they have a chance to struggle any longer with the curse of knowing, they will be delivered. Completely delivered. In fact," his voice was quavering in a quasi-whisper now, "in fact," he crescendoed, "we have one!"

He rubbed his damp palms together and, eyebrows arched maximumly, looked over at Loptoor. "Let's welcome them directly to Z Zone, bypass Level One and Two. What do you say?"

Loptoor was proud to be consulted. He relaxed some, seeing Juristac in such a buoyant state. Juristac rarely overflowed his grand exuberance in this manner. "Yes, yes," Loptoor agreed quickly, "Directly to Z Zone."

Juristac was already maneuvering the Arrival's reception through Level One and Two via conveyer. Craft and all, this life-being was bypassing reception and would arrive directly at Z Zone.

"Let's pulsate them with Euphorisiac, though," Juristac was saying, his pudgy fingers busy over the Z Board. "Let us see, how many?" He leaned back, waiting for the Life Sensor to produce the information. "Two? Oh, all right. Two. Let's take a look. Mmmm, not a large ship."

When the grey snow on the visual screen crystallized into image, even Juristac was stunned, by fear more than anything else, though he would not admit this, especially not to himself. Loptoor felt his entireness wrenched by a more unadmittable reaction. He dismissed it to himself as false sympathy, the trap, his own trap of deceptive sentimentality, his inability to conceive the Grand Order.

It was Juristac who broke the silence. He spoke. It was more of a gasp, actually, and turned into a low, rasping mutter as the name they both knew stuck in his throat. "Aira Flight."

Their attention affixed to the screen.

The Lauryad, still paralyzed, was being transported via conveyer. It was passing Level Two of Station Fifteen. From its portal, its commander's attention was temporarily diverted from her plight and directed dolorously to the beings she witnessed.

Amnesiacs. Deluded, dying into solidity. They were living as complete effects, as slaves to programs and outer influences.

Wake up! Aira thought-reached to them. In protest, she came to their defense. "Remember who you are!" she tried to uplift them, but they could not hear her sound-symbols through the glass plates, and they were petrified beyond being even remotely aware of her thought-convey. Some turned to watch the craft's conveyer ascent up the transparent tunnel. They pointed and smiled and waved as though at a celebratory parade.

Suddenly sound piped into the ship's chamber and Aira could hear them. Prepared slogans which were not their own thoughts, none of which matched their eyes, issued from their body-forms. "Howzit going?" "Whazup?" "Yo babe."

Again, Aira tried to expand beyond her form and outside the ship to pervade the area. But again, she could not proceed past a certain stage of exteriorizing without hitting that peculiar sensation, and she was unable to proceed past it. Now it was more intense. *Pain.* Aira cringed back, startled.

The ship continued on the conveyer into a tunnel. Lights suddenly flashed and pulsated, and currents crackled with increasing volume. The atmosphere was zinging and highly charged, and Aira's attention again turned to the urgency of the situation in which she found herself.

Then the announcement, a detached voice, floated into the cabin. WELCOME AND THANK YOU FOR VOLUNTEERING. YOU ARE REACHING Z ZONE.

She felt a Raze penetrate the ship and knew they were being observed. Funneling her sound-symbols onto the Raze for audio pick-up, Aira stood at Formal Present and heralded, "Liberverus Lauryad!" She repeated it in the seventh vernacular, and introduced herself, "Truth Freedom for the galaxy! This is the Lauryad. I am Aira Flight, here with sensor-mate Onx. Please identify your source."

Fine sub-particles began to snow throughout the cabin. They were highly agitated and moved in tight, circular patterns. As the wavelengths pervaded her, a feeling of euphoric rapture overcame Aira. Onx was moving her head back and forth the way she did when something pleased her tremendously.

Aira struggled to perceive beyond the fabricated E-motion. "It's synthetic, Onx. Please confront!" Hearing Aira's command, Onx mustered her will against the effect.

Artificially induced, Aira kept it under identification, operating through it, keeping her own sense about her. She prepared to emanate for assistance again, this time with resolution not to pull back when she hit against the pain field. She expanded, hit the familiar point, and tried to go beyond it. Her entirety was wracked with electricity, with extreme grid-sensations of heat and cold, until, finally, she evaluated she could not continue to hold the position without severe damage and withdrew.

Aira grappled with what to do next. The Lauryad, her very ship, had been yanked somehow from her control and was completely in the grasp of some strangeness. She could not abandon it, nor Onx, nor her purpose and agreements. Evacuating the existence was not an option.

WELCOME AND THANK YOU FOR VOLUNTEERING. YOU ARE REACHING Z ZONE.

"We have not volunteered," Aira communicated. "There has been an error…"

WELCOME AND THANK YOU FOR VOLUNTEERING. YOU ARE REACHING Z ZONE.

"We have not volunteered," she repeated, and was interrupted once more by the announcement.

WELCOME AND THANK YOU FOR VOLUNTEERING. YOU ARE REACHING Z ZONE.

"We have not volunteered!" Aira yelled with such force that it shook Onx into complete nowness.

The ferocity of her fury surprised herself; she had not felt it in spirals. Then she knew with all the certainty her vastness possessed. The facts lined up: overwhelm of individual perception; enforced reality; two terminal polarity. Only malintent and injustice caused her such white rage. *This is a Station of the Dark Regime.*

The Tribunal had known of one, Station Fifteen, which was still in operation. Supposedly, it was only recycling beings who had already subscribed. Entrapments and involuntary ministration were supposedly no longer active.

It was the Tribunal's plan to salvage these lives after they freed adjoining sectors. First they planned to help and reward those who had at least tried to fight The Conquest by remaining true to Principle Nature. After restoring and rehabilitating the power to these sectors, they would help Aberrees who had programmed themselves to recycle hypnotically in the perpetual downgrade. Eventually, Truth Bearers would even help the ones who had been imprisoned into matter on the outskirt planetary systems.

Station Fifteen was not supposed to be anywhere near her vector-course, Aira pondered as she reviewed the series of events that had led to that point. *It must have been that light-phenomenon. It was bait, a string from a dimension warp that suctioned space-fabric when contacted. An entire portion of space must have been relocated, traveling time-spirals in an instant.*

Aira summoned all she had ever learned about the Dark Regime. She needed to do just the right thing, there was no grace-room for error. If she didn't, the consequences were the closest thing to death for a thought-being. It was death without dying.

Aira Flight was a One of great magnitude, aligned with the Eternal Nature Principle in all its Power. She recalled the history of others who had become targets. They were the very ones her missions were recovering. The Ones of Magnitude had been trapped, forcefully robbed of the knowledge of their very selves. This was loss of Soul. Through force, the sense of who they really were was simply obliterated from their awareness. The Conquest went after those who *daoed*. With these under control, it was much easier to capture the thought-beings of lesser magnitudes. They would have no light-beings, no Supreme Beings as allies.

Aira struggled to overcome the amazement that this could still be an active danger. The consequence of an incorrect solution was almost unconfrontable. She didn't want to confront it, but she had to. It meant her life.

Or death. *Death through unconsciousness, through forgetting.* This is how life died, she knew and shivered against the contact of condensed beings, beings who had once created and *daoed*, now silent and unable to create, no longer cause but only consequence, entombed in solid, stark conglomerates of mass and electrical facsimiles.

In a matter of fractors, she too could be robbed of herself. What did a being have, if not one's self? She would have no recourse. She wouldn't remember.

"How will you explain it to her, Juristac?" Loptoor fretted.

"There is nothing to explain."

"Surely you don't? She is of the Tribunal, you don't intend to…"

The Extractor steadfastly vacuumed the Lauryad toward Phase One Z Zone.

Aira wished she had done the Archaic Condition Prevention training. *Stay in Nowness. Stay to Truth*, Onx sensed.

What is the solution? What is it? The information data had been not initial priority since the Stations were believed disbanded. It had been spirals and spirals ago.

Avidly observing all occurrences taking place, Aira carefully coordinated her every perception with past knowledge in order to reach an undoing of the situation. Then she saw him, through the portal, as the Lauryad emerged from the tunnel. He was standing behind a clear partition. The Lauryad came to a halt at its unpiloted destination.

"Juristac!" Aira cried in relief, stepping through the M/D-barkation panels as they slid apart. "You sensed my call."

Onx's eyes crimsoned. In one swoop she positioned herself in front of Aira and stood ready to fight, her wings stretched to full expanse like two trenchant sails, every gossamer rigid. She hissed fire and her star-tipped tail threatened impalement.

"Onx, it's Juristac. And Loptoor," Aira heard her assurance but simultaneously felt doubt.

Onx was no longer stunned by the synthetic bliss, she was accurately perceiving some danger. *Not Juristac*, Aira began to think, then checked the habit. *If it is, it is. Confront it.* She did so.

Pushing away her suspicion, discarding bias, fear, and even hope, Aira looked—first at Juristac, then Loptoor.

Their gazes met and hung in stalemate.

Aira pervaded Onx. The sensor-mate was intently focused on Juristac and Loptoor, prepared to turn them into targets if necessary. Should they approach as threat or danger, they would not be exempt from Onx's white-fire. Waiting for her cue…

…Onx was suddenly gone.

Aira leapt forward and off the Lauryad's debarkation platform where she and Onx had been standing. She penetrated Juristac's gaze in protest, shattering the shield of illegibility, extricating him so hard with her will that he felt demand for explanation sting his face.

She scrutinized him. He was doing nothing to assist her. Anger began to rise in Aira. It burst against the restraint she exercised. She considered beam-slapping Juristac, but did not want to vindicate only a personal issue. *What would that attain?* She must display only what would attain her desired end. She had to find Onx and get out of this.

Is this even Juristac? Aira wondered. If it was, the entirety of the situation was too preposterous to grasp. She wondered if the massive figure was only a dummy, or some impostor imitating Juristac's manifestation.

It is him, she recognized when she pervaded his space.

The outward appearance seemed so benign. How could she have been fooled? How could the Tribunal not be aware of this treachery? There had been some discussion of doubt, one curve ago. It was incomprehensible. Was it so incomprehensible no one believed it existed? Just as she was now having difficulty believing what was before her very perception? *To willingly destroy, to harm, to entrap life is an incomprehensible.*

Aira again tried granting him the dignity of reason. "Juristac. What happened to Onx?"

"Onx." Juristac smiled. "Is that what you call it? Yes, well, vacation. Onx has won a vacation."

"What are you doing, Juristac?"

"Tsssk. Couldn't resist the mystery, could you? That fascinating little light? You were curious, weren't you?"

His reply appalled Aira. *Confirmed. Hating me. But smiling. Hate?* It seemed unbelievable. An E-motion applicable only to desire for destruction, Aira knew it was a last-solution, a final-solution, a no-solution. *This is why I have not seen it in him,* she thought. *It is unbelievable. So unbelievable it is invisible.* The evil in him, the thrust to death, was so illogical that, not being within confines of reason, it evaded detection.

Aira moved closer to the partition which separated them. "Juristac. Something has happened to you. Don't do this to yourself."

Her earnest attempt to *dao* him was met with a turgid laugh. Then she saw. There was nothing to *dao*. No free-life ran in him. He actually believed that All should be killed. Stopped.

"Myself?" he said, still laughing. "Don't do this to *myself*?" He laughed harder, then stopped abruptly. "Next you will appeal for the sake of those you *benefit*. That they not be deprived of you. And…" He interrupted himself with a roaring laugh from which he seemed unable to recover, but finally quelled enough to continue, "…you actually believe it, that your way of awareness and creation is needed, and good!"

Aira became starkly aware of mostly one thing: his plans for death were now aimed directly at her.

Juristac's countenance suddenly riveted into sobriety. "Most Deserving and Noble Aira Flight," he pronounced solemnly. "You are confused. It is you who I am doing something to. I do nothing to myself, though, granted, it is a sacrifice to be the only one awake."

"If you harm me, it will destroy you," Aira told him, her words weighted with compassion and wrath.

"Harm? My, my. You are about to be rewarded. You should think of this and revel! As for all those who depend on you, who you *dao*, they will be perfectly fine without you. They don't want Truth. They don't want Beauty. You saw. They want sensation. And relief. You deserve a rest."

Aira suddenly felt herself pinned to a location. She could not move. A sensation of degradation overtook her, she could feel it swirling, corroding, dissolving, an insidious liquid invading her very foundation. *Worthless. Nothing.* She fought against being overcome by it. She was feeling as if she were made of sand and being washed away when she was suddenly…

…somewhere else. Surrounded by different dimensions entirely, by the walls of a small, metal cubicle.

"Quickly, now," Juristac bustled. "We must not underestimate the power of her protest."

The atmosphere passage through his form had become rapid. He was sucking it in with his mouth agape, then spitting it out through his teeth as he hunched over the Z Board.

"Come, Loptoor. I honor you. You may help me. This is a great moment. Aira Flight is being relieved of the continual burden of caring for others. She can now be rewarded with thinking only of herself. She will serve herself."

Within the cubicle, Aira could hear Juristac, could feel a frenzy which possessed him. *Onx!* she called out silently, then made contact. The dragon was in close physical proximity, also in a cubicle.

I am ashamed, flowed Onx. She had been unable to protect. She was pinned, unable to exercise any of her abilities.

Do not blame. Only cause. We must not let this occur. Whatever happens, stay with me, Aira conveyed, *even if you have to discard your form, do not fear that.* She felt sick at the brokenness of Onx's spirit. Anger began to boil in her again. "Juristac!" she yelled.

The sound of his name and Aira's tone caused him to look up momentarily from what he was doing.

"I cannot allow you to do this. You are harming, and it only will limit you further. As Envoy of the Tribunal, I command you to stop!"

As Aira Flight's sound-symbols rang in Z Zone, Juristac held his breath.

Aira sensed that her communication had no effect. She wondered how this could be. It was as though he were inanimate, not receiving thought. *Inanimate?* she wondered. *No soul?* She tried again. "You are betraying me and betraying those with whom you interact. Interaction is sacred. By harming me you also harm all those I help. This is Treason!"

This time Aira felt something, but it wasn't Juristac. It was Loptoor. He was considering the way he felt in Aira's presence. With her he felt worthy, calm, able, as though he could do anything he aspired to or dreamed.

Juristac stopped thumbing through a catalogue long enough to flip off the sound monitor, giving it an annoyed look as he did so. Retrieving his place in the catalogue, he soon announced, "Ah! Here we go. I have just the place!" He was programming the system when a sound-symbol made him jump.

"ENOUGH!"

It originated from a spot in the middle of the room, and spread outward in all degrees with such force that it caused Juristac to straighten up erectly and freeze. He double-checked the sound monitor, determining he had turned it off. A wave of fear shot through him. *She is dangerous,* he reminded himself. "You saw that?" He turned to Loptoor. "Despite that twinkling manner of hers, her displays of pathos and tendency for fun, Aira Flight can be deadly." He turned back to his program, adjusting his cape. "She needs a rest."

"JURISTAC. I COMMAND YOU TO STOP. *NOW!* "

He found himself paralyzed first, unable to move, then he felt himself being pushed out and away from the massive form he was occupying. Aira was taking control of his body. Mustering all his intention, Juristac fought for control of his hand. With all his might he pulled and pushed, surrounding it with beams, then forced it to slam down on Blueprint Control. *Crack!* Then, in the same motion, without losing momentum, he swung the volume lever to maximum.

Violent quantities of energy were released. Though aimed at Aira in her Location Cubicle, Juristac felt it because she was pervading him, but he didn't experience the bite of the snarling electrical flood for long. Aira received the brunt of the dose. It sent her into immediate contractions.

While electricity swarmed in Aira like a million hornets, Juristac quickly continued to program the system with his choices for her destiny: BLUEPRINT: CARBON OXYGEN BODY; INCLUDE COMPLETE MIND AND DATA BANK OF SOCIAL REALITY; FACSIMILE MEMORY AND PAST IN SUN'S YEARS, DECADES, ONE, TWO, THREE; REMOTE PLANET; HUMANOID TYPE; FEMALE; ORGANIC; SEX; FETAL DELIVERY.

Juristac paused, debating some options, then continued. "You want to be loved," he stated into the microphone system. "You are looking for the one you love. But you don't remember. If it's love, you'll lose him. You are so afraid of losing that which you love. You must succeed. There is something you have to do. Just forget it. You must win, but you are afraid of it now. Afraid you cannot. So why do it? But you must. Forget it. You will have time. There is something you should be doing. Forget about it."

Juristac went on in a steady drone, amplifying the Forgetter Charge in increments as he talked, pumping megadoses of galvanic force into Aira's chamber.

chapter 5

Every dimension point around Aira was in motion, spinning turbulently. She could not focus on anything.

Simply don't be there. The knowledge glimmered, barely, as though very, very far away. *Don't be there. Don't agree.* It was Onx, valiantly trying to be on duty, sensing and projecting truth data.

That's right, Aira remembered, slowly. *I mustn't agree. That will make it real.*

"Who are you? You are what you see. You'll know. But you don't remember. Let go. Give up. Nothing. Forget it. You are sleeping." The voice droned on and on, and clung to particles which were sticking on her.

It was confusing, difficult to make a distinction now; there was no distance between her and the sound, and the words seemed to emanate from within herself. Yet she hung on to one thing, that she was life.

She couldn't hold onto the sense of herself long before it was bombarded with other thought that seemed like her own, *yet...it was not... but...it was...but was it?*

Now. She would simply consider what she knew. But what was it? *There. No, that wasn't it....There! No.* Juristac leaned on the Full Intensity Activate and Aira was hit with such force that she ceased to comprehend at all.

"All done," Juristac said, relieved, though his clenched jaw still bore pressure that was surging through him. "Now, we'll let her process for a while and work on Cubicle Two."

Juristac coded the blueprint and destination for Onx. "Who am I? I don't know," he was laying phrases into the microphone, deeply engrossed in the final stages of the program.

At least he appeared engrossed to Loptoor who, leaning forward, with his elbow decreased the power that was pumping into Cubicle One where Aira was pinned in a negative-positive vortex.

Juristac would not have otherwise noticed, but when he reached over to press the Transport control, he detected ripples of fear and located Loptoor as their source. When Juristac unflinchingly confronted him, Loptoor flushed with a wave of embarrassed confusion and blurted, "The wattage needed—"

"Mmmyeas?" Juristac calmly prompted him.

"I just thought—"

"Mmyes?" Juristac spotted the change, and turned the power back up to maximum, where he had left it.

"I just thought it would be more interesting if she were allowed to retain *some* of her memory. It would make it more interesting, more confusing." Terror seized Loptoor as he realized Juristac knew he was lying.

"Perhaps you would like to join them, and make it even more interesting?" Juristac offered.

"No."

"They are going to the Game of Opposites. Eh?"

"No."

"No? No-o-o-o-o?" Juristac was appalled. "I see the trap is getting the best of you, Loptoor. You are disagreeing, struggling. Let us rid you of this burden. You need a rest."

Surprising even himself, Loptoor wildly and suddenly threw himself onto the Z board and frantically began undoing Juristac's program. The image of Aira filled him with courage. He could not let this happen. The vision of her pinned to a form, to a carbon-oxygen body which grew from an elementary cell, and her being unconscious as it developed, matured, and died, deceiving her that she was nothing but biological matter…*no, no*….

Loptoor began to function as a soul, his sentience returned and his own thoughts blossomed; he acted despite his fear, propelled by ideals greater than himself.

Not beautiful and good Aira who loves, who grants life, he was thinking as he decreased electrical outputs across the board.

Juristac grabbed Loptoor by the shoulders, wrenched him backward off the board, and sent him sprawling onto the glossy morathene floor.

Pictures and sound-symbols volleyed within Cubicles One and Two. "You're there. Not there. Elsewhere. But here. Forget. You are everything you see." Facsimiles and complete data banks which could act as whole personalities, negatives, positives, pain and pleasure charges, surged and diminished, amplified and withdrew. Hurricanes of electricity, pain riding on its currents, rampaged then subsided, then crackled angrily again.

"You fool!" Juristac blustered. "You've released the containment shield!"

From the floor, Loptoor could see through the partition to the Lauryad's debarkation platform. Cloud-masses of activated programs were seeping out of the Location Cubicles and going rampant in the atmosphere around the debarkation area. Aira, semi-condensed, stunned, contracted, but functioning, stumbled into view, carrying Onx.

"It must be contained!" Juristac gasped, staring at the Z Board to determine what to do. He could have bypassed and shut down, but that would leave an awake Aira Flight with whom to contend.

Loptoor was back on his feet. Something had happened to him. His visage was contorted with joy and anger intermixed. He was acting on a reason other than the avoidance of pain. The sentiment was loyalty, and it felt glorious. It gave him strength as he punched and pulled and pushed, and he felt a glorious power which he had long forgotten he possessed. It was his soul. It was he. He was crying with joy.

His primary objective was to prevent the Forgetter Charge from obliterating Aira's awareness before the Transport was complete. Then, no matter where she ended up, she could at least recover. Even if it took time, she would eventually confront and find her way home again.

Home. Loptoor was wracked with grief, grief of joy and regret. *Home.* It was Love he had connected to, and it was feeding his dry and parched self. Oh, what had ever possessed him to believe Juristac?

He saw Aira by the platform; she had slumped at its edge, struggling for strength to manage aboard the Lauryad. Torrents of voltage and storms of current rampaged in the chamber.

"The Body Blueprint!" Loptoor panicked as he realized it was still activating, still condensing particles into electrical ridges, forming a permanent body around Aira. He lunged for it.

He was whimpering now, shaking with urgency, regret, despair, and love, repeating Aira's name and "This is not right."

Just as he had reached the Body Blueprint and was beginning to twist it off, he felt Juristac stun him. He was suddenly drained and had no more visio. Slowly, his fingers limply slipping off the control and down the board, Loptoor crumpled to the floor.

"I tried, oh, I tried," he wept, unable to move. He sensed Juristac above him. "What," he began, his voice weak and breaking, but he forced the rest out, "did she...ever...do...to you?"

Loptoor's final thought, before final blackness, was the horror of Aira Flight becoming the organic fetus of a carbon-oxygen body.

Juristac looked down at Loptoor in disgust and pity. He was sizzling with contempt and frustration at the stupidity and ignorance of others. *Dangerous.* He punctuated his thought with a kick to Loptoor's side. *They're dangerous.* He kicked him again.

Looking up, Juristac saw that Aira had managed herself and Onx back into the craft. He shuffled to the Z board, surveying damage and options, and quickly readjusted as many settings as he could.

It was impossible to enter the contained area without being affected, Juristac analyzed. He would be unable to isolate Aira and Onx back into their cubicles. The programs were still pumping, but he had no choice other than to activate Transport right then, from right where Aira and Onx stood. *Meaning the craft will have to go, too. Meaning they might not even begin on a cellular time stream. Meaning there's no guarantee parts of their awareness might not splinter off into different dimensions.*

He didn't know what could happen, even though he had reprogrammed the settings. They had been so altered; the procedure had been tampered with while in progress.

Transport. He had to get them out of there. Juristac shrugged as he did so. It wouldn't be the first time that some planet went frantic over seeing an unidentifiable spacecraft crash through its atmosphere, he thought.

Surveying how drastically some of the levers had been swung back and forth, and the settings varied, Juristac shook his head. He watched Aira, Onx and the Lauryad disintegrate before his eyes, the program storms dissolving with them.

If anything, he thought, *they will be a little more…*"Hhaaarrnnnphh," he cleared his throat, *complex. Surely the Forgetter has taken effect. That's what counts most. Their sweet, eternal slumber.*

Juristac shrugged again. He arched his eyebrows maximumly, looked down at Loptoor, then dragged him to a Cubicle for Transport. It was his turn.

chapter 6

A lament rose from the vastness—woe for a presence now missing. Galaxies were robbed of a mirth that had sailed them. And the stars cried to be again the beacons of that warmth.

All elements felt the privation and sent forth a wind which swept disconsolately, both searching and carrying the dirge.

Aira Flight was gone.

chapter  7

"Do you know what the aurora borealis is?" Mendle asked Sandra. He wouldn't have called her, but he had been drinking. She liked him when he was a project, he justified.

"No, Mendle."

There it was, that condescending, patronizing tone. It rankled him, but opposition had its purpose—especially when his own will was not fueling him. Opposition was a primitive incentive for progress.

Mendle smiled to himself and held up the newspaper, pressing the phone to his ear with his right shoulder. "It's in today's paper now, and you tell me what you think. Ready?"

Sandra was going over papers at her desk. As much as she had wanted to hear from him, she detected the dull edges of his words, the challenging attitude. "Yes."

"Okay," Mendle began, then, "'the aurora borealis is one of nature's most dazzling spectacles. When it appears there is often a crackling sound coming from the sky.'" He paused, and when Sandra did not fill in the gap, he continued. "'A huge, luminous arc lights up the black night, and it is in constant motion. Sometimes they flash here and there like giant searchlights, or move up and down suddenly.'"

"What's your point, Mendle?" Sandra oscillated from disgust through concern to annoyance.

"Listen, *listen*," Mendle reprimanded her. "Now I lost my place. Let's see, okay…blah dee da dee da. Mmh-hmm. Here we go. Luminous…bladeeblah blah dumdee, uhhhm, hmmm." He scanned text, reciting it in noises until he caught up to the sentence he had last read. "Here it is."

"Mendle—"

"This is the important part. Now listen to this. 'Science is still not certain regarding exactly what these lights are and what causes them. But it is believed that the rays are due to discharges of electricity in the rare upper atmosphere.'"

She was deafeningly quiet.

"Science is still not sure," Mendle repeated.

Still silence, then finally, "So?"

"So. Do you know what they are and what causes them?"

"No, Mendle. I don't." She almost refrained, but asked, "Do you?" and wished she had not.

"Could," he said between mischief and mystery.

"Could?"

"Perhaps I do. Could. As in might. Perhaps there are…activities going on, about which we earth people know nothing. Electrical activities in the upper atmosphere, and beyond."

"Okay, Mendle. Thanks for the news flash."

"I thought you might find it…interesting."

"Earth-shattering," Sandra carped. A messenger was standing in front of her desk and handed her a memo for the four o'clock deadline to turn in her story. "Mendle, I—"

"That's not all." Anticipating her sign-off, Mendle caught her. "This was in the paper this morning. And, did you see the lightning last night?"

"I heard the thunder, too."

"Yeah, well."

"Yeah well what?"

"Another coincidence."

"Thunder? When there's lightning?"

"No. What I was writing happened again. I was writing about electronics, a battle. And the electrical storm happened outside. I was writing it and it happened. There were storms of high voltage. Now this is in the paper—"

Sandra interrupted him. "There is help for substance abuse, you know."

Her comment triggered a high-pitched laugh. Mendle found it hilarious from his perspective. "You can't abuse a substance," he said. "It abuses you."

Sandra sighed. "Can we talk later?"

"No."

"I'm telling you, it happened. Another coincidence."

"How do you know what happened if you're drunk? Ever think about that?"

"I wasn't drunk when I was working. I saw the lightning. They both happened."

"Mendle, you've been drinking. I have work to do."

"Tell me I'm wrong. Tell me we don't live in one big magnetic field, and that solids are the illusion. Hey, so I've had a couple of drinks. Even drunk I know more what's happening than you do."

She didn't say anything.

Tossing the newspaper to the floor, Mendle said, "I can do mental pirouettes around any genius on the planet, drunk or sober. So I'm being abused by a little substance right now. I'm just trying to keep it interesting, that's it. Do you know how boring—"

"Mendle, I really have to go."

"Wait." He wanted to tell Sandra about the emptiness that had been gnawing at him. Instead, he just told her what he believed was causing it. "She's dead," he announced somberly.

"Who?"

"Aira Flight."

"Mendle. For God's sake, please get some help." Sandra hung up.

Mendle stared at the receiver and vowed he would never call her again. He was glad now he hadn't mentioned that he had also seen Aira. On second thought, he hit Auto Redial, much too hard, and at the sound of Sandra's executive yes, delivered his round.

"Sandra. I finally saw her. She's as beautiful physically as she is in spirit." He hung up.

Mendle rubbed his forehead and rolled his chair away from his desk. He stared at the floor for some moments, the focus going in and out. "Aw, no," he moaned incredulously. "I really didn't do that." His respect for himself developed another fracture.

How did I get here?

He had needed a drink, just one, to relax him. *It might prime where the novel will go next. To celebrate finishing a chapter. It would settle the churning feeling. Just a little warmth to work from the inside out.* There were plenty of reasons.

Mendle inhaled deeply, shifting his gaze to the window. Cascades of red bougainvillaea. Blue sky. It was a good day. *I have no reason to feel terrible.* Yet he did feel an ominous desperation. *What is this damn emptiness?*

He got up and began to pace. He was blocked; he couldn't write. He longed for her, for her companionship, and now she was gone.

Gone? he caught himself. *What the hell am I saying?*

In the chapter Mendle had written the night before, he had done more than feel Aira. He saw her. *It seemed so real. And the danger, when I couldn't feel her anymore.* Mendle calmed himself. It was describing her physically that made him see her, that made it seem real.

He thought about her. She had very big eyes. They were blue, bluer than blue. Her hair was gold, in waves. Her lips were full. She moved gracefully, her motions almost dance-like, yet she was strong. Her body was classical, not thin but lithe in the manner she moved it. Her hands were expressive, with very long fingers, like those of an artist. *Yes, I can still see her.*

"Who's to say what's real, anyway?" Mendle muttered to himself. His thoughts careened forward. *Reality is relative. Time is not linear. The universe is an interplay of thought and matter.*

"Stop!" he commanded his battle of thought. "Quiet." He held his head. *Maybe this is why I drink.*

Mendle began to break up on the inside. In a whirlpool of confusion, he felt so alone he tried turning himself inside out; he sobbed. The sound of his crying made him cry even more. "Me and my pathetic ideas. To think that someone from the pages of a book could come to life and love me. I am going crazy."

Mendle wiped his face. His own whimpering lament sounded strange to him. Even his plaintive words sounded like someone else. *I just wanted someone to care.* The feeling that he was groveling escalated his dolor into anger. "To save me from this excuse for a civilization, run by self-serving, profiteering greed-buckets!"

His eyes narrowing as he thought about it, Mendle pointed accusatively at the air and shouted, "There *is* a purpose to life! I better wise up. Join the club. The fuck and shit club." The pain of solitude and the sting of many miscomprehensions made their way to Mendle's face, escaping as crumpled grimaces. Brandishing his fist as if at a rally, he yelled, "People are even fighting for their rights to hear those words on records and tapes and in movies. It's even called art!"

He became quiet when, in instant retrospect, he saw himself. *Eerie.* He was screaming in pain and simultaneously observing himself again. Even now, the incessant observation and speculation didn't stop. How could it be that he was aching yet coolly watched himself going through it?

It was as though living were some sort of staged event for the purpose of learning. *There's a reason, there's a reason for everything,* Mendle reminded himself. *Maybe that was the real me,* he thought, lowering himself into his chair, *the part that remains bigger than all of it while the rest of me dives headlong into experiences of agony and bliss.*

"That's called 'detached,'" he debated aloud, then silently posed, *But maybe none of it is really real anyway.*

The gas bill was in his line of vision, the red strip reminding him of impending shut-off if he didn't pay it by the coming week. "You're real," Mendle told the bill, pointing at it with accusatory resignation.

He glanced across the room, reestablishing that his portable type-writer was still there. He had purchased it the first time his electricity had been cut off due to nonpayment. Sandra had found him that evening in candlelight, eating caviar which he had purchased in defiance of the occasion. The following day he spent the last of his money on a portable typewriter. "You never know when the electro-magnetic fields are going to shift around this planet," he said, genuinely thinking the electricity episode was fortuitous in that it prepared him. "All computer discs could be wiped out."

"Meanwhile, all the food in your refrigerator is getting wiped out," Sandra had reproached him with disdain, her usual prelude to paying a bill.

Thank God I'll be able to pay her back now.

Mendle lifted the whiskey to his mouth and drank, aware of the burn down his throat when he swallowed. "And money," he declared sardonically, "that's very real!" Setting the bottle down on the table hard made the sound jolt through his body.

"Love? Hey, a friend is someone who can give you something, that's all. Loyalty, Mr. Orion? Hah! Surely you jest. Nobility of character? What's that?"

Mendle stood up and confronted his image in a mirrored wall. He mockingly smiled for himself, holding out an imaginary microphone. "Tell me, Mr. Mystery, I mean Mr. Orion, what are your views on Art today?" he played announcer.

"Art today?" he posed, changing facial expression. "Artists have been replaced by impostors who fondle their sexual organs on stage and clamor for the rights to say four letter words! Saying they're going to liberate us! Those are the ones getting paid! Ooo, we're free now, we're really free. We can say fuck into the microphone."

Mendle suddenly didn't feel so clever; he looked ugly to himself. He wiped his face with his open palm, then made it back to his chair and sat down. His fingers knitted between his knees, he came out of several moments of quietly sitting, realizing he had been staring at the wall beseechingly.

It said nothing to him.

He yelled suddenly, "Doesn't anybody hear me? Isn't there anybody out there?"

He perched on the edge of silence.

"Hell no!" he called out so loudly it created an effect on himself. Wildly he grabbed and aimed the remote control at the television. With a flourish, he commanded it on.

"I knew you wouldn't let me down," he sneered caustically, changing channel to channel. "Yep. Murder. Rape. Shooting. War. Murder. Rape. Robbery. War."

He took a drink of whiskey from the bottle and traced another burn down his throat. *It's so nice to stop the hurt. To stop the noise. To stop it. To not care. To let go.*

Even so, somewhere, from where he had remotely pushed his awareness, Mendle Orion knew it was only a temporary solution.

Before leaving her office, one of the last things Sandra Wilford did was to phone Rex Benton. She knew he was scheduled to be a panelist at the World Science Fiction Convention, but pretended she was just finding out when he told her. She feigned a fluster and said, "I was just calling to see if you wanted to go together, but if you're already—"

"Not at all, dear," Rex agreed in his elaborate manner. "We'll go together."

Sandra was relieved she would not be alone. Attending the convention with Rex would be a good reason for being there.

"Heard from Mendle?"

She decided to tell him. "Rex, I'm very worried about him. He's not doing well."

Having heard of Mendle's recent success, Rex found perverse comfort in hearing of trouble. Mendle J. Orion having problems acted as an anchor of sorts. It didn't allow excellence to rock the boat with comparisons. It meant the world was still safe—no one was better than anybody else. No one had excelled out of the boat. Misery was uniform.

Unable to take comfort in inspiration or hope, Rex found company in limitations. He was a man to be understood more than to be condemned. In his own way, he was only seeking companionship.

chapter  8

As Mendle stood in the doorway of the therapist's office he wondered where he was going to begin. A million things clamored within him to be heard. He wiped his palms against his blue jeans, discreetly, in anticipation of a handshake.

Dr. Alfred Kaufkiff sat behind a desk. Leather everywhere accentuated the seriousness of the room. "Please." He gestured Mendle to a chair.

"You won't tell Miss Wilford?" Mendle asked of the psychiatrist as he sat down.

Dr. Kaufkiff's inquisitive gaze perched on the top rim of his glasses like a bird indecisive about taking flight. Without really extending himself past that point he assured Mendle, "All visits are strictly confidential."

"She's been recommending I come see you for some time," Mendle told him with a little self-effacing laugh as he sat down. "I'd rather tell her myself, if I tell her at all, that I finally did."

"You're not here on Sandra's behalf are you?" Alfred Kaufkiff asked. He executed a preliminary analysis of the new subject. *Under stress. Late thirties. Holds himself tightly in the shoulders.* A laissez-faire about the young man's general appearance bordered on neglect.

"No, oh no. I decided to come. For myself," Mendle told him, running his hand through his brown hair. He could feel Dr. Kaufkiff's scrutiny all over him, but it wasn't as uncomfortable as his preconceptions of therapy. "Well, then, what was it?" A quizzical look from Mendle prompted him to complete his question, "…that made you decide you needed help."

Mendle thought about it. He answered, "The new book I'm writing. Well, not the book actually. I just keep thinking all the time. Wait, let me back up." He sighed, took a deep breath.

"That's all right. Take it easy. Just say whatever comes. You don't have to worry about filtering it," Dr. Kaufkiff soothed.

"That's not it, I just want to express the actuality," Mendle told him. "I want to be accurate in my descriptions." *So you'll know what's going on with me.*

"No defensiveness or denial going on?"

"I'm not sure yet," Mendle introspected. "What's denial?"

"All right, then. Tell me about the book."

"It wasn't the book actually. That's what I was saying—"

"What were you saying?"

Mendle paused to surmount a ridge of annoyance that was densifying. He breathed deep again, stared at the rug. Finally he said, "The girl."

Dr. Kaufkiff was perching over his glasses again, this time in an unspoken question.

Mendle rubbed the inside of his palm with his thumb, alternating between each hand as he spoke. "At first I guess I knew she was based on, well, sort of a fantasy."

"A dream lover?"

"Sort of. Yes. But the more I wrote about her, the more I felt she…" Mendle had difficulty admitting it.

"Yes?"

"The more I felt she…exists," he blurted.

His and the analyst's eyes met, caution at either end.

"The other day I actually believed I…saw her."

"A hallucination?"

"I guess so." Mendle did not want to admit it wasn't real. "I don't know."

"Were you on anything?"

"No," Mendle informed him. "I do drink sometimes. That night I started drinking after I saw her. I wrote about her demise, then I couldn't contact her."

Saw her? Contact her? Dr. Kaufkiff scribbled notes. "Go on," he told Mendle.

"That's the other thing, I haven't been able to write since then. I took a drink. Then went on another binge. Didn't eat for a few days. I become afraid. I think about dying, I think about how easy it is to die. I look at my body and it all seems so futile sometimes."

"Do you ever feel…detached?"

Detached. That's right. I knew that was it. Mendle hung his head. "I suppose so, I suppose that's what it is," he mumbled. "I used to think that was some power I had. I used to think I was some kind of being who—"

A dry little laugh from Dr. Kaufkiff interrupted him. He was scribbling something in a notebook. "I'm with you," he held Mendle at bay while he finished the notes. Dr. Kaufkiff glanced up to find Mendle was looking at him earnestly.

For some reason, Mendle was noticing how pink the psychiatrist's cheeks were; the skin was smooth and pink, reminiscent of a pig's. As Dr. Kaufkiff peered back across the massive desk from behind his fortress of books and leather, an acute desire to laugh seized Mendle. He looked down at his fingers, pretending to be engrossed in an imaginary something on his hand. *What is so funny about pink cheeks?* He checked himself.

It wasn't just the pink, the psychiatrist's entire visage was ludicrous. *All that earnestness is synthetic.* For all the concentration the psychiatrist was sustaining on his carefully prepared, calm visage, Mendle decided he hadn't an inkling to what was going on inside another human being.

He quickly tried to think of something serious, the death of his grandfather, anything to dissolve the laughter that was shaking inside him and threatening to erupt. When he had successfully quelled the nervous internal bobbings that would have escaped as laughter, Mendle looked up again. He managed a serious face to convey interest and close attention. He even knit his eyebrows to muster seriousness. Then he lost it, and laughed.

Had Mendle not been looking directly at the psychiatrist when he burst out laughing, an explanation may have been easier. He could feel the psychiatrist's unwavering evaluation of him, yet the more he tried to stop laughing, the harder laughter seized him. That smooth face, the eyes that perched wisely with no connection to soul seemed hilariously funny.

Suspicion visibly accumulated on the analyst's face. *He's thinking I'm insane. Better do something.* Mendle grappled for control, looking away, grasping at an excuse. "I just thought about the science fiction convention. I'll be receiving an award," he said as he steadied. He rambled on, trying to make sense. "Sometimes problems can seem pretty serious but, put it all into perspective, life is really not so bad. Maybe there's more truth when you're laughing than when you're crying. I feel better already."

That's all I need, someone to clinically diagnose me as insane. Mendle coughed and composed himself in the chair, once more looking up attentively.

"I will look forward to reading your novel," Kaufkiff said.

"Thank you, doctor," Mendle replied.

Alfred Kaufkiff made some notes, "manic-depressive" among them. "Let me ask you this," he preambled while jotting, then looked up, "Can you describe this woman?"

"Yes." Mendle was glad for an opportunity to do so. "She loves justice, and aspires to honor. She loves Beauty. She works at keeping her word, being fair. She's disciplined. She's kind, she's very intelligent. Not just smart, but truly intelligent. You see, she was a spirit."

"A spirit?"

"Yes," Mendle said. "She was a thought-being."

"That's unusual."

"Really? How so?" Mendle asked, looking for some clue to himself.

With a knowing gesture of the eyebrows Kaufkiff said, "Most men don't dream of *thought*. I'll put it that way."

Mendle considered the comment and concluded, "Oh, I don't know. There's a media image, but even the most sex-motivated guys I know secretly crave something else. Especially the ones who go to bed with women they can't stand."

As Mendle noted Kaufkiff's interest become more than clinical, he began getting the sense that he was in control, a sense familiar to him. Once again he was with yet another someone who would not be able to offer any seniority of thought.

"Interesting," Kaufkiff commented, finding it so on a personal level. "What does your fantasy look like?"

"She could make herself appear however she wanted to, when she wanted to be seen."

Alfred Kaufkiff ruminated this. "It is convenient, I suppose, that she can change her appearance at will. Do you have her do so to suit you for, ah, variety?"

"No, it isn't like that at all." Mendle became defensive.

"Tell me about her."

"She's perfect."

The doctor homed in, "Ah, but perfect to you is not perfect to me. Let me give you an example. How tall is she?"

"That's just it. She's really beautiful. She's a soul. It has nothing to do with her body."

"But you said you saw her?"

"In the last chapter, she was trapped. She was being permanently materialized into a human female."

Dr. Kaufkiff pursued a possibility. "When she became 'permanently material,' as you say, did this disappoint you?"

"In a way. I felt worried about her."

"When she took on a physical form, was she...less perfect?" Kaufkiff asked.

"I'm not sure."

"For example, one man might fantasize a woman. Long, thin legs," Dr. Kaufkiff illustrated.

"Modern image used to market dresses. Like Sandra." Mendle interjected.

"Red hair, or black hair," Kaufkiff was saying. "What if when a woman materializes she becomes boring? Is suddenly not as perfect as one dreamed her?"

"No. Not at all. I see where you're going. No. She could have had black hair, or red hair, or green hair, it wouldn't have mattered."

"But what color hair *did* she have?"

"Blonde, as a matter of fact."

"I see." Kaufkiff nodded. "Blue eyes by chance?"

"Well, yes." Mendle found himself becoming defensive.

"Tall? Legs? Bust?"

"She's not skinny. She's not tall. More a classic build. She's...comfortable. But this has nothing to do with her physical appearance *per se.*" Mendle did not like the tone this was taking.

"Now we are getting somewhere."

"We are?"

"Of course."

Mendle watched expectantly.

"She is a contour-image."

"A what?"

"A 'dream girl' is a contour-image of your own mind. She is a comfort and pleases you, whatever makes you feel confident and manly." Dr. Kaufkiff was enunciating with detail. "You are afraid the more real she becomes, or 'permanently material,' as you say, the less perfect she will be. You are outgrowing your fantasy."

"No! But she knows me. She understood me! I felt her." Mendle struggled for words to describe it, "It's like feeling her all over me, inside me. She's there. It's as if one day she's going to come to me..."

"Sure." Alfred Kaufkiff replied assuringly.

"...as if one day I'll find her."

The desperation in Mendle's voice did not go unnoticed. Dr. Kaufkiff emitted a dry little laugh. "It can feel very real," he said, paused, then, as if dropping a bomb, added, "Women like this do not exist. Except in your mind."

"Don't you believe in great love?" Mendle asked.

Alfred Kaufkiff explained, "The true love syndrome is one of the most common, everybody looking for that special someone."

"It's a *syndrome*?" Mendle felt himself sinking.

Dr. Kaufkiff smiled congenially and nodded. "Have you ever wanted to get her out of your mind?"

"No, not really. In fact I've been worried," Mendle admitted confidentially, "I haven't been able to see her lately. Since being turned into a physical human form, it's as if she's dead."

"Dead?" Kaufkiff mused.

"She became matter, flesh. I haven't been able to write since then."

"I see." Kaufkiff pronounced. "Most curious, don't you think?"

"Curious?" Mendle felt hope.

"That you would call her dead when she becomes physical. Usually death means a person *losing* a physical body, not gaining one."

"Yes, I guess so," Mendle admitted earnestly. He began talking mostly to himself. "Maybe she's not dead. Maybe she's just in another world. You can't see the person, but the person just entered a different dimension."

Dr. Kaufkiff confirmed delusion in the patient. "Do you mean perhaps this woman who you once could see in your thoughts has actually become physical somewhere else?"

"I find it difficult to say anything is impossible, doctor," Mendle said solemnly. "A quantum physicist might agree."

"Of course," Kaufkiff said. He approached Mendle from another angle. "Is this fantasy helping or interfering with your sex life?"

"What is a sex life?" Mendle asked. "Do I have an eating life? A sleeping life? A learning life? Why should sex have a separate life?"

Dr. Kaufkiff went off on another ramification. "Does the fantasy keep you from enjoying other women?"

"No. You talk about women as if they're popcorn. The position of 'woman' just isn't filled at the moment." He sat back and felt Dr. Kaufkiff's gaze on him like suction. "Maybe it did, a little. Interfere, I mean, with Sandra. After I knew someone like Aira existed, I compared them."

"Aira?"

"That's her name."

"Ohhhh, I see." Dr. Kaufkiff noted Mendle's referring to her as if she existed. Not knowing where to go for the moment, he said, "Some men use their fantasies, to be with whomever."

"I don't. I wouldn't want to be with a woman and think of someone else if that's what you mean. Although I've done it."

"So you're saving yourself for this woman?" Kaufkiff explored.

Mendle was off in a high-pitched laugh. "That's funny." He laughed some more. "That's funny." When his amusement subsided, Mendle said, "I just believe in concentration, body and soul."

Alfred Kaufkiff studied the young man. He delved into the confidence Mendle seemed to have about his prowess. "You have a high opinion of your sexual performance."

Suddenly somber, "I don't view it as...performance," Mendle said.

"What was the problem with Sandra?"

"She's told you about me, hasn't she?" Mendle didn't expect a reply. He went on, "I just didn't..." He struggled for words to explain it, hurrying so as not to have the psychiatrist finish the sentence for him—a habit he was finding very aggravating, "...didn't want to be intimate with her. Know what I mean?"

"Did that start with the fantasies of the girl?"

"That's what Sandra thought. But I wouldn't have picked Sandra as a friend. She used sex. I didn't like her, but the sensation was pleasurable. I didn't act with integrity. I just couldn't...I couldn't..." His voice trailed off. "I couldn't lie anymore."

Silence swelled in the room.

Kaufkiff spoke. "Would you like to meet the fantasy woman?"

Mendle liked the idea. It surprised him. "Well, yes. I guess so, but how?"

"Hypnosis," Dr. Kaufkiff said. "Now, just come over here." He pushed himself back from his desk and motioned Mendle over to a divan in a corner of the room.

"Am I crazy, doctor?"

"That, I'm afraid, would not be a clinical diagnosis."

"Why not?"

"Let's say it's not specific enough."

Mendle felt foreboding but he sat down anyway and reclined.

"As you can see," Kaufkiff said, "the dreaming of a perfect woman might be inherent to every male of the species. But ask every man to describe the perfect woman and you will come up with as many variations as there are men."

Mendle could not dispute that point but marveled at how the psychiatrist kept diverging from the issue. The point was not that she was perfect, but that he truly loved a woman who, logically, did not exist.

"I think I've cured myself, doctor." Mendle sat up. "You see, the problem is that I love a woman who doesn't exist."

"I think you have a confusion with sex," Dr. Kaufkiff analyzed. "You do not respect the woman once she has become physical."

"Really?" It didn't sound like him, but Mendle was willing to contemplate it.

"Let's discover where this denial is coming from."

"Denial? What's wrong with denial if something isn't true? Sex isn't everything. It's not in my toothpaste like they say. Sex is not all that makes me a man," Mendle protested. "My character, virtues, honor, beauty—"

"Yes, yes, of course," Kaufkiff interrupted. "Close your eyes. You are getting very sleepy. You are becoming sleepy now. Just focus on my voice, listen to my voice, to my words. Relax. You are relaxing. You are letting go."

"This is like the novel!" Mendle uttered to himself, his eyes flying open. Amused by the absurdity of the situation, he quickly propped himself up on his elbow.

The motion was so sudden it startled Alfred Kaufkiff who retracted his neck into his shirt and clutched the lapel of his collar as he listened to Mendle.

"I wrote about a place called Z Zone, where beings are sent to eternal sleep, sentenced to oblivion…and look at what you're doing! Trying to put me to sleep. Everything I write has a parallel in the world around me!"

"Good, good," Dr. Kaufkiff placated him. "Let's see if we can get somewhere with this."

"Sorry, I just had to tell you that," Mendle apologized, lying back down. "It's really amazing all the synchronicity. The co-incidence."

"Yes, of course. Close your eyes. Now listen to my voice. You are getting very, very sleepy. You feel heavy. Relaxed…"

As Dr. Kaufkiff's voice droned on and on, Mendle found himself resisting. *I don't want to go to sleep to find out what's bothering me. I want to be awake. I want to know. Myself.*

chapter  9

Coming out of days of drinking, Mendle groped for a balance. He had been treading the world within and the world without. He sought to mediate the disparity between his own world, where he only needed to think something and it was so, and the world of walls which did not allow one to walk through them. In one, he ruled. The other, called Reality by most, was a tyranny where walls reigned and consistently rebuked him as meaningless. Yet something about it also taunted him. That outer world seemed a ballet of interaction where something else was at play besides sheer force and matter. Somehow he could affect it; he felt he saw evidence of his influence on surrounding reality. *Coincidences. They beckon me like cosmic smiles.* Yet the process of 'perceiving the maze,' as he called his endeavor, and attaining wisdom often defeated Mendle. The crimes and conditions to which humanity seemed 'adjusted' slashed at his awareness as the atrocities they were and caused him unbearable anguish.

Mendle drank to ease the meaningless, unreasoning pain that dug at him daily. Although he held in disdain those who never questioned their existence and fought against what he termed 'The Comfort Zone of Oblivion,' the very thing he cursed was surreptitiously conquering him. He shared with the rest of the human race, it seemed, a desire to escape from that anonymous gnawing pain.

Alfred Kaufkiff accompanied Mendle down the long aseptic corridor toward the elevators. They walked in silence. Haunted by what he had seen through a glass partition in the corridor, Mendle could not liberate himself from the image of a young woman being wheeled away to electroshock against her will. He was told he was not supposed to have seen the involuntary treatment ward. *Her screams, God, those screams.*

He regretted having come to a place he inherently distrusted. Dismissing it as 'just a feeling,' he had ignored his own inner reality. Now he vowed to listen to his instinct. *I may not always know what the reason is, but there is one.*

Allowing himself to be electrically shocked every time he thought about taking a drink of whiskey was not his idea of help. He had a pretty low opinion of himself at times, but reducing himself to the level of a stimulus-response slave flew in the face of everything from which he derived self-respect. *I'm not an organism. I possess a will. I want to be awake. I want to understand.*

Mendle's face darkened the more he thought about having voluntarily put himself on the premises, and he shuddered thinking about some of the others there. These people were not all there of their own volition. Many, like that girl he had seen, had been "signed away," prescribed to have portions of their lives simply 'removed.'

That is not therapy. It was more an admission of failed therapy, Mendle concluded. *Can't fix it, so destroy it.*

"Are you still thinking about the patient?"

Patient, right. "The person I saw?" Mendle said, upholding her as a human being. "A little," he admitted. He tried not to appear glum.

"I'm sorry you had to see that on your tour of the Institute. It's not pleasant, I know," Dr. Kaufkiff told Mendle as he accompanied him to the elevator.

Not pleasant? Mendle rebelled with every iota of his being at the thought. *Just get out of here, just keep it cool and get out of here.* He placed one foot after the other on the shiny, clean floor.

"Some cases only respond to electroshock. After the treatment, she will be fine," Dr. Kaufkiff said. "Her family has her best interests in mind."

They stepped into the elevator. Mendle watched Kaufkiff push the L for Lobby. The thought of the woman made him close his eyes and cringe. Her hair, wild serpents, stuck all over her perspiring face. *Those screams.* She screamed and screamed and screamed, begging them not to do it while they forced her away.

"It is for her own good, that is the foremost thought one must keep in mind," Dr. Kaufkiff was saying.

Obliterating her memory? Electroshocking her past out of existence?

"But let's worry about you."

Me? Mendle reflected. He opened his eyes then laughed nervously. "I'm afraid there is no cure for me, Dr. Kaufkiff," he said affably.

"You may think this way now. You yourself say you are up again, down again. If you change your mind, call and I'll prescribe something."

Drugs, right. Just what I need to help me really get insight into reality. Tried that. Been there.

"Call me when you know your schedule."

As they stepped out of the elevator, Mendle turned and looked squarely at Dr. Kaufkiff. Within the boundaries of seconds, an entire silent soliloquy took place. "Living is a war," Mendle told Dr. Kaufkiff.

The rest he spoke in his head, with his entire being. *Some of us hold out, some give in early. But eventually, it wears you down.*

Someone is mean to us for no good reason. A wish that's dashed and never happens. We lose. The death of someone we know. A betrayal by someone we loved and trusted. Someone cheats us. Someone doesn't care when you need them. A lot of someones just don't give a damn. Too many times alone when somebody should've been there. It adds up—little hurt here, a little wound there. This dream gone. This belief laughed at. This ideal shattered. Eventually you see they just wanted to sell you something. Then, into focus comes the stark, meaningless space and time, and the self-serving protoplasm that populate it.

You try to make home. You go home, with the face looking a little more tired every day, a little more hurt, a little less happy, a little more heavy, a little more lined...and then what? And for what? Eventually, the walls and ground and everything solid laughs at you. Laughs at your beliefs as it counts the last one you pay out for a solution to reality.

You have to put away those beliefs, that's not what the 'real' world operates on. Sure, you learn the ideals in school, but 'ha-ha-ha!' That's not what's being played.

So you pay. You pay out every hope and ideal. You pay belief in love. You pay high ideals bigger than self. Until you're paid out. And broke, and helpless, on your back. Your hair is white if you make it that far, and your skin is sagging. Breath to breath with dying...and Reality, solid and intense goes off, jingling all your dreams in its pocket. Laughing. Laughing at poor, stupid little you who ever dared to dream a thing.

"Do you have a cure for that?" he asked, calmly holding Dr. Kaufkiff in his gaze. To the man's silence, Mendle smiled, shook his head and finally replied for him, "I don't think so."

As they approached the front entrance, Alfred Kaufkiff told Mendle, "You are a smart man. You have some very lucid moments."

Mendle couldn't help but laugh as he said, "That's the problem. We all do." *It's my lucidity that will face and find the problems,* he vowed, *not some artificially imposed program that reduces me to the level of a robot.*

Standing at farewell attention, placing his hands behind his back, Dr. Kaufkiff asked Mendle one last question. "Do you think of yourself as sane?"

"No," Mendle replied, having seen the trick in a movie.

After a quick farewell, Mendle crossed the lobby and stepped out into the morning air. Jaunting down the front steps, he liked the sound of his keys in his pocket.

In the parking lot, tremors peeled off him. *Sleepy, sleepy, sleepy,* he remembered as he unlocked his car door and slid in the seat behind the steering wheel. "Doctor, I can't seem to get drowsy," Mendle re-enacted, then mimicked the analyst's tone, "Hhm, I see," he pronounced, seriously concerned. He played himself as he adjusted the rearview mirror. "What is it, doctor?"

Mendle looked at himself in the rearview mirror and arranged his face the way Dr. Kaufkiff had done. He shook his head slowly back and forth, and rubbed his chin. "You always have to be in control, don't you?"

He had responded, "I like to be. Is there something wrong?"

Back to the doctor. "Just a mild neurosis. Every once in a while we run into some cases who don't go under."

"Under? I don't want to go under."

The doctor was grave. "That's precisely the point. At least you admit it."

Cold crawled up Mendle's back. He became suddenly self-conscious about talking to himself. He looked around to see if anyone were watching. No one had seen him. He inserted and turned the key in the ignition then disengaged the emergency brake and let the engine idle to warm up. *There's nothing wrong with me.*

His thoughts turned to the scene he had inadvertently witnessed of the person being wheeled away to be shocked against her will. Suddenly, Mendle's eyes widened, his mouth opened, and he stared at what seemed to be a clue of some kind—what was happening to the girl in the Institute was essentially the same thing that was happening to his heroine in the novel. His last chapter had been about her struggling to save herself from the doom of her past being taken from her. He was writing that. And now he had seen this. *Another coincidence! This is amazing.*

Mendle maneuvered his automobile out of its parking space. His mouth was still open, his eyes still wide in excitement over the idea of a clue that was offering some insight to his existence. *There is some kind of synchronicity going on here.* Heading toward the gates, he turned on the radio.

"…because I want a girl to call my own, I want a dream lover so I don't have to dream alone…" The song *Dream Lover* played.

"Whoa!" Mendle exclaimed.

Having been notified of Mendle's departure, the security guard had activated the gate opening and was checking off something on a clipboard. The man smiled pleasantly as the silver sedan slowly drove by. "Morning. How are you?"

"Morning. Fine, thanks," Mendle replied cordially.

Past the gates Mendle felt electrical charge zinging up and off of him. "Morning. Yes it is morning. Welcome and thank you for volunteering." He listened to the gears of his silver Toyota wind before changing into the higher one, enjoying the feel of a tight machine operating under his control. "There's nothing wrong with me," he said. He felt the wind on his face. "There's nothing wrong with me," he repeated. *I'm just awake.*

Mendle was glad to be home. If anything, the trip to the Institute finally eliminated what he had mistakenly thought of as being procrastination. He felt better just having confirmed to himself his instinctive doubts and mistrust were justified.

Reclining on a rattan seat outside his small house with a cup of tea on the table beside him, propping his feet one on the other, leaning his head and resting on his hands, Mendle looked up at the sky. Gazing into the blue, he often felt himself going beyond the sky into space. He groped his location in the cosmos with fingers of knowledge; his position in the galaxy was clear to him in concept. He was, at that very moment, on one of nine planets. Earth, a speck of a blue planet that circled an enormous sun, was in its turn orbited by a planetoid called a moon.

Mendle took the perspective of being out in space, experiencing the line-up of those balls of mass around the sun. *Mercury, Venus, Earth, Mars, Jupiter, Saturn, Uranus, Neptune, Pluto.* He felt as though he actually encompassed the solar system. *I can see it.* The ritual was a necessary orientation for him and it was one he often performed, marveling at the microcosms and macrocosms of physical world fabric. The solar system with its nucleus of sun did not by happenstance resemble an atom.

Flight, Mendle imagined, rising, soaring out of his physical body into the perfect blue atmosphere of the morning. *If this mean I'm "detached," so be it.* He smiled.

Watching a silver jet glinting tiny in the distance, Mendle imagined the people within its tubularly compressed air and suddenly saw a stewardess maneuvering a cart down the narrow aisle. *Maybe Thought can actually see.* The airplane was beautiful, swimming through air.

Air isn't nothing. Mendle considered the principle of lift that was keeping the plane in the sky. When in motion, the curved upper surfaces caused faster displacement and lower pressure of the air above the wings, creating that push from the air beneath which lifted the plane off the ground. The first person who knew flight was possible didn't know *how* it was possible. In fact, there were more things, gravity for one, that dictated specifically how it was *not.*

Mendle imagined how the first flight must have seemed like magic; it still seemed like magic. He followed the jet in its path across the morning blue. *Flight.* Seeing a thing unattached and suspended gave the sensation that it could just fall at any minute, but it wasn't magic that kept the plane up. It was lift. Air was not merely the *absence* of solid ground, as people must have at one time viewed it—it was *something.* Though invisible to the human eye, air was a sea of substance.

Miracles are when something fantastic happens and the 'how' hasn't been discovered yet. There is a 'how' possible for all that can be imagined, Mendle speculated. "*Impossibility* is the only illusion," he murmured under his breath. Human beings were certain they could fly before they even knew about lift, rocket power, and the technical aspects to support them or put them into orbit.

When Mendle returned to the point of view of a human looking through biological eyes, he located the sun in the sky and reminded himself of the daily illusion of it rising and setting. The sun didn't move. Yet an entire planet of people persisted in saying it rose and set. *Illusion. Physical limits and barriers are illusion.*

With a little effort, Mendle sat up, perceiving the reality of gravity. Yet because heroes dreamed they could fly, that was real now, too. It seemed to him that most, if not all, things were *secondary* to the will; reality followed. *Perhaps the relationship between thought and reality is totally symbiotic, with thought being the preliminary animator.*

The spirit of flight was the very spirit of imagination to Mendle. No matter how solid 'reality' was, its seed was the dream. *The dream, the dream…* The ability to dream, to conceive, to imagine was his life-source, his power, and Mendle felt it, felt himself, again.

His thoughts went to Aira Flight. Like air, her first name reflected her as a soul, invisible to the human eye but of substance nonetheless. Mendle reached for his cup and pressed the curve of ceramic against his palms.

The moment one is no longer earth-bound, that is the spirit of Flight. He drank the last of his tea, now cooled, and got up from the rattan chair. He felt he could write.

Letting the screen door slam behind him, Mendle went inside the house.

The Lauryad ripped through atmospheres and dimensions. Its travel was not along vectors, nor linear in any way. It traveled as if absorbed and effused by densities and realities.

Out of range of the barrage by overwhelming electrical voltages, Aira was helplessly attached to the Lauryad by energy. As she manifested into molecules, the molecules inextricably interacted with other forms. As she transmuted universe to universe, she was not even aware of herself as herself. The power to create, the power of her very will had been usurped, knocked out of her, occupied by and channeled to activate the very electrical programs that pinned her.

Hurtling away from Z Zone toward other realities, Aira was stunned, spinning in a confusion that eluded her. She was no longer goddess, but dormant in a mishmash of thought and programming, her very essence undermined, fooled into believing that she was everything she felt, not the source of feeling. Beside her was the thought-being known as Onx, also stunned beyond self-awareness, without even a glimmer of awareness of surrounding existence.

"Aira, my Aira," Mendle breathed, desperate for her safety. He could feel her again.

chapter 10

Blackness.

chapter 11

Out of the blackness, Aira adhered to a field. She felt no pain now, she was only dormant Thought, floating along currents of the field's established physical laws. It was a two-terminal field, based on the pole-principle, and currents flowed at different rates between different sets of poles. There was an infinity of twos, and currents between them were perpetual.

Soon the twos were positioned closer and closer to one another. Their locations were in no repetitive pattern. Between two given points, in the space between their spectrum, existed other points, each with their own positive and negative end, and between those existed others, and so on, until they became what appeared to be a complex network of currents within currents, each exerting on the other enough force to prevent a total collapse of points.

The field appeared infinite and contained other fields within it, all in equilibrium and inter-relation. The network became denser and denser, thus more solid, yet it maintained the status of wavelength because, no matter how dense, it was still only particles in motion.

The particles, also comprised of poles with negative-positive ends, were tiny masses. They themselves traveled in wavelengths within the Vast Wavelength and among various points. This created Space.

Some of the masses, because of their speed, could be perceived, or received and absorbed by other masses. The more fluid were Light and Sound. The flow was Energy.

Other masses were rigid bodies and their currents stayed within themselves. Thus their forms remained intact and traveled as a whole unit. These rigid bodies were collections of particles which adhered into a solid shape.

In this manner, within the space created among widely distant points, there was motion of aggregates of particles. These appeared to be solids and objects, positioned in space.

But all of it was Thought made manifest, and the life that catalyzed it had forgotten it was Life. Throughout the conglomerate, unimaginable quanta of life, of lives, slumbered yet were the adhesive, the catalysts, unknowingly maintaining it all only by a decision (though made billeniums before billeniums) to persist.

The magnetic field known as the Vast Wavelength was pinned to Thought by the force of electrical facsimiles, and crosscurrents united it as a whole, creating the erroneous illusion that it was One. Thus it became more and more complex.

This was the wavelength on which Aira and Onx traveled. On this current, toward the interconnecting currents, they were somnambulantly headed, destined to a somniferous complexity. The labyrinth was so convincing that eventually complete inversion occurred, and the creator became the creation and only reacted helplessly, eternally, toward further condensation.

Solid.

Not aware. Never realizing.

With a jolt, she was suddenly awake. Then unconscious. Then awake.

Aira had almost traversed the spectrum and reached the first degree of density. In Z Zone, Juristac had programmed her for the protoplasm line which would grow, cell upon cell, into organs, into organisms. She was headed for the union of negative-positive on a cellular level: the fusion into two properties, joined by an energy vector.

There appeared to be more space, more distance between the particles. But the particles floating in it were planets, and within the planets the physical dictates were maintained in denser form.

There was more density. Less and less space.

In the moments where she was cognizant, Aira was aware of Loptoor. She did not know where she was and she was suffering dazed astonishment which deprived her of all perception and self-awareness other than fleeting glimpses of something. Something to which she was still connected.

Juristac. Loptoor. She knew someone was fighting for her, to free her, to prevent this danger. She felt the dormant thought-being that had been Onx next to her. But who was she? She was herself, yet diffused and dispersed, struggling to stay awake. Then more blackness and compression. She was not aware of it for she was again perceiving nothing.

Then, consciousness glimmered again as a tremendous force lifted. She sensed Loptoor had disengaged the force that was bearing on her. He was fighting Juristac. She knew this, but was instantly submerged once more into absolute nonentity.

The magnetic forces of Juristac's program for Aira aligned with a tiny planet on the outskirts of a galaxy which itself was in a remote corner of a magnetic field comprised of millions of galaxies.

The blueprint for the protoplasmal line was set. That was to be the form.

Facsimiles of the planet's shared reality were rapidly adhering to her: a common mind, an energy machine fully equipped with pictures, data, images to make environ and limitations appear normal. Destination: a pregnant woman… Less than a thousandth of a second before Aira congealed into a sperm-ovum fetus, Loptoor swung a control in Z Zone, then another…

Aira did not electrically adhere to and become the fetus. As a result of the thwarted procedure, she was sufficiently freed for atoms and particles to align to her own concept of her light-body, her own consideration of what she would look like if manifest...She materialized as solid matter in the form of a woman.

Her power as a thought-being surged, yet she was reading light through eyes, looking at photons. She was in a square room and a corpulent native lying on a padded platform was staring at her with a bewildered look, her eyes wide, aghast.

First the lady's mouth opened, then she spoke. "Wow!"

Aira looked down and saw her own body. She was dressed in a tunic, a Tribunal uniform. There beside her she sensed the thought-being Onx, in a new, unknown form, covered with hair from head to tail.

Momentarily in possession of a semblance of senses, Aira looked up and stared back at the inhabitant of the room and repeated what she thought was a greeting, "Wow." Even as she spoke she was already beginning to dematerialize.

She vanished, leaving behind a staring woman, amazed by what she had seen and wondering if she had really seen it.

The repercussions of Loptoor's interference continued. Aira was in the Lauryad again. She could no longer sense Onx next to her. She had seen her dissolve into atmosphere. Some remote knowledge told Aira that the thought-being Onx had been absorbed by another Time/Space, perhaps the one from which Aira just melted away.

Aira's will rallied and she sought to embrace the foremost truth of love and loyalty. She thought-reached to touch all whom she loved and who loved her. *With Love there is no distance. Where are you? Where are you?* Her distress emanated to the universe.

The Lauryad ripped through another atmosphere, then fluctuated into yet another dimension, then re-entered the one just departed. Aira felt a huge impact, then pain. As the debarkation panels opened, she stumbled forward to the opening. It was dark outside, night.

A man wearing blue cotton overalls was standing there, his grinning face luminous with happiness. "I know who ye are," he said. "Welcome. I'm a friend."

Aira felt herself vanishing again, this time away from the Lauryad. Helplessly, she felt it, and saw her hands evaporate off the side panels she gripped for support.

"I'll be back..." Aira heard herself make the noises; they were words. She knew the words because their significance had been installed in a memory bank of some sort, a memory bank that made her feel both adjusted and strange.

The reality upon which she was focusing dissolved from her view. Helplessly, she watched her ship disappear as it remained in the dimension from which she was disintegrating. Elements rebelled at the massive disalignments which were now occurring.

Aira's thought was sporadically free. Her will intermittently imposed itself on the surrounding physical elements. Her focus was fragmented but still powerful. The program fluctuated with extreme polarizations. Nucleic groupings set off their own chain reactions. The havoc and friction resulted in currents, some of which clashed, and an electrical storm raged in full regalia of thunder, lightning, heavy winds, and rainfall.

Aira had congealed with a protoplasmal line. She had avoided the fetus but her body blueprint solidified into a fully developed organism. With lungs she breathed the atmosphere. A heart beat in her chest, blood coursed through veins.

By the sensation of flesh and nerve readings to the brain, she found herself standing in a different environ. She was registering images via light, with eyes, with retinas. Feeling a sense of attachment, she looked down at her feet then held her arms out for inspection. Mesmerized by the appendages, she rotated the hands which she repeatedly opened and clenched.

Looking up, Aira saw grayness and swirling air currents that directed clouds into diaphanous marble. Showering sheets of water made it difficult to keep her eyes open; the drops hit her eyes and stung. Still, she kept her head back and blinked rapidly, as though trying to see between the drops, while planes of water, determined at slightly varied angles by the winds, drenched her.

The sensation simplified her confusion for, if nothing else, she was certain of her skin and it made her feel alive.

Though she possessed a point of view, it was fixed, only uni-directional, and she was not aware of being but only stared, marveling at the objects in motion around her. She did not know them as streets, walls, pavement, trees…she only sensed that life slept in masses so solidly that it could not view her.

Suddenly she was stunned again and her eyes appeared to vacate slightly as she shifted them in order to look at something else. The mind she was accumulating was now replacing her brief stupefaction, clarifying the things she saw. The buildings which stacked from the street matched mental facsimiles she was acquiring; she knew they were buildings; she knew the street as a street; nothing seemed odd.

Telephone poles…At one time she might have analyzed them as curious lines of metal, conductors that relayed electrical impulses to which adhered sound-symbols, mechanical substitutes for concept-relay. She would have known that thought was instantaneous and did not need to travel through distance.

Phone lines would have once indicated a condition of occluded awareness. She would have deduced she was in a society of beings who denied their thought-power and considered their inventions superior to themselves and their inherent abilities. But as she looked now, she simply registered them as "telephone poles."

She did not even question or define their presence.

Bllweaaahhhh. The loud honking of a horn startled her and Aira jumped back onto the sidewalk to avoid the blue Chrysler which turned the corner.

The driver slowed to get a better look at her, and it was for some reason frightening to Aira. Perhaps it was the way the woman craned her head to look through the window; there was something incongruous about the wide span of her grin and the amazement that rounded her eyes. A woman seated next to the driver was pointing at Aira and laughing.

Aira averted her eyes and looked down at herself. She felt her nakedness as others saw it, and felt shame and a need to cover her body. She drop-crouched to her knees and watched the women drive off.

Looking around her, she saw a trash canister. Some newspapers beside it were drenched, but a crumpled brown plastic garbage bag stuck by the leg of the canister remained intact. She shook it out and, still crouching to the sidewalk, adapted it as a covering for her body, poking and tearing openings for her head and arms as she slipped it on.

Slowly, Aira stood up and looked around her. Hesitantly, she decided on a direction and began to walk. The motion was all new to her, but familiar somehow. She passed shop display windows and peered into them, wiping the water from her face and pushing her hair back to see better. Behind the glass, mannequins flourishing bent elbows held permanent poses at exaggerated angles. Hips thrust hither and thither. Propped under a chin or parked on a thigh, their hands gestured at nothing.

Aira wondered why the people bore such angry and arrogant expressions, why they did not move, why they all appeared to be bettering the other. Then she remembered, or extrapolated, somehow the thought entered her mind—they were not alive.

GET THE LOOK HERE. The sign was big and spangled in a window. ULTIMATE FASHION.

What look? she wondered. The angry look? She did not understand. She wondered why they looked so important. They were on platforms as ideal images, manifestations that beckoned aspiration. But they were un-friendly, their posed attitudes seemed to make less of those around them.

A bolt of lightning crackled around her, claps of thunder startled her and rumbled across the sky. Aira started to run.

As Juristac and Loptoor struggled for final control of the channel in which Aira was locked, she fluctuated between confused reactivity and the brink of some sense of self. She ran down the boulevard.

Crystal chandeliers. Lamps. Italian Furniture. Scandinavian Furni-ture. Books. Gold necklaces and colored gems that glistened on black vel-vet. Tiny, immobilized miniature blazes of rubies and luminous emeralds scintillated in gold and silver settings that elevated them for adoration.

Corundum, Aira knew. *A common mineral, aluminum oxide, notable for its hardness.* It went through her head faster than time and she won-dered how she knew it, doubted if what she knew was true, wondered why small chips of it were isolated in a window. DIAMONDS ARE FOR-EVER, the sign read. Concise galaxies of them effulged against more black velvet.

Her body was still running but she realized that, somehow, she re-mained motionless by that window. Lingering in vision only, she had been looking at the diamonds without using her eyes.

Suddenly her awareness snapped to her eyes and she looked through them again. Chocolates in gold boxes. Stuffed cloth bears, giraffes, piglets, cats. More mannequins. Shoes. Purses. Skis. Bicycles. *Want me! Want me! Want me!* the objects seemed to cry out to her as she passed.

Aira looked down at her feet, one thrusting forward after the other, after the other, after the other: left, right, left, right, past the curb and down onto the street...*Blwaaooonkooonnnk*, another horn, louder, longer, and a shrill rubbery screech as a vehicle fishtailed to a stop, barely miss-ing her.

Abruptly, she froze, palpitations in her chest. She simultaneously winced, trembled, and stared in surprise.

"You stupid bitch! Watch where you're going!" The man had manu-ally rolled down his window to tell her that, then, still squinting from the rain that sprayed in his face, he fiercely rolled it back up and took off.

Another angry face, she pondered. She had wanted to communicate. She had felt an urge to tell him she had not meant to cause him trouble or displeasure, but he was gone before she could even begin to do so.

The thought of bringing anything but good to another was painful. Aira crumpled into tears. It wasn't only that incident causing the lachrymal effect; it was something which she could not define but which was as acute and real as the concrete upon which she stood.

She wanted to run; she didn't know where. Gripped by an urgency to vacate where she was standing, she was afraid now and looked around cautiously. Another vehicle was stopped at the corner. There was a man inside it. He was looking at her and waving his hand repetitively across his face.

Suddenly everything seemed suspicious to her, that is, it was strange. She could not define anything in any capacity, had no comparison or reference data. The car was not a car, the body in it was not a body. They were masses in motion with no meaning, no significance, no definition, no prior data with which to compare them, no name or symbol whatsoever.

The driver stopped trying to wave her the right of way to cross the street. He shot her a look of disgust and drove off. Instead of crossing the street, Aira veered right and turned the corner.

Her insides felt congealed; the ache swallowed her so completely that she became the hurt, unaware that it was she who was feeling it. She looked all around her, her eyes darting randomly, her thoughts spinning.

She happened to look at a man on the ground in a doorway. She thought it was garbage at first then noticed that a figure emerged from the newspapers. His hair was matted and filth caked his face and jacket; his feet were calloused and cracked with dirt. His head was craned back, propped against the door, and his entire person lay limp in malodor and despair.

Aira interrupted her gait to look at him. She felt an impulse to go wake him up, then fear harnessed her, then pain, and she felt she could not even bear to look at him. She continued walking away from him, backwards because even though it hurt to look at him, something about it transfixed and amazed her. Aira harbored a sob in her throat and simultaneously gulped for air as she turned away.

It was then that she saw her reflection in a mirrored window.

That's me. She made the connection and looked outward but also introverted, assigning the image cause over her.

Her mind was now functioning anew. Relief flooded her and the tension that had been snapping through her subsided.

The name "Loptoor" came to her on another channel, a sense-channel beyond her mind. But her energy-mind offered data in vias, a deductive relay process, and jammed her ability to simply know. *Loptoor?* she pondered, grappled for data and doubted herself.

As one of the forces which pummeled her slacked even more, she knew: *I am.* And her memory transgressed the built-in, self-protective boundaries of the mind. She reached further into the scintilla. She knew, but she was not knowing it; something perched on the periphery of her knowing, taunting, teasing because she could not grasp it, but it beckoned to her as her right. She reached for it but the closer she came, the further it ebbed away from her, yet it was there, there, *there...*

Something had happened. *Danger.* Now someone was trying to help her.

Harder, harder, harder she stared at the reflection of her eyes. She struggled to go deeper but the image was a dam, beyond it the reservoir in which she sought to plunge, into some source, a calm pool, out of the torrents. If only she could penetrate them. She fought the intangible suppression which circumvented her, grasping desperately into the unknowns and struggling to retain clues of the familiar.

Thought-phrases bombarded her—"I'm crazy. I'm insane. I don't know what I'm doing. I'm nothing."—momentarily debilitating her. She surged again, deciding the bitterness was synthetic, only to be soon inundated with acute humiliation, a sense of foolishness and deep embarrassment that eroded and consumed her from her very veins.

It was her own reflection that seemed to rebuke her. It was suddenly pathetic. The image of herself attempting to find an answer within a mere mirror-image of what itself was merely an image...Aira looked around at the environ...*points of dimension and particles*...and she knew she was not them. She was herself and perceiving them. Just because she was registering them did not make her what she saw and registered.

She looked up at the sky. The rain poured on her face and the wind stung her throat with the droplets and whipped her face with her hair. "I am," she said, first softly. Then she called out into the wind. "I am!"

I am not what I feel, I am not what I see, I am. I am! And I perceive.

She was about to grasp it, grasp something, perhaps only another clue, when her progress thus far was erased, absolutely eradicated. Though she didn't know what "it" was, she knew she had lost it. She was sinking again.

Feebly, from a vacuum of despair, Aira remembered what one of her last thoughts had been. However, all that preceded it, the concept to which it was linked and leading, was not there. Only the thought dangled in *non sequitur* rebuke.

Once a clue, it was now seemingly devoid of any meaning and was itself trying to deny her. Despite its stark ring, it simultaneously pealed refutation. Aira clung to the thought obstinately, repeating it out loud. "I am not what I feel, I am not what I feel…I am not what I feel…I am not what I feel…"

Her voice shrank with each repetition, until it became a whimper and the cracks in it cataclysmed into a chasm of sobs. She did not want to stand up any more. She couldn't.

Her anguish drove her to her knees where she folded over further and weakly wrapped her arms around herself in a futile attempt to protect herself from the woe which lacerated her. Then a silent howl rose from her, mutely shrieking of a wound she could not comprehend, beseeching, imploring for someone to help her, for someone who loved her. She felt wretched and desolate and cried open-mouthed. She didn't care anymore, and could think only of somehow evicting the terrible torment she housed.

Her eyes were closed so she did not witness the occurrence. The environ was again pulled from her, like a tablecloth from a place setting which remained. The space around her vanished, replaced by something else. Aira was immediately elsewhere.

Her weeping had stirred the man in the doorway. He was looking at her, trying to decide whether or not she warranted the effort to sit up straight. When he saw her disappear, he decided he had not seen what he had just seen.

chapter  12

"I didn't know it was supposed to rain today," Rex Benton told Sandra as their bodies traveled north up the Golden State 5 Freeway toward Anaheim at 55 miles per hour.

Sandra was driving. She pushed the seek button on the radio and kept doing so until they received a news channel.

"Those clouds do look pretty dark," she commented, then estimated, "We should be there in a couple of minutes."

"I would have never taken you as being much for science fiction conventions," Rex ventured. "Not after you and Mendle were…no longer together."

"No? I find them fascinating," Sandra said. "I didn't go to science fiction conventions just because of Mendle Orion, you know." Doubts stirred in her at Rex's subsequent silence and, needing to determine she had been convincing, she pursued, "What makes you say that?"

"You're a journalist," Rex answered curtly.

"And?"

"Maybe you always seemed so…pragmatic, next to Mendle…"

"I had to be," Sandra said. She shook her head a little glumly. "He'd try to eat a brick if someone didn't tell him it wasn't digestible."

"Not that there isn't a very pragmatic aspect to the field," Rex proposed. "After all, they say most science fiction is the predecessor of reality."

"I know, I know. Mendle told me. Many times." Sandra glanced admiringly at her freshly manicured nails.

"That might be a good story for you," Rex suggested.

Ignoring his idea, Sandra told Rex what was bothering her. "Mendle has hit a reality warp that I doubt is going to be real any time soon, or ever. That's the problem."

"Has he cut down?"

"Drinking? I don't know. He called me a few weeks ago drunk, because he's bored he says…with existence on the planet. Said he was writing about thunder and lightning and it happened." She sighed. "That's called megalomania."

Rex laughed, looking at the grey clouds ahead. "Maybe he's writing about thunder showers as we speak."

He had barely completed his sentence when the radio aired the weather report. They listened. "…Still have low pressure in the desert, causing a vacuum and pulling in the marine layer with that unexpected cold front moving in from the ocean, causing unexpected thunder storm activity."

"See?" Sandra exclaimed, turning down the radio. "Now, what just happened. We said 'thunder' and then the weather report came on?" She arched an eyebrow, and when Rex nodded, she told him, "Mendle would've called it a coincidence, an omen, or thought he had something to do with it."

They rode in silence some moments.

"But the girl. That's the worst part," Sandra said.

"Yeah, what was that?"

"He thinks some super-intelligent space alien, some blonde goddess, is going to come save him."

Rex laughed. "He doesn't really believe that."

"He actually admitted it. He was serious," Sandra stressed.

"I'll see if I can talk to him—"

Sandra interrupted, "Now he's not talking about it. He won't, and that's worse."

"He actually believes it, as in actually?"

Sandra nodded her head up and down, tightening her lips for emphasis.

"Well, nothing is impossible," Rex quipped and followed with a brief hum of the *Twilight Zone* theme.

Though playful in tone, his comment yanked Sandra's head around. He was smiling at her, but she said, "Don't scare me."

Getting serious, and taking umbrage, Rex told her, "I still know the difference between hypothesis and reality."

"Hey man, where's the beer?" Mendle asked as he straightened up from rummaging through the cooler.

"There's more in the bathtub," somebody shouted.

"There's wine in there, too," said somebody else. "Want me to get you some?"

Mendle decided he'd go for a walk instead, to put some time and distance between himself and the last beers. True, he had been working hard, had written a few more chapters of the book—but beer was not necessarily a reward. *Only advertisers want me to think it is,* he reminded himself.

Another question reached him. "Do you want me to rub your feet?"

Mendle looked in the direction from which the voice came. She was dressed as an elf, in a green tunic, and wore a metal-mesh headdress. He shook his head. "No, no thanks."

Six fans suddenly surrounded him and plopped themselves onto the carpet at his feet. "A quest!" one dressed as a Romulan exclaimed eagerly.

"Give us a quest!"

"A quest!" chimed in the others.

Mendle stepped over and through them, mumbling he would have to think about it. "I'm in the middle of another book," he excused himself. "I'm working, it's going on." He gestured to his temples.

"Say no more, sire," said the elf.

"Quite logical," a Trekkie wearing Spock ears said.

Mendle continued stepping over and around people in the party suite, and finally got out the door, closing it behind him. Walking down long corridors, noticing the coordinated decor, Mendle recognized how people with money, but no taste, decorated their homes like hotels and restaurants, mistaking the ambiance for class and elegance.

No solace wandering the halls, they were jammed with people. Though there was some comfort in being with science fiction aficionados, others who, like him, did not concede limits, Mendle was feeling shy and unprotected from intrusion. He considered going back up to his room—but he had been in there for hours, writing nonstop, eating the hotel's salty food. Besides, alone there he would head for the computer, and he was on an official break. Four chapters done warranted a little relaxation.

Mendle thought of going to Disneyland—it was right down the road, not far—when someone else was suddenly smiling in his face. "You're Mendle J. Orion! I love *The Tunnels of Zoranth!*" It was a boy with red hair and a winsome smile, his eyes traveling happily from Mendle's name-tag to his face.

Mendle smiled back at him. The boy's continuous darting glances to his name-tag prompted a reaction to want to remove it. Mendle's hand shot to the plastic pinned to his shirt, and he began to fumble with it as he listened to the boy.

"Yeah. I really did," the boy went on. "No, really. It was great." The fan's effusive face was eclipsed by a copy of the book. "Will you sign it for me?"

Next, a pen was in Mendle's hand and the open book was being held in front of him, pages flipping awkwardly, finally resting on the first page.

"My name is Stephen," the boy beamed, "with a 'p' and an 'h.'"

Mendle inscribed, "To Stephen. Always dare to wonder. Mendle J. Orion." *No matter how crazy it drives you.*

He handed the pen back and headed once again down the matching monotonies of burgundy and mauve toward the elevators. When a "Thank you!" called out after him reached him, he held up his hand and waved without turning around. Protecting himself with elbows and fore-arms from the tight places in the crowd, he continued to move forward.

At the elevators, Mendle looked at his watch. It was a little before one o'clock. He was due for a discussion panel at two thirty. The eleva-tor doors parted and a mosaic of science fiction fans spilled out. The cos-tumes ranged from Godzilla and Buck Rogers to Ferengi and the Borg.

"You should see the storm outside," someone dressed as Flash Gor-don said.

Surrounded by assorted droids, aliens and humans, Mendle stepped into the elevator. As he took his place, he tried not to meet anyone's gaze. He wondered if anyone noticed his mood swings. *What is wrong with me?* He felt agitated, worried, as if there was something he needed to be doing but he didn't know what. *Why do I feel so damn alone?*

Running his hand across his forehead and back over his brown hair, Mendle took the opportunity to peer discreetly from behind his raised elbow at a few of the faces that surrounded him. Then he suddenly jumped at some internal alert that he had forgotten to press the button. The abrupt motion startled the people adjacent to him. "I thought…the button," he excused himself with a quasi-explanation. "But it's already lit," he apologized. They laughed nervously.

He remembered what he had heard in passing, there was a storm out-side. *Weird. An hour ago the skies were blue. Wasn't calling for rain.*

The elevator reached the lobby with an almost imperceptible bounce, and the doors whooshed open to reveal more faces, grinning, talking, looking, pondering, discussing. Mendle felt people shuffle past him off the elevator.

The World Science Fiction Convention in Anaheim was in full

swing. Booths selling art, souvenirs and memorabilia lined the main room off the lobby. Panel discussions every hour covered topics ranging from Captain Picard's favorite French cuisine to superstrings.

Out beyond his introspective thought, Mendle recognized one of the faces in the crowd watching him as he stood in the elevator while it emptied and refilled.

It was Sandra Wilford.

"Mendle," she said. She smiled, kind of tilted to one side, amused that he had barely remembered to step off before the doors closed again. Then she had him in her arms and he was inhaling her perfume. "It's so good to see you. I've been thinking about you. Congratulations again on the Campbell award. I'm here with Rex."

Inadvertently he had placed one of his hands on Sandra's head when she embraced him. He was now cradling the back of it and became aware of her silken hair. He felt a fleeting yet familiar impulse to pull her tightly to him, more habit than desire. Something in him rebelled and he could not hug her. He discontinued holding her, warning himself against the ruts of habit, and took a step back.

"Hello, Sandra. How are you?" She wasn't beautiful to him now that he could see all of her.

Sandra was determined to make it appear that Mendle was not the reason she was there. After all, she didn't want to be showing up just when he received an award. It didn't look good. "I'm fine. We just got here." Mendle looked around to see who "we" was, but saw no one accompanying her.

"I came with Rex Benton," Sandra told him, tossing her shiny black hair and looking around the lobby at the scores of people the World Convention had drawn. "What a turnout, huh? We drove. Sally couldn't make it but might come tomorrow with Fran and Timothy. How are you? No one ever sees you anymore. You must promise me half an hour at least in the jacuzzi. This place has one. I checked. Not like Capricon I, remember?"

Mendle watched her prattle and look the room over, and wondered if she had even wanted an answer to her inquiry "How are you?"

"Look at all these people!" she exclaimed then quit scouring the room and faced him. "You look great, Mendle. Really. I really do want to talk with you, so promise?"

He had been observing the carefully controlled facial gestures which accompanied Sandra's speech and wondered if she were feigning the cheerfulness, while feeling something else. *Calculated. So planned, it hurts,* he thought, trying to put himself into that frame of thinking for the sake of understanding it.

"Promise?" she demanded, reiterating it with a narrowing of the eyes and a big grin.

"I'm fine, Sandra."

Sandra's face crimped into a quiz. The look was familiar to him, bordering on the one she delivered to let him know he was acting crazy.

"You asked me how I was, a minute ago," Mendle explained. "I thought I'd answer that. I said I'm fine."

"Oh, Mendle!" Her face unraveled and she threw her arms around him again. "You nut. I'm fine, too."

"Good," Mendle said.

He felt her breasts against him and wondered if she were conscious of it. *Probably not,* he decided, giving her the benefit of the doubt. They were just a part of her anatomy, no different than arms or shoulders. They were mammary glands. She couldn't very well push them out of the way. He thought how uncomfortable it would be if he had attention drawn to his penis as often as women did to their breasts. He closed his eyes and felt her hair all over his face. *This is only a friendly embrace born out of exuberance,* he decided. Then he felt her hand change gears on his back.

There was a wistfulness to the caress and Sandra seemed to slow down all over as she traced Mendle's spine with one finger. Up. Down. His neck was beginning to ache from bending over into her embrace.

"It's so good to see you, Mendle," she murmured.

She wanted him. It was a frenzy. The more she felt him unresponsive under her hands, the more determined she was to control him. It wasn't that she wanted to give him pleasure; she wanted to burrow under his skin. She needed the magnets of his blood to jump to her negatives and positives. She hated him for being so much on his own.

"I've really missed you," she said, buttering him with what she called love.

chapter  13

Mendle's biological drive for sex disengaged from his soul. On its own, unintegrated with his personal sentiments, the impulse was an electrical force. The antagonism between Sandra and him increased polarity between terminals. The alcohol in his system impaired analysis of his body's response. The sensation of sexual desire spread in Mendle—an involuntary desire to conquer, to dominate Sandra, as a body. The fact that he didn't like her as a person licensed and fanned it.

"You look fine," Mendle said, returning her embrace yet not liking himself for enjoying the mechanics of being a conduit for flow.

As Mendle and she stood embracing in the middle of the hotel lobby, Sandra didn't want it to stop. "Of course I'm fine," she purred intimately. "And I'm real."

Sandra laughed but Mendle tensed at her last comment. When he started to pull away from her embrace, she tried to make a joke out of her deliberate jab. "I finally got over being jilted for a figment of your imagination!" It angered Mendle further and he stepped away from her.

"Just kidding!" Sandra squealed, pulling Mendle back toward her.

The pin of Mendle's name tag was unhooked from its safety clasp. He had started to remove it earlier but never completed the task. When Sandra yanked him toward her, the pin aimed toward his flesh at an unfortunate angle. When it stuck him, Mendle yelled so loudly that Sandra instantly let go of him.

"Aaoow!" He looked down and fidgeted with the name tag, checking his shirt inside and out for blood.

"Did I stick you? I'm sorry," Sandra gushed, worrying more about people staring at her than about any damage she may have caused.

"Yes, you stuck me. You stuck me with words, with your thoughts, and now this is the physical manifestation of it."

"It was an accident, Mendle."

"It was a synchronous manifestation." He felt disgust at himself.

Sandra stared at him fiddling with the name tag, her incredulity bordering on gawking. "Come on, you're not going to start with that coincidence business?"

She thought she had smelled the acridity of beer on him but up until now he had appeared to be contained and doing all right.

Crack! A loud clap of thunder whacked the air and rumbled through the walls into the lobby, straightening Mendle up abruptly. He looked around the room as if he had been spooked by a ghost then slowly turned toward the lobby entrance. Most heads were turned in that direction.

"Don't tell me you've been writing about thunder and lightning again." Sandra's tone was flat, bordering on caustic.

Mendle slowly faced her and aimed his reply at her on a tight and narrow funnel. "As a matter of fact, I have." He held his gaze steady to keep her at bay but nonetheless felt her on him like tiny tentacles sucking at his life.

Since he was not calculated and rehearsed, Sandra regarded Mendle as prey. She judged his kindness as weakness. So when she moved in on him again in honeyed movements, she was surprised by his steadfast rebuff.

Mendle abruptly turned and faced the large glass doors in the front lobby. He pretended to be more engrossed by the storm than he actually was, welcoming the excuse to place his attention elsewhere, away from her. He further abnegated himself for thinking he needed an excuse to disengage from her. His lowered opinion of himself eroded and insidiously infested him by the minute.

Sandra followed Mendle's gaze to the front entrance of the hotel. Outside, the cumulating clouds had become denser; everything was darker; flailing trees and shrubbery gave evidence of a blustering wind.

"It started off such a beautiful day," Sandra said. She hesitated, unsure of what to say or not to say, but determined the encounter would not turn sour.

"This is very weird," Mendle said watching the rain pelt the plate glass. "It's August. This is California. It just came out of nowhere."

"But they did say on the news that a cold front from the ocean was moving in," Sandra informed him. "Hit this heat and presto. There you have it. Thunderstorm."

"It's fine with me if it just came out of nowhere," Mendle said.

Sandra laughed. "Things don't just come out of nowhere."

"Yes they do," he defended quickly, explaining, "Nowhere is some-times…just…somewhere you can't see."

Sandra jumped at the sharpness of another sudden crack of thunder. The storm seemed to be escalating with prolonged lightning flashes, and it thundered more raucously and frequently. Throughout the entire lobby, explanations were underway, from Time/Space warps to Genesis experiments. The room was again buzzing with a steady gabble.

"There you are!" A voice broke above the drone of lobby conversation.

Mendle turned to see who it was. *Rex Benton.* His hand was suddenly in Mendle's and he was shaking it rigorously. "How do you like this storm?"

I haven't met it yet. Mendle smiled to himself then replied perfunctorily, "It's quite interesting." He wanted to go sit down.

Rex let go of Mendle's hand and said, crossing his arms on his chest, "Congrats on the John Campbell."

"Yes," Sandra interjected as if just remembering. "Rex said if he didn't get the award the only other person he felt deserved it was you."

Rex laughed. "It's all a matter of luck," he said, trimming away at the value.

Mendle reeled a little at the veiled deprecation. He understood envy well enough, he just didn't condone acting on the feeling. After all, within every human being was the potential for anything, from the most vile to the most divine. *At least,* Mendle thought, *when I see success or accomplishment I don't think I have to take someone down a notch.*

He knew envy, the fear of being left behind, of not arriving. He knew hate, revenge, cowardice, even hypocrisy. He knew them firsthand. He let them lie where they belonged, in the pits of his infernos. They were impostors which he would not allow to impersonate him. They were the thieves he met in the internal arenas for battle. They were all admissions of defeat and inability; their existences rooted in the lies of scarcity and incapacity to create—false conditions which people imposed upon themselves.

Mendle withdrew deeper into himself. *Don't I have enough wrong with me that someone could simply rejoice with me over a success without feeling threatened? Without having to diminish it for fear of comparison?*

He had been somewhat dumbly gazing at Rex, with a semi-smile of agreement on his lips for which he began to despise himself even more. He thought about telling Rex to let it serve as an inspiration, but was inhibited by the certainty that Rex would construe such a comment as self-aggrandizement.

A commotion on the other side of the room distracted them all. From where he was standing on the landing near the elevator, Mendle could see a cluster of people in the main lobby jumping up and down and laughing. Some were scurrying around, bent over, running. A bellboy seemed to be on a chase. It was all under the command of a red-coated manager who seemed upset.

Mendle stepped sideways past a column to better see what was going on. He heard barking, like a dog, and the manager was yelling something. Others were gravitating to the scene. As Mendle set off toward the excitement, Sandra and Rex exchanged looks and followed.

"Catch it! Catch it!" the manager yelled.

Mendle saw what they were after. It was a dog—dodging around knees and legs, away from outstretched hands—a white Samoyed.

"Who let that dog in here?" the manager demanded, the intent of his words aimed in all directions. The more he was ignored, the more he inflated with anger. "Whose dog is that?" No one answered him. "Just grab it! Get it!" he crescendoed.

Mendle, as highly capable of amusement as he was of despair, flickered alive with delight. The idea of a game was instant divertissement. "Go, go, go!" he cheered the dog.

Sandra watched him jump and clap his hands, suddenly oblivious to anything else. "Look at him," she pointed out to Rex. "He was just depressed, hostile, melancholy. You saw how sullen he was, and now look at him."

"A happy idiot," Rex narrated. "Saltarello champ."

"I got it!" an anonymous shout rose from the crowd.

Just as the victorious cry rang, the Samoyed maneuvered a ninety degree turn, evading the two hands which were sure to have caught it. The dog tripped, rolled over, righted itself, and scampered off, diving through a hole in the crowd.

Mendle headed in the direction he had seen it scurry across the plushly carpeted lobby, circumventing the bulk of the crowd.

"Get it before it gets to the dining room!"

The battle cry was not far from Mendle's ear now. He glanced to his left and saw that the manager was jogging next to him, holding his glasses securely on the bridge of his nose with one hand. "It had better not get to the dining room!" he threatened, and a rumble of thunder rolled through the lobby as though in ominous reiteration.

Mendle's grin accelerated into outright laughter. The laughing felt good to him, shaking his chest and ribs, shaking his insides loose and running through him. It was beyond his control. He gave it free rein and it screamed out of his mouth like a wild wind passing through a knothole.

"Whhooopeee!" he cried out, the merriment bubbling around his head, taking with it any worries that were stuck there.

The manager looked sideways at him as if he were mad.

"Do you believe this?" Sandra commented, watching everything as she hurried with Rex to catch up to Mendle.

"Go, puppy, go!" Mendle was shouting. He was in the lead now, along with the bellboy and manager. While they took long strides and jaunted, Mendle galloped and leaped, as if riding an imaginary horse. Behind them, a small portion of the lobby trailed in pursuit.

It looked as if the Samoyed would head for the restaurant, but, as it reached the hostess station, it veered, scampering down a corridor where a wall waited at the end. And the end came closer until they were there. The white dog had no further place to turn or run.

"No!" Mendle yelled. "Slow down, puppy!" He cringed as he anticipated the inevitable.

The white Samoyed saw the wall and stiffened its legs to stop, but its momentum was too great. With a dull, smacking thump, it smashed into the wall. The dog fell and lay motionless, long enough to create a hush. Then slowly, it raised its head and looked over its shoulder. There was no outlet in the wall of knees.

Breathing hard, his hands elevated like claws above his head, the manager started to say, "Why you stupid..." Before he could swoop down on the animal, Mendle intercepted him.

Grasping the man's forearm gently but firmly, he told him solemnly, "This is my dog." He thrust his chin slightly forward in challenge.

Rex and Sandra, who had woven their way to the front of the attraction, stood by.

Mendle dropped to the dog's side and caressed it reassuringly. "It's okay," he whispered to it several times, very softly.

The Samoyed held its eyes shut very tightly. It was trembling, as if afraid of being hit. Finally it opened its eyes, barely, and looked up at Mendle. Even the manager, through his ambition, felt there was something poignant about the two of them.

It is rather a cute dog, after all, he thought as he admired its pure white coat, its limpid eyes and little black, shiny nose. He liked the way its breath rose, warm and steamy, like smoke.

Smoke? The man blinked and refocused when he thought he had seen smoke rising from the dog's nostrils. *It's the rain, the humidity. And there are too many people in this hallway.* "All right. It's over. It's all over," he said to dismiss the gathering, burrowing in his pocket for a handkerchief.

He removed his glasses and began to wipe them. "Your dog is not supposed to be here," he informed Mendle courteously.

Mendle looked up. With perfect aplomb he asked, "Did it doo-doo on the carpet?"

"No, he did n…" the manager caught himself about to answer.

Mendle laughed. "I was just being feces-cious!" He howled. "Get it?" Sandra bowed her head and put her hand to her forehead.

The floor manager's job was new; he was not about to blow his responsibilities. It wasn't his sense of duty driving him. The feeling of importance they gave him was like a drug; so was the money. Applying what he had learned at his sensitivity class, he rotely said, "It must be frightened. It's a beautiful animal. Is it a boy or a girl?"

"You know, I'm not sure," Mendle said, spoofing the man's feigned sincerity. "My dog's sex is irrelevant to me anyway." He was back to petting the animal. "Why? Did you want a date?" He laughed then, "Mankind's foremost preoccupation. Hope you used your mouthwash. Someone might sniff you."

Sandra stooped down beside Mendle. She spoke quietly, "Come on, Mendle, let's go."

"Embarrassed?"

"No," she lied. "Let's get some coffee."

The manager had parked his spectacles back onto his nose. To a small group of people still in the hallway, he clapped his hands and announced, "It's all over."

Suddenly he felt shivers up his trousers. The dog was positioned behind him, snarling; he could feel the menacing tone crawling up the backs of his legs and, in terror, envisioned a searing chomp to the calf.

"It's okay, puppy," Mendle said.

The dog rose to its haunches and stood there, its front legs spread as though it were trying to fly.

"What a spectacle," Rex commented when Sandra got up.

The manager carefully tiptoed a few steps forward. He clasped his hands together and rotated his torso. "If you would kindly check with us, we'll be happy to ensure proper accommodations for your pet," he said, then turned abruptly and quickly walked away.

"I'm sorry," Sandra murmured to him as he brushed past.

Mendle looked at her reproachfully. "Sorry?" he reprimanded. "For what are you sorry?"

Sandra looked to Rex for consolation and agreement, and he obliged her with a quick, upward dart of the eyebrows. She looked down at Mendle again. "Is this really your dog, Mendle?" she asked.

Mendle didn't answer her. He turned to the dog. The Samoyed seemed to derive security from his gaze.

Rex said, "It wasn't wearing a collar."

"It's a girl," Sandra told them. "I saw when it stood up."

Mendle glanced up to see Sandra pouring a deprecatory look of sympathy and pity on him. With some effort, he began to rise to his feet. The position in which he had been crouching had put his left foot to sleep and it buckled under him when he put pressure on it. When Mendle stumbled, both Sandra and Rex lunged forward to grab him, but he had already reached for the wall and steadied himself.

It surprised him to be so suddenly flanked. He looked first at Rex, then across at Sandra. Both their faces were embalmed with serious gravity. They let go of him, retracting their arms to their sides. Their solemn expressions ignited a charge of laughter in Mendle.

"Who died?" he chortled.

Sandra and Rex ducked under their cover of smiles as Mendle watched, staring at them openly.

"Was I having too good a time?" Mendle directed the question at Sandra.

"That's paranoid," she said, rankled that he was off her hook, off her line, and she felt no tension between them.

As Mendle looked, first at one, then the other, their insincere smiles became suddenly grotesque and annoying to him. He decided to ignore the matter and took to inspecting his foot. Slowly he increased pressure on it, testing it out. It prickled as the circulation reestablished.

Despite his attempts to carry on, feelings of isolation and humiliation encroached on Mendle. He felt betrayed, as if Sandra and Rex had been talking about him behind his back and were really against him. "Damn it!" he snapped. "Why don't you just worry about your own lives? If I'm so crazy, why don't you just leave me the hell alone?"

"What on Earth is your problem, Mendle?" Sandra exclaimed defensively, but behind her portrayal of victim she knew what he was saying.

Rex interceded, "Hey, relax. We were just trying to be helpful."

"Okay, okay." Mendle waved them away to say that he didn't want to discuss it further.

Putting his full weight down on the foot, Mendle momentarily started down the hall and beckoned the dog, which followed him. Sandra watched him walk away, limping only a little. His hands were in his pockets, his head slightly bent forward.

"Mendle," she called out. "I'll see you in a little while."

The eagerness in her voice produced a small upheaval of discomfort for Rex. When Sandra turned, she saw it cross his face. Ever alert and expert at detecting others' buttons and strings for personal advantage, she quickly mimed a look of pity for Mendle, feeding Rex's need to feel superior. She shook her head and said, "He's a mess."

Rex nodded in agreement. "His hands were shaking," he said.

"I saw."

His self-importance fueled by deprecation of Mendle, Rex called out affably after him, feeling he could afford to be generous. "We'll see you later."

A portly woman ran by Mendle as he neared the hotel front desk. She called out to someone, huffing as she caught her breath to speak, "Wow, man! Someone just appeared to me in my room!"

"So time doesn't happen in any sequence, really," someone else was saying. "It's not linear."

"One second Earth-time can be billions of years somewhen else, if you speed up faster than the speed of light."

Things Mendle heard in passing began to engage his thoughts, but he stopped himself. It was too confusing, keeping track of all the coincidences, determining the meaning and interrelation of everything. *Maybe none of it means anything. It means I'm at a science fiction convention.*

Thunder permeated the building and rumbled away.

Standing in front of the elevator, Mendle pushed the Up button again, even though it was lit.

Everyone around them gone, Sandra and Rex presented smiles to one another.

He's a small man. His work is banal, Sandra thought about Rex as she smiled at him.

She's manipulative but this is something to do, Rex thought as he smiled. He didn't like things unless they had a twist. *And her hips are narrow, like a boy's.*

"Want to get something to eat?" Rex asked.

"Sounds good," Sandra said.

She glanced at Mendle ahead in the distance. He seemed forlorn, standing there at the elevators, the stray in tow.

"I didn't know he had a dog," Rex said.

"He doesn't," Sandra told him.

chapter  14

"You coming back to the fanzine party?" The question came from one in a small group of fans getting off the elevator at the third floor.

Mendle shook his head no, then, before the doors shut, added, "Maybe in a little while." The elevator continued its ascent.

At the sixth floor, the white dog followed him obediently and together they headed down the color-schemed corridor. When they arrived at his room, Mendle saw he had forgotten to lock it; the knob turned with no need of a key.

Pushing the door and holding it open with his foot, he prompted the dog, "Go on. Go ahead." The white Samoyed trotted a few feet in and lay down by the bathroom door.

Mendle was relieved to see the unlocked room had not been violated; his computer was still there. He tossed the plastic key-card onto the dresser, where it landed by the television bolted to the wall.

"Aaahhh," he exhaled, glad to be away from the crowd.

For the third time since checking in, he did a hotel-drawer-inspection, one by one, first the dresser, then the desk and nightstand: Bible, stationery, pencil, note pad, City Business Directory, Room Service Menu.

Then he sat on the bed. Falling backward, spread-eagled, Mendle stretched out in the space and luxuriated in the privacy. He rolled over, picked up the phone and rang the front desk.

"This is Mendle Orion in room 618. Has Rex Benton checked in?"

"One moment." There was a pause out of which the receptionist replied, "Yes he has."

"What room?"

"We are not allowed to give out that information."

"I just need to call him."

"We are not allowed to give out th—"

"This is Mendle Orion, I'm a guest here."

"Anyone could say that, sir. We can't give that out."

"Why not?" Mendle wondered.

"We just aren't allowed to give out that information."

Mendle thought about it. "You mean in case someone wants to go to their room who isn't supposed to? Like a killer, or bill collector, or maybe a crazed fan?"

"Maybe, sir." The operator added, "It's for your protection, sir."

"What a way to live…"

"I can connect you."

"Thank you. Will you connect me? He may not be there yet but…"

"One moment."

Mendle sat up, slid to the edge of the bed, bent down and untied his shoes. He listened to the electronic voice-mail message answer for the room as he slipped each shoe off with the opposite foot, pushing at the back of the heel.

At the beep he said, "Rex. It's Mendle. Listen, I'm due on a panel in about forty minutes. I was hoping you could take my place. Let me know. I'm in 618." He hung up.

As he walked across the floor in his socks, Mendle noticed his feet become damp. "The floor's wet," he said, puzzled. *It feels like when I've been walking around on the carpet after a shower.*

He looked at the Samoyed. It had not moved since entering the room and posting itself between the front and bathroom doors. In fact, it appeared frozen, staring straight ahead.

"You okay?" Mendle asked, thinking the dog looked stupefied, stunned. When it resumed panting, Mendle's attention went back to the floor. "How did it get wet in here?"

He looked over at the window. Rain descended in flowing strata against the glass, and thunder boomed and grumbled in the distance.

Lightning suddenly flashed. In fast rhythm, it seemed to pulsate in the middle of the room, tails of it flashing and flickering, crashing into immediate thunder.

"Whoa! Did you see that?" Mendle laughed, a backlash of excitement.

It was good to relax, not to have people everywhere. He dragged the round table a little further from the window then reached in his sweater pocket and took out a miniature whiskey bottle, unscrewing the cap and sucking the contents out. He felt it burn all the way to his stomach.

Next, he brought the television remote to the round table and sat down, leisurely settling into the stuffed upholstery of a chair. He aimed the remote at the radio unit of the television and pushed the on button.

"Dream lover, where are you with a love oh so true?…"

'Dream Lover!' again. Mid-century classic, but every time I turn on a radio lately, it plays. Another coincidence…it's telling me something. A cosmic smile!

"…I want a dream lover so I don't have to dream alone. Some day, I don't know how, I hope she'll hear my pleas…Some way, I don't know how, she'll bring her love to me…"

As he listened, Mendle picked up a pencil. He idly marked a line on some blank paper on the table, then turned the doodle into the outline of an eye, almond shaped, tilted slightly upward, lids, eyelashes. He drew another, until two large eyes were on the page. He feathered in eyebrows, then started drawing lips next, full lips, slightly dimpled at the corners. Then curls. Mendle shaded the ringlets, shadowed a little cheekbone.

"Hi."

The voice startled him right out of the chair. She was standing right next to him.

"My God, Sandra. How the hell did you get in here?"

He glanced over at the dog; it hadn't budged or given any warning.

"The door was unlocked," Sandra told him. "Sorry I startled you." She felt him instantly start to ignore her.

Critically, she began to take in the scenario of the room, papers and books strewn about. Knowing Mendle's fixation which bordered on superstition for songs that happened to be playing on the radio, Sandra tuned in to the music and recognized *Dream Lover.* Deeming the balloon needed popping, in her most cheerful manner, holding projected sincerity as a shield, she pricked, "How's the dreaming coming?"

The phone rang.

"There are some strange people at these conventions," she quickly changed the subject, motioning with her thumb to the outside. "I just passed four gnomes. Why dress up like a gnome?"

Pushing against the floor with his feet, Mendle rolled his chair to the nightstand and picked up the phone. "Hello? Yes, hello, Rex."

"Don't tell him I'm here," Sandra whispered intently.

Mendle turned away from her to hear Rex more clearly on the phone. "Great, so you can sit in for me?"

"Delighted, Mendle," Rex replied tersely. "How generous of you to offer me a spot in your panel."

"It would be doing me a favor, actually. I have some work I have to finish. I'm just not feeling up to it."

"Right," Sandra commented under her breath, noticing the empty liquor bottle on the table. Mendle's pronunciation was a little round.

"I understand," Rex sympathized, thinking this would be good publicity.

"You sure?" Mendle checked.

"Sure, hey. I'm just waiting on Sandra to get back with some ice. We're getting a little something to eat in the room."

Mendle glanced over at Sandra pacing the room as he listened to Rex.

"We'll go as soon as she gets back," Rex was saying. "What's the topic?"

Mendle kneeled down by the nightstand and pulled a steno pad out of his satchel. "Here," he said, then read from his notes, "Human beings as we know them have coexisted with various quasi-human forms for millions of years."

"As in we aren't apes?"

"I guess not," Mendle said, playing it as big news. He scanned his notebook as he told Rex, "They've discovered apes were a different species than humans. And modern man existed *alongside* Neanderthals, Cro-Magnon."

"I'm getting a pencil."

"Listen to this." Mendle read off more notes, "A skull and other skeletal remains of modern man were found at Castenedolo, Italy, in Pliocene deposits over 2 million years old. Discovered in 1860, Professor Raggazoni. Later in 1880 such remains of two children and a woman were found in the 2 to 7 million year old strata."

"Wait, I'm writing," Rex told him.

Mendle glanced at Sandra. She was moving toward his work table. "I'll spell the names later," he told Rex.

"Mind if I throw in the possibility of space ancestors?" Rex suggested, leaving a way out with a laugh.

"Take it where you want," Mendle said as he watched Sandra pick up the paper with the face he had been sketching. Mendle continued, "Dr. Hans Reck, in 1913, discovered a skeleton of modern man in the strata depth that made it contemporary with Peking and Java man. That was in East Africa's Olduvai Gorge."

The sight of Sandra poking around his work table went beyond irritating. "I'll tell you what Rex," Mendle said, "I'll just give these notes to old Sandra here, she'll bring them down to you."

Sandra turned on her heel accusatively, her face a contortion of anger and protest. Mendle hung up the phone, ripped the pages from the steno book and stepped over to her.

"Why did you tell him I was here?" Sandra demanded, employing a technique of putting Mendle on the defensive.

Handing the notes to her, and removing the drawing of the girl's face from her hand, Mendle said, "Rex is expecting these. And you." Motioning for her to leave, Mendle dumped his body into the chair, reached in his pocket and pulled out another mini-bottle of whiskey. He unscrewed it, tilted his head back, and poured it into his mouth as if it were a glass. When he sat up straight and looked defiantly at Sandra his eyes were watering from gulping.

Sandra decided to put her anger second, or, plainly, there would be a collision. She was not about to leave out of control. She toned herself down. "Mendle, why? Why the bitterness?"

"I want simplicity. Aren't you supposed to be getting some ice? Walk your crap out of here, man." He was becoming rude and didn't like it.

Sandra glanced back down at the drawing and stopped her pacing. She mustered a smile, straining for it to reach her eyes. "You better get something to eat," she said, trying to sound warm. That was a good idea, he couldn't dispute it.

The radio station started airing the Neil Diamond song "I Am...I Said." Mendle tuned in to the words.

"I love this song," Mendle muttered to himself. He sang along with words he knew, humming the melody to the parts he didn't know, then said, "I was just writing something about that."

Sandra pulled out the other chair by the round table and sat down. "Want me to order something for you?"

Mendle shook his head. He propped his elbows on the table and dropped his face into his hands.

"Cute dog," he heard her say.

Sandra looked over at the white animal again and noticed it seemed to be having trouble breathing. *It looks stupid. It's just staring at the wall. It's dumb. And sick.* "What's its name?"

"Onx," Mendle said for want of a name, and smiled to himself behind his hands.

The name sounded familiar to her. Sandra felt Mendle lowering his shields. He was about ready. Just one more move. "Want some coffee?" she offered nicely.

Mendle rubbed his face in his cupped hands. "I'll get some later."

"Onx," she repeated. "Where have I heard that?"

Mendle shrugged. "It's the Egyptian symbol of eternal life," he kiddingly misinformed her.

"Maybe that's it," she mused, unsatisfied. "By the way, how is your book coming?" she finally asked.

He didn't answer her.

"Is that drawing for the book?"

Mendle removed his hands from his face and glared at Sandra.

"Is it…one of the characters?" she ventured.

"No." He felt himself diminish internally at the untruth.

Sandra's smile bordered on a sneer. "You despise me for not wanting Rex to know I'm here in your room, and look at you. You lie, too. Everybody does."

"No, everybody does not lie!" he pushed back the chair and shouted as he struggled a little to stand up. He was standing up for the human race.

Sandra stared him down knowingly.

"Okay, everybody has probably lied, but some people have different motives!"

She smirked with satisfaction then got up. "Now Mendle, the drawing is obvi—"

"What do you do? Be nice to me just so you can piss me off again?" Mendle interrupted. "You're a churl."

"That's girl. Listen to you, you can't even enunciate!"

"That's churl. You're churlish. As in a rude and surly person."

"And what are you? Prince Charming?" Sandra retorted, letting her rhetoric mirror the disgusting way she perceived him.

"That's better," Mendle applauded. "You're letting it out, instead of being so nice and pulling all your little strings, sticking your little pins in me behind the curtains!"

Sandra changed gears. "I felt you respond to me."

"It wasn't me."

She stared at him challengingly.

"I don't love you, Sandra."

"What was it?"

He bowed his head. "Biological functions," he apologized frankly.

"And you're saving it for when you get married?" She said it derisively. "For the woman you love," she ridiculed him. Mistaking any semblance of virtue as her nemesis, Sandra was quick to draw sword against it, and, ironically, anything which might serve as her own beacon.

"Maybe I am, yes."

"A regular modern day Cyrano," she scoffed.

"Honor does exist!" Mendle screamed so hard he felt the volume scrape his throat.

"Except you ain't no virgin." Sandra put him in check. Then she lowered her voice. "I'm worried about you, that's all, Mendle. Your hostility…"

"I'm hostile because you're pissing me off!"

"…the drinking, and your delusions, and…"

"You're not worried about me."

"…this…this contour-image woman of yours taking up all your thought…"

"'Contour-image?' You've been listening to Dr. Kaufkiff's meaningless garbage," he jeered.

"How did you know that's what he calls it?" Sandra's eyes narrowed in smug scrutiny. "You went to him, didn't you?"

"Your anal-ist?" Mendle walked over to the dresser and brought the menu over to the phone, regretting his mention of Kaufkiff.

"You went to see him. I'm so glad," Sandra said.

"The ice is melting, Sandra. You know, your alibi, the ice you're supposed to be getting. Rex is waiting. Please let me get back to work. Please let me order something to eat. Please leave before you drive me to drink more…"

"So now I'm responsible, am I?" Sandra took a hard edge. "You know, Mendle, maybe you've just been around these bizarre science fiction things too long. Why don't you go pitch some hay in Oklahoma for a while, hang around some real people."

"And what are real people? People with B.O. and tooth decay? The more flawed the more real? Huh? Is that what's real to you? Are people who shop at Sears real people? People who settle? People who eat hot dogs? People who make errors? They're real people, huh? News flash! We're *all* real, baby! Even excellence is real! From the scumsuckingest to the highest dreaming, we're all real people."

Mendle turned away from her. *She got me.* He felt sickened that he was fighting, using language for shock value. His hands trembled as he poured himself a glass of water. He inhaled deeply then drank the water, set the glass down and collected every ounce and atom of himself.

When he faced her again he smiled, very neatly. Careful to omit even the smallest sardonic nuance, he said, "It's not you, Sandra. I am totally responsible for my own life. Do get those notes to Rex. Panel starts soon."

He turned his back to her, knowing he had her to thank for that last maneuver; he learned it from her. Slick on the outside. He felt a piece of his childhood die.

Satisfied that she had earned a few points, Sandra made her exit. On her way out, she stopped by the white Samoyed. "There's something wrong with this dog. It looks like it's been hit by a car," she lashed, then added, sardonically applauding Mendle's communication as a performance, "Oh, and Bra-vo," before closing the door behind her.

Quiet. He turned to look. Safe. She was gone. The dog was facing the door, silent, but its teeth bared, as if growling.

"Hey. Dog." It didn't move.

The thought of it having rabies crossed Mendle's range of possibilities. The dog turned and looked at him.

"You okay?" It whined.

"I'll order something for us to eat."

Thunder rumbled in the distance. *And coffee for me. Lucidity is definitely the key needed here.* "Room service? This is Mendle Orion in 618. I'd like to order some food." *Something solid.*

"Yes, sir. What will you have?" a chipper voice asked.

"I will have," he fumbled for the menu, "we will have," he stalled, playing for time to glance it over, "uh, two Hamburger Royales." He looked at the size of the dog and quickly corrected his order, "Make that four Hamburger Royales."

"How would you like them?"

The dog sprang into a spastic motion. It seemed to be vigorously shaking its head in the negative.

"No?" Mendle asked it, perplexed. It stopped the motion. "For a minute I thought my dog said no," he laughed into the phone.

"How would you like them?" Room Service repeated.

"I will be ingesting them through my mouth, so they should be delicious."

The person taking his order did not share his jocosity. "Rare, medium, or well?"

"Definitely well. No ill hamburgers in this room." He tried again.

"That will be four Hamburger Royales, well done. Will there be anything else?"

"What are you? An automaton?" Mendle exploded.

"Pardon me?"

"Where is your active intelligence? What is this monotonous routine?"

"I'm sorry, sir, but—"

"Never mind, never mind," Mendle grumbled, exasperated. He suddenly saw himself deluded by some self-inflated image that he was clever. Seeing himself sitting there as the epitome of a jerk deflated the merrymaking and he said resignedly, "Hamburgers well done, yes, thank you."

"Anything else, sir?"

"Coffee."

"That'll be about fifteen minutes, sir."

Mendle hung up.

"Coffee," he said again. He tightened his lips and shook his head. "Automatons," he lamented. Then the louder, more insistent reality in his mind barraged him: he had made cheap puns; he was hostile; he lied; he liked control; he was no better than anyone else, yet demanded perfection.

"I need a shower," he decided. "A hot, riveting shower."

Lightning flashed and thunder fell instantly afterward, crashing into the room so hard it vibrated the walls.

That was nearby.

The dog didn't seem fazed at all. The thought occurred to Mendle as he crossed the room that there might be something wrong with the animal. It appeared deaf, in a world of its own. He leaned over and gave it a little pat.

Mendle thought to lock the room door, and double-checked it.

As he prepared to enter the bathroom, he decided he just couldn't think about things now. His thinking felt entangled, like a group of coat hangers; he tugged on one question and it pulled three or four others with it. He wasn't going to wonder who the dog belonged to, or what he was going to do with it, or why Sandra was the way she was, or why he felt the way he did, or what it all meant. For now, all Mendle wanted was to feel hot, soothing water on his skin.

chapter  15

Mendle stepped out of his tan trousers, pulled off his forest green sweat shirt and slipped off his socks. He draped his clothes across a chair and, after one last concerned look at the stray dog, backed into the bathroom. The tiles were cold to his feet. He shut the door so steam would accumulate in the room and searched the wall for a heat lamp.

When he turned around, Mendle saw he was not alone. The sight of another unexpected presence startled him so much, he jerked open the door, stepped out of the bathroom and, once on the other side, leaned hard against the door in case he needed to keep it forcefully shut. Feeling safer by the door imposed between them, he tried to identify from memory the glimpse he had gotten of the strange figure crouching by the commode.

Mendle caught his breath from the scare. He glanced at the dog. It was still staring blankly. An eerie sensation permeated him, an intense unfamiliarity accompanied by subsequent distrust. Something was strange. It was himself, his mind, the dog, what was in the bathroom, some of it or all of it, he didn't know.

Abruptly letting go of the door, Mendle quickly ran for his pants, grabbed them, then ran back to his spot outside the door, where he yanked them on. He held still and listened—*nothing*—then zipped his pants. He tried knocking. When nothing happened, he cautiously turned the doorknob, very slowly pulled the door slightly ajar, and peered in.

There was somebody in the bathroom.

He held his breath.

She hadn't moved. She was sitting on the edge of the bathtub by the toilet. She was nude, doubled over, her face buried in her hands. Wet ringlets covered her profile. Wetness dripped from the hair glistening down her long neck, down her arms; her body was wet.

"Are you okay?" Mendle asked, opening the door wider.

She didn't respond, and, when the dog whimpered, Mendle let himself into the room and pulled the door closed behind him. The girl did not respond at all to any of the noise.

Not because she was naked, but because she was wet and appeared to be shivering, Mendle pulled a towel off the rack and hesitantly draped it over her shoulders. All he could do was stand and look at her. He wondered who she was and how she got into his room, and debated on what to say next when she began to move.

Slowly, the woman lifted her head from her hands, keeping them cupped and prepared to shelter her face again. Unsure, she turned her head to look, as if afraid of what she would see. When she looked at him, she searched Mendle's face expectantly, beseechingly, as though hoping he had an answer to something. She appeared frightened, confused, her hair a tempest.

Mendle found himself very quiet. He stood frozen, quelling all thought, almost not wanting to breathe.

Her eyes were the brightest blue he had ever seen; the sensation was a slow-motion fall into liquid jewels when he looked into them. Her lips were generous, colored like roses. And her hands, long and graceful, hovered like dove wings where she suspended their motion.

It's her. The girl, the face I was just drawing.

She pulled the towel off her shoulders and wiped her arms, her chest, then held it to her body. All Mendle could do when she looked at him was nod. A fraction of happiness seemed to pass through her, then her gaze leveled as if expecting him to say something.

He couldn't speak. *It's her, it's her. It's you,* was all he could think. Then, ever so slowly, Mendle reached from the solitary fortress to which he had resigned himself all his life; he extended his arm and held his hand out to the woman, shedding all personal affliction and thinking only of tending to her sorrow, whatever it might be.

She glanced at Mendle's hand apprehensively, then back to his face again. He didn't know what else to do. She was obviously badly shaken by something. She seemed tired and ravaged. Mendle kept holding his hand out, very still, as one does to a wild animal to show it good faith. He watched her as if she were a sunrise, or a doe in her own woodland—some type of natural phenomena to which he was afraid to add any ingredient lest he spoil it. Finally, she took his hand, and in that small motion, Mendle felt the movement of the planets.

With that touch of her hand on his, Mendle realized he had been treasonous to himself; something stirred inside him and by contrast he knew he had been negating himself. He felt sentiment, unrehearsed, revive and quicken until it swept through him with such power that he remembered what it was to be alive.

Nothing else existed—the walls, the bathroom, the people, the hotel, the world—none of it existed. Only her face, her eyes, their contact and something he knew with such intensity that he didn't even care to define it but let it wash through him like an only truth. He pressed his fingers around her hand and held it with concentrated being. Then he took a step toward her and carefully kneeled, lowering himself to the floor by the bathtub beside her.

The apprehension on her face was replaced by gratitude. She tightened her hold on his hand then placed her other hand on his shoulder as if he were a buoy and her only promise of salvation, the only hope she would not drown.

Mendle assisted her as she lowered herself from the side of the tub onto the floor next to him where, to his amazed fulfillment, she familiarly nestled into his arms and rested her head on his chest for refuge.

"I wished for you," she whispered. Then her body slumped as if releasing the weight of a huge burden, and she began to sob.

It was happening, it was here, Mendle knew, but part of him did not believe it. Yet feelings loomed in him so concretely that they overtook the rationale process that prattled "incredible" and hastened to cross-reference "knowing" with data and fact. Mendle tried to understand logically that which he simply knew. It felt irrefutable but was inexplicable. He had no way to explain, only to know, and—whatever it was—the power of it overwhelmed him.

Reverent of the woman's anguish, he caressed her head when grief began to shake her. He did not speak when she cried audibly but only held her and allowed her to hold onto him, which she did desperately.

After some minutes, her lament subsided; she stopped crying and wiped her eyes. When she finally looked up at Mendle, she did so with wonder, as though surprised to find him still there.

There was a different look about her, he thought. The shift in her condition seemed oddly abrupt.

"Where am I?" she asked, then clasped her hands to her throat as if marveling at the sound of her own voice.

"In a bathroom," he replied. Her question surprised Mendle a little; it somehow seemed anti-climactic. He had been about to tell her he loved her.

She looked at Mendle as though his answer had not been sufficient. So he continued, "In a hotel…Holiday Inn or Marriott or something."

She was still looking at him that way, as if he weren't making sense.

"Anaheim, California?" he obliged. The tone of his voice questioned whether any of this meant anything to her.

She stared at the floor now, trying hard to figure something out, then turned that look on him again.

The possibility of this being a joke posed itself to Mendle. "You know, the United States of America?" he prompted, seeing if that jogged anything. "Between the Pacific and Atlantic oceans? Planet Earth."

"Oh, no!" she gasped.

Mendle might have concluded that this must be a prank, perhaps instigated by Rex, or Sandra—the girl was so earnestly horrified; it bordered on the unreal. He remembered the carpet being wet in the room and wondered if it had been her, walking around there earlier.

"Who are you?" His words spilled out of his mouth before he had decided to speak them.

She looked as if she wanted to answer but drew a blank. Then she just stared at him.

Trying to encourage her, he offered, "My name is Mendle." After a long minute of that same unwavering look from her that poured on him like a blend of headlights and evening sun, he ventured again, "Who are you?"

Mendle's heart was beating very fast. He held onto her upper arms as she rubbed her forehead then stared into space, as if she could extrapolate the answer from the air.

Then she started to speak, as if coming out of a trance, "I am," she enunciated slowly. She appeared to be staring at the very sound of her words and remained that way, motionless, then repeated, this time faster, "I am."

Mendle was facing an impending conclusion that loomed in his own mind. *It's you.* The other mental process jabbered, *This is not happening. This can't be real. This is incredible.*

"Were you in the storm?" he asked her, dabbing some water off her arm with a corner of towel.

Urgency widened her eyes, and she nodded, unsure.

"Don't you know who I am?" Mendle asked her.

She shook her head, afraid and about to cry.

"Why did you say you wished for me?" Mendle asked, hoping to hear some sign of recognition.

"I don't know. Because I don't remember. Because I needed help?"

"Oh." He fought off a twinge of disappointment.

On the other side of the door, the Samoyed barked.

The woman's eyes widened. "I was looking for...I was looking for..." Then she pointed at the door and her mouth moved as if she were stammering, but no sound issued.

"Your dog?" Mendle finished for her. "Of course!" he exclaimed. "What's it name?"

She dropped her head, thought a moment, then covered her face. "I can't remember anything," she bemoaned, astonished and perturbed, her voice small.

She's something like a child, Mendle thought. *Like a child-woman.* He brushed her hair, smoothing it back off her face and untangling curls with his fingers, feeling as if she were his only friend in the world, and he hers.

She started, as if about to remember something, then stopped. "I look. There's nothing there," she said, becoming more upset. "It's...blank."

It's you. "You have amnesia. It's all right. I know who you are," he told her.

Mendle remembered what he had been writing. "I won't remember, I'll forget who I am," she had desperately cried in that chapter. *This is her.* He recalled his agitation, his panic, the feeling of utter helplessness to do anything.

The girl was looking at him as if he were a saint.

Mendle challenged his own sanity, then took a stand. Resolutely, he told her, "Your name is Aira. Aira Flight. And your dog's name is Onx."

The woman looked at him trustingly, appearing to float with no connection to anything except what he had just told her. Mendle felt elated. He felt like doing things. He wanted to brush his teeth, shave, shower, use mouthwash, go to the panel. He wished he hadn't drunk anything.

The panel, he remembered. "I was supposed to do a panel. I was going to...uh...not go. I said I would be there, then I just didn't feel like it, I guess," he confided.

"You said you would be there?" she repeated what he said. Her voice was whispery, lilting, each word endowed with her breath, and she spoke slowly.

Mendle inhaled and exhaled thoroughly, his chest heaving up and down as he nodded yes. He liked the way she was carefully picking each word, *like going through a bowl of cherries for the firm, dark ones.*

"Then you should try and keep your word if you gave it," she said.

Her expression was kind and soft. As soon as she said something, she looked around, acting as if she herself didn't know where her thoughts or words were coming from.

It's her, it's her. Mendle wanted to scream it for joy. Instead he told her fervently, "Just stay with me, things will come back to you. Meanwhile stay with me, let me make sure you're safe." He amazed himself with his ardor. The woman nodded matter-of-factly.

Explanation clamored for the floor as Mendle looked at her, wondering how this could be possible. He looked into her eyes, *thoroughfares to heaven.* It was a human phenomena, going to great lengths to disprove anything too wonderful, he reminded himself. Like people winning prize money on the radio babbling, "You're kidding. I don't believe it. Incredible." A phenomenon that served nothing.

She was feeling her face, brushing it with the palms of her hands. "Do you know me?" she asked Mendle.

Mendle's throat began to tighten as he attempted to stop the uprising of emotion which threatened to seize him. He took in a deep breath to try to dissipate the beginnings of a tidal wave gaining momentum inside him, and tightly held the breath in. He tightened his grasp on her arms and pulled her gently toward him, mostly so she could not see his face. *Do I know you?* The only air he allowed to escape was the amount necessary to form his next words.

"Yes." Emotion bit the back of Mendle's throat as it struggled to vent itself.

"Does it happen to you? Blankness and forgetting?" she asked him.

Mendle felt as though all his life prior to that moment had been a dream. He could no longer contain the profundity of his sentiment which begged outpouring; he held her to him harder than he wanted to, desperately embracing her, and sobbed. He was crying and he did not understand why. The tears issued from his very soul, releasing wounds and joy which had no name. In all his life of loneliness he had never cried this way.

Am I going mad? Mendle wondered again if this were an illusion that, like every other shining illusion, would be soaked up by reality. *No!* he shouted silently. It was real, as was all the glowing ideal he ever imagined. He felt dignity restored that the daily world surrounding him constantly tried to rob. *Love is real! There is more to life than the governing decay the news professes.*

He vowed he would not be robbed again. *No matter if no one agrees with me, ever. No matter if I am scorned, taunted, ridiculed more than ever.*

No matter if I die of solitude, and every face around me continues to regard me with smiles that pretend to understand but eyes that judge me as mad.

There was more to life than met the physical eye and Mendle felt he was holding living proof in his arms. His world was real, and she had been real, more real than the hard floor on which they sat. Perhaps she was buried now, in human vestment, as he was buried. He didn't understand it all, but he vowed he would never doubt himself again.

Mendle J. Orion clung to the woman in the bathroom as though she were his only witness, the only proof of his sanity, the only friend in a world which had been alien to his most golden aspirations and dreams, a world to which he felt he never belonged.

She gently put her hands on him then returned his embrace. Close to her, Mendle felt his emotions were valid reason enough by themselves. He did not feel compelled to tell her why he cried. He needed neither to excuse his tears nor justify them. He was sure she understood him; even though she seemed disoriented, he was convinced she knew on some level.

When he finally stopped, Mendle pulled away from the girl and bent down to wipe his face with the towel. He used the towel as a shelter against the uncovered vulnerability and tenderness inside him before finally venturing to look at her.

His eyes offered passage to his soul and though the girl could not grasp any details, she responded to, if anything, the relief of a kindred isolation. She appeared to relax and a small smile blossomed. While she looked at him, with those eyes he readily welcomed and understood, Mendle's thoughts turned to her plight.

Unabashedly open, she was looking at him. Despite the seriousness of her predicament, she didn't even appear to think anything much was awry now. Her countenance was like a newborn's, just taking everything in without filter or defense.

Her eyes were very large, a realm of aquamarine and sapphire, bright and open, joyful and sorrowful all at once, as if they had witnessed the birth and death of a million things—yet it was as if a curtain had lowered in them. Nonetheless, the spirit behind those eyes, so new and receptive, so agelessly ancient, reminded Mendle of his place in the cosmos.

chapter  16

Sandra Wilford used the swing of her body to toss her hair back and forth behind her as she walked, and flexed the muscles of her buttocks with each stride, taking the corridor as an opportunity for exercise. She turned down the right wing, and when she saw a white-jacketed hotel employee wheeling a room service cart, she quickened her pace.

As soon as she determined his destination was Mendle's room, she stopped the man from knocking while managing a bill out of the wallet belted to her waist. "Excuse me," she said, handing him the money. "618, right?"

He nodded and smiled gratefully, his timid demeanor telling her he didn't speak much English.

"Thanks," she told him and took over the cart.

Watching the man go his way, Sandra secured the wallet, smoothed her hair, and adjusted her yellow dress, taking long enough for him to put distance between them. She knocked on 618 very lightly without the intention of being heard. When she went to open it, she found the door locked.

Through the shut bathroom door, Mendle heard a sharp knock on the outer door of his hotel room.

"Your hamburgers are here." It was Sandra's voice.

"My hamburgers are here," Mendle told Aira matter-of-factly with a matter-of-fact nod of the head and an accompanying matter-of-fact gesture with his mouth. He readjusted to the space and time of the moment, where they sat on a bathroom floor. They had been wandering silent in thought as they held each other.

"Hey!" Another knock rapped louder than the first. Then came the edict. "Your hamburgers are here."

"My hamburgers are here," Mendle repeated, and a grin tugged at the corners of his mouth.

The situation, his entire life, seemed suddenly ludicrous. Sandra and all the things about which he had ever tormented himself seemed mere specks. He felt elated, all-powerful. He began to laugh.

Sandra called through the door. "Mendle? Are you all right?" She pulled her hair back and pressed her ear to the door. She could hear laughter followed by Mendle calling out, "I'm fine!"

"Didn't you hear me?" she shouted insistently even though she was sure he had. "I said your hamburgers are here!" Such seriousness about a hamburger juxtaposed with a glimpse of the cosmos sent more laughing sweeping through him.

"I'm coming in," Sandra warned.

As Mendle heard her jiggling the doorknob, he imagined the expression on Sandra's face as she continued making a senate hearing out of hamburgers. Aira was swept up on his mirth and twinkles sparked in her eyes as she watched him.

"Your hamburgers are here and they're getting cold!" The finality in Sandra's tone, the disgust and exasperation in it, promised that this was the last time she was going to say it. It was official. This was a grave matter.

Mendle was laughing happily and wildly. When Sandra repeated her pronouncement yet again, it was the punch-line to his life—a commentary on the importance of all that had tormented him. He couldn't stop laughing; he didn't want to.

"What are you doing in there, Mendle?"

Seeing a change in Aira's expression cooled Mendle's merriment. Something about her face had changed. A look of pained acquiescence had descended over her, remote but most definitely there, even as she tried to smile. It was disconcerting.

Mendle managed to his feet and held his hands out to help the girl up. While doing so, he saw his reflection in the mirror. He looked at his body as though he had never seen himself before.

He wasn't looking to check if the defects were still there. He looked to see. He did not instantly attack himself with criticisms as he used to do. When Aira stood up, Mendle stepped closer to the mirror. Something hovered on the periphery of his awareness about himself, something he knew yet didn't know. He struggled within the image of his eyes, searching into his very pupils, to find it.

Aira stood behind him now. She was staring at her own reflection, much the same way. He turned and faced her. She was obviously trying hard to orient herself. She looked up at him with such plain simplicity that Mendle felt the urge to kiss her.

"Do you remember something?" he asked her.

"Panel?" she tried, grasping for some direction.

"Yes," he told her, disappointed not to hear her say the words for which he longed yet happy to hear her voice something which was important to him. He thanked her softly for remembering what he had said, feeling warmed that someone should care about him enough to want him to keep his word. "I'll shower and we'll go."

Mendle burst with a jubilee of gratitude for the panacea of her presence. What a glorious feeling gratitude was, triumph and humility combined. It dampened his parched soul. He expanded, pressed against and stretched all his edges. In his heart a thousand birds sang of morning.

Aira turned and stared at the door, then her wrist jumped, as if visibly receiving an impulse from her brain, and she reached for the handle. The motion seemed mechanical, and, as Mendle observed it, a small fear jolted through him and mushroomed. He feared the innumerable ways he could lose what he had found.

"Aira..." The girl turned, accepting the name as hers.

Everything came to him to say all at once and stuck, too big to come out in words. So, to begin with, Mendle picked, "This is a strange place. We have to be careful."

She looked at him, trust making her eyes seem even wider than they already were, and nodded agreeably. He nodded back and she turned around to go. There was a vagueness about her, a distance.

"Oh!" she exclaimed, excited when she saw the white dog outside the bathroom door. She quickly went to it. The animal collapsed into her embrace. The dog seemed relieved, as if it knew her.

"Is that your dog?" Mendle asked.

She didn't answer. It appeared she couldn't answer, and she gave Mendle an apologetic look as she continued embracing the dog and nestling her cheek against its fur.

Mendle watched them for a moment then said, "Onx."

"Onx?" Aira repeated.

"Right," Mendle said.

The dog opened its eyes and blinked up at Mendle. He took it as a confirmation that sent chills through him.

Sandra had been pacing to the elevators and back, debating with herself whether to report an emergency and get someone from the front desk to open the door. *After all, Mendle does drink, he may have hurt himself in there. It might be embarrassing, but it might teach him to listen the next time.* A vindictive desire writhed in her.

On her second time to the elevator, she decided to give him one more chance and turned around. From the hallway Sandra could hear music and the sound of water running through wall plumbing. She thought she had heard a female voice within but wasn't certain. Surmising Mendle was in the shower, she planned to wait until the water stopped before knocking again, but exasperation and impatience compelled her to lift her knuckles to the door once again. She delivered three swift raps.

The door swung smoothly open, surprising her. A girl stood there. Barefoot. Dressed in a trash bag.

Sandra stiffened. "Hello." She could hear the shower running in the bathroom.

"Hello."

"I'm Sandra Wilford."

"I'm," she paused, "Aira Flight."

"I...just wanted to let Mendle know. His hamburgers are here," Sandra said curtly. Motioning to the room service cart, she turned abruptly and left.

It was intermission. Rex and Sandra sat in brown folding chairs along the wall of the conference room where the panel discussion was about to begin. Still agitated from her encounters with Mendle and that woman who opened the door to his room, Sandra continued flipping through a catalogue of possible explanations for this latest development. Yet she could only surmise.

"Well, then who is she?"

"I don't know. Why didn't you ask her?" Rex said.

"I was stunned."

"It's probably some fan playing games with Mendle."

"Just what he needs in his condition." Sandra fumed as she thought back. "She was wearing a plastic bag, a garbage bag," she said incredulously.

"You have to admit, his goddess come to save him in a trash bag is pretty amusing," Rex giggled.

"I'm pretty sure she said that's her name. The name of his character. I remember. Aira Flight." Sandra shook her head and pronounced, "I see nothing funny about this." She was incensed that someone had intimate access to Mendle, especially now that he was beginning to acquire some success and recognition. "He might've been hiding her in the room when I was up there," Sandra conjectured, enraged at his audacity.

Rex turned to see Sandra wide-eyed with her mouth agape. "Onx!" she said, snapping her fingers. She placed the name that had been puzzling her, remembering having earlier read it on a page of Mendle's manuscript. "Now I know where I've heard that!" *It's not the damn Egyptian symbol of eternal life!* "Onx was the name of a dragon in the novel he's writing." *Onx. Not 'ankh.' What in hell is going on?*

Bewildered, Rex looked at her.

"He said that dog's name was Onx!" Sandra rampaged. "The dog. The white dog." She waved a nevermind at Rex and kept on. "He said that was its name."

"Maybe it's a," Rex took a significant pause and emphasized it with two upward darts of his eyebrows, "coincidence."

Cold marble slabs of hate were building up in Sandra, congealing into a feeling so frozen it burned to the touch. Desire for revenge was a sensation of flames about her head.

"I wouldn't jump to conclusions, Sandra," Rex told her. "It's probably someone he picked up here at the convention. Fans act out scenarios. I mean there are probably at least fifty Scottys here, needing 'more time Captain,' ya know? I passed a guy being Jean Luc Picard, who said "Make it so" to someone pushing the elevator button."

"Mendle's book isn't published yet," Sandra said dryly.

"You've read parts of it. Maybe others have, too. Mendle has fans."

"What...if...if...if...if..."

"Sandra, you're stuttering."

"I'm concerned." Sandra inhaled deeply for control, reminding herself to get those subliminal self-progress tapes out of the car.

"That's probably all it is," Rex said, "he found some fan to act things out."

Sandra turned to him, proposing in a stressed, hushed voice, "What if it's some opportunist? Someone who wants to take advantage of him? I wouldn't worry if Mendle were in his right mind. But he's, well, you saw him. I'm telling you, he believes it."

Rex leaned discreetly toward her. "What? You think he would really believe some girl who told him she was his soul mate from outer space?"

Sandra arched an eyebrow and let the question hang rhetorically.

Up in 618, Mendle took another bite of hamburger and decided he didn't like hamburgers. Three remained on the tray because the dog would not eat them.

"I ordered it because I thought that's what a dog would like," Mendle said, drinking the coffee, anxious to eliminate all whiskey from his system. "Maybe it'll be hungry later." Onx barked once. She shook her head from side to side; the motion became spasmodic, then suddenly stopped.

Whoa. Or maybe it doesn't eat, Mendle thought as he took a hard look at the dog. An eerie feeling was breaking the horizon in Mendle, and his logic worked hard at putting pieces of this puzzle together. He looked from one to the other as Aira sat on the floor next to the white Samoyed and petted it.

The girl consumed his attention. It pained him to see her wearing a plastic trash bag. He decided it was too acutely a commentary on the condition of the society.

"Where did you get the, um, the dress?" he asked her. "Come on, I'll help you up."

She looked around the room, wondering about it herself. Settling on something, she pointed to an oblong cardboard dispenser of plastic drycleaning bags by the luggage rack. She extended her hand to him.

"Were you out in the storm earlier?" Mendle asked her for the second time as he pulled her to her feet.

Her Bambi eyes displayed a struggle to remember, then she shook her head and relinquished her attempt to surmount failure. Mendle continued his efforts to gather and assemble pieces of the enigma. "Do you have anything with you?" he asked kindly.

She thought about his question, but appeared to be wondering more than thinking. "Me," she finally said, content to have been able to answer something.

"It's okay," Mendle reassured her.

He hadn't brought extra clothes, not even a tee shirt. He thought of using his pocket knife to modify a pillow case, but it wasn't his property so he planned to buy something downstairs.

He wasn't about to leave the girl in the room. Though he felt some trepidation about bringing her with him, his elated spirit did not focus on predicting and avoiding any problems that might arise in doing so. Mendle was excited. His thoughts rapidly knitted together entire pieces of the picture where they could, fitting this to that to solve puzzles, and posing questions that he wondered how to ask. For the most part, however, he floated on a glow of unthinking satori.

Collecting his money and keys from the dresser, Mendle ventured, "Do you eat?" He turned just in time to see her take a chomp out of one of the hamburgers.

In the conference room, the panel discussion had resumed with the host recapping and summarizing the discussion of the first half.

"Nobel-laureate physicist, Werner Heisenberg, said, quote, 'It turns out we can no longer talk of the behavior of the particle apart from the process of observation...'"

Rex, surprised to see Mendle come through the doors, leaned toward Sandra and whispered, "There's Mendle."

She turned to see; he was holding hands with the girl who had opened the door.

"I guess she must've changed out of her trash bag," Sandra commented caustically as she watched them. She scrutinized what the girl was wearing, some type of space costume, a tunic and tights.

"Looks like she slipped back into the outfit she flew in on," Rex commented wryly, then broke into giggles.

Even Sandra laughed a little. "She's short," she said.

"Average," Rex corrected, being of moderate height himself.
Then, "What a view," he smirked.

Mendle was beaming and holding the hand of the girl, who walked a little behind him, looking around as if she were in wonderland.

Assuming that Mendle was searching the room for him, Rex stood up a little and elevated one hand over his head. Sitting down when Mendle had spotted him, he narrated to Sandra, "King Mendle and his Space Goddess," then worked to keep his face straight.

Mendle reached Rex and crouched beside him. He said, "We thought it best I keep my word and make the appearance."

The word "we" punctured Sandra. The sudden show of righteousness seared her.

"Fine, fine," Rex started to bow out. He hastily handed Mendle the notes, concealing his disappointment.

Mendle stopped him, placing his hand on Rex's forearm, "I wish you would join me in the panel. I'll be happy to introduce you."

"Rex has his own panel in an hour," Sandra informed Mendle.

"That's all right," Rex interrupted her. This panel had a bigger draw; there were editors from DAW and TOR Books, as well as several newspaper and film people in attendance.

The host on the platform had been delivering his introductory segment, a preamble to the second group about to appear. He was introducing the guests and, as he called for the panelists to take the table, Mendle insisted, pulling Rex up off the chair to his feet.

"Most magnanimous of you," Rex said, making less of Mendle's gesture with an exaggerated and aggrandizing manner. Following Mendle, he tossed Sandra a glance and shrugged.

"How rude of me," Mendle remembered, suddenly turning and taking a few steps back. "Rex Benton. Sandra Wilford. This is Aira Flight."

Her face impassive, Sandra directed an alarmed look through her eyes to Rex.

chapter  17

The room was throbbing with multi-colored lights that flashed and pulsated to the beat. Green. Red. Blue, blue. Yellow. Blue, blue. Green. Yellow. Red. The hotel nightclub was an intriguing cavern of wavelengths that beckoned Aira's curiosity as she paused outside its doors to listen to the music. Despite Mendle's reluctance, at Sandra's and Rex's insistence, they entered and sat together.

The bar was filled mostly with out-of-town people: some on business, a few families visiting nearby Disneyland, and some of the science fiction convention attendees.

While they decided on a table that satellited the dance floor, Sandra studied Mendle with sideways probes. She continued to do so as the waitress took their order and brought their drinks. This was Mendle as Sandra had never seen him. He was calm. He was courteous and good humored. He acted as if the world were his to give.

One thought comforted her. When Mendle was happy, all shields were down, he was open house.

They were sitting next to a table of women who aspired to be rich and famous stars. Of the credo that stardom was a matter of having low body weight and collagen-pumped lips such as theirs, they exuded altitude and criticized other women in their vicinity. Targeting various failures of perfection in surrounding female bodies, they searched and sifted for people—producers, wealthy men, executives, anyone—who would serve them.

Sandra had smiled to herself when they took the adjacent table, anticipating it would be only minutes before Mendle would observe them and bitterly begin ranting about the degraded state of civilization. Yet Mendle, who often buckled under social settings containing varieties of human weakness, said nothing when he saw their comportment and haughty stares. He noted the persistent looks and seductive poses they aimed at him, and likened them to so many fishing lines with delectably baited hooks. Deciding to terminate this nuisance, he did so with casual indifference.

"Excuse me, women," he leaned over and addressed them. "To be confronted with thigh and cleavage intentionally as a communication is quite an interesting phenomenon. I myself am not into having my sex buttons pushed today. Your bra size does not interest me. I assume you are human beings and hope you start acting with some intelligence."

He quietly sat back with aplomb and sipped his orange soda, leaving the table giggling and exchanging marveled looks.

"Mendle, a prude?" Rex joked. He craned his head to look at the women. "I'll trade places with you if the view is bothering you."

"They're supposed to be people," Mendle stated.

Rex turned to get a look at them again. "I'm afraid I don't see your point," he said lasciviously. "Not with those accoutrements."

Sandra felt embarrassed. Her plan to use Rex as leverage with Mendle was fading.

"People are known to be…sexy, you know," Rex finished, restoring some of Sandra's confidence.

Often a person's innermost opinions, when disagreeable, vent only with anger or upset. Yet Mendle spoke, although bluntly, without any attitude of superiority. The benign tone enpowered his words. "It isn't that you can't see my point," he told Rex calmly. "It's that you won't. You prefer the grotesque, that's what you write about. Why even discuss it?"

Rex smirked. The comment stung. It felt unfamiliar for Rex to be on the receiving end. It was Mendle, opinionated, but not twirled into knots over something that offended his ideals. It was clean opinion. Direct, even kind, no pain about it, a statement such as Mendle's was definitely more threatening.

Sandra concealed her machinations. From behind a cool facade, she glowered at Mendle thinking, *What's he raving about now? Who the hell does he think he is?*

Mendle's beneficent air irritated Sandra as much as if not more than the naivety with which the blonde girl next to him sat looking at everything. Acid thoughts fumed in Sandra's mind as she viewed the scenario. She noted that Mendle had not ordered alcohol, but orange soda. He had even recommended a fruit punch to this person who had the audacity to lie about her name. *Whatever is she up to?*

Sandra held up her glass, "Cheers," she toasted, nodding toward her adversary and stressing the name, "Aira Flight."

In vino veritas, Sandra justified silently as she watched the girl start on her second glass of punch. A tip and a promising wink slipped to the bartender earlier ensured that the tropical fruit punch held the nectar of more than fruits, and now Sandra anticipated a return for her investment.

Aira, who had been watching the dancers on the floor, slowly pushed back her chair and walked forward, as if in a daze, to join in.

"Mendle, you looked great accepting your award up there," Sandra quickly engaged him. Hiding behind a chipper veneer, playing with her cocktail napkin as she spoke, she was set on taking full advantage of Mendle's exuberance. "This is your second significant award."

"I suppose so," Mendle said as he curiously watched Aira step onto the dance floor and start moving to the music.

"So, that's her, huh?" Sandra filled the lull, keeping him at the table. *She looks like one tired babe.*

Sandra shifted a quick look at Rex, seeking his agreement, but he didn't return her silent verdict. Still stinging and feeling distracted at being topped by Mendle, Rex only grinned and shrugged.

When Mendle abruptly turned to face Sandra, he caught her off guard before she nervously transformed into smiles. Seeing Mendle's brow furrow, she worried that he had caught the cross-flow between Rex and herself. Mendle's preoccupation, however, was with a new danger that presented itself—Aira had to be protected.

"Her?" Mendle acted puzzled by Sandra's question.

"Her," Sandra probed, knowing he knew full well what she meant. "Is that...*her?*" Sandra repeated, careful to maintain a reverent tone.

Mendle twiddled with his straw, sat silent, then looked away. Sandra followed his gaze to the dance floor, where the woman was beginning to move ever more wildy to the music.

"I guess super-intelligent life knows how to shake tail feather," Sandra commented, and she shut Rex up quickly with a sharp look when he started to laugh.

"I guess it probably would," Mendle replied without giving a satisfying answer.

As Sandra observed Mendle watching the woman dance, it amazed her that he seemed actually impressed by this person. She was average at best. She looked a little worn out, actually. No make up, didn't seem to care much about her appearance. She looked rather plain, even stressed, except for the platinum in her hair. Earlier, when Sandra asked her where she was from, Aira had looked at her a little vapidly. *As if to make me feel it was a stupid question,* she decided. Then, after darting a look at Mendle, the girl had finally replied, "I'm from right here and now," as if the answer should have been obvious.

Sandra smiled to herself as she watched her now, not particularly dancing with anyone but jumping and twisting to the music, completely in orbit in the small sea of bodies. *I wonder how old she is. She seems childish, but...* She reached for her wine and took a sip, deliberately using the raised glass as shield while she probed Mendle with a scrutinizing look.

"She does somewhat resemble the girl you described," Sandra feigned casual earnestness as she set her glass down. "Except I imagined the character as much prettier." She let that hang a moment, then added, "Your dream girl. You know."

Rex looked at Sandra quietly from across the table then lowered his eyes.

When Mendle didn't reply, Sandra zeroed in a little closer. "It's such a pleasure to, well, to, you know, to meet her, to finally meet the girl in the novel."

"That's not the girl in my book," Mendle said.

"Oh, I'm sorry. Isn't her name Aira Flight? She said it was. When she opened the door. To your room. You introduced her—"

"That's a coincidence," Mendle said, cutting her off. To avoid lying, he further detoured, "How can she be the girl in my book when she's the girl right here?"

His laugh seemed forced to Sandra, and she layered one on top of his, louder. Hers was tight, controlled, patronizing and condescending. In the silence following that laugh, she cleared the air space further with a look and admonished, "Oh, Mendle, Mendle—what am I going to do with you?"

"You don't need to do a thing with me," he replied politely, and Rex laughed.

Propelled by a desire to keep Mendle at what she considered a suitable size, Sandra said, "I'm personally going to take you to see Dr. Kaufkiff again."

"Yes I've been," Mendle admitted openly, undermining her attempt to embarrass him. "Do you know what the diagnosis was?" He sipped his orange soda, aware of the apprehension at the table.

He seems so sure of himself, this is unlike him, Sandra thought as she waited to hear what he was going to say.

"As an anal-ist I found him duly anally retentive. In other words: Full. Of. Shh—"

"Oh, Mendle," Sandra interrupted him, disgusted. Looking away, she saw the bartender talking to Aira at the edge of the dance floor. Panic flitted through her as she wondered what he was telling her.

Rex blinked and pushed his spectacles securely onto the bridge of his nose. A habit begun to gain needed time for rebuttals had now become a mannerism accompanying most any thinking process. It bothered him that neither arrogance nor the omniscience of his smile seemed to have an effect on Mendle anymore. There was no question in Rex's mind as to which of them was the superior. Mendle possessed charm, looks. *But he is not as qualified, not as educated, as I.* Deciding the arena would be intelligence and the weapon debate, Rex busied himself again on how to create an opportunity. He didn't want to appear as though he were trying to acerbate Mendle out of sport.

As Sandra watched Aira returning to the table, she flippantly narrated, "Here comes your super intelligence."

Everyone turned to see Aira walking loosely toward them. The big smile on her face caused her to resemble a suburban girl in a shopping mall with unlimited credit. "Oh wow! That was fun!" she exclaimed as she plopped into her seat.

Mendle speculated about the body of the woman he had dubbed Aira Flight. She was sweating. He found himself wondering how she had arrived, whether the body contained blood and organs. *Could she suddenly vanish?* The thought left him cold.

"The bartender asked me where I was sitting," Aira said. "I told him I wasn't sitting, I was standing. Then he asked what table was mine. I didn't know they gave you the tables here."

"Mendle, are you listening to this?" Sandra asked, and turned and saw that he was.

All three of them at the table stared at Aira, each transfixed for different reasons.

"Do they give you the tables here? Is this table mine?" the girl asked ebulliently.

The three of them shook their heads no, in near unison.

Each watched her with varying degrees of amazement as she said "Oh." Pleased to recount something evidently of interest to her new friends, she went on, "Then he asked where I was sitting before I was standing, and I pointed. And he said he wanted to send me another drink and said you were paying. I declared 'Why should they pay? They haven't done anything wrong!'"

She stopped her discourse abruptly and started to look idly around the room. When she became so suddenly silent, Mendle, Rex, and Sandra all inadvertently craned their necks forward. Soon it was plain she wasn't going to continue; she was bobbing her head to the beat of the music, leaving her listeners dangling, wanting to hear the rest of the story.

"Then what?" Rex prompted.

"Oh," Aira came around with a wide-eyed look. "He laughed and said not to worry, he meant you were paying as in money. You know, those pieces of paper?" They nodded.

"I told him I didn't have any money and said I would be happy to bring him some if he could tell me where to get it. He made a noise through his nose and said he was busy and was just going to put it on the tab, and to let you know about it." She pointed her finger at Sandra, to demonstrate what the bartender did. "He said you would know what he meant."

"Sure, sure, everything's on me," Sandra said. Acting nonchalant, she sat further back in her chair and felt relieved the bartender had not divulged that she paid him to add a punch to the punch.

"Amazing. What a vision," Rex muttered.

So, he's smitten by the helpless routine, Sandra concluded about Mendle. *After all these years I've strived to be independent and never need anything, does he respect a self-sufficient woman? No, here he is falling for the needy routine. He seems amused, cheerful, oblivious to the idiocy she's displaying. She can't be for real.* Sandra decided, *It's an act. It has to be. Contrived coyness at its best.* Her determination to find out who the woman really was increased.

Sandra smiled at Aira, then casually took her reading glasses out of her belt pouch and put them on. Her intent was to show, by contrast, *the brainlessness of the girl.* She mustered her composure preparatory to continuing her line of questioning when Aira, who had been watching with fascination, said effusively, "You know, they *do* give you an appearance of authority."

Responding to Sandra's indignant look, Aira explained, "You thought they made you look intelligent when you put them on. They do somewhat have that effect." She spoke with genuine interest, trying to be agreeable and glowing with innocent friendliness.

Even though there had not been the slightest hint of malice in Aira's voice, her statement unbalanced Sandra. Platformed in her mind now was the fact that, unlike most people who used the optical aid to improve vision, she did on occasion use her glasses as a way of emanating being smart.

"What, you have ESP or something?" Sandra's rebuttal was derisive. It dispelled Aira's comment as ridiculous and succeeded in making her appear, and feel, foolish for having said it.

"Can I get you another round?" a hotel waitress interrupted as she set a glass of punch in front of Aira.

"You can prevent another round," Sandra played the victim. "Here I am getting dragged into something," she said, acting distraught, "and I didn't do anything."

Mendle was temporarily off in his own world. He had been sporadically tracing his novel in his mind, deriving inspiration from his observations. "Can I borrow that?" He took the pen from the waitress's tray and wrote on a napkin, so he wouldn't forget, the words, "CHAPTER EIGHT—Life played, its forms disguising it from itself."

The waitress nodded and smiled politely at Sandra, even though she didn't know what she was talking about. Her low-cut blouse and micro-skirt revealing black lace bloomers underneath was vibrating one of Rex's wavelengths.

"My, my, my," Rex responded to what was real to him. "Does the hotel provide these uniforms?"

The waitress smiled obligingly. "Can I get you something else here?" she repeated cordially.

"Based on your configuration, I could most assuredly help you realize your innermost cravings," Rex announced pompously.

"Come on, Rex." Mendle replaced the pen on the waitress's tray.

Rex would not be dissuaded. "Then…completely ravaged, driven wild, veritably consumed but still in the frenzy of lust, you would indeed be pleased to get me anything I requested. Anything at all." A sardonic grimace frozen on his face, he punctuated his recitative display with a pointed stare at her breasts.

As Mendle watched him sit back all pleased with himself, he realized that this wasn't flattery at all, Rex was thriving on the woman's embarrassment. It was a mockery, a masquerade, a pretense of liking sex, when, in fact, he was only degrading it. It pained Mendle to see the waitress feeling degraded but hesitating to speak her mind for fear of losing her job.

Suddenly the nightclub scene engaged Mendle for other reasons. It paralleled a chapter in his book, where doll-bodies were offering "euphorisiacs" on trays to arrivals in Z Zone. Devoid of soul-life, asleep, they were coerced into believing they were nothing but machines.

I don't want to forget. Mendle looked around him at the people. *Soul-death.* Beings believing they were matter, organic or otherwise.

In his novel, the personification of soul-death, Juristac, gloated with derogatory glee over beings who became trapped in material bodies. *Another coincidence,* Mendle thought. Another thing he had been writing, and here it was…happening. Well, almost. There were similarities, parallels; this couldn't be denied. He felt an increasing excitement. *Another glimpse, I saw it. These are clues. Clues to some universal order. To the Theory of Everything.*

Focusing back on the scene at hand, Mendle realized that it wasn't that he didn't like sex—and he had been beginning to wonder about himself. It was that he loved sex and protected it from degradation. "That makes me a real man," Mendle suddenly blurted out his conclusion, and no one knew what he was talking about.

"The bartender said to give you this," the waitress told Sandra, handing her a tab.

"Fine, fine," Sandra rushed to take care of it, pulling a charge card out of her wallet.

"Yes sir. Mighty fine," Rex muttered at the waitress through tight lips.

Aira, who was watching Rex, spontaneously exclaimed like a ray of sun through dark clouds. "Wow! How genetic!"

"Yes!" Mendle exclaimed.

It sickened Sandra to see Mendle respond to the girl as if she had uttered a decree of genius.

"Not just genetic, though. Influenced by individual aberration," Mendle added.

Aira looked around with saucer eyes, from face to face surrounding her. "This is so interesting!" she enthused.

"This is human interaction," Mendle said to her.

It appalled and amazed Sandra the way he was talking to the girl, as if she were a three-year-old at a zoo.

Aira asked, "Is it a form of social play that underneath the words people say there is a different conversation going on?" Her voice and expression seemed the pinnacle of innocence.

Sandra arched an eyebrow. "So. You *are* psychic."

"No," Aira replied.

"You must be from outer space," Sandra pronounced, getting more aggressive.

Mendle froze.

"I am?" Aira asked, then quickly, after staring into nothing as she did, "No, I think I am from inner space."

"You certainly seem psychic to me," Sandra insisted dryly. "Wouldn't you say, Rex?"

"Indubitably," he said, with difficulty restraining himself from laughing.

"Psychic," Aira pondered.

Sandra seized an opportunity to illustrate the girl's dimness. "The word means telepathic," she explained condescendingly. "As in the ability to read minds or the future. Don't you read minds?"

"No," Aira said.

"But you said you read my mind, said I put on my glasses to seem smart," Sandra challenged, twisting to produce Aira's retraction of the comment.

"I wasn't reading your mind. It just came to me out of nowhere. Just like that. This thought came to me. As something I knew. You wanted to look smart and make me appear brainless."

Sandra winced on the interior. She hadn't counted on her repeating it. She turned from the topic and dove into a loophole for cover. "How could I hope to prove you brainless?" she denied. "You have to have a brain, obviously, what person doesn't?" She forced a laugh.

"Intelligence doesn't stem from the brain," Aira said, looking off into somewhere in front of her.

Sandra let that statement hang in silence for magnification of the way the girl said it. *Staring off like some circus clairvoyant.*

Sensing Mendle's impatience to leave, Rex launched the tactic he had been harboring. "You know, I notice you incorporate archaic forms in your work," he challenged.

"What a delightful evening," Mendle sighed.

Rex ploughed ahead. "For one, your use of 'said John,' as opposed to 'John said.'"

"That's not archaic. I just used it in my last novel," Mendle replied.

Rex insisted, "It's archaic. The proper way now is 'John said,' not 'said John.'"

"Probably just a trend thought up by some critic who really wanted to be a writer, or a professor who can't contribute ideas of his own so alters another's work, to feel intellectual."

"You're saying to never change anything?"

"Did I say that? No. I was talking about trends. Degradation can't come up with anything original. It can only lessen some ideal that exists."

Rex cleared his throat and pushed his glasses closer to his head. "I see. So you're saying that—"

"Rex, I'm not an intellectual. I'm just a writer. I know you've developed an excellent mind at Harvard, you needn't prove it." He paused for a moment then, got halfway up from his chair and abruptly shouted as if in distress, "Oh, no, my preposition is dangling!" Heads turned toward him.

"Mendle, please," Sandra hushed him. She had seen this routine before.

Rex smiled. "Ah yes. And I've heard you contend the brain is like a computer, a mere computer."

"Well, it is," Mendle said, sitting back down. "It's the soul that creates. From nothing. That's why it's called 'original,' as in…*origin.*"

Rex took things down a notch to what he considered more solid ground. "Certainly one cannot dispute the value of education," he said eruditely.

Mendle settled back into the chair before finally answering. "Education is one thing. Regurgitation of facts another."

"I don't understand your point," Rex said.

"In writing, for example…'The gift of words is no such great matter; a man is not made a hunter or a warrior by the mere possession of a firearm.'" Mendle quoted idly.

"Joseph Conrad!" Rex returned the serve—which wasn't intended as a serve—adroitly, but he missed the point. His eagerness to vent knowledge only to intimidate others loomed in the silence.

Mendle tried restating his point. "What makes a great writer is what he or she perceives and has to say, secondary and subservient is use of language."

Rex shrugged. "Never heard of it. Who said that?"

"That's my point. The point of education is knowing what these things mean, not peacocking by reciting names and references."

Aira interjected, "This is fascinating. I'm noticing a concern about being intelligent…but…we are intelligence."

"How profound," Sandra pronounced in mock-reverence.

Mendle turned to Aira. "More than a concern about being intelligent, what you are perceiving is a concern about being somebody," he said sadly.

"Why worry about being somebody when you already are?" Aira happily offered her solution.

"A regular dynamo," Sandra quipped, nodding at Aira.

The waitress returned Sandra's credit card. As she waited for Sandra to sign the slip, Rex mustered the lustful grimace on his face. He followed her with his gaze when she walked away.

"Why do you make a display of wanting to copulate with that woman?" Aira asked him.

The simplicity with which Aira spoke caused Sandra to laugh, a laugh which, though directed to being disparaging of Aira, stemmed from pain rooted in lost innocence.

Rex only levelled a calm grin at her.

"Let's just say he was being archaic," Mendle replied.

"Oh? Archaic? How so?" Rex asked, acting amused.

Mendle spoke as though quoting an encyclopedia. "Animalismo: An antiquated impulse. A genetic reaction originally rooted in a thrust to perpetuate the species. With higher life forms, reason is usually employed in conducting the organism. The act has evolved to an expression of love and creation. The impulse in the human is most desirable when integrated with sentiments of affection and admiration for the person present, as well as the body."

Mendle was on a roll. "In some," he continued, "the sex impulse remains in the realm of mere genetic response. This is, in and of itself, a productive and pleasurable activity. However, in still others, the sex impulse is not even in the archaic realm of simple procreative function, but has degenerated rather than evolved. Degenerated into a means of degradation and humiliation, to serve as a means of conquest, perverted or otherwise. All this, of course, under the pretense of having a genuine desire for sex, or under the anthem 'there is nothing wrong with sex.'"

Before silence could completely fall on the table, he added, "And some think it is the sole purpose of life. Why even toothpaste, cars, modes of hygiene and transportation, are sexy."

"How fascinating!' Aira exclaimed.

Sandra rolled her eyes.

"If only I had a pen," Mendle said.

"Ah yes!" Rex quoted Lord Byron, "'A small drop of ink, falling like dew upon a thought, makes millions think.'"

"A small drop of ink falling upon doo, makes the world stink," Mendle converted, amused by his instant wit in adapting the quote to the situation.

"What do you mean by that rephrasing?"

"Just what do you like to make them think about?" Mendle posed rhetorically.

Sandra thought of Rex's last novel about a group of eunuchs that tried to conquer the world, collected male body parts and killed children. She wished Mendle hadn't asked the question.

"Only what I'm qualified to write," Rex retorted, puffing up, but his comment did not command the respect he had intended.

"Precisely!" Mendle declared and started laughing. Though he had never particularly needed agreement from others to condone his actions, Mendle felt reinforced by feeling the girl at his side. He was reckless from the elation. "Why do you quote Lord Byron? You don't support his ideas," he challenged Rex. "You glamorize distortion and crimes, and it isn't at all that you aren't responsible for your effects on society, it's that you actually derive pleasure from deviation."

"People buy what I write," Rex said, cooly.

"I guess that's what a deviate is. Deviation, deviate," Mendle mulled aloud, ignoring Rex's comment. He threw in with mock pompousness, "And you may quote me!"

Rex grinned. "People are stupid. It's what the masses want. That's why they pay me."

"To calculate on their weaknesses and push their buttons?"

"Perhaps you should do that a while, too. Unless of course you can pawn your literary awards for cash," Rex delivered. "Or do you dream they'll come to life as food or a rent check?"

Aira shook her head, sending her curls bobbing. "No, no, people are not stupid," she insisted plaintively, her words so simplistic they were poignant.

A Science Fiction Costume Contest was letting out and a few Borgs and Klingons wandered in from the lobby, taking a vacant table nearby. Sandra glanced over at them and wished for the night to be over. She grabbed the wheel of the conversation and threw it into a fast turn. "Where did you and Mendle meet?" she addressed the girl.

Before Mendle could intercede, Aira answered, "In the bathroom."

"How cosmic. You're a devoted fan, are you?" Sandra pried.

Mendle felt uneasy even though Sandra was all smiles. It alarmed him that Aira was looking at her so trustingly.

"I'm not sure," Aira answered.

"How about that," Sandra replied.

The sarcasm did not escape Mendle. He had become all too familiar with Sandra's knack for layering it into friendly-sounding comments. It was the kind of expert veiling that left one wondering why they felt so deflated after being with such a nice person.

"You've read Mendle's work haven't you?" Sandra asked, aiming to blow the whistle on the charade and get to the facts.

As Sandra's intentions became obvious, Mendle's alarm increased. Though he had not pursued a logical explanation for the girl's presence in his hotel bathroom, instinct told him that, whatever her story, others would not regard it the same way he did. She herself didn't seem to remember a thing. *It's her, it's her, though, I know.* He realized it would stir up trouble, even if others only knew she had no memory.

"No. I…I've read Einstein," Aira was replying, then volunteered, "I think mostly I don't learn about things. I just know them."

"What do you mean?" Sandra delved. "Just know things?"

"It's an active ability."

"I see," Sandra mused, pretending to agree. "So you just know everything, I see." Though amusement flickered at the corners of her mouth, more for Mendle's benefit than anything, she felt a jab of worry that the girl possessed some smarts. Venturing the risk, she asked, "What of Einstein do you like?"

Mendle wondered how it was possible Aira had ever read Einstein. *Was it sent up in Voyager?* He caught what he was thinking. *Am I mad?* He wondered if he had wanted to believe in her so much that he had tricked himself into seeing something that was only in his mind. *Who is she? And what was she doing in my room?*

" 'Imagination is more important than knowledge,' " Aira quoted

Albert Einstein. Then, with that way she had of seeming to be extracting knowledge, she struggled to explain, staring at the air as if it were giving her the answer, "Science gives great importance to fact...But first, before facts, one can know something...and find it only after one knows it first."

Her words suddenly resonated a chime in Mendle. "I know just what you mean!" he exclaimed, dispelling his doubts, impulsively grabbing her hands in happiness.

Rolling her eyes, Sandra conveyed her unspoken evaluation at Rex across the table. *Mendle has gone over the edge.*

The girl hiccuped then said, "Don't ask me how I knew what I did but I did. I just knew it." She added, "And I know just what Einstein means."

"Meant," Sandra corrected. "He's dead."

"I'm sure he still means it," Aira said ingenuously. "Beings don't die."

Just the sort of thing Mendle loves to hear, Sandra thought as she took in the sight of him gazing at Aira as if she were Botticelli's Venus incarnate.

Sandra proceeded to close in. "Have you read Einstein's book of essays?"

"No. I read it on a calendar," Aira said, pointing as she referred to the merchandise displays in the hotel lobby.

"Einstein in a calendar," Sandra said, nodding. With a toss of her meticulously groomed mane, she addressed Mendle, "By the way, they loved my last piece at the magazine. I'm getting a raise. I'll be writing features and special assignments as well as reviews."

"I'm happy to hear that, Sandra," Mendle congratulated her.

The undercurrents that had been criss-crossing at the table were beginning to pull him down and he wanted to leave before succumbing to the undertow. He was starting to feel leeched, depleted, drained. Pushing himself back from the table, Mendle excused himself. Still holding onto Aira's hands as he stood up, he told her, "Don't go away." He carefully let go of her, almost in slow motion. "I'll be right back. Then we'll go," he said fervently.

A little too intense, Sandra thought. As Mendle turned to go to the rest room, she quickly scooted her chair back and jumped into his flow of exit, determined to get a level answer.

And thus splintered that contingent of humans at play.

chapter  18

Aira sat erectly in her chair, watching Mendle and Sandra until they were out of sight, then leaned back.

"Tired?" Rex asked, studying the girl.

Aira sighed. "This mind feels tired," she said.

With oiled words, Rex played along. "Time travel can be exhausting."

Aira looked at him surprised. She sat up a little straighter. "Time," she pondered aloud. She looked around her as if realizing something. "We're traveling in time."

He grinned, then said, "Look, you can relax with me."

"Thank you."

Rex found her charming. Perhaps it was her vagueness, obviously calculated to create a mystique, but any attempt at illusion was seemingly sweet and harmless, not for deception, but rather for glamor, like a little girl playing grown-up.

Back from staring open-mouthed at the flashing colored lights over the dance floor, she focused on him.

"Yes?" Rex urged.

Aira told him, "My mind, I was thinking about this. There is data in it. Language. But some of it is blocked. Listen to me. I don't know why I'm talking like this. It's strange. I don't think I've ever had a mind before. That's odd isn't it? But maybe it's because I don't remember."

Rex giggled. "That's good," he applauded. That anyone could actually be so naive was beyond him. *She's not stupid,* he decided, speculating the girl was just used to being able to fool people, to charm them into getting her way. *Probably a sheltered childhood. It would be a pleasure to introduce her to reality.* He encouraged her, "Don't remember?"

"It's just…blank," Aira described.

Rex felt an increasing urge to sully her, to etch her with experience.

It was the innocence of her face that kindled him. The wonder with which she looked at everything, with a gaze that rivaled white in purity, as though she were seeing everything—the most mundane, common, everyday things—for the first time, spurred hunger in him. Her simplicity beckoned him as virgin territory does an explorer eager to be the first to set foot on the terrain, to stab untraveled soil with his flag, to name it and then put it on the map with his mark. Rex imagined her unrehearsed responses as she felt things for the first time, things she could not control.

"Do you know how I can unblock it?" Aira asked when Rex didn't offer any helpful suggestion to her. He was just staring and grinning.

"Let me think about it," he placated her.

She began looking around the room again, with wide-eyed and unabashed observation. As she did so, she felt her thoughts glimmer from her eyes, and she felt as though she were actually bestowing everything in sight with well-being, by an outpouring of love and well-wishing. *Within me is the power to touch and bring something to life.*

"Isn't it glorious to be alive?" Aira suddenly exclaimed ardently.

Her apparent spontaneity disarmed Rex and he shifted his plump body in his chair as an excuse to look away from her. Something which had long been dormant in him stirred ever so slightly, so slightly that he was not even aware of what it was, but only of a fleeting surge of the unfamiliar. He quickly braced himself against it; it was strange, and the sentience threatening.

"Is there such a word as dao?" she was asking.

"As in T-A-O? The Chinese writings."

"No, no, no," she fast-fired. Her mind seemed to be racing, as if scanning a data base, the speed of her speech increasing as she mused aloud. "'D.' With a 'D.' D-A-O. An action. Verb. Like granting life. Love. Loving something so much you enhance its life? Give it life. Give life! Pure gift? Gratuitous. Like the sun."

The way she was speaking chilled him. The speed became, first of all, astounding. At least it had seemed so, but Rex now disputed what he had actually heard. *It couldn't have been that fast.* He remembered the word "dao" as a term coined by Mendle for one of his books.

Rex smiled slyly. "I thought you hadn't read any Mendle Orion," he taunted, his voice tinged with reprimand.

"I haven't," Aira told him innocently.

"Then how do you know that word?"

"It just seemed to come to me from somewhere."

Rex smiled disbelievingly.

"I just…knew it…somehow." Aira's face crumpled in exasperation. "Oh!" she exclaimed, seeming frustrated. "It's blocked! I just can't seem to remember."

Rex's smile broadened, his amusement increasing as he played along. "I have something that will unblock it," he offered. "Interested?"

"Yes!" Aira unconditionally welcomed the idea.

"We have to go for a walk," Rex said.

As they rose from the table, Aira asked about Mendle and Sandra.

"They'll just…*know* where we are," Rex said, cunningly playing along.

"Oh!" Aira exclaimed happily. "So you *do* know what I meant when I said that? I was beginning to doubt myself."

"Of course," Rex said.

"This will unblock me?"

"Yes, yes. Guaranteed."

"Wait, Mendle, wait," Sandra said desperately. She grabbed his arm. This was the second time she tried to stop him from going into the bathroom.

"We have to get back," Mendle repeated.

"I like her. I'm happy for you!" Sandra lied enthusiastically.

"You do?"

"Yes!" Sandra insisted convincingly. "And she does look like your description." *And so do a million other women who have blonde hair and blue eyes,* she finished silently.

"You actually saw that?"

He was nibbling. Sandra nodded carefully, concealing her amazement at his admission. *So you do think it's your dream.*

"It is pretty amazing how she was right there in my room, I mean how did she get there? How did she know, of all the places she could have gone?" Mendle began sharing some of what he was thinking with her.

"Do you think she's from some planet?" It sounded too contrived, Sandra knew the moment she said it.

Mendle became suspicious. "Could be." He broke from her grasp and turned around with a smile. "Earth is a planet, you know."

"Let's stop playing games right now," Sandra snapped, dropping her facade and taking a step closer to him. "You can deny all you want to. All right. I'll believe you. But think about this. When she answered the door, when you were in the shower, that girl told me her name was Aira Flight.

Why would she do that?"

Mendle shrugged. "Maybe that's her name."

"Do you believe that's her name?"

"If she says so. Why not?" Mendle dodged the point.

"You said so, too. You don't believe it, do you?"

"What's in a name?"

"Look," Sandra laid down terms with no-nonense steeliness. "You know what's going on between you two. You don't have to tell me. But if she's going along with you, I would seriously start wondering who the hell this person is."

Mendle gazed calmly at her.

"Who is she, Mendle?" Sandra asked again firmly yet softly, this time her voice also billowy with concern. "Do you know? That's all I want to know."

Doubts perking, Mendle turned away from her and went into the bathroom.

On the roof of the hotel, underneath the night sky, Aira gazed up at the twinkling glimmers in the blackness.

Almost reverently, her face tilted upward to the expanse of night above, she whispered, "Gosh, look at all those stars."

"'Gosh?' Haven't heard that word in a while!" Rex marveled, amused. She didn't react to his comment and he wondered if she was from the midwest or watched a lot of old family shows on television. "Pretty cosmic," Rex said, deciding he had better find some point of agreement. When he turned and saw her eyebrows were slightly contracted in puzzlement, he asked, "What are you thinking about?" The grin was by now a permanent fixture on his face.

After a brief pause, Aira, still looking up at the stars, sighed. Her thoughts seemed very far away when she finally said, "I felt as if I was about to know something. There's a mystery up there. Or an answer." She lowered her head and sighed. "I don't know," she said, shaking her head.

She turned her gaze on Rex, it caught him off guard and he squirmed. His eyes narrowed involuntarily, like eyes do when first receiving daylight after being in the dark. When Aira began to speak, he realized that he had been holding his breath.

Very confidingly, her voice a near-whisper, she asked, "Do you ever get the feeling that you're very, very far from home?"

She was looking at him very earnestly. Rex found himself almost taken in by her manner. He broke up into giggles "Do you?" he asked, enjoying this.

Her mouth tautened and she lightly bit her bottom lip with her front teeth as she thought about it. "I do now," she answered. "Do you?"

"Depends on where I am," Rex said, still smiling. "Right now I'm about, oh, a hundred miles from home."

When the girl smiled at him, she did so as though she were forgiving him for something and Rex wondered why. She said, "I meant far away from home like you don't belong here. I meant very, very far."

"Ooooh!" Rex pretended to finally get it. "Very, verrry far."

"Yes!" she exclaimed, happy he got what she meant.

Rex abruptly pulled a deadpan face and asked, "How far?"

Aira looked disappointed. Somberly, she said, "Millions and billions of miles."

"Billions and billions of stars," Rex did his Carl Sagan imitation.

Aira looked up again. "They're so strange. Yet so familiar. It makes me sad."

"You probably cry during *The Wizard of Oz*, when Dorothy clicks her heels together and says 'There's no place like home.' The concept of home makes a lot of people cry."

"Why?" Aira asked, glad somebody knew about such things.

"I don't know," Rex said. He pushed his spectacles firmly onto the bridge of his nose before carefully maneuvering the marijuana and yellow paper between his fingers into a cigarette.

"Or *E.T.* There's another one," he said. "That Phone Home business. Many people get emotional because it subliminally sets off a feeling in them that they can never go home."

"Why can't we go home?" Aira wailed, dismayed. She blinked at Rex, the epitome of innocence.

He actually did a double take, the eyes were so wide and sincere. His need for flattery outweighed any cynical thoughts about her sincerity, and, happy to be consulted as an authority, he duly replied, "It's actually a wish return to childhood. Which, of course, is impossible. Once you've lost it, it's over. Past."

Rex fumbled to light a match and stopped talking as he sucked in his breath, hissing air and smoke. As the marijuana burned his lungs, he narrowed his eyes. The aroma was insidiously sweet, as if promising the gift of pleasure then depriving one of sight to avoid pain.

Mendle scoured the dance floor and every corner of the hotel night-club and returned to the table, his hands on his hips. He was seething.

"Just sit down. They'll be back," Sandra said.

Mendle wouldn't. He called the waitress and asked if she knew where Rex and Aira had gone. She didn't.

"Look, just sit down," Sandra said firmly. "They'll be back."

Mendle took a seat but continued nervously to scan the room.

"Are you all right?" Sandra asked.

He leveled a gaze on her, his eyes nearly bulging with intensity. The voice was restrained as he began. "Well, let's see now. I question existence. War *bothers* me. Pollution and environmental crime *bother* me…"

"Okay, Mendle. Can't you keep it a simple answer?"

"My own shortcomings *bother* me. Crime and violence bother me. Everywhere I look someone's flashing sex or blood, trying to get a rise out of me. It bothers me—"

"Mendle, you're shouting," Sandra said, looking around. People were beginning to stare. She never forgave him these scenes, but she was used to them.

"These things *really bother* me. So, yes, I must still be all right!" Mendle angrily got up and started walking out of the bar toward the lobby. Midway there, he stopped and yelled, "No, maybe I'm part right!" then kept on going.

He's nuts. "Mendle, wait. Where are you going?" Sandra called after him as she followed him across the lobby to the elevators. She managed to scurry in before the doors closed. It was crowded inside the elevator. A chance for her to stand close to him. She touched his arm. "Mendle," she murmured.

"Sex, please," he called out to someone by the buttons. "I mean six."

A few people giggled.

"Mendle, it's okay," she whispered, emanating physicality to him.

"I know it's okay," he replied, his tone more conversational. "Because to me people aren't a bunch of asses and thighs. Hey, you see it on TV. Decapitated butts on parade. What happened to faces? Character? Soul?"

"It's okay," Sandra said soothingly, making sympathetic eye contact with a few people in the elevator.

"I know it's okay!" Mendle said. "It's okay because my inconsistencies do bother me. The universe beckons me. Coincidence fascinates me, I am not numb…"

"This is six," Sandra informed him when the elevator doors opened. She filed out behind him.

"Maybe I'm not all right, maybe I'm part right. But at least I'm not asleep!" he declared, starting down the hall.

She dared to say it as she hastened to keep up with him down the corridor. "No, you're just drunk."

"I'm not."

"Maybe not as much right now, but—"

Mendle stopped in the middle of the hallway, spun around and faced her. "That doesn't change what I know."

Sandra calmly returned his defiant glare and said flatly, "Just don't make any major decisions."

Her words shook his confidence but he held on to what he knew, some core of him that was unshakably right. "You know what your problem is?" Mendle challenged her. "The magic is gone out of your life. If you can't eat it, wear it, or seduce it, it doesn't exist for you. Because you can't put your clammy hands on it."

It was the first time he ever stood up for himself after she mentioned his drinking. Standing outside the door to his suite, while he fumbled for his key in his jacket pocket, Sandra resorted to a last desperate attempt. She firmly took hold of his shoulders and started working the muscles. "Relax," she said lightly, lacing her voice with a little laughter.

As Sandra felt Mendle soften a little, she murmured, "That's right. Calm down." A massage and she knew he'd listen to just about anything, as long as she kept relieving the tension in his shoulders. She did have something for which to thank his many hours at the computer.

"That woman said she met you in a bathroom? It wasn't this bathroom was it?"

Sandra felt Mendle instantly tense up under her hands. He knocked on the door and called out.

"Aira!"

"She's not here, Mendle. Unless, of course, Rex decided to…maybe we should go check our room."

Mendle turned and glared at her.

Sandra was quick to justify her insinuation. "She told me she you met in a bathroom. I assume it was this bathroom. Was it? I mean if a woman gets together with a total stranger in a bathroom, no telling what she'll do."

"What if she just happened to appear in the bathroom?" Mendle retorted defensively as he managed the key card in the door slot.

He's so easy, Sandra thought, at the same time amazed at his seriousness. "Appeared? You don't really think…? Mendle!"

"Yeah? Well how did she get in there? Tell me that." Mendle's anger continued to preclude his caution.

He unlocked the door and pushed it open. No one there, except the white dog. It was asleep on the floor.

"Great watch dog," Sandra joked as Mendle kneeled beside the animal.

Sandra got on her knees alongside Mendle and started petting the dog. Suddenly she turned, took Mendle's face between her hands, and went to kiss him. Mendle recoiled. Shoving as he got up from her, he inadvertently pushed Sandra over. She could've prevented it but didn't; in fact, she helped the motion, going all the way down to the floor, acting hurt.

"I'm sorry," Mendle said.

He started to go to her, but this time, he caught the manic, euphoric spark of glee in her eyes as she watched him realize he may have hurt her. Up until that moment, he had started to implode, to feel culpable of some gloomy thing. Now he saw her tactic. Sandra invited people to be mean to her as a method of controlling them. A few carefully received offenses on her part put anyone with a heart in the position of propitiating to her to make amends.

When Mendle didn't respond to her injured look, Sandra changed gears. "Don't tell me you didn't feel something," she said seductively, extending her legs in front of her.

Well toned, but they speak of vanity louder than health, Mendle thought. He was seeing her more clearly than ever. *That's her,* he marveled, seeing a shadowy, fuscous mass.

"Of course I felt something," he admitted. "Though not much," he realized somewhat happily. "You have no respect for men whatsoever, you know that? If you did, you wouldn't be manipulating my inherent bodily reactions. You'd have some respect for me and not a desire to activate my body." He turned and adjusted his shirt, sadly wishing she were capable of simply being.

Unbelievable. "Aren't you going to help me up?"

"I'm sorry. I just don't like this hitting below the belt." Mendle extended his hand to her.

Sandra brushed imaginary dirt off her yellow dress, hating him. She thought about telling him she loved him, but decided it wouldn't do any good.

Mendle looked at the dog, which hadn't budged. "Onx!" he commanded. To his partial surprise the dog sat straight up instantly and riveted her attention on him.

"Aira." Mendle stressed the name as he had seen done on Lassie re-runs as a boy. "Where's Aira?" he repeated excitedly.

The dog seemed to space out for a moment, then got up and started whimpering, going around and around in a tight circle.

"See there?" Mendle said.

"It's just responding to the manic tone in your voice," Sandra said. "That animal's sick."

The dog suddenly looked at the door and trotted out of the room. Mendle followed, quickly ushering Sandra out with him.

"Come on, Mendle, *think*," Sandra pleaded. "It probably has to go pee." Mendle took off running after the dog.

Sandra stared after him incredulously then looked at the room door he had neglected to close. Exasperated, she yanked it shut behind her. "You leave doors unlocked a lot! I walked right in earlier. That's how that woman got in your bathroom!" she blared after him furiously.

chapter 19

From the hotel roof, yellow and red predominated the night city-scape. Lights sparkled crisply in the dark through air that had been washed by afternoon thunderstorms. Aira and Rex were both sitting on the ledge holding their breath in and idly staring at the gravel on the rooftop when Aira suddenly erupted into laughter. The smoke's forceful exit from her lungs rasped her throat and she began to cough violently. She was dou-bled over, still coughing, and Rex was laughing, patting her back, when

Onx bounded out the service entrance. Whining and acting very perturbed, the dog reached Aira and nuzzled her hands which were cupped
over her face as she coughed.

"Onx," Aira sputtered. "Onx!" She threw her arms around the dog
and buried her face in the furry neck. "What are you doing here? How
did you find me?"

The sound of footsteps caused Rex to sit up. His fear was amplified
into panic by the weed's influence as he looked in the direction of the
sound. It was Mendle, with Sandra not far behind.

When Aira looked up from Onx's white mane, she was happy to see
Mendle. Though Mendle was relieved to have found her, the sight of the
girl's condition pierced him. He smelled the dope; her eyes were glazed;
she was smiling vapidly. Immediate protest flooded him, starting rivulets
of anger which soon spread, infesting his entirety.

Rex held out a joint. "Come contemplate the *primum mobile*," he offered, grinning. "That's what we're doing."

"What's that?" Aira asked, her voice scratchy from the cough. Her
eyes were watery and felt prickly.

"*Primum mobile.* The outermost of ten concentric spheres of the universe that makes a complete revolution every twenty-four hours. Thus
causing everything else to move," Rex pontificated.

He seems to be doing an imitation of himself, Mendle thought then
deemed the man incapable of stepping outside of himself in order to do so.

"Really? The outermost sphere that turns?" Aira gasped.

Rex nodded. "Completes a turn every twenty-four hours."

"There are ten of them?" Aira asked, laughing.

"Indeed."

Aira began to giggle then said, "I don't believe it. A sphere doesn't
make things move! Life makes things move!" She leapt to her feet, pro-
claiming "Life!" and took off, doing a type of *jeté* over the roof, singing
her own accompaniment to the dance. "Life! Life! We're free! We're free!
Free! We're free!"

"Wild outfit she's wearing, isn't it?" Rex commented. "What a
spectacle."

"Why did you get her stoned?" Mendle demanded, his vehemence
shocking both Rex and Sandra. "Look at her!" he continued, outraged.
"She's a mess! You've altered her perception! I can't believe you would do
this."

"Look who's talking," Rex chortled.

"Really," Sandra jumped in, her words boiling in resentment at Mendle's protectiveness of Aira. "I didn't think I'd ever see the day when you'd be adverse to 'altering perception'!"

"And since when did you start defending it?" Mendle shouted back. The readiness of Sandra's caustic reply astonished him. He began pacing back and forth, raving, "Now I know why drugs and whiskey are garbage. It alters perception. It messes up being able to see your way out of here!"

"You do it, you 'alter perception,' Mendle. That's all I was trying to say," Sandra justified.

Mendle felt Sandra's derision tugging at him, pulling him like a barbed hook toward a reality to which he had subscribed. *I have the right to change my mind,* he thought. "Just because I did it doesn't mean it's right!" Mendle yelled bitterly. His words rang into the night and echoed in the hollowness of his stare.

Rex and Sandra watched him, mesmerized.

"I've done a lot of things. That doesn't mean I have to keep doing them," he yelled.

"Ah-hum! A transformation!" Rex proclaimed.

Mendle tried elucidating the matter. "It's more a matter of physics than morality! That's what right and wrong is about anyway! Life and death of the very self!"

"Come off it, Mendle," Sandra said. "Who do you think you are anyway? So self-righteous when you're no better than the rest of us."

"I'm not trying to be." Mendle breathed deeply. He turned and put his hands in his pockets, dejected. "That's not the point. Why is it when someone strives for excellence in this dump everyone holds him back, accusing him of trying to be better than everybody else?"

He stared desolately at Aira who was still improvising a dance across the rooftop. *Her grace is hampered.* The sight angered him.

"Answer me that!" Mendle snapped, taking his hands out of his pockets and throwing his clenched fists to his sides. He turned and glowered at Sandra. "Maybe I'm just trying to be better than my own worst. Ever think of that?"

Sandra opened her mouth to say something, but Mendle raved on. "Oh no! See a little decency and hurry to find some mud, some smut, make sure it isn't really that good, make sure it's defective just like everything else so nobody has to worry that they themselves don't measure up. Don't let him get too high and mighty. That's too good to be true; let's find what's *real* about it."

"You're shouting, Mendle," Rex said. Suddenly nervous about being arrested, he spit between his fingers, extinguished and swallowed the last bit he was smoking, then looked around.

"Loosen up, Mendle," Sandra chimed in. "Look at you. You're becoming a raving lunatic." Smugly, she added, glancing toward Aira demonstratively, "You might as well face it. None of us are perfect."

"It is true, all of us are standing in the mud, but some of us are looking at the stars!" Mendle was both sad and valiant as he proclaimed the phrase, his hand reaching up toward the vast night above. He suddenly felt very small.

"Your friend was looking at the stars earlier," Rex laughed, then "That was Oscar Wilde, right?" he asked with the intent of showing he recognized the quote.

"I don't believe it. She just gets here and what happens? She gets drugged first thing!" Mendle exploded.

Rex and Sandra exchanged worried looks.

"Just gets here?" Rex repeated, completely amused.

"Mendle..." Sandra began.

"Well, she'll have a lot to talk about when she goes back to Mars," Rex jibed, catapulting himself into a laughing fit.

"Mendle, you've taken this too far. Settle down. Don't be so defensive. You just have to face the real world." Sandra's words seemed to Mendle to roll and spill automatically out of her mouth, as though they had been pre-thought and said somewhere else, and merely traveled across the conveyor belt of her tongue.

"Yes. Relax, Earth man," Rex kidded.

Mendle whirled on Rex and held him in an accusative glare. "Did you see her eyes?" he demanded.

Rex gazed across the rooftop at Aira who was still leaping and dancing. "I think they look rather patriotic," he mused. "All red, white and blue," he completed his analogy and laughed some more, fat with pleasure at his cleverness.

"Mendle, Mendle, Mendle," Sandra chided soothingly. "Lighten up. You're so big on freedom." She continued, "There you have it," gesturing toward Aira, "the epitome of freedom."

Mendle looked at Aira as she skipped and pirouetted to her euphoric sing-song chant. *It's a trap*, he thought. *It feels like freedom. It gets you deeper into the chains of matter, detours you into mazes of altered perception.* He saw it more clearly than he ever had, the synthetic well-being brought on by chemicals, the illusion of relief while the communication systems of sight, sound, and nerve impulses were being poisoned, sabotaged from functioning. "It's a trap. To keep people enslaved!" Mendle blurted out.

"Don't be so paranoid," Sandra complained, beginning to lose patience.

"It's pushed for economic and power reasons! It's true. Look at it. While the planet goes to hell, everybody is just asleep, drugged or floating on their six pack! Z Zone!"

"What?" Sandra and Rex uttered in unison, not knowing what he was talking about.

Mendle suddenly took some deft steps toward Rex. Fulminating him with the intention that poured out of his eyes, he hissed threateningly, "Don't you ever contaminate anyone I know with that crap again."

Fearing that Mendle was about to become violent, Rex held his hands up. "Okay, Mendle. Okay."

Mendle held the gaze a moment for emphasis, then backed off. He turned around and realized he was breathing hard. He felt amazed at himself for his outburst toward Rex, then recognized *he seems so benevolent yet there's something underlying that grin.*

It happened very fast.

Aira was jumping and running with Onx at her heels. Mendle saw her precariously close to a portion of the roof which was not fenced, merely lined with cement blocks about two feet high. Desperately, he called her name, but his warning came too late. The girl spun and stumbled against the border. Her momentum carried her past and over the edge of the roof.

The threesome stood petrified long enough to watch Onx run toward the spot Aira went over and take a flying leap after her.

"Oh my God," muttered Sandra, but her words were lost in the commotion and scrunch of gravel underfoot as they desperately ran to the edge.

Faster than time, between the seconds, Aira's thoughts unraveled. Desperately, she tried to stop herself by bracing against the air with some invisible force, but her intention was to no avail and nothing complied. Falling through substance she could not grasp, her body plummeted toward the concrete.

Pain and death loomed. Terror gagged in her throat as she screamed, "Stop!" Then it was as if she suddenly evacuated the body so as to not feel its injury when it hit, and she saw her body falling.

Mendle reached the rooftop edge before the others. He skidded to his knees and braked himself with his hands against the border of cement blocks, oblivious to the rasp of concrete against his palms and the bite of jagged gravel into his knees. Vaguely, he felt Sandra's fingers clasp his shoulders. She was standing behind him. Rex was to his right.

When Sandra looked down and saw Aira's pathetic form on the ground below, remorse encased her like shrinking plastic. She felt her insides wither. Silently and futilely she shrieked a cry of regret over having wished harm to the girl, over having wanted to make less of her. She wished that the girl was everything Mendle claimed her to be.

Sandra's voice shattered as she gasped, "Oh my God. She's dead. I didn't really want to hurt her."

On the brink of losing his balance, Mendle bolted toward the service entrance. He tried to defy time and distance as he rushed down the exit stairs. All he could think of was getting to Aira and he cursed himself for the moments lost in trying to stop her from falling. *As if my intention actually could make a difference.*

A memory flashed through his mind of a similar experience…he was driving a car, the brakes went out. As he careened toward a wall, he seemed to shoot out of himself as if he could, by sheer thought, stop his car that way.

He couldn't run down the stairs fast enough. He took them in twos and threes, belittling himself for thinking this girl was superhuman as he pictured her body lying on the ground below. *I'm nuts,* Mendle thought. *But the dog,* he remembered, *just before it hit, what was that? Oh stop it, stop it,* Mendle hissed at himself to silence the internal debates and speculations. Clenching the metal bar on the fire door with both hands, he jammed it forward and open with all his force.

Out of the stairwell and into the night air, he looked up at the roof to confirm his bearings, then dashed to the right, around the corner where she would be. When he got there, he didn't see her. He looked up again to confirm the location. *That was it,* he determined, aligning the roof, the marquee, the surroundings. She wasn't there. She wasn't anywhere.

She's gone. Mendle felt utter and total panic. Then he heard it, his name, carried to him on the summer wind.

"Mendle." The voice which spoke his name was thin. It was barely audible.

The way she called my name when she was just a dream. He jerked his head to the direction from which it came but saw no one.

Just as he wondered if it had been his imagination, he heard it again.

"Mendle." It was Aira's voice.

Mendle looked frantically but he didn't see her anywhere until she repeated it again. Then he saw her, huddled in the bushes like some wounded animal. *Aira.* His soul leapt to her. When he reached her and crouched beside her, he stopped an impulse to embrace her and hold her tight for fear of disturbing a severe injury.

She looked at him imploringly. As though apologizing for impending death, he thought.

"Don't," he begged crazily, "don't go. You'll be all right." His mind offered all manner of internal injuries she was suffering. "They've gone to call an ambulance," he assured her.

Her eyes were huge and sad and bewildered. "Oh, Mendle," she finally said. "I don't know what's going on."

"What does it feel like?" His fear of losing her was a frenzy he was trying to contain inside of him.

"Something happened to me when I was falling," she told him. "I could see myself falling. But how is that possible? It was like I was... separated from this body. I could see it." She shook her head slowly, concluding, "I don't know how, or why, but I know I'm not this body. Because I saw it."

That's what that is. Mendle could barely nod his head as he listened to her describe the essence of what he had experienced trying to stop his car when the brakes gave out. *I separated from my body.*

She held her hands out and examined them, staring somewhat dumbfounded, as if the appendages were something strange. "I know it," she whispered fervently. "But I'm stuck with it. And I'm not even hurt, except for this."

As she showed Mendle her leg, scraped and bleeding, the truth sank in creepily—it was the only injury from a sixteen-story fall. Mendle craned his head back and looked up, his mouth open from awe.

"I know," Aira said. Looking up at the building which towered above them, she knew what he was thinking. She spoke slowly and deliberately. "I was falling, and so much time seemed to happen in a few seconds. It seemed like forever. Then I saw myself falling. I actually saw...this body falling. Then...I saw my mind. This mind, it has things and facts and language in it."

Her gaze traveled downward, trailing the distance she had fallen. When she and Mendle looked at each other, they searched for an explanation in each other's eyes.

"I feel myself," she told him. "And I feel like I'm fighting to know something."

"I wish Rex hadn't—"

"I know," she stopped him quietly, focusing on the artificial, drug-induced effects in her body. "I don't like it." She dropped her face into her hands and rubbed her eyes, her temples. Her voice was plaintive. She said, "That must be what I saw then."

"What?"

"I'm not sure. I'm not sure what I saw."

"Tell me," Mendle urged, his heart pounding. Aira shook her head.

"I understand the problem," Mendle told her. "The only way out of this mess is to know what you see," he said, half to himself. "It's tricky. Most people spend their time either not looking, messing with their vision, or convincing themselves they're not seeing what they see."

Aira looked at him and saw he understood.

"Try to sift it out," he urged her. "What really happened?"

She decided to tell him. "I should be dead," she began. "But Onx..." Mendle followed her gaze to the white dog. It was sitting nearby, panting happily. Making eye-contact with the dog for a moment before it quickly averted its gaze, the thought crossed Mendle's mind that the ignorance and oblivion the animal was exuding seemed feigned.

"Go on," Mendle encouraged, waiting to hear if she would say what he thought she might.

"Just before I hit...oh, it's incredible."

"Tell me."

"Well, I swear..." Aira looked at Onx. She spoke with disbelief. "I swear...she turned into a creature," Aira said incredulously. "I saw this swoosh of wings and smoke, like a dragon or something, with green and white scales. She broke my fall. It sounds crazy but—"

"It doesn't sound crazy," Mendle uttered, his voice low with amazement.

"Good weed, huh?" It was Rex, joking nervously. "Lucky thing there was that awning up there." He pointed up to the green and white striped canvas awning stretched above the veranda.

Somewhere was Truth. Perhaps each person held a piece of the whole picture.

chapter  20

The woman he had named Aira Flight, had been living in the room over his garage ever since they met. Her presence was a comforting reality he confirmed often through a glance or with the exchange of a word with her, anything that reaffirmed and celebrated her presence. She was in his life.

From his place on the couch, Mendle could see through the dining room to where she knelt by the sliding door; she was brushing out the white dog's coat. He set his notebook down and watched. The stray's white coat set off the silvery blonde of her hair. They seemed matched somehow. It was so uncanny that he sometimes wondered if the dog had been hers, and if anyone missed either of them.

Yet, other than puzzling occasionally over a few such mysteries, Mendle's perpetual preoccupation with the details of existence ceased. Since meeting Aira, some missing element of life seemed finally supplied. For the most part, he had given up trying to explain it rationally. Her presence in his life was some truth at work; that became sufficient reason for him.

Something was at work. He didn't know exactly what, but he recognized it as the very something behind the weaving of coincidences of everyday life. Whatever the facts about her would turn out to be, Mendle was convinced the details didn't matter anymore.

She was no longer the woman of his dreams, of his novel. She was the woman right there. Buying her a toothbrush and clothes were bliss. Aira could have remembered she was a bowling alley attendant from Topeka, Kansas, yet it would not have demoted her from the pedestal on which he proclaimed her goddess. The only relevant fact which mattered to Mendle Orion was that she was there, everyday.

And days passed.

Days of pastel, impressionistic bliss.

Love is not blind. Love sees what is most true.

Mendle picked up his notebook again, transforming his thoughts into a flow of black ink, he wrote, "Love is not blind. Love sees what is most true."

Even in this world there exists what is "most true." The joy of Mozart. Vivaldi violins—resonating geometric harmonies. Elevated sentiment at the threshold of heaven. To the most mundane things. Lambs leaping. Strawberries. Tropical fish. The miracle of flowers. Roses, jasmine blossoms. Iced cream. September days, gold heat. Rainbows. Water. Reggae. Silence. Languid rolling out in a stretch of time with nothing to do. The glory of appreciation—round and budding, soaring upward. If only others knew the orchestration, heard the miraculous symphony in play, every moment in perfection, each day would be an occasion!

When life is right, the human spirit soars and glides, like a skater breaking the barrier of physicalness into music poetry. Ballet of Thought and Matter.

Green lawns, cropped rows underneath bare feet. Tomatoes spilling sunshine into the mouth with enzyme-active vine flavor. Sweet basil combining taste and smell into harmony The inhaling and exhaling of air.

Eyes. Portals. Someone across a distance understands. An idea's successful travel and landing…and another's eyes illumine in receipt. There is no hospitality like understanding.

The excellence of the human shines in its one most basic need: to care. Most of us find it so 'good to know' when we were of help to another.

Love is the power to give life, yet its source is never seen, because the source becomes something new. This is my very core, the center of myself.

As he signed his name, "Mendle J. Orion," Mendle looked up. He wanted to tell Aira he loved her.

She was setting the dog's dish of broccoli outside the glass door. Mendle studied Onx eating the greens. It was curious, the dog did not eat meat. *The oddest thing I can see about her is that vegetarian dog,* Mendle mused, considering how daily living with the young woman was proving to be not so unusual. Aira was exceptionally kind, and very quick to learn. *But she eats, sleeps, drinks fluids, has female cycles.*

As he visually scanned her body up and down, he wanted her in a way he had never wanted a woman before. It wasn't her looks that did it, it wasn't particularly her body he wanted, not in and of itself. Other than extremely large eyes and full lips, she bordered on looking plain. Yet he was magnetized by her. Although she was ethereal and graceful, he found her more sensual than women who worked hard at looking erotic.

Though ebullient, she was shy and reserved about things that ran deep. Sentiments and ideas flared and bloomed in her as if each were new and unrehearsed. The essence of her set him on fire but the flames, though white-hot, didn't burn.

Aira smiled at him from across the dining room as she went to put the steamer in the sink and Mendle felt washed in warmth. That smile, he had never seen anything like it. It twinkled. It was all-knowing, all-forgiving, all-understanding. Unlike many women he knew, she was genuinely capable of platonic love. She didn't use her body on him. They shared hours and hours of exchanging ideas when they stayed up nights talking. They had gone to museums, read, listened to music. The sublimation was euphoric.

There was that time, Mendle thought, *she felt something physical for me. Her face became so…delicious, vulnerable. Then she quickly looked away, confused. It's as if she contains her potential with reverence. That's it,* he determined looking at her, realizing she didn't just randomly emanate emotions, sex, thought, attitude, at whoever happened to be there.

A reverence for sex. For the power. And for me, Mendle contemplated. *And isn't it a power? Where a very life can begin?*

He thought of her physically now but wasn't in a state of uncomfortable desire. Most of what he felt was rapture. He isolated and identified his sex currents for her; they were pulsating through him, literally an electricity pulsing through his body. But there was more. The energy did not generate from the body organism as some impersonal, generalized thrust. The energy was connected to, and in fact triggered by, intense admiration and respect. It was not compartmentalized, but total; unified body and soul. His profound ecstasy for her occasionally wracked his body to want to respond in suit, but that was only a fraction of the rapture.

"I've abused things," he found himself revealing to her when she came in and sat in the chair next to the sofa.

Under her quizzical look, he unfolded. "I, well, you know when we first met? At the hotel in the nightclub, I made that speech to those women in there? About their using their cleavages and thighs as communication devices?"

"Maybe it was the best way they knew how to get love," Aira mused.

"I guess," Mendle said, her compassion giving him an insight. He thought about how he had addressed the girls and realized it was one of his many attempts to perform surgery on others' shortcomings with an incisive stroke of a phrase. Most people looked back blankly, or responded with hatred, or confusion, or laughter.

Aira smiled at him.

"I guess I can't expect to force someone to see it all in a minute," Mendle said, realizing that's what he had been doing.

Aira nodded.

"I used to be into that sort of thing." Mendle looked carefully for Aira's reaction. When he felt no condemnation, he continued. "Maybe part of the reason I wasn't so kind to those girls was because they reminded me of something I had done that I didn't want to face," he admitted. He began to burn with embarrassment. "It was an addiction, sensation, like to anything, I guess. I had to feel something. I wanted that buzz, the bang."

Aira's gaze didn't waiver.

"I spent hours doing nothing but thinking of ways to get someone in bed. I've been intimate with people I couldn't stand," he confessed. *It was because you weren't here. It was because I wondered where you were. It was because I thought you didn't exist.* The thoughts welled in him and surprised him. He felt like crying.

When he contemplated Aira—wanting her, having her—it was like stepping into an illuminated arena; his every spot showed. He was having trouble looking at her as he thought about things he had done, not only sexual transgressions, but all things of which he was not proud. To others they may have seemed insignificant—lies, stealing when he was a kid, neglecting responsibilities, going to bed with someone he didn't love —but they ballooned in his mind and occupied his thinking. Past compromises slithered inside him, rebuking him, threatening to congeal into a pact with imperfection. "I know the streets as well as royalty. I've seen and done, well, the antithesis of everything I stand up for." In this space of understanding, Mendle was free to admit and not be wrong. Guilt and shame detached from him. He released himself from his own condemnation. He said, "I guess I was getting used to this body here. I let something other than me do my thinking."

"I understand."

Aira smiled at him. Mendle smiled back and wondered what it was about her that inspired him to tell her what he just had—things about himself he had reviled and hidden, all the while loudly spouting the ideals to which he desperately clung.

In her presence, all that fell short of the ideal rose like scum to the surface. She seemed to look past it all, to his soul. Letting it rise into view didn't condemn him. Facing it, he felt absolved. All the dreams remained. His valiance was left standing, unsullied.

A contradictory duality resolved when Mendle realized he was neither 'good' nor 'bad.' He was capable of being both, as was any human being. Yet his past transgressions against his ideals had not negated the inextinguishable light that was his innermost, truest self. As he felt himself regain his way back to his integrity, his relief was enormous. He knew his worst did not obliterate all the best of him. His very self was, in fact, the beacon, the lodestar of the ideal! That was home. Where all tears and suffering stopped.

Mendle smiled gratefully. "I suppose it would be a lot easier if a training manual were issued at puberty," he said, grinning. "First chapter: what your body is feeling isn't necessarily you."

His words stirred something in Aira. She felt it surge, but she could not grasp it. She looked away, "I wish I remembered puberty," she told Mendle quietly.

Her words sent a twinge of panic through him. She had been content to let time pass with no outside interference, hoping for a natural return of her memory. He sensed a shift; he couldn't keep their world inviolate much longer. A wistfulness pervaded that afternoon, and now Mendle saw it in Aira's eyes as she gazed back at him.

There had been a problem with a medical visit, even a simple trip to the grocery store stimulated questions and an increasing urgency for an identity.

Who was she? Not only who, but "what" seemed to be a mandatory matter in the world. A person had to be a "doctor," a "singer," a "photographer," a "salesman," a "secretary." Anything, as long as it was some thing.

Only pat identities qualified. Many people became confused if an individual had more than one "what," as if doing two things were incomprehensible. "Well, which do you really like to do the most?" "Which do you really want to be?" That one-dimensional tab was needed to label and file, label and file, label and file. "Lawyer." "Housewife." "Driver."

When Mendle considered Leonardo da Vinci—poet, inventor, statesman, sculptor, engineer, painter, architect, botanist, geologist, biologist—he was curious and saddened to speculate what twenty-first century man's treatment of him would be. "What do you do?"

The girl felt like his only oasis in a strange desert. It was ironic that she was the one who expressed wonder at what she'd do without him. They had resolved what to do about her dilemma by deciding that her memory would eventually return on its own. He had managed to sequester her in his home for a couple of months, away from outside influence. The world, however, did not go away. He had only postponed the search for an answer with a temporary vacation.

The moment had finally arrived. She quietly asserted, "I want to know who I am."

"You know who you are…you're you," Mendle started to comfort her, but his argument sounded weak to him.

"I want to go see a therapist," Aira announced. She got up from her chair and sat on the edge of the sofa.

Mendle sat up. "But I thought we agreed that—"

"It's been almost three months now."

"Where did you get the therapist idea? How will that help you?"

"Sandra said she knows someone who does something called regression. Through hypnosis."

"Sandra Wilford's advice isn't all that trustworthy," Mendle tried to explain. An ominous foreboding washed through him. *Like a shark, able to smell a drop of blood up to a mile away.* Sandra just wouldn't let up with her phone calls.

"Did she call again?" he asked.

"This morning, when you went to get strawberries. She asked me if everything was still a blank."

"How did she know about the blank?" Mendle asked.

"Rex. It was before I promised not to talk about it. I told him the night on the roof."

Mendle nodded. *Just like her,* he started seething about Sandra. *She knows my Sunday morning ritual of fresh strawberries and calls when she knows I'm at the market.* He patted the couch beside him, and Aira moved closer to him.

She was looking at Mendle expectantly, her countenance alert, earnest, quizzical. Her face was one of the sweetest, most innocent he had ever seen, and yet it contained all the wisdom of a mature woman. He liked that she didn't have to resist, contradict, or disagree out of some erroneous datum that it meant 'independence.' Her clothes made her look like something out of a television family of the 1950's. Tailored, happy, neat, hair curled. *The epitome of an earth girl,* Mendle thought. It was charming, but a little poignant.

"I like your dress, and the…" Mendle motioned to the necklace of pearls.

"This is what we bought the other day," she reminded him, pleased. "At the thrift store. I styled it after the favorite popular show, 'The Donna Reed Show.'"

Mendle smiled, somewhat pained, then looked down at his hands, rubbing one palm then the other. "The Donna Reed Show" hadn't been popular for decades. It was reruns she had seen.

He reflected on the fairness of keeping her sequestered as he had been doing. Wasn't it her prerogative to recall enough about the past to know what was current or changed fashion? She was somewhat touching, sitting there so eagerly, as if doing her best to portray what she thought a woman should be. *Like an alien adapting to...*

No, Mendle caught the thought and corrected himself, *Like an amnesiac.* He wanted to stop fooling himself.

Some people laughed when Aira spoke to them. *It's out of some sort of relief,* Mendle thought, *more than ridicule.* He contemplated how people reacted to her. She was kind and courteous, aware of others. When she spoke, she was considerate of the person in front of her, as if there were no other life like that one in the world. She funneled undivided attention on strangers, spotlighting them with her gaze. Sincere care flowed from her heart with such gratuitous, warm candor that it naturally sunnied others. She left trails of smiling faces.

"It's called regression," Aira repeated to Mendle eagerly. "I can go back and find out what happened, who I am."

The prospect frightened him. He looked up at her and stopped fiddling with his hands. It didn't matter to him anymore who she was. It was fine with him that she was a blonde, blue-eyed girl with a ready smile, who loved all his favorite poets, music, flowers, animals, paintings, dancing, and the ocean. She was herself. What did details matter?

Mendle nodded now, to let her know he had heard her, then looked out the window at the cascade of red. He thought, *Life is seen in pieces. The mind, body chemicals, other's evaluations, Time itself, all can fluctuate the total picture, or allow one to see only bits and corners, or only what one wants to see. What is the whole story?* The mystery beckoned him. While he could contend he knew her on some level—if only recognition of an essence—missing facts still teased him.

Aira was still looking at him earnestly. The sight of her drew him. Again he wanted to tell her that his love for her owned his entire being in a way that had no rational explanation.

He didn't know how to warn her about Sandra. He started to say, "Life isn't all wonderful." He remembered when his mother told him that —very sadly, in exactly those words—one day in the kitchen when he was nine. He had jauntily come in from playing in a nearby stream. She was worried about him being there, near the woods alone. Coming from a world of moss, tadpoles, dragonflies, skipping stones and sunny reflection pools, he felt by contrast only his mother's distinct sadness etched in his memory. Her face bore the tiredness of guardianship and love as she said it. He had looked up at her in wonder and had not known at all what she meant. He hadn't yet learned about war, about hate, about perversion, about greed, about insanity, about death.

Life isn't all wonderful. He decided not to say it. Nobody could tell another about it. *One finds out soon enough. Experience is a personally reserved seat for each person born onto the Earth.*

chapter 21

The irritation that had begun to percolate in Mendle amplified the noise of Dr. Kaufkiff's pencil as it scratched across the paper. The sound-proof office blocked out all outside noise, and the lead scribbling across the page, accented by an occasional, important-sounding flourish, dominated the room which had fallen silent.

Mendle became aware of the sound of his own breathing. The thought of Sandra waiting in reception provoked the beginning of a spasm in his left shoulder. She was gloating by now, he imagined, now that everyone was in the same boat getting "professional help." He did not trust a profession that, while claiming the title of doctor, deplored the impossibility of any cure and classified "dreams" as "dangerous," the human being, an "animal."

Sandra Wilford was always nicer to Mendle when he was broke, broken, or in some misery. It was a statistic; he reviewed the evidence—when he was down, Sandra was chipper.

Personally, Mendle preferred an angry man to a sobbing one. *But the electro-shock boys don't see it that way, and neither does Sandra. For them, a crying, broken man is safer. An apathetic man safer yet. Dead is too obvious, but the closer to it, the better in their book.*

So he seethed in the corner of the office, swelling up and down on the waves of personal rage and deep concern for Aira's welfare.

He watched Dr. Kaufkiff and wondered how another person could possibly sit and tell others what was going on with them. Being evaluated in that manner was different than really being listened to.

So far, Aira had been regressed and Dr. Kaufkiff was astonished and bewildered by the fact that she, as he put it, "appeared to have no subconscious." Nothing, nothing, nothing. Now she was up and sitting eagerly in her chair again.

Dr. Kaufkiff stopped scribbling. The therapist seemed to hang in suspended motion for a moment. Just as Mendle wondered what he was going to do next, the man twirled the pencil in his fingers, tapped the pad of paper with the eraser and, not moving his head, rolled his eyes up to peer over the top of his glasses.

A brief laugh effervesced out of Aira. When Kaufkiff's eyebrows curved up in question, she explained, "You think they make you look intelligent, too! Your glasses. I don't understand it. Why should failing eyesight, a deficiency of the organism, indicate intelligence? Perhaps because using glasses signifies a person has used their eyes to read? And is therefore intelligent?"

Aira shook her head, carrying on with herself. "That doesn't really follow logically, but may be what some people conclude."

Kaufkiff was fascinated by her discourse and noted how she rambled on, posing and answering her own questions. "Tell me," he coaxed her. "Do you often talk to yourself?"

"How do you mean?"

He pointed out, with careful enunciation, "Just now, for example—"

"Oh yes," Aira interrupted him, having determined what he was going to say before he finished explaining. "I do that when I want to know something," she told him. "I pose a question about something I have never thought of. And then I know the answer. If I don't ask or wonder, I won't know."

"I see."

The therapist pursed his lips and glanced over his data sheet. In perplexity, he returned to the most curious fact of all: the girl's I.Q. measured 220—well beyond 140 where genius range began. Yet, her entire demeanor—the insouciance, the open, unguarded gaze, the light temperament—none of it to him was indicative of intelligence.

Kaufkiff looked for stolid, supercilious seriousness as the sign of intelligence. Though Einstein, Mozart and other prodigies had childlike temperaments, enamored of wonder, the therapist's school of experience dealt with posturing superiority. It didn't occur to him that perhaps jocosity and candid simplicity were traits, direct reflections, of a facility that came from Mastery, and pompous cogitation was merely the low-level effort to pass for virtuosity.

"I have no subconscious?" Aira pondered. "Could it be I have a blocked conscious?"

"I said it *appears* you don't," Dr. Kaufkiff said.

"Maybe I have an *ab*-conscious."

"Do you mind if I ask you a few questions?" the therapist asked, ignoring the comment.

"No, I appreciate your concern."

"Good." He smiled tersely, then his face went serious. "Do you often feel this…phenomena…what you described. As though you are not your body?"

"Yes. All the time," Aira told him.

Kaufkiff transferred a scrutinizing look back and forth—to Mendle, who was sitting behind Aira by some book shelves, then back to her. "At those times," he resumed, "do you feel disassociated from anything else?"

"What do you mean?"

"Detached. Disassociated."

Oh no, Mendle thought. *Not this routine.*

"Yes. All the time," Aira replied eagerly. "When I was getting the medical examination, I could see the smallest letters at the bottom of the chart. The physician was amazed and kept pulling it further and further away. But, you see, I was not looking at the chart with my eyes."

"Were you experiencing a sense of far awayness?"

"No."

"Did things seem vague to you? Unreal?"

"No."

Dr. Kaufkiff glanced at his notes, "You just were not *seeing* with your *eyes?*"

"Right. Even though I was looking through them to perceive some things. I was also looking without them."

"I see."

"Oh, good. It happened after I fell off the roof. That was when I noticed it."

"Of course, of course. And you remember nothing before the day you fell off the roof? Correct?"

Aira nodded yes, pushing a strand of wavy ringlets behind her ear.

"I see."

"Oh good!"

Dr. Kaufkiff sat up a little straighter. He took a moment to think, trying to ignore her outbursts. "You found yourself in the bathroom. You were wet, wearing a trash bag...is that right? Wearing a trash bag?" He paused, as though that were particularly significant, until Aira confirmed it with a nod. "...and you don't remember how you got there."

"Correct. It's just blank."

"Had you been in the shower?"

"I don't know." The absence of memory frustrated and amazed her anew. "I just don't know."

Kaufkiff lowered and warmed his voice. "How do you feel about Mendle?"

She didn't hesitate. "I like him."

"I see."

"Oh, good."

Kaufkiff again chose to ignore the literalness with which Aira took his manner of speaking. Keeping on the earlier track, he pursued, "You like him. Would you describe that for me, please."

Buoyant with hope that the doctor was understanding something she didn't, Aira swiveled a little in her seat to see Mendle better. She smiled. Then she faced Dr. Kaufkiff again and told him, "He oxidizes me."

"I beg your pardon."

"That's okay. You didn't do anything wrong," Aira assured him kindly.

The therapist noted the fluctuations in her personality. She seemed outstandingly lucid at times, and other times confused. As Kaufkiff leaned back in his chair, he scribbled his observation. *Lapses in being able to discern figurative speech. Seems only able to take things literally.* Without looking up from his notes he asked Aira, "Would you explain what you mean by that?"

"Oxidizes me? You know. Oxidize. To increase the valence of an element in a positive direction."

"You derive a sense of well-being from him?"

"Yes."

"Does he remind you of anyone?" Kaufkiff asked, drawing out the word 'remind' as though it were of great significance. "Family perhaps?" he fished. "Father? Boss? Brother?"

"I think so, I don't know." She thought about it and concluded, "He seems familiar, friendly," then looked at Kaufkiff with dismay. "But I don't even know if I have a father."

Mendle's speculations about the woman instantly revived. He wondered, feeling the gocse-bumps begin, what if she *did* remember something about herself so incredible she might be classified as insane?

Kaufkiff was chiding her patronizingly. "Now, now. Let's look at this. Do you feel abandoned at all?"

Abandoned. Maybe she was abandoned as a child, has a childhood too terrible to remember. Maybe she is crazy, has done things she wants to forget. Mendle cautioned himself. *I have to be willing to accept anything about her, whatever it is.*

"Not abandoned, no, I just don't know about my past. So it feels as if I don't have one."

"Of course, of course," Kaufkiff said, checking himself from saying 'I see', wondering if she referred to a past or a father.

Aira looked over at Mendle for reassurance. He let go a small smile.

"Let's try this before we finish for today." Kaufkiff instructed Aira. "I'll say something to you and I want you to tell me the first thing that comes to mind when I snap my fingers."

He determined by her expression that Aira understood what he meant, then asked, "Ready?"

She nodded.

"Chair," the doctor said, then snapped his fingers.

"Chair," Aira responded.

"Woman," he said and snapped his fingers.

"Woman."

"Man." Sharp finger snap.

"Man," Aira replied.

"Banana!" Snap.

"Banana."

Dr. Kaufkiff was perturbed. "Now Aira, tell me what is going on?"

The condescension in his voice caused her to introvert a little. "Am I doing something wrong?" she asked.

"What *are* you doing?"

"I'm doing what you asked me to do," she told him.

"But you are only repeating what I say," Kaufkiff said.

"No I'm not. I'm telling you what I think of."

"Now let's face this. Everything I have said, you have repeated. Is that not so?"

"No, I haven't, Dr. Kaufkiff."

He was surprised at her adamancy. "How would you describe it?" he asked her. A brief but somewhat heavy exhale betrayed his exasperation.

"I've been telling you what comes to mind when you say what you say," Aira explained.

Kaufkiff was silent. He felt a little ruffled, as though being proven wrong. He took a moment to regain his composure, comforting himself against the frustration of dealing with mental disorders. "All right, then," the doctor resumed smoothly. "Shall we continue then? Close your eyes this time."

Aira complied.

"The first thing that comes to mind," he reminded her, then proceeded from where he had left off. "Banana." He snapped his fingers.

"Banana," Aira responded.

"Apple!" he called out and snapped.

"Apple," Aira said.

"Pond." Snap.

"Pond."

Then faster. "River." Snap.

"River."

"Snake." Snap.

"Snake," Aira replied, faster.

"House." Snap.

"House."

Dr. Kaufkiff was increasing his tempo.

"Ocean." Snap!

"Ocean."

"Car." Snap.

"Car."

"Sex." Snap.

"Sex."

Now he stopped once more. "Aira?" he asked.

There was silence. Her eyes were still closed. Finally, "You didn't snap your fingers," she told him.

"You may open your eyes now," Dr. Kaufkiff informed her. When she did, he checked, "Don't you think of anything when I say those things?"

Bewildered by his question, Aira answered, "Yes. When you said 'house,' I thought of a house."

"Don't these things signify anything to you? Don't they mean anything?"

Aira was absolutely perplexed. "Of course they mean something. They mean what they are."

"Don't they bring anything to mind?"

"You mean anything other than what they are?" she asked curiously.

"Some people, when I say 'snake,' think of bite. Or when I say 'pencil,' some people think of paper, or school, or airplane." After citing examples, Kaufkiff sat back in his leather chair expectantly. He inwardly chided himself that he shouldn't be feeling disconcerted with the patient.

Aira simply stared at him.

"Does anything like that come to mind at all?" he prompted her.

"No," Aira marveled. "Why would anyone think of an airplane when you say pencil?"

Mendle concealed his amusement. He had no trouble understanding her. The fact that she did not think of objects as symbols but saw them as what they were was an indication of sanity to him.

"What do you think of when I say 'knife'?" Dr. Kaufkiff pitched like a last minute curve ball then snapped his fingers.

"Knife," Aira answered.

"Pain." Snap.

"Pain."

"Remember." Snap.

"Remember."

"All right," the therapist surrendered as though it had been war.

Mendle interceded, concealing his merriment under a studious countenance. "Excuse me, doctor." He scratched the side of his head a little and earnestly asked, "What do most people think of when you say…'banana?'"

"It varies," Kaufkiff said, busy with his notes. *She is not cooperating. She's working against me.*

"Have I done something wrong?" Aira asked.

Her question earned a sharp glance from Dr. Kaufkiff which he mollified into a smile. "Do you feel as though you have?"

She thought about it. "Yes, I do."

"Do you feel this way often? As though you have upset someone?"

"No."

"Do you often feel as though people are angry with you?"

"You're not upset?" Aira asked him.

Deciding his own emotions were not pertinent, Kaufkiff steered Aira further. "Perhaps you feel others are working against you? Or that people don't like you?"

"You weren't just a little upset with me?" Aira asked again.

Dr. Kaufkiff decided it best not to complicate the session by entering his personal non-clinical opinion. *Besides,* he concluded, *any twinge of irritation I felt in dealing with her was only transitory, and therefore irrelevant. To hell with her.*

"I'm not upset with you, dear," he told her.

Aira's heart began to race.

"Well," Kaufkiff concluded somberly, his shoulders moving up and down as he heaved a conclusive sigh. "This is our first visit. We both agree you need help. You are suffering from an identity crisis. Obviously, there is something in your past which you do not want to remember, thus the amnesia. You say there was no evidence from the medical exam of physical injury, nor blows to the head. Therefore, it is probably safe to assume it is a severe emotional trauma of some—"

Now Aira's chest heaved as her breathing quickened. "You're lying to me," she accused suddenly.

Mendle leaned forward, alarmed. Kaufkiff's interest perked.

Gone was the soft, mellifluous voice. Aira had started to perspire. Some words were bordering on strident. "Don't you know how harmful it is to disorient a person's reality that way? You are directly messing with my sanity!"

She was speaking louder than Mendle had ever heard her.

"To tell a person something is *not* so when, in fact, it *is*? What do you think that does?" she demanded, then accused, "You are sitting there pretending to have my best interest in mind when you just lied to me. You intentionally undermined my sense of observation and judgement!" A split pause, then, "You were upset with me moments ago. Admit it. You wanted me to go to hell!"

Mendle noticed sweat breaking on her forehead.

"All right, yes, all right," Kaufkiff tried to soothe her.

After a tense moment, Aira said, "Thank you." She sat back a little. "A person's observation and sense of reality is really very important, you know," she explained, looking nervous and unsure. "What I feel is real, what I see is real. You can't say it isn't real when it is real. It is real. It is."

"Of course it is," Dr. Kaufkiff told her. Her sudden shift in comportment confirmed his speculations. His silent conclusion: *schizophrenic with paranoid tendencies.*

Aira looked at him, grabbed the sides of her chair and inched forward again. "That's not it," she said. "You think I'm schizoid but I'm not."

Silence vacuumed the room again.

"Miss Flight, I was only giving you certain reasons, certain theories if you will, about the amnesia, I said nothing about—"

"Those aren't reasons! You call those reasons?" She was gripping the arm rests and now pushed herself up to her feet. "Hey!" she challenged defiantly. "Something is going on here and I want to know what it is! And you haven't given me anything to go on!"

Dr. Kaufkiff was unflinching as he calmly observed and let her continue.

The major crazies are always the quiet, unflinching ones, Mendle thought. He knew that one buzz away were means of forceful restraint, from jackets to drugs. *An arm's length away.* All the doctor had to do was reach over and press a button.

"I'm not schizophrenic!" Aira insisted petulantly, her eyes wide.

Perspiration trickled down her neck into dark spots on her dress, and her arms were sudorous, too. As Mendle noticed her rage and abnormal sweat, it called up the memory of the electro-shock patient he had seen in his last visit to the facility.

Sandra's warnings about the girl clamored next. *A crazed fan out for a free ride.* Then his own speculations. *Space goddess.* His thoughts began to jumble in his thinking process like clothes in a dryer, and he only saw cuffs, collars, and corners roll past.

"I said nothing of schizophrenia, dear," Dr. Kaufkiff was assuring Aira, assuming she had made a paranoic guess.

"But you were thinking it. I know what it means. Hey, what do you think I am? This piece of meat I'm walking around in? Flesh and blood and guts?"

"Well, I think we're getting somewhere, past that cheery personality you offer at first."

His statement filled Aira with indignation, it exploded onto her face. "What?" she cried. "You upset me like this and tell me we're making progress?"

"Aira." Mendle stepped over to her and grasped her upper arm firmly. She turned on him, her eyes flashing like he'd never seen, they were wild with incomprehension and rage. He could feel her trembling.

"It isn't fair!" she insisted. "That's how to drive a person crazy. Keep telling them what they see and feel isn't real, it's only in their head." She pointed at Kaufkiff and accused, "He was thinking things about me and denied it! There's a reason I'm upset, and it's not because I'm crazy! I know what I see."

"I understand," Mendle told her.

Her upset decreased a fraction. "There's a reason for what I feel." A whimper undulated her tone.

"Sure. There is. There is a reason," Mendle assured her.

As her breathing quieted some, Aira began to feel amazed about her reaction.

"Just because I changed emotions does not mean I became another personality," she defended herself.

"Of course, of course," Kaufkiff said, jotting down some notes and recommendations.

Mendle knew he had to do something to take control of the situation. To conceal his trepidation, he stretched, as if bored, and he was about to initiate their exit but didn't manage soon enough.

"Electro-shock?" Aira whispered incredulously, then wheeled around and glared at the doctor.

As Dr. Kaufkiff rose from his chair, he attributed her correct guess about what he had just written in her file as another paranoic jab in the dark. *They can be quite clever.* Characteristic of the personality type, he surmised, she was covering her bases, trying to outguess people, hoping to stay a step ahead of their moves against her.

"I'm sure you'll be fine," Dr. Kaufkiff said, trying to dismiss the tension with a little forced laugh.

Mendle joined in. "Sure." He was at Aira's side and rapidly stepped forward and extended a hand which the doctor accepted and shook. "Dr. Kaufkiff, thank you very much."

"Interesting custom," Aira said, watching them. "Shaking hands. Originates from the days when it was done to show the parties bore no weapons. Today the weapons are more invisible." She was looking at their hands but not focusing. She sounded drained.

"A few more visits and you'll find them getting more pleasant, you'll even look forward to coming here," Dr. Kaufkiff placated her. "If you find yourself too upset, there is something I can prescribe, a medication that will help you."

"Thank you for your help," Mendle intercepted, thinking, *Drugs, just what she needs to help her get oriented.* He quickly turned to face Aira. Sure that his back was completely to Dr. Kaufkiff, he implored her with his eyes to say no more. He tried to gesture and pour his understanding to her. Then, arching his eyebrows dramatically for her to get the hint, he said, "You've done *very well* for your first visit."

Aira decided to trust in him and fell silent in his care.

So as not to appear in a panic to leave, Mendle asked the doctor, "Do you have a Kleenex?" Then, noticing a box on the corner of the desk, he said, "Ah, here. Thanks."

He could feel his heart beat as he wiped sweat off Aira's neck and face. He thought of nothing but getting her out of there without seeming too abrupt and, finally, maneuvered it.

In a waiting area, Sandra flipped through a magazine, barely seeing the pages, mostly looking at her own ruminations. She was pleased the woman with Mendle was even less pretty than she remembered. *Exotic, maybe, but a model she is not.* She was not tall, which to Sandra was everything. It was difficult to pinpoint her age because she had a childlike appearance about her, yet she had to be at least thirty-five, Sandra guessed. Perhaps it was the oval face, the chin which was not strong, and the big eyes. Her hair appeared more platinum than when she first saw her, yet she denied having it done. *She lied. That color is not natural. The waves have to be a perm. She's wearing chiffon. Who wears chiffon in the afternoon?*

When Sandra noticed Mendle and Aira approaching down the hall, she did a mental check of her posture and composure. *Legs crossed and extended. Back straight.* Ensuring that her head was in the position she had planned to affect Mendle—with the sunlight sparkling through the plate glass window onto her hair—Sandra stopped thumbing through the magazine and pretended to be engrossed reading.

Mendle is looking less haunted these days, she thought. His arm around Aira sent a pang through her, but she tempered her anger and sat there as attractively as she could, silently racing through options of what to say. *'How did it go?' 'Oh! There you are!' 'Isn't he a wonderful man?' 'Did he help you?' 'What is your problem?' Who the hell are you?*

She gauged her timing, looked up, feigned surprise, and was about to open her mouth to speak when Mendle and Aira walked right past her. "Mendle! Aira!" she called after them as she discarded the magazine.

He could hear Sandra's heels clattering behind them across the reception area and down the steps. Following them across the parking lot, Sandra maneuvered herself in front of Aira and Mendle. "What happened?"

"Go home."

Sandra aimed a distraught expression at Aira, targeting her as the more accessible. "What happened? What's the matter?"

Aira resisted Mendle's yanking her forward. "She's only trying to help us," she protested.

"That is exactly what she is not doing," Mendle said, unlocking the silver car door. He held it open for Aira to get in, then shut it and brusquely crossed to the driver's side. He could feel Sandra's glare on him, trying first to singe then incinerate him, and he was relieved to be in the car with the door shut.

The car windows were up but Sandra could hear Aira's eruption into sobs. The voice was muffled but she could make out, "There's a reason for what I feel. What I feel is real!" An almost wailing lament turned into sobs.

"There is a reason. There is. I know that," Mendle assured her. "Even though we don't know what it is."

Sandra bent down to look through the window and saw Mendle lean toward Aira and caress her hair. He was being reassuring, telling her, "The right reason won't upset you. Don't worry, we'll find out what it is", then their voices were overtaken by the volume of engine as he turned the key in the ignition.

As Sandra watched them back out of the parking spot and drive away, her obsession became malignant. She was determined with a vengeance. "Damn right we'll find out what it is."

chapter  22

They drove without speaking for some ten minutes. Finally, Aira said, "What's wrong? I just don't understand what came over me."

Mendle didn't either, but he believed if a person felt crazy, there was something causing it. He didn't know the reason for her angst, or, for that matter, his own but, he did know what he told her next. "I guess even if it's just your imagination, there's a reason you're imagining it."

Gravel scrunched under the tires as he steered the silver car onto a patch of dirt off Mulholland Road. He turned off the engine and sat quietly with Aira, overlooking the panorama of Los Angeles.

Mendle was pleased with the restraint he had shown in Dr. Kaufkiff's office. He used to blurt out whatever he was thinking, without considering either to whom he spoke or of the effect his words would have. He now realized, communication served a purpose—a bigger purpose than simply letting off steam.

It wasn't a matter of of being 'open' or 'honest.' Revealed confidences were used by some to demean or hinder. Others simply didn't know how to help. *Why communicate to someone who isn't going to understand? Or twists anything said to use as artillery against you, or uses it for perverse entertainment, such as gossip.* This was how he could begin to tell the girl about Sandra, Mendle thought. Perhaps the most important thing one could do in life, he realized and reaffirmed to himself, was to know the definition of the word "friend."

"Aira," he said, paused, then started by giving her his definition of the word, "A friend is someone you know, like, and trust. Someone who has your well-being at heart." He continued with his point, "You think everyone is a friend. And why? Because *you* like them and wish them well. But does your being a person's friend mean he or she is also yours?"

Aira thought about it. "Not necessarily."

"Right. Someone being a friend is based on what is in their heart for you, as well as what's in your heart toward them," Mendle said. He pointed to someone walking down the road. "That man isn't my friend just because I wish him well…who knows what's on his mind."

"If I'm someone's friend doesn't necessarily mean that person is a friend to me," Aira let him know she understood. She traced a seam on the seat cover with her finger then looked up. "But why would someone not want to be my friend?" she posed, puzzled by the thought.

Mendle gazed over the top of his steering wheel. "Fear, distrust, betrayal." He shrugged apologetically. "Welcome to planet Earth," he said wryly, not without bitterness.

"Earth is beautiful." Her words sounded wistful, as if wishing would make it so. They sat in silence, then Aira spoke. "I guess could still be a friend to those who aren't my friends," she resolved, "As long as I don't let them hurt me while I'm trying to help them."

She was still feeling ashamed of how she had behaved at the Institute. The emotions had triggered in her without warning—the cold and confused sensation that came over her when she began to sweat. Something about the place and Dr. Kaufkiff had set it off. The upset clung to her like velcro, but the mesh onto which it was sticking was invisible. Thinking about it gave her no answers, and she was becoming desperate to know.

Sensitive to Aira's despondence, Mendle asked her if she wanted to go sit outside, thinking it would help. She nodded, and they both got out of the car and walked to a rocky vantage point overlooking the canyon. There was a hot, dry Santa Ana wind blowing through the craggy boulders and low brush that surrounded them. Distance miniaturized bright green squares of sprinkler-induced paradises on hillsides across the canyon.

Mendle stretched, feeling good without any toxic substances braiding his thoughts. When they took a place on the flat part of a large boulder, he consoled Aira. "You were upset. I don't blame you for being upset. I don't think that place is equipped to help you." It rang true to him as he said it, and he elaborated, "Maybe you just sensed that instinctively. Like a danger or something."

"Danger. Yes, that's what it felt like," Aira said.

Mendle let out a satiric noise resembling a laugh as supportive commentary. "No wonder. Look, do you know what they do to people there?" As he described psychosurgery, the removal of brain tissue to modify people into behaving in desirable ways, heavy 'personality' drugs, and electroshock, he became angry. "They call it 'behavior modification,' but they're modifying human beings, not behavior! They can't cure the ailment so they just squash the person, make them quiet. I mean they obliterate entire portions of a life, zap it right out of existence—" The parallel of the absence of the girl's own memory suddenly hit him.

Mendle quit talking. Aira had buried her face in her hands. He touched her. He could feel her trembling. As he gently brushed her hair back from her forehead, he felt it damp from sweat.

"I'm just trying to understand," Aira moaned. "I was thinking about what you said, about danger, and the feeling started again. It's cold, confusing. So I throw myself into the shaking, and I started feeling it again. It's a clue to something. But I don't know what." She started to sob again.

Mendle didn't know what to do. He considered suggesting they file with missing persons. Sandra's warnings chimed in, about the girl being a calculating, crazed fan. His inner clamoring stopped at what Aira said next.

"Juristac!" She blurted it out in a half-whisper. It echoed in the silence that followed.

"What did you say?"

"I don't know what it is. A name, a place. It's a thought, it came to me, and I, maybe I remembered it..."

She was talking fast, excited by the possibility that she had remembered something. Mendle thoroughly scrutinized her every move and expression for a reading.

"Why did you say that?" he asked somewhat suspiciously.

"I don't know." She looked at him blankly. "Why?"

He didn't want to tell her about what he had written in his new novel. It was too weird, but there it was. She just said the name of one of his characters. He wondered if she had seen his notes, maybe some pages about Z Zone with the name Juristac on them. He looked hard into her face, her eyes. *No, she can't be lying, she isn't lying.* "Sounds like a name," Mendle said, trying to be nonchalant.

Aira broke their long gaze and shook her head in frustration. "Have you heard of it?" she asked.

"Yes." He decided to tell her, "It's a name. In a book I'm writing."

She looked at him, still wide-eyed, as if she had been spooked or was about to discover something earth-shaking. Suddenly, she dropped once more to despondence. "Oh. Maybe that's where. I read it and don't recall," she said.

"But it isn't published."

"Maybe I saw your computer...That's the second time."

"Second time what?"

"The night we met, Rex asked me if I read your work. Because I was thinking about a word, I asked him about the word. Dao."

She was about to spell it. Mendle did first, "D–A–O?"

"Yes!" she said fervently. "To love…"

"…so much it gives life," they both finished together.

They were silent as they stared each other.

That he had once considered this girl of flesh and blood in front of him was the legend of his space adventures seemed somehow too incredible to him now. Not only incredible, a little ludicrous.

Earlier, Mendle had found himself wondering about the dog again, wondering who owned it and what its name had been. Perhaps some child or person out there was mourning its loss. Then the same things occurred to him about her. Here he had assigned her this name out of his fiction, while some parent, or sibling, or spouse could be frantically searching for this woman.

"I probably have read your work, and just don't remember," Aira was saying.

Mendle grappled with his own confusion. His pragmatism questioned this particular coincidence. *How else could she have known the word?* He heard her sigh into tears and turned to her. "Tell me," he gently murmured.

"I don't know," Aira wept. "I was looking at you. At the way your hair grows at your neck. At your arms, and shoulders. I thought I loved you, but then I became afraid."

Mendle felt motionless in an amazing suspension of time. It felt like the grip of his own destiny.

"I'm afraid," she said. It was painful for her to say what she wanted to tell him next. "Because I thought I was going to lose you. I'm so afraid of losing you." She abandoned herself to utter grief.

"You won't lose me," Mendle told her as he slid closer and put his arm around her. "I know what you mean," he said. He did recognize something with his entire being, but he didn't know what to make of it.

Aira cried, "I feel things and I don't know why. I know things, but don't remember others. I wonder where I am, and what this is all for. And I feel afraid. Then I don't know why. Who am I? What does it all mean?"

"I've asked the same thing, believe me," Mendle comforted her. He held her while she cried. When Aira's emotion was spent, they sat quietly, the warm wind blowing around them.

Mendle's attention turned to Los Angeles sprawled in the basin below. He wished it could be washed as simply as throwing in a few giant cups of detergent with the next rain. Everyone could wake up clean.

He thought of humanity and it was ugly to him. Not even the diaphanous pink and apricot-gold glow that washed the hillside in late afternoon was any solace. *What good is beauty in a world of crime, war, and envy, and slavery?* "I mean, just the fact that someone is going to die is enough to ruin their life," Mendle finished his thinking aloud.

"Die?" Aira wondered. "What does that mean?"

"You're asking me?" Mendle said. "I really can't figure it out." He held onto her a little tighter, as if to protect her. Aware of it, he considered the irony and said, "I thought you'd have all the answers."

Aira pulled away to look at him. "Me?" she said, wiping her eyes and nose. "Why me?"

Mendle thought about it, then shrugged. *Because you're special,* was what he thought. "Because I guess when a person finally meets someone special, they're expected to know everything," was what he said.

Aira delivered a half-smile then leaned against him wistfully. She found comfort in the feel of Mendle's body, and she stretched across the rock, accommodating herself into his lap.

Looking down at Aira as she rested on him, her body and hips in a comfortable compromise against the boulder, Mendle felt grateful and proud, as if he'd been given the keys to heaven. *At last, company.* Having her, however, opened the door to the potential of losing her. The idea of mortality punched him, and he internally boxed with the concept of death. It was agony, panic, terror, protest, all at once. The thought that someone he loved could be taken from him without warning was the ultimate blasphemy. Yet it could happen, from one second to the next.

Without her, life would be meaningless, he thought, feeling the warmth of Aira nestling against him. When he was younger, he felt he had so many friends. Through the years, the disparity between his dreams and the world in which he found himself had become a chasm. There was desperation in Mendle's feeling that Aira was the only person in the world who understood him, and he began to love her with religious passion, as a hope of his own salvation.

He gazed out over the hazy smog layering the city. Pictures of people he knew seemed to leer at him. Those indelible faces of his first hosts to trickeries of the world. He remembered clearly his first taste of hate, of betrayal. Portraitures loomed of people who had robbed him, manipulated him to his detriment to serve their own ends. The incomprehensibility of their having done so remained.

I feel things and I don't know why. I know things, but don't remember others. I wonder where I am, and what this is all for. And I feel afraid. Then I don't know why. Who am I? What does it all mean? Many of the questions that troubled Aira were what Mendle had been asking himself. He had become unreachable but not by choice. It was as if he were quarantined, lest his ideas and protests disturb the Great Slumber. *Inquiring what is wrong with the picture disrupts nap time.*

Rejections and rebukes left him feeling he wasn't good enough. *It was I who should have quarantined the world,* he thought. *It's contaminated.*

Mendle stroked Aira's curls. "We don't have the answers yet…at least we're asking."

She turned her head to look upward at him and, after a while, said, "It takes courage to be afraid."

Hundreds and millions of them out there, crawling underneath bill-boards, he imagined the city in detail. From where he sat he saw rectangular slabs of twenty-storied, mirror-buildings looking smaller than an inch and shining like postage stamps of bright sun. They were filled with thousands of people who, eyes glazed with sleep, floated up and down on elevators and orbited around desks.

Was this life? A life-span seemed like a blink of an eye. The more he lived, the less time fifty, sixty, seventy, even a hundred years seemed. He could not concede that the only purpose of life was the avoidance of pain and death of an organism…which was, in the end, inevitable anyway.

Below, he imagined, rose the moans of the damned.

Across town Sandra Wilford worked five-pound weights in front of a mirror at the gym. She checked out the thighs and buttocks of the women who walked past her, comparing them to her own. "One, two, three, four," she pumped out her repetitions, all the while thinking while she sweated, *The best. I'm going to be the best. The best. The best.*

The sun was pulling the last of its light to another side of the globe and Los Angeles began to glitter with electricity. In another hour, the city would be twinkling in the blackness, imitating the night sky. It was quiet where Mendle and Aira sat, except for the faint chorus of crickets and occasional sighs of wind through the canyon.

Aira turned her head sideways. Her knees were drawn to her chest, her arms clasped around them and, when she turned, she rested her cheek on her knees and leveled a steady, wistful gaze on Mendle.

Her eyes invaded him.

"You're special, too," she told him softly.

Not like you. He wanted to tell her. She was special. But he wasn't sure how anymore. She did seem to have the ability, although not consistent, to read thought. Maybe she had read his mind to get the names and words. His eyes narrowed as he wondered again what her memory would reveal when it returned. She was certainly different from most of what was running around down there, he thought looking at the city— if only because she was kind and caring, sweet and simple.

"What are you thinking?" Aira asked.

"Aw. This planet is a dump," Mendle said, disgusted.

Aira propped her chin on her hands and joined his gaze over the city, holding her hair to keep it from being blown into her face as she looked over the vast grey metropolis. She was beginning to see what he meant.

"But, you know," she said sadly, "All those people out there…they, too, have their reasons."

They had stopped by the house to pick up Onx and made it to the California coast for the sunset. As they traveled up Pacific Coast Highway, Aira saw a white dove flying alongside her side of the car. It kept pace with them, parallel to her window.

"How beautiful!" Aira exclaimed. "It's pure life reaching out to touch us!"

Mendle smiled at the sight and a feeling of well-being stayed with him as they drove up the coast to Paradise Cove and parked.

Aira and Mendle locked the car in the parking lot and walked toward the sea. The sand was rumpled from the day's millions of footsteps. The beach was not peopled at all. In the distance, the small figure of a man jogged away. Several hundred yards down the coast, a couple was preparing to leave. With Onx trailing alongside them, they walked until they found a place on the sand, and there they waited for the sunset.

"The term 'sunset' is misleading," Mendle said, feeling the beneficence of being with someone who liked the things he thought about. "Doesn't the word imply that the sun is moving?"

Aira nodded. "You're right. The sun doesn't set."

"'Sunrise' doesn't work either."

"What should it be called?"

"The earth-turn," he said.

"It *is* the earth that's moving," Aira agreed, mulling it over. "Night earth-turn and day earth-turn."

"Or night-turn and day-turn." They both liked it.

"Oh, look! How lucky!" Aira suddenly squealed, excited and pointing her finger.

Directly in front of them in the sea right off the shore, dolphins were leaping. There were some twenty of them frolicking, including a baby or two. They sprang from the water in arches, diving and leaping up and down the shore line.

Aira clasped her hands together and rose to her knees, enraptured with the abandon of a child. When Mendle turned to smile with her, he noted the peculiar way she had of sometimes looking eleven or twelve. Yet she was a completely mature woman.

He turned to the dolphins. *They're the materialization of pure Joy.*

"How fortunate we are! How lucky!" Aira enthused, half-whispering. Her voice was a mixture of delight and reverence. "Oh, let's go closer!"

The dolphins skimmed through the waves, twenty feet from shore, taking turns leaping, laughing and chattering mid-air.

"Yes, yes, yes!" Aira told them, extending her arms wide. "I love you! I love you! I love you!"

The late sky, the ocean, the dolphins all breathed into Mendle the sighs of eternity; he was inspired; it exhaled as thought. As he watched Aira joyfully skipping up the beach alongside the dolphins, Mendle began to speak the poetry in him, recording it on his pocket recorder.

"Life that loved her, sought her. As the sweet lushness of ripe fruit, as quenching water on her tongue, as sea in which she bathed—it found a way. If it had to be strokes of luck that appeared like miracles, the singing of a bird at her windowsill, the butterfly that landed on her hand, the flight of a dove alongside her journey, Life kissed her however it could.

"It rallied to foil the person who meant her ill, to turn her head just in time for her to see what she needed to see. In whatever way and however Life could manifest to love her, it stretched, like hands from some heaven, coming out as shape and form on the other side, where she now lived in a world of forms.

"It was only natural affinity. She was smiled upon by That to which she had always been devoted. Around her, she found manifestations of the pure fabric of her origin."

The earth's night-turn was rising above the sun which, from Mendle and Aira's position, appeared an orange semi-circle on the horizon. A star's pallid light faintly dotted a twilight sky of mauve and tangerine, lilac wisped by pearl and dark pink translucence. Earth continued to rotate by degrees into the first shades of night which revealed, ever brightening, the first twinkling evening beacons.

Mendle had secured his shoes, microcassette recorder and shirt in the sand, and joined Aira in skipping and running along the waves. Soon they were in knee-deep, being bashed and thoroughly soaked, and their exhilaration grew such that they didn't pay much attention to the cold water or to their clothes. Aira played swishing her chiffon dress through the sea and, laughter escalating, they proceeded until the water came waist-deep. Then they both dove in to swim and splash with the dolphins.

Time proceeded and their position on the planet's surface continued to move in relation to the sun. The immense solar star was now out of their line of vision, but, from somewhere down there in space, its glow broadcast past the horizon. Another part of the blue-green planet, some other turning curve of the globe presenting itself for morning light, was receiving the sunlight directly.

As the Earth, like a sunbather, rotated in ritual worship of warmth and light to be evenly kissed and energized, Mendle and Aira played with the dolphins, and Onx danced along the shore by the shiny, scalloped wavelets.

Graced by the dolphins that surrounded them, Mendle and Aira threw themselves to each other in laughing, spontaneous embraces. Underneath the beginnings of a starry expanse, they held onto each other and swayed in waves that tugged and pushed them. They sought to capture the warmth of each other's bodies in their embraces, resting, becoming quiet, feeling one another through their silence.

As the cold Pacific water continued to drain them of body heat, they began to shiver. They looked at one another, then around them. Their bodies felt very small but their eyes sparkled with the huge expanse of awareness, and they felt it, the vastness, as an inkling to their true selves.

"Shall we remove our bodies from this freezing water?" Mendle asked. Aira agreed emphatically, vocalizing her shivering.

Stumbling for balance against the waves at their backs, they made it out of the sea and were greeted by Onx who continued to cavort happily around them as they walked up the sand to pick up Mendle's shirt and things. The dolphins slipped off to other parts of their realm, and soon, the joyous banter gone, there remained only the lulling lapping of waves and the rushing white noise of breaking surf.

"Did it really happen?" Aira whispered, looking at the sea.

Mendle shook sand out of his shirt and carefully replaced his pocket recorder. He looked over at the brink of their worlds, where the marine visitors had come from the water. *To greet and love us.* "I know what you mean," he told Aira.

Aira smiled at him. "But it was so good, it *was* true."

Onx barked.

"That's right," Aira answered back playfully, shivering hard to keep warm.

"Nothing drains body heat faster than water," Mendle said. Their pace back to the car turned into a run, then into a race, and soon they arrived, heaving with laughter as their hands hit the vehicle in a near tie.

"Maybe you should step out of those," Mendle told Aira as he fumbled through his pocket for his keys. The soaked chiffon clung to her; it was cold, he imagined. "I have a blanket in the trunk."

"You liked that, didn't you?" Aira played with Onx as she rubbed her arms and hopped from foot to foot to warm up.

"Earth *is* beautiful," Mendle told Aira as he unlocked the car and went around to the trunk.

It was as if reality around him had first lived inside him, and was reminding him…*of what?* John Milton's words from Paradise Lost came to him, '*The mind is its own place, and in itself can make a heaven of hell, and a hell of heaven.*'

Their bodies came and went places in space and time, making it appear as though they were motion—but it suddenly seemed the reverse was true: motion moved through them, and they had been, as static thought, right where they had always been. *It was a peek at something,* he knew; fleeting, gone as quickly as it had revealed itself. Mendle often felt as if he were nose to nose with it. Too close, he couldn't see it. He saw signals. *Glimpses, clues, glimpses of clues.*

"Brrr, brr," Aira was shivering.

"And I'm hungry," Mendle commiserated

"Me, too," Aira seconded, her teeth chattering.

"Go ahead, get it off," Mendle told her as he pulled the blanket out of the trunk.

Aira unzipped the dress. As she struggled out of the wet fabric, pulling it with some difficulty over her arms and head, Mendle's gaze traveled down her body.

That's when he first noticed. Stunned, amazed, incredulous, reverent, chastised, afraid, excited, aghast—all of that and more was what he felt when he saw.

She didn't have a navel.

chapter  23

Under the fluorescence of gas station lights in downtown Los Angeles, Mendle fueled his car. When the gas hose clicked off from hitting full, he replaced the nozzle on the pump then headed to the attendant booth to collect his change.

Chaos increased on entering the city; it was a different world. Names, initials, shock words were sloppily spray-painted on walls and street signs. The sprayed scrawlings were attempts to claim space by a vagrant loneliness which felt it had no home. Echoing desolation, property was neglected and vandalized. Cans, bottles, and papers lined the streets. Everywhere, unguided by the touch of a soul, things fell to disrepair and turned to rubble.

Broken people wandered without destination or reason. Many spoke to themselves, to invisible or nonexistent companions, or to the mind-demons. They walked their nightmares in the streets, desperately seeking witnesses for the horror that plagued them.

Sirens spiraled hysterically from different points in the night. Helicopters chopped the air, droning restlessly, pursuing justice by breaking the dark with roving spotlights. Some people drove in polished automobiles, their faces casting their own dark to hide their violations. Crime needed the dark.

"Does something seem…wrong around here to you?" Aira asked Mendle as he got in the car.

"Glad it's not just me who thinks so," Mendle said, cranking the engine. *No navel? Did I see that?* His wonder ballooned.

Aira looked at a poster on the side of a bus as they pulled out of the gas station into traffic. The design of advertisement aimed at attracting children, but the viewer rating was restricted. "Look. Hideous violence. Straight out of torment. Why is it on lunch boxes, school books, clothing? Why not give children beautiful toys and images?"

Mendle thought about what he had seen in some of the stores and conjectured, "Maybe it's an attempt at immunization against the world they're about to enter."

"See? We try to make some sort of sense out of it, when it has none," Aira declared. "Violence in toys and television is no vaccine, it's part of what *creates* that ugly world," she said adamantly. "And why prepare anyone for crime anyway? Why not prepare them against it? Instead of thinking it's normal." She was exasperated. "I don't understand."

Mendle commiserated, "I guess violence is where reason and understanding fail." He shook his head. "It's no accident. It's *individuals* putting out that pollution."

At a red light, Mendle glanced over to the passenger side at Aira. He followed her gaze toward a magazine stand on the street corner. People straggled and loitered about the racks of newspapers and magazines, some leaned against the brick building. A prostitute and her pimp caught Aira's gaze and haughtily stared back at her. They challenged her with mocking faces, a reaction to feeling judged.

Mendle understood her as she turned toward him. "Lock your door," he told her, softly but seriously, then returned his attention to the road. The light turned green.

As he thought about it, Mendle concluded that while many clamored for rights and special privileges as minority underdogs in the world, it was really those who tried to build a better world who were the truly underprivileged. Those who clung to dreams, those who aspired to excellence were perhaps the only real minority.

People with above-average intelligence were a minority. Yet smart people weren't a group over which charity-mongers could feel superior. After all, feeling good about one's self, not helping others, seemed to be the purpose of pseudo-charity. They couldn't loom over brilliance and excellence, positive solutions and creation, that didn't make them feel better about themselves. *What would happen to her if she didn't have me for a friend?* Mendle wondered, glancing at Aira, fearing the treatment her aspirations would receive.

The true minority, people who were the most capable, generally worked for the benefit of many and society. Yet it was unrecognized. Not only were they unhelped, they were the most hindered. There was no room allowed to the good and the bright for error. They were a minority that had to fight to accomplish their noble aims, noble aims which, ironically, had in mind the benefit all of humanity.

The disparity was never clearer to him.

The history of the planet was a trail of excellence taxed and ability penalized. All one had to do was find achievement of any type—art, science, prosperity, kindness, beauty—and there one would find the most severe criticisms and attacks.

Gods were crucified, scientists and inventors tortured and persecuted, artists slandered. Despite their obvious good, the best did not serve to inspire the media; they were attacked for the smallest speck of flaw or error and, if none could be found, imaginary ones were provided. The true minority had to bear gossip for the most benign of faults, were given faults if they didn't have enough of their own, while the rest, criminals, derelicts, the self-serving, dunces, materialists, and less noble of heart, got pampered and protected with "compassion" and benefits.

The thought of what Diogenes of Sinope said echoed in Mendle's mind. He had read it in *Forbes* magazine that morning. *'Beggars get handouts before philosophers because people have some idea of what it's like to be blind and lame.'*

From her side of the car, Aira quietly watched traffic and people. She thought about the daily ration of what was called "the news." There appeared to be complete tolerance for degradation of the human spirit, as if that were a normal condition. Crime, from theft to murder to calumny, did not seem to appall anyone.

She puzzled over what she considered a state of twisted life and questioned the phenomena of persons embracing things which made less of them. *They are so much more.* Some, she saw, pretended decency by their material riches, justified grotesque products by the earning of profit, and, further, they called it survival.

Why be less than what you are? It bewildered her.

A sentiment welled up in Aira. She wanted to cry out. What—she didn't know. As she looked at people around her, a flood of pathos surged from her to rally them to break free from what encased them.

Her voice was imbued with compassion, heavy with their grief and demise. "So many seem…lost…and broken," she said to Mendle.

The tormented, horror-etched faces were her personal sadness, her loss. Some old, some younger. All so…lonely. *Doesn't anyone love you?* Her very soul cried out to the depleted, ravaged faces, to a man who looked as if all had been taken from him. *Doesn't anyone love you?*

"I feel I *know* them." Aira's words to Mendle sounded like a plea. "They're broken."

She wanted to embrace the disconsolate, to embrace each of the lonely or hardened people she saw, and comfort them. *If only each one had someone who loved him or her and wouldn't let go.*

When he stopped for a red light, Mendle looked at a small group of people, desolate, congregated on the sidewalk, staring into nothing. *Estranged*, Mendle thought as he focused on the unhappy faces. They were estranged from what he, too, imagined possible for the human race. *They're embracing the dark as all they know.*

The signal turned green and, as they drove off, Aira took a lingering look back at them, then she covered her face in her hands.

Even after some months with her, Mendle was not used to it and still rejoiced at the company of another who wouldn't accept travesties as "normal life." Her response to them was even more disquieted than his own. He listened to her crying, familiar with the doleful mourning he had seen sometimes when she saw what was called "the news" on television. Reports of wars, of murders, robbery, environmental plundering and hunger affected her as if it were happening to her personally. She was also moved to tears by acts of heroism which she described as 'service to more than personal comfort and desire, despite threat of loss or death.'

"What is wrong with us?" she bemoaned.

Us?

"When will we get it right?"

We? Mendle protested her use of terms. *How can she lump herself in with the rest of the human race?* He had wanted to ask about her navel, or the lack of one, but hadn't. It became harder to bring up, for some reason, the more he wondered how to do so.

They were crossing the intersection just before their freeway exit when an approaching vehicle turned left directly in front of him. Mendle slammed his palm on the horn, flattening it into a blaring honk. The blast jolted Aira. She looked up, scared. They barely missed a van. As they skidded across the road, Mendle turned the wheel into the spin. He maneuvered to avoid hitting another car in the oncoming lane. The sound of the horn seemed to go on forever.

"Stupid idiot!" Mendle cursed as he got the car back into control. He looked in his rearview mirror and saw the van speed off. "I don't believe some people on the road." He turned to Aira. "Are you all right?"

She barely heard him. She was looking at Onx who was in the back seat. The white dog was sitting squarely on her haunches, petrified in that position with her front paws in the air, looking like a statue ready for take-off. Just as Aira was getting seriously concerned, the dog came out of it and started panting happily.

"Everything's fine," Aira murmured, turning back around in her seat.

"What's that?" Mendle asked. He sat up a little to angle his gaze into the back seat through the rearview mirror. His eyes made contact with the dog's and the animal looked away, as if caught at something. "Smelled like sulphur, or something burning," Mendle said.

When Aira didn't say anything, he glanced over at her. She was staring straight ahead, her mouth slightly agape. Mendle managed to divide his attention between the road and glances to her.

Her voice sounding vaporous, nearly whispering, she said, "I remembered something."

Her statement had a major impact on Mendle, and he waited for her to go on.

"I know it was something. It just flashed, like a definite something there, something from my past. There was really something there!"

Mendle steadied the car in his fast-moving lane heading north on the 101 freeway.

Aira shook her head. She let out a little laugh. "It was the horn. The sound of the horn triggered something. I saw cars. And heard a horn. Only it was in my past, I know it was my memory. It was really loud, and it came closer. I was standing in the road." She paused, then conjectured, "I think I was hit by a car."

Of course, an injury or an accident was the most feasible reason for the girl's amnesia, but disappointment was Mendle's instant response. "What happened?" he asked her.

Aira thought about it. "It's an actual memory," she said, pleased to have it. "It's right there. I saw a car." She closed her eyes and reveled in being able to think back and touch an actual piece of past. The sense of being able to look backward and see something, even if only for moments, felt like an anchor of relief in a horizonless sea.

Mendle swallowed hard. "Good, great, wow." He made utterances of happiness for her—sincere, even though mixed with other emotions.

"I saw it," Aira exuberated, reaching for the memory again. "The street. It was wet. It was raining. And the horn. I was running. The horn is blaring. I turn, and there's a car…coming at me."

"Okay…" Mendle encouraged her.

"There's screeching rubber. It was trying to stop, and the horn…" Aira trailed off when she saw nothing more. "I don't know." She sighed a long exhale. "Everything goes black. I think I was hit. I see stars." She marveled over it for some seconds then desperation for more edged her voice as she said, "That was all I saw, like a flash."

"That's okay," Mendle assured her. "See, it'll come back to you. Just as we said. Just don't worry, and you'll see."

Suffering amnesia as a result of a car accident was not what he had expected to hear. He settled back in his driver's seat and fought off a threat of loss. He wasn't sure exactly why the feeling was impending.

"I'm hungry," Aira said.

"Me too," Mendle told her. "It's the sea air. Always makes me hungry."

"Let's have some fruit juice!"

Mendle nodded. She had the way of suggesting the simplest thing and making it sound like it was the most fabulous, original idea in the universe.

Running his hand back through his hair, gently tugging on it, Mendle wished his mental dilemma would be over. For the millionth time, he wished something, just one thing, could be clear-cut, black or white. What was his lot, to be continually sifting through thoughts, through appearances, trying to determine reality from illusion? An all-too-familiar irritation returned like sandpaper to his insides. He gripped the steering wheel tighter and set his jaw. The traffic and surroundings assigned him his place, and he resigned himself to being just one insignificant peon in a long chain of luminescent red taillights.

"What's troubling you?" Aira's voice was soft, mellifluous.

Mendle shook his head, then didn't resist confiding. "I get confused," he told her, feeling her in attendance as an understanding witness of his life. "I don't feel very comfortable sometimes." He struggled how to explain it. "Sometimes I feel like I don't belong. As though I'm apart, and don't fit. Things just seem…crazy. I don't know. I wonder what's real."

Quiet filled the car as they drove through darkness in the glow of dashboard controls. Long red and white lights snaked the highway.

"Well it *does* seem a little crazy around here," Aira answered out of the silence.

"Yeah, but compared to what?" Mendle asked her.

"I guess compared to ideals," she decided, sighing. "Sometimes I feel like I want to go home. I look at other people, I think they want to go home, too." She shrugged. "Maybe we all feel strange here."

Mendle shot her a quick look, trying to pierce what she meant. She was looking ahead out the windshield. Concentrating on his driving, he silently reproached and chastised himself for always having to attach outer space or cosmic implications to everything. He reached over and turned on the radio, admonishing himself, *Home isn't necessarily Mars or Venus.*

"…that mission to Mars was in July 1976." A talk show was in progress. "The satellite pictures that came back of the Cydonia Desert clearly showed, on the surface of Mars, a one mile long and 1500 feet high humanoid face, and a collection of pyramids. These were NASA photographs," the host confirmed.

Mendle's arm hairs rose as he registered the topic of the talk show. He glanced over to check Aira's reaction. She appeared involved in her own thoughts, her face beautiful in the rhythmed illuminations cast by passing car headlights. She did not appear fazed or interested in the topic.

Another coincidence. It means something, Mendle thought. *My thought 'Mars' coincided with the word on the broadcast.* He challenged himself. He pushed another tuner button on the radio. The frequency slid and stopped. "…I want a dream lover…" *That song.* He listened to it play. "…so I don't have to dream alone…Dream Lover…"

It was like feeling the finger of Existence tapping him on the shoulder, but he never turned to look quickly enough. As soon as he looked, it had…reabsorbed into "normalcy."

Mendle pushed the tuner button again. "UFO. Hoax or reality? Tune in Saturday on NBC. More than four million Americans have reported abductions by aliens. It's a special you won't want to miss."

"Would you like me to find something?" Aira asked.

Mendle withdrew his right hand which was hovering over the radio controls. "Sure," he told her, leaning back. "Okay."

He sighed. *Quantum theory proposes that matter does not seem able to exist without Thought to perceive it. What is the relationship? What is reality?*

He reined in his thoughts and scoffed at himself as freeway traffic thickened from a flow to an ooze. *One car in a string of thousands, and I'm trying to prove that it all means something, that I mean something.*

Sandra didn't turn on the light. She kept the flashlight low to the floor as she forced her vision around the garage room where Mendle's "guest" was staying. *This chick is hiding something, two and two are not adding up to four,* Sandra justified using the extra key she had never returned to Mendle. As she looked at the cot in the corner of the room, she wondered if the girl was sleeping there or with Mendle in the house. She had watched her turn out the light up there one night when she was surveilling. *They've got to be sleeping together by now,* Sandra speculated. *Unless he's past that phase and into his need-my-space celibacy stage.*

She directed the light beam around the room, careful not to flash by any windows. The circle of light landed on the closet where it isolated the handles as a good place for prints. As she stealthily dusted the area and lifted fingerprints, her heart was in her throat; the beating kept her on-edge-alert to sounds of any approaching cars.

All too neat, all too coy, she thought, glancing at some cut-out stars and planets she assumed Aira had pasted on the window.

And the books, she mentally hissed at a small stack mathematics books as they came into the circular illumination she directed across the table. *And this is definitely weird,* Sandra thought, holding the light on a stack of Zaxxon Space Scout decals and other game posters. *Isn't she a little too old for video games?* Sandra picked up one of the silvery decals. *Contrived or what? Nut targets science fiction writer. What better bait than what's in a person's own mind?*

"Pushing his buttons," she fumed under her breath as she got up.

As she was taping another set of prints from the bathroom door another car drove by. Sandra froze and couldn't bear the apprehension any longer. *These are enough prints,* she decided, counting six plates she had taped. She carefully placed everything back into her gym bag, wiped the lampblack off the bathroom door, and tiptoed to her exit.

One last look over the room satisfied her. *I've got your fingerprints, babe.* She clicked off her flashlight, made sure the door was locked behind her, and started down the side stairs behind the garage.

Well, if you don't know who you are, let's see if somebody else might, she was thinking as she removed her gloves and slipped them into her bag.

She cut across the lawn and quickly headed down the sidewalk leading to the side street where her car was parked out of sight. Before turning the corner, she looked back and saw a set of headlights on Valleyheart Drive; they slowed down and turned into Mendle's driveway.

Just in time, Sandra gloated as she slipped into her driver's seat. The car felt good. It was new, shiny; she looked rich.

Around the globe, night and day revolved into one another. Some people on the planet were aware of deciding what they were doing, others were not knowing and just reacting. Some questioned Life; others didn't.

In some places it was night; in other places it was day. Some people said the sky was black and there were stars in it. Some people said the sky was blue and the sun was in it. Some only saw clouds. They were all right.

chapter

24

The Video Arcade was a cacophony of dings, buzzes, and electronic phrases. Occasional seven-note melodies rose above the din. Aira glanced at the wall clock and decided she had time to play one more game before heading back to meet Mendle at the house. He had only recently relaxed about her being out unaccompanied; she didn't want to worry him by being gone too long.

Slipping her coins into the Zaxxon machine, she was off. The craft hovered over the enemy gate. Aira successfully maneuvered it through the narrow opening.

Zoom. She swooped down and discharged three missiles. *Blam.* The fuel depot exploded. *Blam! Blam!* Two enemy planes gone.

An electrically barbed fence. She had to act fast and pulled back on the controls, zipping up just in time to avoid it.

Close call, she thought. *Zip,* to the left to avoid the enemy's defense missiles that hurtled at her. *Zip,* to the right to avoid the massive brick wall, then up—a little slower to ensure passage through another tight channel—then down.

Pweeoo, pweeo, pweeo, pweeo, four more missiles discharged; she hit two enemy ships, missed the fuel depot, but got a radar tracking device. The enemy defense squad was coming at her now. Faster. She had to dodge and fire with more dexterity, with total attention; there was absolutely no margin for error.

She got through it with no damage and now carefully gauged her exit through another narrow passage at the end of the enemy field. Aira leaned back a little in relief, but only for a moment.

She had to prepare for the next level. Her left hand rested agilely on the missile control, her right hand clasped the flight control. She knew she had yet to face the worst—the closer she got to Zaxxon, the tighter the defenses would be.

Another wall up ahead. It was a little different. She had to think fast. Getting past this one was not only a tight squeeze, but also a dangerous maneuver. As soon as she cleared it, she would have to nose-dive thirty feet immediately to avoid the radar net, then swerve sharply to the right to avoid being exploded by the mine.

She held her breath, her grip tightened on the controls as she gauged her distances. She kept her wrist flexible.

A deft maneuver, another, then another, and she made it back up to cruise altitude. She exhaled quickly but couldn't relax because unexpected scouter crafts hurtled at her.

Pweeo. Pweeeo. She fired. She hit two and avoided being blown up by the rest.

It was then that she became aware of another presence, standing behind her, a little to her left. She tried to ignore it, but it took just enough of her attention that she misjudged clearance through a gate. *Smash.* Her craft slammed into it and was obliterated into disintegration.

She stomped her foot and slammed her hand on the cabinet, then looked over her shoulder to see who it was. Someone was waiting to play. Aira turned back to her controls. She still had another run to go.

"You got twenty minutes off one quarter," a boy said to her when she finished. A small group of admirers had gathered around her.

"You were really into it," somebody said.

"That was a pretty good run," Aira said, satisfied, her tone ardent, as if she were talking about the real thing, not a game. She refocused on her surroundings as she stepped back to relinquish the game. It had seemed so real.

A voice interrupted her thoughts. "You're good at that."

Aira turned to see a lanky man grinning at her, scratching his chin. "Cool shoes," he pointed at her metallic silver oxfords.

By the time Aira nodded and was about to thank him, he was saying, "Check out the jacket," referring to the silver baseball jacket she was wearing.

There was a group of girls leaning on the video machine next to them who overheard him, even though he lowered his voice. "Uh, you want to go out sometime?" he asked Aira. As the girls were reaching puberty and their bodies were preparing to reproduce, this was a topic of some interest to them, so they made an effort to listen closely.

"Out where?" Aira asked, curious.

He laughed. "Pretty wild," he said, then, "We could get it on."

The lack of expression on Aira's face confounded him. He stuck his hands in his pockets and pulled his shoulders in a little tighter around his neck and waited. Then he lowered his voice some more and said, "I mean, if you're as good in bed as you are at that," he nodded toward the video game, "we can have a pretty good time."

"How amazingly genetic," Aira marveled.

"What?"

"I'm curious." Aira wondered. "Did I do something to give you the impression that I would want to merge with you?"

The girls standing behind them started giggling. It began as a low snicker, but the more they tried to control it, the harder it seemed to push through them. Their eyes kindled each other whenever they made contact and soon the laughter was cross-flowing in moderate squeals.

The man turned to look at them, his hands still in his pockets. They covered their mouths with their hands, as though that would stop or conceal their laughter, and turned their heads away, darting only sidelong glances at him.

Embarrassment burned his ears, but he forced himself to laugh. It came out as a guffaw. He meant to project that he was willing to be the brunt of fun; in fact, he wasn't, but he kept on grinning.

"Merge?" he smirked. "I've never heard it called that. Genetic?"

"Totally genetic!" one of the girls bantered under her breath to her friends. The others followed suit, the phrase making them laugh all over again each time they said it.

Sensitive to his discomfort, Aira assured, "I'm not making fun of you. I just wondered what I did, if I gave some sign to make you think I wanted to merge, you know, mate, have sex with you. I find this all very interesting."

"Wild." He scratched his head.

"I'm observing all this," she explained.

Torn between believing the earnest expression on Aira's face and fear of being taken for a fool, he shrugged. "Body language," he finally answered. "You're good-looking and you play it up. Your hair. You know."

Aira thought about what he had said. He looked on as she considered it. "I love beauty," she finally said, "I love it in all things, but I don't understand how it's a signal for sex."

He was staring at her, at the way she talked, at what she was saying, finding her mesmerizing in an incomprehensible, slightly scary way.

She was saying, "I've thought about it, about merging in sex, but I can't leave myself out of things. I don't think I like you that much, and you don't seem to really like or even see me."

"Huh?"

"I've noticed my body does have certain impulses," Aira explained, "but I could not let it merge with another and leave myself out of it. Don't you see?"

They stared at one another, she eager to communicate ideas, he beginning to become suspicious.

"It has impulses?" he asked thickly.

Aira scanned his face then explained, "Well, sure." Happy to stumble on a conclusion, she added, "I think perhaps you're just feeling a thrust, but it's not coming from you since you don't really know me. Maybe it's coming from your organs."

She was fervently sincere, but her words caused the girls to scream with laughter.

"Wild," he said. "Pretty far out." He leaned over a little and mumbled, "You high?"

Aira thought it. "I'm about five feet and five inches," she told him.

He started laughing and Aira felt a flood of pleasure about the interaction of new friendships.

Wanting to make his offer for a date more enticing, the man wound down his laughter and next muttered to Aira, so low it was barely audible to her, "I've got some great coke. Or acid if you're into that."

"Oh no!" Aira gasped, alarmed, realizing what he meant. "Do I look like I want to damage myself?"

"Hey!" He scowled and motioned with his hands for her to quiet down. When she looked at him curiously he told her, "I'm doing some right now," as though he were a very important person. "It's phenomenal."

Aira felt intense compassion for the stupidity she perceived in the person's face. No wonder he wasn't seeing her, she realized, the person was obfuscated by delusions and fears. There was a synthetic energy pouring off him, an electrification that at first deceptively seemed like enthusiasm. *His synapses are frying.*

She held herself back from speaking, not wanting to create the wrong effect on him. *The drugs increase risk of misunderstanding or disorientation,* she was thinking, but when he told her that he had come down from an acid trip yesterday and was "riding on coke," she thought she had better say something. Aira gasped, "Don't you know?"

"What?"

"Lysergic acid was devised as a warfare technique. By psychiatrists in World War II. To put in water systems to disorient entire populations."

"Naw."

"Yes!" she affirmed emphatically. "Why warp your view of things? I mean, by observing, by really looking and seeing, you can have heights and freedom beyond your dreams. You're playing into their hands. That's it! That's it, I just saw it."

"Whad'you see? You psychic? What's your sign?"

"No, it's about making people into slaves. A drug culture. Asleep, enmeshed in sensation, forgetting. Listen, befriend yourself…"

Aira thought the man was really getting what she herself was realizing as she spoke. He was looking at her intently, but he suddenly squawked, "Are you for real?"

Aira started to consider his question. *Am I for real?*

He continued. "Who needs reality? I'm bored with reality," he told her, with disgust for both it and her.

"But a drug doesn't give you any powers…"

"Not so loud."

"…it saps them, and scrambles you up. It's a low level divertissement, getting little jolts of thrills of sensory sensation, and—"

"Hey. Yo. Divertwhat?"

"French, it means amusement. Amazing, I just knew that somehow."

"I don't speak no French, baby, except when I kiss maybe. Ha ha."

She regarded him calmly, then apologized. "You're right." She pervaded him and extrapolated a language from him. "Listen man, I'll tell you a thing or two. You talk about being outta your gourd, but it's because you got poison up your ass."

Now she was speaking a language he understood. He took a step back and his eyes widened as his attention became riveted on her. When she finished, he smiled slyly. "What's your game, baby?"

"I must be a linguist," Aira told him, marveling herself at an ability that seemed to spontaneously come to her. "Last week I didn't even speak French."

"Go on, you jive turkey."

Seeing she was losing him, she went back to his idiom. "Listen, dude, chemicals in your body make it a prison. No shit. Is that what you want? You want your body to be a prison?" Her words triggered something and she suddenly stared off.

"Whoa, man, you just lit up. Or is that me? You just glowed, man. Or am I seeing things? Didn't you?"

She glanced at a reflection of herself in the Arcade mirror wall and, for a split instance, saw an incandescent aura around her body.

A realization flashed. "Wow!"

"You saw it, too? Geez. Trails, man."

"I didn't used to have a body!" She turned away from him all agog in her own personal excitement.

"Anyone ever tell you you're str-a-a-n-nge?"

"That was me!"

"Get off it." He looked overhead. "It was the lights." He laughed. "Strange girl."

"I remember. For a moment, I could feel it! I didn't use to have a body!" Aira was enthusiastic.

"Well you sure as fuck got one now." He grinned.

Aira looked at him hard. "It's sad that your idea of freedom is the use of supposedly forbidden words. You could be much more free."

The idea made it over to him.

"My dog's outside, I have to go," she announced.

"Okay, okay. I got some really good weed. A couple a hits. You could use it. Mellow out, man."

"No, no," Aira declined, shaking her head, annoyed with him now. "Don't you get it?"

"This I gotta hear." Some mental mechanisms in him had rallied to keep him locked inside, but he was in there listening.

"*Cannabis sativa* confuses time relativity," she told him.

"What the fuck are you talking about?"

"Time relativity. You know. Memory placing things in time. What happened—when—in what sequence." Aira focused on him again. He wasn't getting it. So with steel intention that hit him like fifty pounds, she said it in his language. "I don't want to be fucked up."

The man pulled his hands out of his pockets and reached for a soda he had parked on one of the game machines. He paused, perching above the can he lifted to his lips, then sneered. "Who needs time?" before taking a big gulp.

"You're living in it," Aira said, flatly serious.

He shrugged and turned away from her. "Hey, whas goin' on? Whas happenin'?" he called out to the girls nearby.

His greeting landed like the punch line of a joke; the girls' laughter was intermixed with teenage panoplies of disdain and make-up.

"Totally genetic," quipped the redhead to her friend. They embraced, and abandoned themselves to giggling.

"Yo, shit," he said, then turned. He was going to kiddingly tell Aira, "Now look what you've done," but she was gone. He shook his head as he looked around. Suddenly self-conscious, he pretended to spot someone across the room. He waved to the imaginary destination and set off in that direction, so no one would think he was alone.

The wind was in her hair; the day was sunny. Aira walked on exhilaration derived from the sensation of flying through space. The pride of operating a ship, as she had vividly imagined while playing the game Zaxxon Space Scouts, still pulsed in her. Onx, happy finally to be redeemed at the entrance of the Arcade, trotted happily beside Aira in the afternoon sunshine.

"Onx, you beautiful, noble creature," Aira stopped a moment to pet and tousle the animal's coat. As she straightened up she said, "I just don't understand why people use chemicals to lessen their thinking capacity."

She resumed walking, thinking about the man who had approached her at the Arcade. He appeared shocked when she attributed his sexual impulse to biological origins, sex organs. When she mentioned his organs directly, his facial expression evidenced a feeling of being violated, even though he had first alluded to having sex with her.

How strange, Aira pondered curiously, *that sex is something which seems to be done with such facility, yet to address it logically or communicate about it is apparently taboo. It seems as though people use sex to prevent getting to know each other.*

In looking around her now, and also drawing from observations made while watching television, Aira concluded that the civilization virtually pivoted around being sexually attractive. Images of buttocks, bulging shoulders, and shiny women's lips were even used to sell products which, to her point of view, had nothing to do with sex. Transportation for instance. *What is a sexy car? What do automobiles have to do with sexual sensation, or even the purpose of procreating the species?*

The "old movies," as Mendle called them, though she had no recollection of seeing them before, were different. They focused more on the faces and individual characters of human beings, and on the dialogue, which was unique to each person. But media of current years highlighted body parts—legs, breasts, shoulders, and buttocks—as if it were those things having relationships.

This was still a matter of curiosity to her, and, just as she was ruminating on it, her gaze met a huge billboard across the street of buttocks clad in blue jeans. It fueled her perplexity. *There are mostly such bill-*

boards lining the street, she noticed as she made her way down Ventura Boulevard. Any human faces she did see on the ads seemed arrogant, or angry, or perched on a sexual pain-beauty peak.

There was a movie she had seen one late night on television called *Babes On Broadway.* In trying to discern what was different about it that she liked, she decided it was because things happened on the inside of the people. *More like real living.* It was so in many of the "old" movies.

Survival of the spirit, she pondered as she looked down at her feet stepping one in front of the other, then at her hands. She opened and clenched her fists. *That is not me.*

"Oh wow," she mumbled under her breath, then looked up in amazement at the thought.

She watched people around her, getting into their cars, walking into shops, riding bicycles. "They actually think they are nothing more than organisms," she gasped. She stopped walking, amazed, and stared at people around her. So many seemed empty.

Aira suddenly knew the only way a person could really die. *And when they die, they become walking, talking vacant shells.*

Death occurred by compromising love, caring, and duties, by going against one's own beliefs because of imagined "survival." Even though actions that compromised personal belief could put food on the table and provide housing, survival was an illusion at that level because the body ate well, but the person died a slow death.

It's by going against dear principles, that's how a splintering takes place which disintegrates a being's very self. Aira's newfound conclusion excited her, and she felt an urge to share it. If she could tell people around her of this discovery, they might be happier. *Sure. They're forgetting about what they really are,* she decided, surging with a feeling that she could be of service. That was what she liked about those old movies, they were about survival of the true person.

Joy welled in Aira at the thought of being able to create a good effect, at being of service. Anything seemed possible. She felt as though she were awakening from a long sleep. Frustration began to peel off her, and the day felt like a jubilee.

"It's the word integrity!" she concluded aloud, turning the head of a woman walking by. "Integrity. It means whole and undivided! Not broken into pieces." She continued walking down the sidewalk.

Onx trotted beside Aira, tapping into her joyful mood as she thought aloud. "Of course! The word 'corrupt' comes from *corumpere,* Latin, to break into pieces. Wow! How did I know that?"

Aira looked down at Onx. Spontaneously, she interrupted her gait to drop to her knees and embrace the dog. "Oh, Onx!" she exclaimed happily. "I saw some truth! Living really is about love. We have to let the others know!"

An attorney and his client sidestepped her and the animal on the sidewalk, briefly casting an amused second glance at them over their shoulders.

"Onx!" Aira said, looking into the dog's eyes. "If only I could be completely as I am on the inside, I could do anything!"

She felt herself regenerating. "I'm my dreams, my thoughts, my ideals, I'm *me*. I'm not *matter*." She looked up. "It's not really inside even. I'm just moving around, connected to…this body. It's…as if…I, my very self, is something different than anything I see. *That's* what I have to keep alive!" She stared at her arms and down at her torso curiously again. "That's what has to survive. Me." *The light. The thought.* She transferred her pondering gaze to Onx. "Could that be?"

Onx suddenly averted her eyes. Her tongue, which had been happily lolling out of the side of her mouth, retracted. She hung her head.

"Onx. What's the matter?"

Aira's question elicited a small whine. Onx made sheepish eye contact in sidelong glances; the animal seemed embarrassed.

"Did you understand me, Onx?" Aira cajoled. Onx feigned a blank look at the ankles of a passerby.

"You did!" Aira exclaimed. "You did, didn't you? You understand words! And you're embarrassed because you're content to be a dog, and don't want to let on you know any more. That's it, isn't it?" Onx dropped her head again and looked at Aira from the corner of one eye.

A woman quickly tugged her child past Aira and Onx on the sidewalk.

"It's all right, Onx. You can take on as much responsibility as you want. There's a lot to being a dog," Aira assured her. "You're wonderful. You're loyal, courageous, and very beautiful. You're the most noble dog in the universe."

Aira was petting Onx's thick white fur as she spoke. The dog sat up straighter with every word until her stance was proud and erect. Soon she was blissfully panting again.

"And," Aira finished playfully, holding her finger out in mock scolding, "you pretend to be a lot dumber than you really are!"

Just as she said the words, before they were even complete, Aira was seized by a distinct sense that she had said them before. The very words, the very scene, seemed to jar something familiar, as if she had done it all before, but anything specific completely alluded her. She straightened up and got off her knees, curiously wondering about it.

In the office building's Coffee Shop, Sandra Wilford waited in line to pay for a cappuccino and a strawberry yogurt. She perused the news stand, her eyes resting on the cover of a fashion magazine where, from a photo, a cheery, if vapid, model smiled over the top of abundant, if silicone, cleavage. Sandra thought the woman was beautiful; it angered her. Hatred for the model's projected confident attitude began to swarm in her, and she did not even consider it strange. Sandra was filled with a desire to undo, to kill, to damage, and she related to this as healthy, competitive aggression.

She released the internal chaos by inconspicuously resting her thumb on some chocolate Christmas candies and systematically puncturing six Santas. It was as senseless as that. When Sandra looked down and saw the maimed, cracked holiday merchandise she had damaged, the satisfaction that buoyed up in her was translated by herself to be good "drive."

"Is that all you're having?" an office worker asked, coming up behind her and startling her.

Sandra tossed a dismayed scowl over her shoulder. "You scared me", she whined, seeing it was Karen from the advertising department. She wondered if the woman saw her poke in the faces on the chocolate Santa Clauses.

"I'm sorry," the woman apologized.

"That's all right, Karen."

"Actually I should take a hint from you," the co-employee said, nodding at Sandra's coffee and yogurt, and waving her package of pink coconut-spreckled Choco-balls in comparison.

"Oh," Sandra said tautly, taking quick inventory of Karen's body: brow lines, dark roots showing at the hairline, a little pudgy. "Don't worry about it. Your look is popular."

"Look at this," the woman said, noticing the trashed candies. "Somebody did this on purpose," she declared, holding them up.

"Disgusting," Sandra pronounced idly.

"Who would do such a thing?"

Sandra shook her head. "It's despicable. People like that should be shot," she said self-righteously, distracting her attention from the candy to the magazine rack once again. Her gaze traveled to a headline in the tabloid section: **SPACE ANGELS MYSTERY SOLVED.**

"It's uncanny, isn't it?" Sandra mused to Karen as she picked up *The World Weekly*. "When we think about something we start seeing things we never saw before. Like buying a car, I guess. Before you or a friend buy a certain model or color, you never notice how many there are on the road. Buy it, you suddenly start seeing them everywhere."

"Have you been thinking about Space Angels?" the woman kidded about the tabloid.

Sandra snorted. "Right." She thumbed to the inside story, then turned back to peruse the cover. "I have a friend who's a science fiction writer," she told her as she scanned the introductory paragraph:

> Russian cosmonauts who sighted a band of gigantic angels on a space mission last summer saw immortal super-beings of pure energy, says a top Russian scientist. Dr. Yury Kovmana said he hoped to dismiss the celestial sighting as a hallucination, but was unable to do so. (Story continued on centerfold)

"I like the one they had last month," Karen said when she finished reading over Sandra's shoulder. "The alien playing golf with the President, advising him on world issues. It was an actual photograph." She laughed. "Did you see that?"

"No," Sandra said. When a passing glance determined the manager at the check-out counter was admiring her, she tossed her sleek hair nonchalantly.

Encouraging Sandra to go ahead and read the story, Karen referred to the people in line ahead of them. "Looks like it'll be at least a couple of more minutes."

Sandra shot an impatient look to the new cashier who was familiarizing herself with the register under a manager's supervision.

"It's either this or 'Ten Pound Baby Born Out of Forty-three Year Old Man,'" Karen joked, reading off another headline on the rack.

Sandra opened the paper and they both leaned in to read the article:

> RUSSIANS SOLVE SPACE ANGELS MYSTERY.....Reports that Russian cosmonauts sighted a band of angels on a space mission last summer have been disputed by a Russian researcher who says the celestial apparitions were actually fields of pure energy and alien intellect.
>
> In an interview with French journalist Andre Dezure, Dr. Kovmana said the cosmonauts initially referred to the beings as angels simply because they had wings. But now that all the facts are in, he said there can be no doubt: The creatures descended from a race of humanoids who shed their bodies after reaching the top of the evolutionary ladder.

They read into the smaller print:

> As reported in *The World Weekly* last October, the cosmonauts claimed to have seen the beings while orbiting the earth in Salyut 9 three months earlier. Accounts of the incident smuggled to the West quoted the cosmonauts as saying that a brilliant orange glow engulfed their craft. The source of the light, they said, "was seven giant figures in the form of humans, but with wings and mist-like halos." Accounts were signed by all three cosmonauts.
>
> The 43 seconds of film they got were enormously revealing, says the scientist. "The forms seem to change continually," he said. "The beings appear solid, then misty."
>
> Curiously, government officials who once denied that the cosmonauts saw anything extraordinary now respond to queries with "no comment."

Sandra shook her head as she folded the paper up and put it back in the rack.

"What if it really is true, and we think it's just too incredible to believe, have you ever thought of that?" Karen proposed.

"Right," Sandra said. "And JFK is alive in Argentina."

"He is?"

Sandra disguised her disdain for the woman's stupidity under cajoling incredulity. "Right. He married Evita." She rolled her eyes and, her tone between jab and jest, complained, "Some people'll believe anything."

Upstairs, Sandra launched a quick smile into the room of co-workers as she backed into her office. The smile evaporated the instant she stepped inside and closed the door behind her. Her eyes narrowed with a sense of pragmatism all her own as she hoisted her briefcase onto her desk. "Let's get down to facts," she briskly told herself.

She accessed a database on her computer and had it dial the number she was looking for.

"Scientific Services," someone answered.

"Fingerprint department. John Hobbins, please."

As she waited for the inspector to come to the phone, Sandra admired her Cocoa Rouge nail polish, then pressed the latches to open her briefcase. She checked on the little plates she had carefully secured in the zippered pocket.

"Mr. Hobbins," she greeted him efficiently when he came to the phone. "Sandra Wilford. You remember, last year? United Press. I was doing the story on the war crime. The conviction that took place as a result of a fingerprint found on that postcard from 1942?"

"Oh yeah. Sure."

"Did you ever get the copy of the article?"

"Yes, I did. Appreciate it."

"It's my pleasure. Anything to help justice in any small way I can," Sandra politicalized. "I want to thank you again for your cooperation, Mr. Hobbins." She carefully inserted his name to give an impression of sincerity. "Your information was invaluable."

"Happy it was of help."

"Couldn't have done it without you. What you and Detective Sims showed me about lifting fingerprints was useful to me recently. Your abilities amaze me." Sandra layered in a flow of nearly imperceptible sensual tonality. In the silence that followed, she read that flattery wasn't a particular vulnerability of his. She continued, "In fact, that's what I'm calling about. Research on another story. Finding people. Missing people. Double identities. Things like that. I was wondering if I might not be able to drop by. It's a fascinating article. Some of your expertise on finding out about…certain individuals, would be invaluable to the public. 'Pro bono publicum' and all."

"Well, I…"

Overriding the hesitancy in his voice before it densified, Sandra interjected, "It won't take but a few minutes." She laced in mystery for adhesive. "It's a very delicate…uh…*confidential* matter. Your expertise on my research would be very greatly appreciated."

He toppled into agreement after a split moment of indecision. "That'll be fine," he told her. "Just set it up anytime between eight and four."

Sandra acted surprised. "Why thank you, Mr. Hobbins." A smile in her voice, none on her face, she set it up. "How about today?"

"How soon can you get here?"

Glancing at the chrome and crystal wall clock, she answered, "Let's see…West Beverly. I can be there after lunch. Let's say by two thirty?"

"See you then."

Sandra replaced the phone receiver in its cradle and sighed as she swiveled her chair away from the desk. *I'm going to have to improvise,* she thought as she stared out the window. She would be more convincing in person, she decided.

Contemplating the fingerprints, Sandra thought it was a long shot that the strange woman living with Mendle was wanted or had a record anywhere. It could be, however, that the prints were of record on something as simple as a driver's license somewhere.

It was only a string. But she had it between her fingers. She started to pull on it. And all strings led somewhere.

chapter

25

Her silver jacket and shoes glinted with sunlight. "Come on!" Aira broke into a run from skipping down the sidewalk then headed across the street, Onx bounding after her.

A shrill whistle pierced the air. Somehow Aira knew it was meant for her and she stopped, turning to look. A uniformed policeman sauntered toward her, cheek muscles rippling from a clenched jaw. As Aira hopped back onto the curb, he asked, "Do you see a crosswalk there?"

"Crosswalk? Oh! The painted lines." She looked, "No."

"I'm afraid I'm going to have to ticket you for jaywalking," he informed her.

"Oh, don't be afraid," she cooed reassuringly, taking him literally. She inspected the spot she had crossed the road. "You're right, I did jaywalk," she said. "I didn't know what jaywalking was until you just told me. I had to think about it, then I knew. That's how I know things. First I don't know, then I think about them, and *know*. Most things anyway."

The officer studied her.

"I did it twice, in fact," Aira realized. "When I came back to see what you wanted, I jaywalked again."

Not taking his eyes off her as he pulled out his ticket pad, the officer tried to determine if the citizen was ridiculing authority. He started tapping the pad with his pen, tightening and releasing his jaw, as if he were chewing something.

Aira looked at the pad. "A ticket," she realized, then told the officer nicely, "You don't have to go to all that trouble." She was proud to tell him, "I'm easy to correct."

Noting the furrowing brow over the man's hazel eyes, she explained, "I don't need penalties, you see. I correct myself, and reason works quite well with me. That's the best method of control in a social order. I understand now, the reason for this law." She paused, then added, beaming, "It's only logical for us all to work together."

They hung in a moment of suspense as they looked at each other—Aira an earnest smile on her face, the officer trying to congruate her naive appearance and the concepts she was spouting.

"Why weren't you watching where you were going?" he quizzed.

"I was. I looked both ways. There wasn't any traffic approaching," Aira explained enthusiastically.

As her buoyancy increased, so did the officer's suspicion. *Pupils are dilated,* he noted. "What are we so happy about today?" he asked.

"How nice of you to inquire," Aira expressed, pleased by his interest. "I was thinking about integrity and survival, and I realized—"

She had barely launched her account when the officer interrupted her, "You on something?"

Aira looked around, then down at her feet. "I'm on the sidewalk," she obliged him.

"Don't get smart."

"You don't like intelligence, either?"

"Your pupils look a little wide there."

"They always do when I'm in deep concentration," Aira explained, then went on with her account. "I also think that sex is used by many people as a way of avoiding real communication. I was also thinking about sexy cars, and realized if such a thing really existed it might be very convenient because a person could purchase two, a male and female, and they would procreate a new car. I understand cars are a major expense and—"

Deciding the girl was being evasive, "All right, all right," he stopped her. "Let's not get smart."

The statement again made no sense whatsoever to Aira. "Why not?" She wanted to know. Being smart, she thought, was a desirable attainment.

Before their interchange could continue, however, Onx began to growl.

"Onx," Aira said, surprised.

She reached down and petted the dog, and was suddenly alarmed by a small puff of smoke she noticed issuing out of the Samoyed's nose. It was phosphorescent and had an acrid, sulfuric odor. Aira dissipated the smoke with some quick waves of her hand. When she looked up perplexed, the officer didn't seem to have noticed.

"Hope you got some I.D. on you," he demanded.

Onx began to rumble some low, voracious-sounding growls that Aira had never heard before. The officer laughed and said, looking at the animal's cute face, "Vicious dog there."

"Don't let her bother you," Aira told him. She dropped to Onx's side and put her arms around her.

Patting his gun, the officer replied, "No one is going to bother me."

Aira poured a pleading look on Onx. "Don't, Onx." She squeezed the animal, feeling afraid. "What's the matter?"

When she saw the dog's eyes flash a candescent yellow, Aira sensed it was somehow connected to her, to her own fear. *Protect,* everything about the animal seemed to say.

She buried her face in Onx's neck. "I'm all right," she whispered, "Everything is okay," and when she raised her head, she noticed the dog's white fur was turning a bluish color.

The officer repeated his request for identification.

"I don't have any, except my body," Aira hastily explained to the policeman. "You can see it's me, I was just taking a walk."

"Your dog's not on a leash, either," the officer said, tapping the ticket book as his glance darted around the street.

Aira felt a pressure on the inside of the forearm with which she was embracing Onx. When she curiously lifted her arm to look under there, she was aghast by what she saw. A formation was bulging out of the dog's back. Two protrusions were trying to unfold...wings? Her heart began pounding between bewilderment and panic as she quickly lowered her arm again. *Wings.* She thought she had seen wings the night she fell from the rooftop.

Embracing Onx tighter, Aira hovered over the animal as she looked up at the officer. She had learned one thing—people either attacked or ridiculed that which they did not understand.

The officer looked down at them. "Shame," he said. "Dying such a nice animal's fur blue. If it was meant for people to have blue and pink and purple hair, don't you think you would've been made that way?"

"Please," Aira begged him. "Be nice to me."

The earnestness in her voice touched him. He instantly felt better. He was commanding respect. The officer placed his hand on his hip.

Looking at the policeman, Aira saw how he put his very life in danger everyday. *It isn't that he wants me to feel badly. He's just been fought, and is frustrated because all he really wants to do is help others.* She had read on the cars and badges "To Protect and To Serve." *Just like you, Onx,* she thought, and felt Onx settling down within her embrace. It was as if her realization about the man soothed the animal by transference. *He wants to feel he's doing his job, and he's doing it the only way he knows how.*

The policeman conceded a resigned, "All right," then said, "I wouldn't want you, or a motorist, being hurt."

"I appreciate your looking out for my welfare," Aira told him.

"I'll just leave it at a warning this time." He tucked his ticket pad away and let go a small smile, then affably quoted her, "You can correct yourself." As he sauntered off, he said, "Heaven knows the court system could use a break."

He had walked off some twenty feet before Aira registered to speak. "Thank you!" she called after him.

Looking down at Onx, she slowly let go of the animal. The wings that had begun forming out of her back were gone. Aira ran her hand up and down the animal's back. It was smooth. *Incredible.* She doubted herself. *Did I really see that? Did it happen?*

"What are you?" Aira asked Onx, her voice cracking a little.

A whine and several short whimpers came back in response.

Aira slowly rose to her feet, in a daze of wonder. It couldn't have happened, and yet she had felt it physically. She remembered the pressure on the inside of her arm. *I saw them.* She rubbed her arm where she had felt the push against it.

She continued walking, wrapped in thought. Everything seemed bizarre to her. Even prior to what had just happened, she realized, Aira had been observing the environment as though it were all bizarre; as though she weren't used to the things around her; as though she were seeing it all for the first time.

What is this place? She wondered as she looked at the street lined with fast-food stops and unhappy faces. She looked down at Onx. The dog's coat was completely white again. But it had been blue. The officer had even seen it, he had commented on it; it was blue.

Molecules…atoms…This is not solid. Looking around, Aira mused, *Maybe this is my first time here.*

The thought was not preposterous to her. In fact, it seemed to fit. Even supported by a string of known facts, it somehow made sense on its own.

Aira looked down at Onx again, keeping pace beside her. Three weeks ago the dog used to walk differently. She padded along with her nose to the ground, intent on sniffing everything that came into her path. Not anymore. Now she held her head up and looked straight ahead. She didn't sleep all the time, either. They both seemed to be regaining something…but what?

Aira flashed on an image, but it went by so fast she didn't fully see it.

Something was blocking it, it had to do with Onx; at least she thought it did, she wasn't sure; Aira looked at the dog again to see if she could retrieve it, get some sense of memory.

"What a cute dog," someone said in passing. "I used to have a Samoyed."

You are cute, Aira thought, looking at Onx trotting beside her, seeing absolutely nothing odd or strange about the animal. She turned a corner and headed down the alley which was the short cut back to Mendle's home on Valleyheart Drive.

Suddenly Aira felt a hand grip her shoulder then an arm press her throat. She was yanked backward, then shoved against a cement wall where she remained, the wind knocked out of her; she looked into a pair of crazed eyes. They seemed propped open by invisible bars, and tiny red rivulets navigated the sides of both irises.

Becoming acutely aware of the sensation of cold metal pressed against her throat, Aira cast her eyes down but couldn't see past the man's arm; she knew, however, he was threatening death. When she looked again into the eyes of her assailant, his voice spilled out hoarsely and the foulness of his breath was wretched. He nervously rasped, over and over, "The money. The money. The money. Gimme the money."

Incredible. She had a difficult time believing what was actually occurring. Then, only one thought filled her: in an instant, she could be dead. Her terror reached a state of exaltation. She sought to control it. She reasoned to stay calm, but her body's blood felt cold in her veins. She opened her mouth and was about to say something.

"Shut up or I'll kill you."

Aira wondered what would happen to her after that. *Nobody can kill me,* she thought, then immediately knew her body could die. *Then what?*

"It's all right," she told her assailant, controlling her voice, trying to calm him.

His nostrils were flared and he was breathing heavily. "The money. Money. Money. Gimme the money." He kept repeating the word "money" in a hypnotic craze.

Through her terror, Aira suddenly felt heartbroken over the pathetic figure presenting himself to her. Her voice small and plaintive, she asked, "What's happened to you?"

"Shut up. Gimme the money," he ordered desperately, and he forced the flat edge of his blade further into her neck.

She was alive, and she wanted to keep it that way. *No one has the right to threaten my life and well-being,* she thought. It was hers. Her life, her body, and, for that matter, her money.

Then again, she only had a few quarters on her, maybe three dollars, and what were a few dollars in exchange for keeping one's life? Nothing.

But the principle bothered her. It was outrageous. "Let me get this straight," Aira asked, speaking carefully. "You'll let me keep my life if I pay you?"

"Gimme the money," he hissed.

Aira despairingly admitted to herself she was a coward. She wondered how she was going to keep both, her money and her life. It wasn't so much a matter of keeping the money that was at stake. Wasting her life to preserve dollars would not necessarily be, in and of itself, a noble act of courage, she decided. But another principle was involved; it dealt with allowing a human being to commit a crime. *To let him do it,* she concluded, *would be committing a crime on him.*

"I can't move." She started to bargain. "Let go of me."

The man registered willingness to cooperate. He released pressure against Aira's neck and withdrew his hand, making sure she could see the large, gleaming blade. He lowered the knife to her ribs, and held it there, his arm cocked, elbow bent and ready to thrust.

"The money," he said. He nervously looked her over and, spotting the small purse fastened to her belt under her jacket, lunged for it.

Aira quickly jumped to the left, away from the blade, also escaping the grab with his free hand. Though anger was surging in her, her attitude was only annoyed when she said, "You feel worthless enough already! You think I should contribute to that?"

Her back was to the alley wall. Their eyes met halfway in challenge. Slowly, almost imperceptibly, Aira shifted, and the two began a ritual of swaying to the right, then to the left, shifting weight, faster and faster until they were scrambling back and forth along the wall. He was looking for a moment to stab her. She was trying to create the space to bolt past him.

Suddenly seeing an aerial perspective of themselves, Aira laughed. "Look, I refuse to be a victim," she told him.

His eyes were crazy on her. There was absolutely zero reception.

The tense, dodging interplay resumed.

"There's a policeman down the street," Aira informed him as she scuffled back and forth. "You should find him and let him give you a ticket. You don't seem very self-correcting to me."

The man appeared to be completely elsewhere, caught in a pattern which he wasn't even questioning, but playing out like a puppet. Being spoken to the way Aira scolded him, like a petulant Shirley Temple, was not what he might have expected from his target, but there was no personal contact; he couldn't reason; he was stuck.

"If you need help you could ask for it," Aira started telling him. "Needing money is one thing, but this is…" She was going to say "unacceptable", but the word remained unspoken when she glanced past him. There, standing in the alley, in turquoise-green and lavender living color, was a beautiful small dragon, about the size Onx had been, rearing on its haunches. It stood about four and a half feet tall. Its wings were extended.

The sight instantly unraveled Aira's face through a gamut of emotions to surprise. Her mouth dropped open, her eyes widened to maximum capacity, her eyebrows arched, her hands flew to her face as if making sure it was still there, to hold onto something she knew was real.

The abruptness of her surprise was just enough to send the man's head in a nervous jerk over his shoulder. When he saw the dragon, too, he jittered his knife back and forth from one hand to the other, then turned a horrified look on Aira, as though she might be able to provide an answer. When she just stared at the creature, he panicked, burst around and took a slashing lunge through the air toward the threatening hazard.

The creature's face turned as mean as it was beautiful.

A dragon! That was the image, Aira remembered, the image that had fleeted through her mind about Onx. *It's a memory,* she knew. The reality standing in front of her matched something familiar, jarred a tangible but unavailable recognition, but she couldn't place anything specific about it.

Smoke and heat began to spew from the animal's mouth.

The man's arms dropped to his sides and he screamed a short, hollow-sounding noise. He screamed again, this time it sounded as if it started in his stomach. It didn't start very loud but the timbre expanded, getting huge, until the pain mixed in the outcry sounded as though his throat were being stretched into a larger cylinder to make room for the volume passing through it.

Aira slowly stepped forward. She watched in amazement and awe.

When Onx breathed white fire, the man turned to run, slashing at Aira as he pushed past her. The sharp steel sliced through her flesh, severing the index finger of her left hand. Though Aira felt no pain at first, she felt the blow. When she looked at her hand, the finger was gone. The sight of spurting blood weakened her instantly.

She located the appendage which had been part of her lying on the asphalt. She stared at it in fear and disbelief, the oddest thought striking her before stooping to pick it up off the ground. *A moment ago I would've called that 'me.'* The fact that it was only part of the body seemed as stark as the dismembered digit lying there.

Steadying the rush of pain and fear of death flooding her, Aira looked down the alley and saw Onx swoop on the mugger and pin him against a large trash canister. The small dragon held the criminal there, fiercely spewing fire in streams to either side of the mugger's face.

The man was in sheer terror, certain that the heat was within degrees of frying his flesh. He heard the girl's voice. "All right, Onx. Just hold him." The fiery fences and choking smell of phosphorus and sulphur stopped. He could move his head but felt himself securely gripped at the shoulders by what felt like iron. The man groped for his face. It wasn't burned, just completely slick with sweat.

Aira was standing in front of him now. He looked on as she pondered her mutilated hand. Brooding over everything, she finally held her severed finger in front of his face with her right hand. Next to it she held up the bloody oozing left. The man grunted in fear and revulsion.

Inside a small brick building which faced the alley, a Mexican woman heard something which sounded like a dull scream. She went to the window and saw nothing unusual outside. Her husband smelled a peculiar acrid odor, and asked her if she, too, smelled it. "It must be tar," they agreed, answering their unknown with a something that was better than nothing. They even filled in the details around it—the construction crew was probably melting tar again, and they both hoped the main road would soon be patched. Bored, the woman shut the window to keep out the smoke and dust.

Aira confronted her assailant. The steel was hers now—not a knife, but a gaze. "Yeah," she responded, nodding her head to his horrified expression. "What do you have to say for yourself now?"

He could only stare at her chopped, bloody hand, at her severed finger, and the words he tried to speak came out only as little burps in the back of this throat.

Aira sadly cradled her hands in front of her. She positioned the finger where it was supposed to be and tightly gripped it in place, pushing hard to stop the bleeding. "Well?" she demanded of him.

"I, I, I, I," the man gurgled.

"You what? That was *my* finger, you know." Aira's voice was sullen and forceful, not angry, but intense, and that increased its impact.

The man began quivering, feeling his skulking insolence liquify inside of him. It was her eyes, the way she was looking at him. The girl's mouth was slightly pulled to one side as she held him in a long gaze, a blend of disgust, pathos, and boredom. She wasn't raging mad, she was smouldering with a vengeance that wasn't personal or arbitrary. Mixed with her fury, he also saw the despicable pity with which she regarded him.

"I, I'm," he gasped, then heaved out the last word, "sorry."

The man's eyes were a tunnel through which she traveled, traversing his hatreds and loves, his failures and domination, his anguish, his pleasures, his regrets, his dreams, his convictions, his self-betrayal, his pain. *The only way a person truly dies forever is by going against one's own self,* she thought.

He seemed to go back millennia. Hate and numbness were his final solutions before total death.

As she sought to understand him, she saw he had gone against himself so often that he was splintered and diluted. He blamed everything around him—but, in fact, it was he who had made the choices. He had reduced himself to thinking his heart didn't exist because he could not bear to feel his own pain and remorse. He deluded himself that this was a way of surviving—even though the very stuff of which he was made was now nearly nonexistent as a result. The only things he allowed himself to feel now were injuries done to him by others, because these motivated and justified his crimes.

By fooling himself that he hadn't created any of his life, by blaming others instead, by denying his decisions, he finally fulfilled his own creation—he could not create, could not decide. Others caused everything. His light had extinguished.

Yet buried in the dark there was still a spark, a dim glimmer of reason. Contracted, cowering, yet alive, it had been shunned and denied, scorned and negated. That spark was him.

Aira saw him as he was in the beginning, though she didn't know when that was. He was still there, almost a remnant of himself, but still an ember. She understood then that the only reason he had been slowly killing himself was because he had been good in the first place.

Understanding granted the basic life of him love—love, in turn, granted more understanding. The symbiosis promoted perception of how all life-beings were interrelated. Only confusion turned life-beings upon themselves and upon one another. By seeing this, the mechanisms of how it came to be focused into view. He was spun in his own confusions; wrong solutions had rendered him further ignorant and dense with regret. Perceiving, reason glimmered, and his self became restored. So Evil, the parasite, was rendered powerless.

Aira sighed, and the breath was long and deep, continuing into infinity long after she had finished suspiring. She knew fully then why it would have harmed the man to allow him to commit another crime; she had not wanted to give him another reason to die further.

Returning from the tunnel of his eyes, Aira focused on the man's face. He was crying.

She became aware of her tight grip on the severed finger she was holding in place. Looking back down at her hand, she slowly loosened it, then withdrew her right hand from the injured one.

Her index finger remained properly attached to the hand.

Slowly, she lifted it, and turned it, inspecting the back of the hand and the palm, especially the point where the finger had been severed. By degrees, she curled and straightened the fingers. All of them moved perfectly. It seemed natural, though a reverence accompanied the power she knew was hers. It was the power of life, and she knew it to be synonymous with the power of love. Aira knew then, with her entire being, that her will was more real than any solidity which surrounded her.

The voice that came out of her body was kind and soft and fiercely huge at once as she told the man, "When Onx lets go of you, don't run away from me."

Onx unclenched her claws and perched above him on the trash canister. The man stood there. He didn't run. He heard what sounded like a whoosh of wings behind him, then heard clicking on the asphalt. A white dog come around from behind the canister.

Aira looked at the man intently. He returned her gaze. Though she spoke softly, the two words she uttered hit him like a projectile. "Wake up."

chapter

26

The sound of piano and ethereal singing floated in from the other room.

> Stars sparkle secrets, hopes, and dreams.
> Stars hold the mystery answer it seems.
> Out there.
> It's so strange yet so familiar.
> When I look up in the night,
> light years far, but close and bright,
> I wonder what I am.
>
> Why do I feel so far from home?
> Where is it that I really belong?
> Still nights.
> Skies of stars and moonlight.
> Something pulls me from above.
> If the air were made of love,
> I'd know home wasn't far.
>
> Dreams are denied and robbed from my soul.
> Life isn't dreams, it's war I am told.
> Love cries.
> It is so shunned and abandoned.
> But I can't believe that's real.
> There is more than this ordeal.
> I know Ideals can be.

Lonely faces, all the faces
of the people who forgot.

Home is all the good you are,
Magic isn't something far.
Home is you. You brought it here
to play Time and form again.

Home is the very fabric of you.
You are all the good that's true.
It is real.
All the beauty you imagine.
It's to beauty we belong.
We are souls of light and song.
It's all there. Home is you…

Aira's voice faded into a near whisper, "…Home is you." Over cascades of lilting piano notes in 6/8 time, she narrated, "You're from home. Remember? It's still there. All the beauty you imagine. You are the beauty. You are the magic. *You*…are home."

Mendle closed his eyes. He was on the verge of crying as he listened to Aira singing in the other room but his insides felt as though they had been scooped out of him, leaving nothing but the ache burning in him. *What does any of it matter, anyway? How insignificant we're all proven to be,* he thought bitterly, again feeling the gnashing torment.

"Stop it," he reproached himself, and opened his eyes. *I can control this,* he thought, forcing himself to look at his surroundings, at the soup bowl on his desk, at the work he had to do. *I somehow hold a key to reality.*

He knew that. One example was how sometimes he could look very ugly to himself in a mirror, very definitely ugly, pathetic, mortal, and flawed. Moments later, with nothing changed but his frame of mind, he would look radiant, handsome, and venerable.

It was within him to believe either side. He could believe the superiority of Thought over Matter, he could understand the principle of how goodness was Life itself and would therefore always win—or he could believe the solid wall's constant reminder, decency was a joke, force was king, and he was going to die, end of story.

Mendle extroverted onto the computer screen in front of him. The grey blur focused into the name "Aira Flight." Once wishful thinking and Courier 12 point font, now she was a flesh and blood woman living in his house.

He swiveled his chair to a bowl of alphabet soup he had prepared for himself, picked up the spoon, and dabbled in the letters floating in broth. "M," for Mendle. He parked it on the side of the bowl. As he spooned some into his mouth, Mendle thought about the letters he was eating. *When I finish the soup, all the letters will come out as wonderful words and I'll write another chapter.*

A demon voice fought back when he swallowed; it told him those letters were heading only one direction when he was done digesting… down. They were not going to come out as thought, they were going to come out as…

"Shit!" Mendle spun his chair and banged the wall with his fist.

The loud jolt woke Onx. The dog's eyes shot open and it yelped, looking disoriented. "Go back to sleep," Mendle waved at it, and Onx nestled its nose back on its paws. Mendle's gaze lingered on it after it closed its eyes. Looking at the Samoyed's sweet face, it was difficult to believe what he knew about the animal.

Mendle cursed himself for the remaining alcohol that slogged his system. He wished he hadn't drunk again and reached for the B vitamins in his desk drawer. Taking two, he swallowed them with a spoonful of soup, then gulped coffee.

There has to be some other way to dull the thinking when it gets to be too much, he vowed. *Some other way to vacation without decreasing IQ and damaging brain cells.*

He reached for his notebook of companions and saints, opened to a random page, and began to read a clipping of an interview with Karl Pribram, a Stanford neurophysiologist, "It isn't that the world of appearances is wrong; it isn't that there aren't objects out there, at one level of reality. It's that if you penetrate through…" Mendle broke eye-contact with the page and scanned the room. *It's as though I'm in a virtual reality,* he pondered as he studied the lamps, walls, furniture and objects surrounding him. *Somehow it's interactive. My thoughts can affect events. Other people's thoughts affect their lives. It's like a mutual playing field.*

He returned his attention to the notebook and thumbed through collected thoughts of other poets and scientists that made him feel less alone.

But could that woman and that animal have actually materialized straight out of my consciousness? Affecting matter, he could contemplate; actually *creating* it loomed as the ultimate Art. *That woman is more than just matter, however,* he contemplated.

He focused on the computer, at a section he had scrolled up from Chapter Three, and read it.

RELOCATE. RESUME VECTOR: HOME BASE ORIGINAL DESTINATION
PROGRAM.

"Are you sure you want to keep the dragon life-form,
Onx?" Aira asked playfully as she finished entering the
commands. "You seem capable of reasoning rather well.
You could operate as..."

Onx feigned limited potential and blinked up at Aira.
Yet her stance was nonetheless alert, prepared to respond
to a potential emergency. That she could do. *Sense, identify danger, combat, protect.* She was good at that and
that was all she was about to aspire to.

"Blinking blankly, eh?" Aira chided Onx then turned
back to the control board.

Mendle crossed his arms in front of him and turned away from what
he had written just months ago, before a flesh-and-blood Aira Flight sat
in his living room and an Onx padded around the house.

He found himself wishing the girl's memory would return now, to
put an end to this torment. *What is her real name? I'm the one who gave
her that name. Who is she really? Is she from Georgia, Alabama, Wyoming?*
It would be a relief. Yet she continued to wax into a persona larger than
life.

He reflected on the morning she had started speaking French. Two
months prior she didn't even know what *"Merci"* meant in a French restaurant, she thought the waiter had done something wrong and was asking to
be pardoned. Over the month of January she had learned to speak six languages fluently. Learned or remembered, they weren't sure which.

Recently she had diagnosed a problem with his car and fixed it, adjusting the butterfly valve in the carburetor. Not an act needing a rocket
scientist, true, but it was the way she did it. She seemed to change from
knowing absolutely nothing about it to knowing a great deal about the

combustion engine, rambling aloud about crank shaft, rods, pistons, air-fuel ratio. She moved from ground zero knowledge through a super-fast deductive process to a conclusion. She fixed the problem, and she said she just "knew" it.

It was most disconcerting, this way she seemed to extrapolate knowledge out of nowhere about things she claimed she previously knew absolutely nothing about. Her eyes would widen a little, she'd pose a question, and she seemed to suck knowledge right out of him, the air, anyone standing by, or anything she was looking at.

And she insisted this was normal. Maybe she had been a language teacher, maybe she had been a car mechanic.

She could draw, paint, formulate mathematical equations, sculpt, dance. Now she was playing the piano and composing music. Amazingly, she continued to sprout shoots, like some unfathomable rhizome; Mendle wondered what else lay beneath the surface.

Then there was the dog. He turned and looked at it again, over in the corner, staring at it sullenly as he pondered the "transformation" Aira had told him about.

Mendle reminded himself of what St. Augustine said. *'Miracles don't occur in opposition to Nature, but in opposition to what we know about Nature.'* He knew all this, he *knew* it, but seeing it for himself, with his physical eyes, in space and time, defying space and time—that definitely had its impact. It was about ten days later, when the gas man had come to read the meter, that Mendle saw some of that "transformation" phenomena himself. Onx's white fur began to modify before his eyes, to blue, and two growths did indeed begin to protrude out of its back, until Aira reprimanded it into submission.

Referring to the incident, Aira had replied, "There is a perfectly logical explanation." If she didn't know what the explanation was, she would just say, "The data just isn't available yet."

It had to do with electrons, Mendle conjectured. *If matter is broken into smaller and smaller pieces, eventually the parts become atomic, then subatomic—electrons and other particles.* He looked at the matter surrounding him, and imagined its atomic contruction. *Except an electron,* he reminded himself, *is not even a "thing."* He knew it could behave as a particle, or a wave. *And now they say particles don't even exist. On close inspection, they disappear.*

Light and radio waves, too for instance, could change from waves to particles and back. There was a vast field of something beyond subatomic that was the fabric of the material existence in which he found himself. It appeared solid. *Appeared.*

Physicists had even labeled the sub-atomic phenomena that should not be classified as either waves or particles; as a single category, they were always somehow both: Quanta. The stuff of which the entire universe was made. *And there is some evidence that the only time quanta ever manifest as particles is when we are looking at them,* Mendle ventured further. Which would mean Life and living was an inter-active virtual reality, from wavelength into patterned particles of visible realities.

Modified daily by thought? Thus coincidences? Mendle suddenly felt the sensation of floating, in a fluid of time, space, energy, and potentials. Then it was gone.

No wonder his frustration. Again, it tapped him on the shoulder, and when he turned to look, it turned to ordinary, solid reality.

Exasperated, he sat back in his chair, thinking he should have known better than to wrestle with it—it was mercurial and stayed in the hand only when one did not grab. Frustration welled up in him that it evaded him. He was so close, yet wasn't there at all.

Back to his notebook, Mendle turned to the pages that listed the co-incidences in his life: Old phone numbers of his that were coincidentally a friend's number backwards—more than once, in a city of millions. Times he was speaking of some person who coincidentally called or showed up in a public place. Names of streets that coincided with relatives. Coincidentally reading some obscure book, not a best seller, at the same time as a friend was reading that book in a different country.

And the historic. Presidents Lincoln and Kennedy died on Fridays, in 1860 and 1960. Each was warned to avoid the death place, one by his secretary, Kennedy, the other by his secretary, Lincoln. Each was succeeded by a Southern Democrat, an ex-senator named Johnson, one born in 1808, the other in 1908.

Mendle flung the notebook like a frisbee to a corner of the room behind him with a sharp surrender. "It's just weird!"

"I've been told I'm weird, strange, not for real." It was Aira. "But I think there are many more really strange things in this world than me. Don't you?"

She was there, smiling and looking at him from across the room. *Aaaahhhh,* Mendle mock-screamed to himself. *I don't know about that.* She was part of his puzzle, and here she was talking to him about it. He had to admit, "Sure. War, and death. There's two, definitely stranger than you," then managed the semblance of a smile by tautening his lips.

"What's weird?" she asked, leaning in the doorway.

"Nothing, Aira. I'm tired. My mind is tired. Tired of trying to figure all this out."

"Figure what out?"

You for one. "Let's just drop it. I don't want to be serious all the time. Do we have to talk about serious things all the time?"

Mendle's attitude astonished Aira. He had never spoken to her with that kind of an edge in his voice, not directed at her personally, and it cut. "Could you be more precise?" she asked him. She wanted to know how she had displeased him.

Her innocent, unabashed hurt pierced him. Nevertheless, he tossed out, "Like when you came in last week and wanted to discuss saving the world."

Aira thought about it.

Mendle got up from his desk. "Let's think about saving ourselves first. Or let's just start having some damn fun. Some stupid goddam fun!" He hurled his body onto the small sofa. "Save the world," he bantered.

"Don't you think we can?" Aira asked.

It sounded trite. She was earnest. *Like talking about changing a tire.* The dream was becoming a nightmare. Amazed that she would actually ask such a thing seriously, Mendle regarded her with indignation. His look seemed to blame her for every departure and failure in his life. Then, "Sure," he quipped. "Let me check my calendar." He hyperbolically jumped up and ran to his wall calendar. "Let's see. I'm not doing anything tomorrow. Let's save the world!"

She smiled a little, but just underneath was a fresh wound. She cast her eyes downward. "You yourself say every reality begins with the idea," she started to murmur, feeling humiliated and silly, and worse, helpless and of no value.

"Stop it. You're just simplistic. Things aren't as simple, as pat, as la-dee-dah as you make them. I'm sick of La La Land." He gave his chair a spin for emphasis as he walked by it. "This ain't Kansas!"

Mendle's words sounded strange, even to himself, but his momentum kept spitting them out. He looked at Onx in the corner. "We're not in Kansas anymore, Toto," he accused caustically, pointing at the dog.

"What do you want me to talk about?" Aira asked. "I talk about things that interest me. I thought they interested you, too. I thought you liked intelligence and…"

Mendle lifted his hand to his lips and blew a fanfare through a mock trumpet,then started calling out, "Freedom for the Galaxy! The world can be saved!"

It was absolutely incomprehensible to Aira that Mendle was ridiculing her, attacking the sentiments she held dearest, her very core. She wasn't at all prepared for it, and the sheer betrayal catapulted her into confusion. Even though it was a reflex to protect herself, she shrank with self-disgust as she retorted with a disparaging imitation of him. "I've found you my truest love, I've found you. Where have you been all my life? You've come to me. Where have you been?" She forced herself to glare boldly at him and let it sink in. "Is that what you'd prefer to talk about?"

"I was drunk!" Mendle snapped, instantly regretting it. "What about you?" he mocked and derisively taunted, "I think I love you. I'm afraid of losing you."

His words hit a mark. She did have a desperate, inexplicable fear of losing him. "Sure," Aira quipped, "I said that. I love you, I love Onx, I love Sandra…" She forced insouciance to cover a need that was suddenly not safe with him.

The inferno was being fanned. "Yes!" Mendle exclaimed. "The Cosmic Kid! You *love* don't you? Miss Ideal Universe." He pirouetted and danced on tiptoe in a disparaging impersonation of her, speaking in falsetto. "Man is wonderful and should be freed! I love people. Let's save the world."

He stopped suddenly, confronting her angrily. "Well I'll tell you something. It's all shit. People are rotten, disgusting and hard. Cold! This planet is a hellhole if you haven't noticed. A meaningless wasteland of zinging atomic rot. I'll tell you what people are. Bags of blood and guts that eat, shit, get old, and die!"

"No!" Aira cried out, horrified.

"Yes!" He glared at her as if his eyes would pound truth into her. Still, his heart yearned for her, admired the way she valiantly defended some ideal that tombstones daily defied. "And Love! Love does not exist. Maybe an occasional hand out, but believe me, there's always a selfish reason at the other end."

"That's not true! Love is not an emotion! It's Life itself! It's the very reason for life…we are much more than organisms—"

Mendle cut her off, "That's right! Excuse me, I forgot." He mimicked her again, "These are but shells. We are not our bodies! Heavens no, not these nasty little organisms!" Though he felt smaller with every word he spoke, he couldn't stop. Something propelled him, yet he fought it. Though he was resigned to what he was saying, he also rebelled against it.

A scenario went through his mind, to pull down his pants and yank out his penis and scream, "This is not an illusion. Look at it! It's a cock.

And it's real. It's mine. And I feel it, and it ain't no costume."

"I didn't say it like that!" Aira was shouting. "I didn't say bodies were bad or there's something wrong with them!" Her voice was defiant, but there was a wail in it.

Behind his activated panoply of responses, Mendle felt awful. Aira was on the verge of tears. He wanted to run and hold her, but something held him back and he felt further degraded and confused. He refrained from saying any more because nothing had been coming out accurately anyway.

This was life: cruel and unfeeling. Traps everywhere. Traps of feelings, words, miscomprehensions, false hopes, reacting in opposites. He found himself turning on a person who understood him, who lived and breathed all he embraced as most dear.

He was turning on himself, he saw.

Aira was crying now. He listened, and made himself turn to look at her. Her grief tumbled over its last remnants of restraint. She sat on the chair in the corner and sobbed, "I'm so afraid. I want to go home."

"Aira," Mendle said softly, forcing himself past the paralysis brought on by his pain.

"People are good," she insistently sobbed. "They would never feel bad about anything if they weren't good."

"Yes," Mendle said, rubbing his face. "You have a point."

"You think I'm bad now," Aira cried.

"No. See, things just aren't simple like that."

"I am bad. I just tried to hurt you. And I thought I served things that were pure..."

"No, see, that's what gets me sometimes. See, you are different, there is something a little different about you, and you just breeze around acting as if it's all...business as usual or something." Mendle handed her a tissue.

"I don't know why you expect me to be so special." Aira blew her nose. "I'm not different from you or anyone." She started to cry again.

"But you have to admit. The way you read...I mean, two hundred pages an hour." He thought about the way he had seen her read—she just set books in front of her and vacuumed entire pages in a second. Her eyes didn't even travel across individual words and sentences. It was as if with one look she could suck up everything there.

"And the languages." Mendle started pacing the room, listing things, her knack with mechanics, her seemingly instant musical ability. He avoided mentioning her lack of a navel, but pointed out, "You know what people are thinking…it's inhuman." There, he had said it.

"Inhuman?" Aira looked up at him, thought about it and said, "I saw someone who spoke every language in the world on television last week."

Mendle had also seen the show.

"And what about those people who knew what others were thinking? Some even knew events that happened in other people's lives who they never met. That's just telepathy. It's human."

True, there were also shamans, and Sathya Sai Baba. Witnessed by literally thousands, he materialized food, gold, flowers, an endless supply of things, right out of air, or molecules, or wavelengths.

"And you've talked of artists who were also scientists, astronomers, poets, painters," Aira was saying, "who did many more things than I do. You yourself know physics, write novels, music…your IQ is over 180."

Mendle didn't know what to say.

"I'm no different than you," she told him quietly. "Or anybody."

"Okay. You're just…well, there aren't many around like you," he said.

"I know." Aira wiped her eyes and blew her nose again.

"You do?" He was surprised and felt himself calm down.

Aira nodded. "I know now I'm weird," she despaired, the grief starting up again. "I always thought I was good, but just now when you hurt me so deeply, I yelled at you to create the same effect back."

"That's okay. That's understandable."

"It isn't acceptable," Aira wailed. "It was hurtful."

"It was just a momentary lapse," Mendle explained to her. "I understand."

"But I didn't even act that way when the man sliced off my finger."

Her words zipped Mendle into dumbfounded silence. He checked her hand and counted, ten, all there. "What? Did you remember something…?"

As Aira told him about the mugging in the alley, he moved closer to her and sat in a chair opposite her. Mendle picked up her hands, listening carefully. He gently caressed her long, graceful fingers as she described how the finger had fused back with her hand.

To his marveling, transfixed attentiveness, she finished, "I saw a film of a man who performed surgery with his hands. In the Philippines. He not only fused flesh together, he could cut it apart, enter bodies and perform healing surgery with his bare hands. It's called…"

"Faith healing, I know," Mendle finished for her.

"I can't do that. In fact, I don't even know exactly how I did what I did, or if I can do it again," she said, pulling her hands out of his to inspect them.

Mendle nodded. "I'm sorry, Aira," he said. He shook his head, letting go his grasp to hold her sacred. He ventured, "There are times I feel like a god. Then other times I'm smacked in the face. Usually by myself. Something that sets me in my place about any notion of eternity or decency or meaning."

"It isn't true," she consoled him, fervency in her voice. "Those are just barriers, not the bigger picture." She mulled over what she just said, trying to take it further. "There must be more to all this," she reassured.

When Mendle looked at her searchingly, she squeezed his hands warmly. He looked at her a long time. Her eyes were oceans, skies. Her face was so…good.

"Why didn't you tell me about the finger?" *Now, now you can ask her about the navel.*

Aira looked sad. "I started to tell you about Onx transforming that day. I didn't tell you the rest because…because you had been tampering with your reality, you were…"

"Drinking." Mendle finished for her.

They both fell quiet.

It wasn't near as much as before he met her. It had only been two or three times over months. *Even so.* Finally Mendle said, "I know." He sighed. "I'm sorry." He disrobed himself of excuses, including regret and guilt. "Don't worry about it. It's my problem."

Aira looked at him, filled with a care for him that was now inseparable from her very self.

"No," she said. "It's not your problem. It's your solution."

In the silence, across the distance, Truth groped in the dark, knowing it could feel what it could not yet completely see.

Mendle and Aira embraced, staying close and still, feeling like a miracle to one another.

chapter  27

"Is the pattern of a fingerprint always detectable by the naked eye?"

"Well, yes. Just look at your own hand."

"And it's always one of those three patterns?"

"That's right. Loop. Whorl. Arch. Most of the general population, about eighty-five to ninety percent, have a combination of loops and whorls. About ten to fifteen percent have one or two arches. Only four percent have three or more arches."

"What might be considered rare?"

"Out of one thousand individuals, only one will have an arch on each finger."

"There is no other type of fingerprint?"

"Nope."

She had paused to think, Sandra Wilford remembered, then thought to ask, "In what instances might no prints be left?"

"It can depend on many things. Metabolism is one. Or let's say you have someone who washes his hands every day, often, a doctor or something. The oil is gone off the fingers then, for a minute or so. So, no prints will be left."

"Is there any instance whatsoever in which the print can't be seen except with magnifying equipment?"

"You mean after we process what we got with the lampblack?"

"Yes."

"After prints are processed, they can be seen. They're not microscopic. In this case, Miss Wilford, it's not someone who isn't leaving prints. This is definitely some type of print that's been lifted off here. But nothing like I've ever seen." She remembered Hobbins' face as he examined the plates. He asked, "Are you sure you didn't mar this?"

"I may have."

There was a prolonged silence.

Keeping the steering wheel steady with one hand, Sandra turned up the volume on the microcassette tape recorder that had been in her lap then set it in the passenger's seat beside her.

"These don't look like any fingerprints I've ever seen," John Hobbins' voice came out of his silence. "There's no real dermatoglyphic evidence to speak of. Just a few dots." Another moment of silence. "This one does have an actual pattern on it. Look at that."

Sandra recalled the magnification he held up.

"A tiny star," John Hobbins was pointing out, "made up of little dots."

"You know what these remind me of?" he said next, giving the impression that there was something he had been trying to place. "About thirty, oh, maybe forty years ago, there was a case run through here. Supposed to be top security at the time. A government project, it was being supervised from the east coast. Turned out to be a UFO hoax or something, I don't know."

"Hoax?"

"They brought in some piece of something all hush-hush, said it was a control panel of some damn space ship."

"And?"

"And there were prints on it all right. There were a couple with that star, described like that. Others they said looked like maps, inside the finger, you know. Constellations or something."

"In the finger prints?"

"Or what someone would have wanted us to *think* were fingerprints. It wouldn't have fooled me."

"I wonder if that pattern wasn't some emblem on a piece of rubber I was using to press down. What did the lab find out about those others?"

"Nothing," Hobbins said, a little laugh in his voice. "Then the file was missing. There was a big to-do. *The Probe* got ahold of it, you know that sensational rag. Some leak. Somebody probably made a few bucks. You know, it turned into one of those Martians-Have-Landed stories. Of course, nobody believed it. I think somebody needed some money or publicity."

"Whatever happened to the evidence?"

John Hobbins laughed. "The whole thing got yanked. I saw something about it when I was going through backlogs. Now seeing this thing reminded me. Sims was asking me about it just the other day. Someone from Lockheed had been checking on it. Government wasn't very clear about it. Guess they have a hard time being wrong."

"They were wrong?"

"That's what they finally admitted, formally."

"Of course." She paused. "Does every human being have fingerprints?"

There was another silence and she could feel John Hobbins judging her question as strange. He answered as though he thought everybody knew. "Yes. Their own. Unless they're removed, surgically, acid, something."

"Of course, of course," Sandra said. "What I mean is, are there any exceptions?"

"No."

Sandra reached down onto the seat and with her thumb punched the tape recorder off.

Are there any exceptions? No. The words echoed in her mind as she circled Mendle's house.

His car was gone. The garage lights were off. She parked her car around the corner.

When the brass-colored key slid into the lock, memories triggered in Sandra of when she used to live there. She rang the door bell once more and waited before turning the key, then bolstered herself and pushed open the door.

"Hello!" she called out cheerfully, clasping a set of *Scientific American* magazines, her alibi, to her chest. Silence within. She quickly stepped inside and shut the door quietly behind her. She listened again, and when she heard nothing, she relaxed. Aira was at dance class until eight-thirty. And—Sandra ran through her story—she had called and left a message on Mendle's machine that she might drop by with some magazines. They wouldn't have wanted her to wait outside.

Smoke screens and backups set, Sandra looked around at signs of Mendle's life, the familiar smell of the house filling her with nostalgia.

The sight of a cozy setting by the fireplace caused her stomach to feel like burning ice—especially the two pillows on the floor, two tea cups, a Vangelis compact disc. Bristling with rancor, she tended to her objective. Within a minute she had dusted the cups, taken prints off each, and wiped them clean of lampblack.

Odd, she was thinking, *these prints don't seem any different from the ones I got in the garage apartment. And I've been so careful.*

Coldly, she turned her attention to scan the room. She moved through the dining room to the study. Nothing much new in there—still books and papers and notes. At the desk, a blue vinyl folder, the kind made of transparent tinted plastic, caught her attention. Through the cover she read: "Gain for the Vain," © Aira Flight Corp.

A worry surfaced that Mendle and the woman might have started making money. She flipped through the pages and saw it was a marketing plan for waterproof books that people could read while in their tubs, pools, or jacuzzis. "Printing poetry and worthy reading materials on plastic to give incentive to reading as play."

Sandra snorted at Mendle's penchant for fantasy and tossed it back on the table, then cocked her head sideways to read a few bills. One was overdue. It comforted her to know that nothing was going to rise suddenly up out of her reach. *He shouldn't be rewarded anyway, not until he learns to face what the real world is all about.*

If they came home unexpectedly, the best place to be would be the kitchen, Sandra calculated. She could be having coffee, with her stack of magazines, a favor for them, after all.

She made a stop in the bathroom. Seeing herself in the mirror was an irresistible attraction. After inspection of her face, Sandra draped her jacket over the basin and set her bag and magazines on the floor next to the sink. She took an eyeliner pencil, some blush and a coral lipstick out of her purse, removed her gloves, and applied the cosmetics to her face.

I am so beautiful, Sandra thought, checking everything out. *Perfect.*

She took a step back and, never breaking the connection with her own eyes, tossed her glistening hair and practiced seductive looks at her own reflection. She liked it when the front shock of hair draped dramatically forward and partially covered one of her eyes. Pleased, she returned the cosmetics to her purse, carefully replaced the gloves, picked up her belongings, and moved on, feeling totally together. The kitchen promised to be rich with fingerprints.

She was halfway through the dining room when she heard Mendle's voice. He wasn't alone, he was talking to someone, coming up the walk. She looked, it wasn't even eight o'clock yet.

The kitchen. Sandra coolly fed herself her backup, tightened her clench on the magazines, and made for the back of the house. As she scooted into a chair at the dinette table and thought to pretend she had fallen asleep, Sandra heard the key in the front door.

"I'm not sure, it happened so fast." It was Aira's voice. There was an urgency to it, almost like a whisper, intense, as though about to divulge something. She said, "I just suddenly saw the entirety of the universe."

"Should I leave the door open?" Mendle asked.

"No. She'll bark when she's ready to come in."

Sandra wondered if she should call out "Hello" or come out brandishing her apologies with the magazines. *Which would work better?*

The door shut. Mendle spoke next. "Let's sit down. Are you all right?"

Aira said, "Yes, the shaking has stopped."

Their voices traveled, coming from the living room now.

"You may have been right about me," Aira said.

"What do you mean?"

There was quiet, longer than an ordinary pause. Then Aira said, "This is my first time here. I wondered before, but now I know. I might be a little different."

Sandra held her breath.

"I just know I've never been here. I'm not from Earth," Aira went on. "I don't have a childhood. I wasn't born as a baby."

"Give me a break," Sandra muttered under her breath, vexed at the girl's audacity. *He must be in pig's heaven,* she speculated on Mendle's reaction, annoyed that he was being given any satisfaction.

"I know it sounds strange."

"No, I'm not surprised," Mendle said matter-of-factly, but his adrenalin was pumping, his heart racing, his breathing accelerating.

"I feel as though something is wearing off, some type of spell," Aira told him. "It's happening so fast. When the memory came, I started to shake like that. Two weeks ago I remembered the car and the loud horn. I thought I was hit."

"I remember," Mendle recalled.

"But I wasn't," Aira told him. "It was raining. There was a storm, thunder and lightning. I was on the street, running. Before that, I somehow adhered to an electrical facsimile, and it has to do with electromagnetic fields. I materialized."

Sandra realized her gloves looked suspicious and tugged them off. She stuffed them into her jacket pocket as she listened.

"Somehow, I've…manifested," Aira said, not knowing what else to call it. "I didn't use to have a body," she said plainly.

She then explained how she was in possession of a mind of some type that made the universe appear normal once she entered it.

A mind of some type that makes the universe appear normal once you enter it, Sandra reflected dryly.

"It's where the common reality is stored," Aira was saying, "but it isn't me. I use it. The mind linked me in to everything. That's why I just accepted everything as it was. It's like a data base for this universe…

but...I've materialized. I used to not be here. I don't know how else to describe the feeling."

"I understand," Mendle soothed her, sensitive to her struggling to explain. "You're talking about having condensed on some molecular level."

What? Sandra silently challenged them. *Sure. String together a few more quantum tricks you picked up in those books.*

Aira was perturbed. "I don't know much else, no details..."

There was silence.

When Aira asked Mendle to tell her what he was thinking, he stumbled over a couple of beginnings. This was where, Sandra was certain, he would tell Aira the part about being in love with her all his life, and she was the woman out of his dreams and fantasies. Instead, Mendle told Aira he wondered about it when he saw she didn't have a navel.

No navel? They've both flipped completely, Sandra thought, *I shouldn't have stayed away for so long.*

"But it's a completely normal body," Aira said.

"Okay, so it wasn't reproduced biologically," Mendle said. "I suppose it's based on some type of electromagnetic blueprint. Like anything else, for that matter." He hummed, then, "Can it reproduce?"

Sandra seethed internally. *Oh right. As if you didn't know. What's next? Doctor?*

"It is a human body," Aira said. "It operates in all functions, involuntarily. It's an organism, a machine. Solid. Confined and interrelated to all the laws of physics. It's a human female body."

Oh really? As if you didn't notice, Sandra mentally jeered at Mendle, hating the way the girl talked. *She looks and sounds like some Marilynesque deep-space version of Pollyanna and Flash Gordon combined.* Sandra couldn't figure it out. *It's so unreal. She has no sense of style. One day she's in baggy khaki fatigues. Another she dresses like Doris Day. Then she's in the metallic spandex motif. Like she's trying too hard. She's hiding something.*

Something about Mendle's tone when he spoke next set Sandra's arm hair on end. His voice was suddenly subdued; he sounded afraid.

"Do you know you're doing that?" he asked, awed.

"What?" Aira said.

Careful not to make a sound, Sandra rose from her chair, tiptoed to the kitchen door, and peered through the crack in the swinging panels. She could see through the dining room into part of the living room. She could see Mendle, but Aira was across the room, out of her line of vision. Sandra guessed she was looking at herself in the baroque mirror by the french doors. Mendle stared in that direction, his eyes like saucers.

"You just lit up," he said, aghast. "I just saw your light. A light around you."

"That *is* me," she cooed, herself marveling.

Aira came back into sight and sat down across from Mendle, by the coffee table. Sandra didn't see any glow. But Mendle was looking at her as if she were an egg about to hatch.

"*That's* you?" Mendle asked, all agog.

Aira nodded.

She did suddenly look a little luminescent to Sandra. *It's the hair color,* she decided in disgust. *Those "ethereal" blonde highlights she claims aren't touched up.*

"We're in a time stream," Aira said.

There's that look again, Sandra inwardly commented, *that two-bit clairvoyant look, as if she's seeing something nobody else can. And Mendle— more gullible than ever.* Her anger was turning to rage. She leaned back to rest her eyes and breathe deeply.

"Wwhhoooo." It was Mendle, sounding like a little boy. "How did you do that?"

Sandra quickly focused her eye to the crack again.

"I spotted it in its exact time continuum!" Aira was telling him in that super-tizzy that Sandra knew so well. Whatever the feat was, she missed it.

"Where are you from?" Mendle asked.

He looks pathetic, Sandra thought as she watched him. *He looks gaunt. He looks sick, tormented. That man is not well, and he's not getting better. There she goes pretending to get a vision, the clairvoyant-at-a-seance bit.*

Aira shook her head and looked disappointed. "I can't remember. There are only certain things I'm beginning to know now."

Sure. Sandra thought. *Convenient.*

"I'm having trouble with it," Aira said. "Sometimes I look around, and I see matter as a wavelength. But then, the reality is so intense, it solidifies. It seems incredible to me also."

"I know what you mean," Mendle said, excited. "Try to do it again."

Sandra watched closely through the crack in the door as Aira leaned over and put her hands on a large oriental blue and white vase on the coffee table. She lifted it up and over. There, in the space the vase had occupied, in the exact shape of the vase, remained an oscillating black hole.

Slowly replacing the vase, Aira explained, "This universe is only a dimension. It appears solid. But it isn't. These *things*," she emphasized, indicating various objects surrounding them, "the chairs, the walls, the lamps, our bodies, they are frequencies on interference patterns." The vase and its black image merged.

Aira and Mendle began virtually gawking around the room. Sandra narrowed her eyes. She questioned if she had really seen what she thought she did.

"That vase," Aira said looking at it again, "is connected to everything in existence."

Mendle stared at the object. "How did you do it?"

"I had to think of the entire universe," Aira said. "No part is without the whole. And no whole without each part."

"Relatively independent subtotalities," Mendle said. "That's how David Bohm refers to 'things' in *Wholeness and the Implicate Order.*" He was smiling. "And, in the words of William Blake: 'To see a world in a grain of sand…And heaven in a wildflower, Hold infinity in the palm of your hand And eternity in an hour.'"

"Yes. That's right," Aira affirmed, her voice sounding almost like a little girl's.

"Have you read that?" Mendle asked.

"No."

Right. Sandra's contained fury was getting more bestial by the minute. She would kill this woman to protect Mendle. She turned away from the door, unsure of what to think or do. She kept listening carefully.

"When I was playing video games at the Arcade, I thought of a space-ship," she heard Aira say. "It's different from flying because it's not a mass propelled through space and time. It travels through a process of disassembling and reassembling in different space."

As Mendle watched and listened to Aira, he was ecstatic, delighted, fearful in a good way, and totally out of his mind on the brink of unrehearsed, raw quantum life. He surfed the crest of his passion, where he lived, the heights, widths, breadths of…potential, power, verity. The juice of Life itself. He never knew what the phrase meant before, but he knew it now. This was the moment he had been waiting for all his life. He was outside of himself with pleasure.

Aira was intently summarizing, "…so I've worked out some equations on a possible theory. The first involves moving space-time to the ship. My equation calculates the outer periphery of Time. So it's not a *propulsion* method for spacecraft, rather a shifting of space and time. I may have isolated and theoretically broken the Time Barrier. Moving a space *to* the craft, rather than propelling a mass, or 'independent sub-totality' as Bohm calls it, through space."

What a pile of monkey rot. Sandra was feeling sickened.

Mendle asked, "Are you from another galaxy?"

A silent howl of appalled protest rose from Sandra.

"I don't know if it's a memory or a discovery," Aira said, adding, "Maybe both." Then she smiled.

"Why are you smiling?" He loved her smile. Sweet, but with the wisdom of the ages.

"I was just looking at you," Aira said shyly. "I saw you more than I ever have." She bit her lip a little, then told him, "You've had the courage to navigate…where there are no compass readings."

Sandra was burning, her skin literally eruptive with discomfort. It enraged her seeing someone being nice to Mendle. *The pain he put me through, and all I'm trying to do is help him.* It made sense to her.

"What you did with the vase, can you do it at will?" Mendle was awash with sentiment. His many years of loneliness were repaid now with joy that surged in him, too huge for a thank you or any word.

"I'll try," Aira said, her gaze lingering on him. There was more she wanted to say to him, it trembled in her, but she didn't know exactly what it was. "It's not a hundred percent," she said, getting up from the sofa.

Sandra quickly repositioned herself at the door.

Aira walked over to a floor lamp by the white reading chair. She picked the lamp up and moved it aside about a foot. An oscillating impression remained in the space it had occupied.

The girl seemed to radiate. If not light, it was intense joy; something poured from her. She didn't set the lamp back into position, as she had the vase. She let it go, and it seemed to float back, to be molecularly re-absorbed into position.

Having done it again, she tried to define it better. "I was able to see matter as a wavelength, and disconnect the object from space-time by creating a different space-time for it." Aira mulled over what she just said. "Otherwise, it's impossible."

She sat down in the white chair.

"If that one lamp were to disappear, so would the entire universe have to," she said. "And, it's all rigged to our brains somehow, to the way the minds that we're equipped with *perceive*."

Mendle nodded.

They both sat in silence, both in their own worlds.

Mendle looked at objects around him. He pondered materialization. *This environment is made up of illusions of light, time, space, and we're in-*

tertwined with our brains and minds. He looked at Aira's body. *If a person can spontaneously combust, I suppose one can spontaneously condense.* Mendle asked, sudden worry in his voice. "Can it...Can you...dematerialize?"

Aira shook her head. "I'm here," she said, as if to say she were stuck.

This woman is dangerous, Sandra thought.

Mendle asked again, "Are you sure?"

"I'm human," Aira said.

Though he felt the impulse to refute it, Mendle could not argue. Undeniably, there she sat. Flesh and blood.

Quietly stepping back to the dinette table, Sandra puzzled over everything she had seen and heard. Though she was breathing harder than she had been some minutes ago, she was still thinking evenly. Under the circumstances, she decided it best she leave the back way, to avoid their suspicion she had heard or seen anything. She picked up her things. When she turned toward the back door, what she saw at the window was so shocking it caused her heart to jump, freeze, and skip a beat.

On the other side of the glass, a bluish-lavender creature was staring at her.

Its nostrils were pressed against the window, the pressure of the glass deflecting a stream of smoke that was emitting from them. The porch light only partially illuminated the creature's face, while pools of night and shadows obscured the rest. Tongue flickering, eyes flashing orange-yellow, it was glaring right at her.

Sandra jerked her head away from the window. She stood paralyzed in a quandary. Her data systems were unable to process the information. Yet she could not dispute that she, in fact, had seen what she had seen.

In the living room, Mendle was about to bring up the fact to Aira that he had named her out of his novel when she suddenly said, "Where's Onx?" Realizing the dog hadn't barked to come in, Aira went to the front door to call and whistle for her.

When Sandra forced herself to look back at the window, there was nothing there. She couldn't believe she had just seen what she did. *But I saw it. Didn't I? Did I? It was there.* Yet she wasn't sure. She suddenly wanted to be out of there more than anything in the world.

Nervously, she slid back the bolt, looking over her shoulder at the window every few moments, then slipped out the back door. She felt undignified and embarrassed when she chipped a nail, and more so when she tore her stockings going through some bushes. Hate burned in her at the degradation she was subjected to by this woman in Mendle's life. Cutting through a neighbor's backyard and across the street, she took to her car in a near run.

Bounding into the foyer, Onx exuberantly shook her white coat from tail to nose. She moved her head around in circles, her unique way of showing she was happy to see Aira again. It was almost comical, and often she kept doing it until told to stop.

"This is for you," Aira said, picking up a "Costumes—Special Effects" movie studio sign from the coffee table. "In case you transform into a dragon again. That way nobody will think you're too unusual and take you away."

"That's right, Onx," Mendle echoed. "You know what they do to unusual people around this place. Just look in any Christian church."

"It is relatively certain that only threats of danger cause her to transform," Aira said, patting the dog's head.

"That sign's a good safety measure to implement," Mendle said, his voice starting to sound far away. "If we leave her in the car, or something happens."

"You fluffy white dog. You're so pretty," Aira was telling her when Onx suddenly bounded toward the kitchen.

"Maybe she's thirsty," Mendle said. "I got broccoli for her."

What about the book? He wanted to ask Aira. *What about all I was writing, about you and the dragon?* It was eerie. He felt as if he was being surrounded by his own imagination come to life. *There has to be an explanation for all this.*

"Have you heard from Sandra?" Aira asked him.

"No, why?" Mendle asked, getting up to open the kitchen door for Onx.

Aira shrugged. "I was thinking about her, don't know why."

He stopped to pick up a message that blinked on the answering machine.

"Hello you guys. I have some fabulous issues of *Scientific American* for you!" It was a cheery message from Sandra.

chapter

28

Sandra Wilford listened to her heels clacking down the Lockheed corridor. Their clipped sound gave her a sense of confidence, and she was aware of the way her hair swung back and forth in rhythm with her steps. Looking at room numbers and peering into offices as she passed them enroute to her destination, she assembled a feel for the place.

Subdued energy cloyed the atmosphere and the stark normality of the place, accentuated by fluorescent lighting, was so overstated it seemed surreal. Sandra was having second thoughts about what she had decided to do. Not so much about the rightness of her decision as just how she was going to accomplish it; it had to be done in such a way that would guarantee discovery of the truth.

She wanted to instigate a relentless undertaking. Interest had to be stoked. That would take drastic measures. Yet she had her reputation to protect. She decided she would straddle both sides of the fence—conceal her personal involvement in the matter and, at the same time, secure a promise to give her first break on the story.

Soon, the truth, whatever it was, would be out. At best, it might be the story of the century—provide scientific breakthroughs, bring money and fame, or capture some escapee. At worst, it would reveal the home-town and identity of a delusionary nobody trying to make life interesting. In any scenario, it would eliminate the duress—possibly even danger—from Mendle's life.

Undue duress, she justified, *and distraction he doesn't need. Mendle needs peace. He needs rest. He needs me. I balance him. I keep him grounded. We could go to Hawaii. I could get an assignment there. We'd go together. A room overlooking the ocean. Tropical nights, bonfires on the beach...*

"Yes?"

"I'm Sandra Wilford. Mr. Toor is expecting me."

His black-rimmed glasses made his ferret-like eyes appear even more remote, smaller than they already were. He was toying with a yellow pencil and did not interrupt the motion of twirling it as he pushed himself an inch off his chair in token gesture of standing.

"Sandra. Please sit down."

"Hello, Paul."

Firmly secured back into his chair, he smiled at her from behind his desk. Sandra returned his cordiality confidently. Leaning forward, she extended her hand, which surprised him, but he took it and they firmly shook before she finally sat down in the burgundy chair to which he motioned.

"How have you been?" he asked, so merrily that it seemed out of character.

"Staying busy," Sandra replied, casually taking in the room in measured glances. She did not waste time executing her first move. "Nice to see fewer job cuts as a result of that story I did."

"Yes, the Hubble telescope is doing fine."

"I was happy my story helped Lockheed get that contract." Sandra let that sparkle in a setting of silence, then, "How are you?"

"Hanging in there. Can't complain." Paul thought about his liver, about the terrible pains he had been having in his side, but didn't mention it. "You certainly look well."

"Thank you."

There was a pause. Both of them began to fill it with their thoughts when Paul came to the point. A few moments in the room with her and he was reminded of her efficiency. It left little room for grace. "What can I do for you?" he asked point-blank.

"Well, Paul, I thought you might be able to point me in the right direction regarding some research," she lied.

"If I can. What is it you need?"

"You did say once, didn't you, that the government had its act together? Anybody born after 1963 could be tracked by prints? Provided they weren't born in the Amazon or on a sidewalk."

Paul let a little laugh out. It sounded nervous, Sandra thought. "I suppose what with hospitals, schools, DMV's..."

"As common as Social Security numbers now, isn't it?"

"I wouldn't say..." He was trying to underplay it.

"How do you find proof that someone legally exists?" she asked, baiting his curiosity.

"What do you mean, 'legally exists'?"

"Let's just say someone is in the country, and there is a suspicion no birth record exists," Sandra embroidered.

"You mean an illegal alien?" Paul Toor asked.

Sandra smiled with calculated reserve. "You might say that. Would you have the means to run some kind of query. You know, state to state? Maybe internationally?" she asked, underplaying any seriousness.

Paul Toor bristled slightly as he scrutinized Sandra, and she detected it.

"Let's say," Sandra quickly added, "fingerprints were available. And, let's say the person in question had access to information about aircraft that would change the entire field as we know it?" She hadn't planned on saying that, but it sounded good, she thought.

Paul did not change his facial expression whatsoever. "Well, Sandra," he finally said. "I see your career as a journalist is taking you down some interesting avenues. This is certainly a step up from features in the style pages."

They both laughed.

She sent a laugh dovetailing into his, more to oblige him than anything else, but underneath it Sandra was thinking fast, and on the tail of her tittering agreement, with an underlying tone of granite, she interjected, "And what I know would certainly be a step up for you from overseeing reports of aircraft testing and research."

Paul Toor stopped fiddling with his pencil and slowly raised his eyes. He steadied and narrowed his sights on Sandra and waited expectantly.

He appeared unimpressed. Except for three rapid blinks of his eyes. Those had not escaped her.

Sandra relaxed a little in her chair. With newscaster aplomb, careful not to interject any personal emotion lest it discredit her facts, she said, "I think I am on to something that has national, possibly international, ramifications of very great significance. Maybe more than that."

The smile that had been threatening to flicker in the corners of Paul Toor's mouth disappeared now.

Sandra casually glanced at her manicure, playing for time enough for her words to sink in. When she felt they had echoed in his head long enough, she calmly looked up at him. He had leaned back in his chair. One hand was to his temple, the other was holding his side. His brow was a little crumpled, and Sandra thought he appeared to be in pain. Pleased that he was thinking so hard, and intoxicated with the control she had so successfully exerted, she went one step further, though she had not planned this.

Sandra let her words fly on an arrow of certainty. "I know the whereabouts of a bona fide extraterrestrial."

chapter

29

Around the blue-green planet, Life played in many disquises.

chapter

30

Onx was restless. She was lying in the ivy, and, though she rested her leonine head on folded paws, her lids didn't droop shut for long before flicking open again to survey the goings-on in the garden. Her eyes opened, shifted left and right, then down the deep green cascade of ivy to the sidewalk and street below, then shut again. From time to time, her ears twitched to the tune of small gnats which buzzed at them. Sporadically, she snapped her head to her side, to dive her clipping teeth into a patch of fur, or her rear leg would burst into a frenzy of scratching.

Fleas! Onx abominated silently as her paw thumped furiously against her side. Parasites were the ultimate insult.

She didn't know which was worse—the fact that her very blood and flesh were being used as food, or that Aira had been leaving her alone more frequently. It was equally miserable, she thought; except the feeling of being not needed did bite a little more acutely. What good was she if she could not serve?

Not moving her head, just using her eyes, Onx trailed a local dog who was passing on the sidewalk below. *Click, click, click*—its nails sounded against the sidewalk. Then it stopped.

Oh, no, disgusted Onx as she watched it poke its nose through the fence and sniff a pile of feces. *I don't go around smelling yours,* she thought disdainfully, turning away in aversion.

Mercury, the silver Himalayan cat who lived next door, was in Onx's line of vision now. The cat had managed to enter the vicinity without making a sound—a game he was very fond of—and now sat perfectly still by the rock garden, his blue eyes transfixed. Onx silently transmitted a greeting to him, sending with it admiration for the cat's resourceful stealth, benign arrogance, and exquisite composure.

Mercury accepted the compliments as his due. He opened his mouth in a meowing motion, though no sound emerged. Still basking in the admiration, he abruptly rose, pivoting his weight in perfect distribution amongst four paws. He stretched fluently, his paws under him as though balancing on a pinnacle, and arched his back, all in one elegant flow. After punctuating his exquisite flourish with a yawn, Mercury sauntered over to Onx. Though the feline's eyes lackadaisically drooped into slits, he was in total command. Alert, but feigning indifference, he deigned to touch noses.

The friendly contact alleviated some of Onx's misery and indignation. She raised her head. Her tongue lolled happily from her mouth when she smiled, and Mercury soaked up the benevolence that bathed him from the dog's eyes.

Then a squirrel scampered past them and the cat went off like an alarm. His idle complacence instantly congealed into channeled aggression, and he sprang out of his aloofness, claws leading the way.

Onx dropped her head back into her paws and watched the chase. She didn't like being part of the cat and mouse, dog and flea game. It was an energy trap, a mechanism inherent in the genetic structure of most life forms that surrounded her. Responses to stimuli automatically sprang into action—without the consent or volition of the participants.

For the most part, Onx had made friends with some of the local inhabitants. One afternoon, she recalled, when she was in particularly good spirits, she had managed to get them out of it for a time. She considered it a triumphant victory, though no one was there to acknowledge it. Had Aira seen it, Onx was sure she would have been given a medal. It was a beautiful sight, one that Aira would have especially loved. Birds and cats and dogs and squirrels and rabbits lounged around the garden together.

It had been all too short-lived, however. They were stuck to forms in a system in which they had to consume each other for energy. The duration of amiability between them lasted only as long as Onx could dissipate the energy flows that locked them into their roles of cause and effect.

There were other systems. There could be. Somewhere Onx had known them, though the knowledge was just beyond the periphery of her grasp. Meanwhile, life in this garden left little room for unique encounters. The squirrel made it safely up a palm tree and was pummeling Mercury with abrasive chatter.

Suddenly, Onx felt the fur of her back stand on end. She turned to face the direction from which she sensed danger. It was Podo—a large, gnarly, brown dog who had been coming around lately, insistent on one thing—copulation. Now he was generating extreme animosity toward her. After tearing at the ground with his paws, sending dirt and ivy bits flying behind him as he did so, the dog approached her with his head bent and his tail slung low.

Rising up, Onx took a firm stand on all fours. The last time he had been there, just three days past, a terrible fight had ensued between them when he tried to mount her and she wouldn't let him. She was appalled that, again, without any other attempt to communicate, he immediately began trying to sniff her tail.

Onx rumbled a low growl at Podo and kept swinging away from him, trying to face him while he pursued her tail end. Any thought Onx tried to project was to no effect; the dog was dense, its stimulus-response mechanism intensely in gear.

Three other dogs were scuffling and scrambling onto some boxes that were piled up by the trash on the other side of the fence, and, by the time Onx noticed them, they had entered the yard and were approaching. It seemed they were all reacting to the likes of Onx being unknown in the dog kingdom. The dogs had some type of system going; they started moving in unison with Podo. The animals seemed to derive confidence from one another. They assembled, sticking together in a semi-circle, about three feet in front of the white Samoyed. Their mouths curled back, baring the menacing glisten of their fangs, and they snarled as though they were one entity, one mind, on the wavelength that Onx should be destroyed because she was different. Ever-growling, they jumped forward in springy little starts to taunt her.

When Onx sized up the situation, it held absolutely no interest for her. She had no desire to oppose these creatures, nor any wish further to attempt to be understood. It was their problem, not hers, and she flatly refused to receive what they were trying to push on her.

In one deft maneuver, Onx bounded past them and darted across the front yard where, half-way down the ivy slope, she leaped into the air and sailed over the fence. Even Mercury, hiding in the fuchsia bushes, was impressed. Smugly and stealthily, he crept off around the side of the house, leaving behind the hysterical crew of dogs now stuck in the yard.

Onx kept running. The sensation made her feel as though she were leaving behind disgust, boredom, and all she could not comprehend. Up the winding canyon road she ran, aware of the fleeting pavement under her paws and the wind against her face.

Evening flowered in pink and mauve, and, with warm gold, the sun varnished a completed day before going off to begin a new one elsewhere.

Color lifted off the surroundings; the air grew fuscous, and night spread between remnants of light until all color was absorbed and blackness was intact.

It wasn't until dark that, back at the house, Aira noticed the strange dogs in the yard—none of them Onx. It was just about this time, too, that Onx thought of Aira and felt a pull to go back to her. She was feeling sheepish for having doubted Aira's love for her.

Of course I am needed, Onx thought, *and loved.* Just because their activities together had been less demanding, and less frequent, did not mean they were no longer a team. In fact, if there were ever a time when Aira needed her, this was it. It began to dawn on Onx that this was the worst predicament, the most forsaken and degraded of dimensions they had ever been in.

Onx had picked up her pace and was moving back down the canyon at a good trot when something that had been brewing for some fifteen minutes spilled into action. A pack of coyotes which had been tracking her downwind moved in for the kill. In a split instant they were all over Onx—one at her throat, two on her back trying to push and flip her to the ground—while the younger pups circled.

The fact that they were a pack of five, coupled with their severe hunger, forced them to overcome their cowardice and attack such unusually large prey. The hysterically shrill yelps they discharged to confuse their victim were soon the gnarling and gnashing of teeth about Onx's ears. All of it, as well as her own pitiful yelps of pain, was too fast, too incomprehensible, too much of a shock, too much randomness. Onx could not create her own space in time to begin to transform.

Frantically, she locked her forelegs and yanked her head free. She could feel the flesh around her throat rip as she did so. She struggled for distance, but, when a third coyote leapt on her, she lost her balance and slipped. With a solid thud, her ribs hit the ground.

She tried to roll away but one of the coyotes, too wily to miss the exposed belly, leapt for her stomach and voraciously ripped at her flesh with its teeth and nails. Onx's legs flailed in the air, and she tried desperately to twist over, to grip the ground with her paws so she could right herself. The sensation of being devoured caused a conflict of perceptions and feelings. One of them was sexual and she could not understand it until she saw it was the body's thrust to reproduce in the face of death.

She managed to lock her jaws onto one coyote's shoulder and, using its body, pulled against it to get upright again. With mustered and concentrated effort, Onx heaved and twisted onto her feet. It wasn't even pain that she was feeling anymore, but a delirium of panic as the reality of the situation continually focused in ever-sharper degrees: they were going to eat her.

I'm not prey. The concept of being a victim was the ultimate insult, and her sense of dignity surged in acute protest and determination not to allow it. Onx's transformation process surged to activate, but her present form was too engaged in operation.

One of the coyotes was diving for her underside again. She was losing blood fast; she could feel it, as she could feel that its odor and warmth were driving the creatures into a wilder frenzy.

From Onx's gut and from her entire spirit pulsated only one desire: to keep her life, to survive. In the violent tornado of vicious growling, of snarling, and ripping and clawing of flesh, she tried to find the eyes of her assailants. In glimpses, however, she saw there was no calm to be met in those discs that were glazed and yellow. Only an absence occupied them.

In this contact, she saw the difference: she could reason and they could not. The life that animated them was so amnesiac that it was being stimulus-response machinery. It was machinery, mental and biological, that had taken over and engulfed them; any life that was extant was only obeying the machinery's dictate—eat to survive. So, life clashed in a conflict of different purposes; both sides were fighting to live, one side mechanically executing the precept that the other must die in order for it to survive.

Onx registered beams of light filtering through the trees, and, the next thing she knew, the coyotes were slinking off. Weak and humiliated, she collapsed, knotted in the abomination that life itself must even struggle to live. From very far away, like a dream, the sound of Aira's voice came to her, calling out her name. "Onx! Onx!"

She heard footsteps, and, "Over here. I heard it over here." There was the sound of a car door slamming shut. Then more footsteps, fast, crackling through leaves. Onx strained to open her eyes, and she saw the blurred image of Aira kneeling beside her. Unable to keep her eyelids open for long, she let them close, succumbing to their heaviness and to blackness.

It is a universe of force, she projected faintly to Aira.

Oh, Onx. I know, I know. Aira wept. She looked at Onx's bleeding body, at the open gashes and torn flesh, and felt the lacerations as her own. "Oh no, no, no."

Mendle was behind her. He had taken off his shirt and was ripping it into strips for bandages.

I am embarrassed for you to see me this way.

"You're not this way, Onx. You're not. You *are* life. This is only your form," Aira was saying. Then she collapsed her body over Onx and embraced her, sobbing. "But it's damaged…you could die…please don't. Don't die. Don't leave me. Oh, how can this be?"

Mendle was kneeling beside them now, and had begun wrapping the strips of cloth around the more gaping wounds.

"I'll never find you in this maze. What if I don't find you again if you go away?" Aira whispered. Then, suddenly, she became very, very still.

In the dark, Mendle saw her body begin to glow with a dim incandescence, almost imperceptible. He felt as though he were in the presence of something holy and became filled with an awe which made him stop everything he was doing except breathing—and even his breathing slowed down, as if to disengage from time.

Some moments elapsed before Aira let go of Onx. She slowly sat up. Her face and shirt and arms and hands were smeared with red blood, but her expression was very tranquil.

Mendle followed Aira's gaze to the dog's body. Onx's wounds had stopped bleeding. Not only that, a section of her belly that had been gouged open, from which entrails had been protruding, was now healed shut, and a dry scab had formed.

The three remained huddled in the small patch of woods for some minutes, suspended in the silence of unadulterated life. When Aira touched Mendle lightly on the shoulder, he looked at her and saw that the incandescence was gone. His instinct was to reach to her face and wipe off the blood that stained it.

Aira started to speak but her voice gave out, and she had to clear her throat before starting over again. "She's still a little weak," she told Mendle. "Can you carry her to the car?"

Mendle nodded. His eyes questioned her and she answered.

"I can accelerate a body's own repair system," she said sadly. "I'm not fully in control over it, though."

She hung her head a little and thought for a moment. When she looked up, Aira appeared somewhat shaken. She continued, "When one understands certain mechanics, one can control them. Maybe full and complete understanding is Love. And Love…" she paused, then went on, "…is granting full life. But this is a strange place." Her eyes wandered as she repeated it, almost gasping. "This is a strange place."

Abruptly, Aira looked at Mendle. Both fear and a plea for an answer occupied her eyes. "Oh, Mendle," she said, aghast, "I can't control it."

She stared down at herself, studied her forearms, her hands. "I'm not totally in control of this." She looked up in amazement. "I can *die*," she gasped, stunned and perplexed. Slowly turning her gaze to Onx, she almost whispered as she grasped the nearly unbearable fact, "Just as if she had been dead...I would have lost her."

chapter

31

"Ev'ry night I hope and pray a dream lover will come my way. A girl to hold in my arms and know the magic of her charms. 'Cause I want a girl to call my own, I want a dream lover, so I don't have to dream alone. Dream lover where are you with a love oh so true..."

It was enough to make Sandra Wilford get off the sofa, even though the song was about over.

"...Someday I don't know how, I hope she'll hear my pleas. Some way, I don't know how, she'll bring her love to me..."

"Yeah, right, she's gonna hear you from outer space," Sandra muttered through the remnants of sleep clinging to her. "She'll zip down in her space ship," she suggested sardonically, rankled by the memory of Mendle's connections to the song which he called a "mid-twentieth century Earth Classic." She felt for the seek button and pushed it. "I doubt that's what Bobby Darin had in mind," she grumbled.

The radio settled on another frequency. Lush orchestrations of the Moody Blues filled the room. "I love you, ooo yes, I love you. Oh how I love you…oohhh…"

Another one of Mendle's favorite 'classics.' Thank heaven you're not here,
Mendle. You'd think this was some coincidence that meant something. Hugely
significant.

The phone rang.

"Another coincidence," Sandra cracked caustically, heading for the
portable. "Must *mean* something."

"Hello?"

"Hello, Sandra. Paul Toor here."

Wondering why he was calling her on a Saturday, she toned down
her abruptness. "Yes, Paul."

In different locations Paul Toor and Sandra Wilford stared out of
their respective windows as they conversed.

It was one of those California winter days when, from indoors, the elements appeared savage. The sky was low and grey. Some trees relinquished their brown and orange leaves to winds that promised cold, but
the palm trees and other tropical foliage called the weather's bluff.
Nonetheless, one could succumb to the illusion of winter for fashion's or
change's sake.

Despite Paul Toor's nonchalant approach, Sandra cunningly detected
tension in his voice; she recognized a restrained pacing. When Paul finally came to the point, she was curious about his seeming effort to underplay what he told her. "By the way, regarding the matter you came to
me about. I did check into it thoroughly. Seem to have found something
from Iowa, Idaho, somewhere."

It was too good to be true. She, too, played bored. "Really? Which is it?"

A pause, then, "Iowa."

"And?"

"Nothing much."

"Nothing?" then, into his silence Sandra lightly tugged, "What do
you mean nothing?"

"Just some Jane Shmane from Iowa. Nothing more," he finally met
Sandra's interrogative silence.

"How did you trace the prints?"

"Standard Driver's License I.D." He cleared his throat, then, "No
'bona-fide extra-terrestrial.'" He laughed.

As Sandra calculated, she steadied her voice and calmed the gloat of satisfaction that was mounting. The ploy worked. He hadn't been able to resist
the incredible. "Well, let me know what you have on her. Who is she?"

"Not from Mars," Paul said dryly, a terse attempt to introvert her.

Sandra forced a laugh to camouflage her anxiousness. "My apologies. I feel a little silly now," she contrived. "However, checking out leads, law of journalism number one, don't rule out any possibilities." She was fully awake from her nap, excited she was about to finally find out who this woman was. "Let me get a pencil."

"Why don't you arrange for us all to go to a show or something," Paul suggested casually.

Another abrupt silence. This time a vacuum from Sandra's end. His tone was mild disgust. So, what was his interest?

"A show? What interest would—"

He cut her off neatly, his voice still on a perfectly even keel. "Never mind then, Sandra." He changed slant. "Anyway, I'm sure you understand I can't let you have access to information privileged by my position. I suppose you can be content I verified your initial, uh, hypothesis, as incorrect."

She knew the game. *Quid pro quo*—something for something. "A show. What a great idea. How about the ballet? A concert."

"Either might be nice."

"I'll arrange something. I've been in the mood for music lately."

"Yes." Toor paused. "Perhaps we can talk sometime, when I'm at the office," he alluded.

Before she could finish saying "thank you," he hung up.

Sandra's attention stuck on the conversation. She speculated on Paul Toor's suggestion they go out, wondering if he had personal interest in her. He wasn't a type popular with ladies, that was for sure; probably shy about dinner alone with her, this was his way of arranging a date. *Every man I meet wants me.* He couldn't resist her body, Sandra understood, and the information she wanted from him was a way he could ensure seeing her again.

I like this new haircut, Sandra thought, catching her reflection in the mirror across the room, admiring her bangs. *Totally hot.*

Her thoughts turned to the girl. *From Iowa? I wonder what her real name is, how old she is, what her life is about. And won't Mendle be...surprised.* Sandra imagined telling him, *'Yes, she's from a planet called...Iowa,'* then handing it to him, *'Here's her driver's license, Mendle.'* She contemplated his devastation. *It's time he adjusted to reality,* she decided.

"I love you, ooo, yes, I love you. Oh how I love you...oohhh..."

In his studio, Mendle Orion's thoughts undulated with the music-poetry of the Moody Blues. Power was in his hands, he felt the taut reins of something he harnessed. He had taken to painting, a desire he had had since childhood. Now, as he brushed canvas with strokes of colors, he indulged in vibrancies—blue, violet, yellow, white, orange, green. Each emanated the beginning of color itself to him as he painted. In love with them, he moved his brush to the music.

There are artists who are fluent in one medium. And there are artists who speak in two, or more, or all mediums—music, invention, color, form, motion, words. He quickly exchanged the paint brush for a pen to make notes. *Master artists. The degree of mastery is the degree of evolution, to some pre-divine stage,* his pen touched the page and thoughts flowed as ink. *Metamorphosis, perhaps, occurs at arrival. A return to a previous state, or a transformation into an even more evolved state of existence and being. An evolved being is the master of matter itself. There, one doesn't even need sound, and music, and color, or words, but rather creates mediums with which to speak…out of nothing. The artist returns to, or achieves, the state of Creator.*

He trailed off on that thought and read over what he finished writing. Conceptualizing was exquisite. Gone were the days when rage had pushed up from his insides, protesting the indignities that affronted his dreams.

Mendle set down the pen, and the brush was back in his hand. The large canvas pictured the Cosmos and was interwoven with portals and gateways to other dimensions.

His days of hell seemed far gone, impossible now even to have existed. It used to be that his aspirations to the sublime—glimpses of comprehension, of beauty, nobility of sentiment—all seemed to end in death. Senseless violence and cruelties shouted to be what was real, barraging the decency and love in which he believed. Once it had nearly destroyed him.

Media broadcasts touted rage and rights for minorities, magnified demands to license departures from common sense. It seemed the practitioners of every possible aberrant human conduct were being made into a minority needing civil rights, while, conversely, those who strived for excellence were taunted, shunned, ridiculed.

It was criticized as elitism or bigotry by "politically correct underdogs" if geniuses insisted they be allowed the right to create a better world for all. The good-hearted were attacked if they demanded the world be honest, fair, and kind, or if they pointed the finger at criminals.

Mendle had the picture now. Lowering the standards for scores on SAT tests was viewed in education as a solution to the problem of fewer people passing. It amazed him that educators actually discussed it as an alternative. Doing this was like shortening the length of a football field because athletes, out of shape from bad diets, thought it was too far to run. Lower the standard, don't find the real problem. *Be less, don't feel bad, we'll all be less.*

In this world excellence was fought. Criminals were defended as "under privileged." Beauty and compassion were fought harder than twisted insanities. "Don't dare champion excellence, it'll make others feel bad." But only excellence could *inspire* and *uplift!* His rage was no longer red about it. It was white-hot, bordering on the blue. It surpassed anger and became intention.

Mendle did not put himself above others, but he knew the planet's population was asleep and being enslaved further. They had bought the biggest dupe of all: they mistook those of valor as their enemies. Clenching the rot pumped to them by those who would keep them slaves, they found false comfort in the propaganda promoted on TV aimed at making aberrations "okay." They wallowed in filth because what they had lost and forfeited was too painful to bear, so they accused perfection, believing it rebuked them. They attacked ideals, believing they did not have any within them. They escaped their true selves by embracing the dark, thinking the light would expose their dirt. *But you are the light. You are the light.*

"Z Zone," he mumbled, thinking about the last chapters he had written, about those who wanted to forget, to sleep, to be numb. He understood it in them from having understood it in himself.

He was strong now, determined to communicate his vision. He would somehow get past the impostor publishers and the producers whose specialty was speculating on push-button reactive trends for profit. He would find ways to give people the elixir of his soul, to offer portals to the excellence that was the core of every human being.

As he worked, his dreams and purposes burned in him, bordering on blue heat. No more implosions of defeat. This time he had seen it—a glimpse of that part of life that could affect the solid, physical reality. He did not have the whole picture, but he was not about to let go of the clue he saw.

It had to do with *her.* Her. She filled him and he sailed her, like an ether. She was synonymous with his dreams. He had known it from the moment he saw her. Before he saw her. Since finding the girl that afternoon in Anaheim, a nightmare had ended. The oppression of lowest common denominator, of "everybody is just like everybody and it's all crap" was over. He was renewed. He was writing. He was painting. He was sculpting. Power. He felt the power of creation. The power of gods—this was certainly it—raced in him.

If everyone were themselves, each would be a unique deity…no common denominator slogans and acquired-personality mannerisms. Thinking about Aira, the sentiment vibrated more than just Mendle's cells, it reverberated the very essence of his being.

He wanted more. He wanted her as a woman. And, yet, he wanted her in a way he had wanted no other woman. This was different.

Mendle put down the brush and closed his eyes, feeling the want of her. He wanted her nude, pressed against him. He wanted to feel her lips, her mouth on his. He imagined the wetness of her mouth, her tongue. He wanted to merge with her and hold her. He wanted to feel her under his hands, her thighs, legs. He wanted to feel the heat of her tightly around him, her arms holding him, her hands on him. He wanted to make love to her, to tell her he loved her. He wanted to feel her feeling him. She would whisper and moan and writhe with pleasure. *Finally.* Yet that was only part of it. It was *her* that he wanted to touch.

"Are you concerned?" He heard her voice.

Mendle held still. He took a deep breath and opened his eyes. Aira had entered the room.

He shrugged, shook his head. "Sometimes I think about the future. I wonder what's going to happen."

She was looking at him with that innocence, transparent as a clear mountain stream. "We could look at it like a video game," she offered.

"A video game?"

"Yes. You're the commander, the player, see?"

"Okay."

"Okay. So, you're running the ship, and the screen is life. Well, if you knew everything that was coming up on the screen, it wouldn't be as much fun. Right?"

"I guess, not if I knew everything that was coming up." He looked at the floor realizing she hadn't understood what he meant, then he looked up at her again. *I love you. I love you.* The way he was feeling, it amazed him she didn't know.

She wasn't looking at him, she was saying, "Right. It wouldn't be a game if we knew everything that was coming up on the screen."

Mendle felt a twinge of annoyance that she was making pinball analogies. Here he was on the living pulse of Love itself, surfing a wave from the beginning of Source that carried the full momentum of that stretch. *I could just go over and take her.*

Aira sighed, blowing the air out of her pursed lips. Resigned, her thoughts turned to her personal dilemma. "*My* problem is I can't even see the past, let alone what's coming up in the future," she said.

"I'm not worried about what you'll find out about yourself," Mendle told her, adding, "as long as you'll be in my life."

She beamed a smile. "I don't think anything is an accident."

"Why did you say that?" He jumped on her statement.

"Because it's true."

Mendle searched the girl's face expectantly, then picked up a paint brush saturated in indigos and turned back to his canvas. No, he didn't want to *take* her.

After admiring Mendle's painting for some moments, Aira resumed talking, "But the good thing is that no matter what comes up, you're at the controls."

She was back to the space video game analogy. Although she had a point, as Mendle listened to her, she began to sound as though going to the mall was having its effect. "Sometimes you have to dodge, sometimes you have to swoop, or slow down, or speed up, or blast something, or refuel, and sometimes you can just cruise."

"And sometimes something is at work that is...not *planned*," Mendle said, his attention still on the 'nothing happens by accident' comment. "It might as well have been because it's perfect. So it's no *mere* coincidence." With a small laugh, he relinquished trying to explore it.

"I know what you mean. About the coincidence stuff," Aira assured him. Out of the blue, she said, "I'm glad I studied about money."

The change of subject threw him a little. "I guess I am, too," he admitted, thinking about the idea they had placed with his agent. "That Bath Book is going to be a real commercial trend..."

"Because, thanks to you and your agent, we have traded it with society for money," Aira pointed out.

"That's one way of putting it, I guess."

Aira's idea of printing books for people to read in water on a patented paper-plastic formula had brought a nice licensing fee. She had agreed to Mendle's suggestion that it be paid in his name to avoid complications about a Social Security number. *What am I afraid of finding out about her? That she has one? Or that she doesn't?*

"You know, this entire planet is under one economic hoax. It's designed slavery," Aira said earnestly, as if she were making a discovery that very moment. "Those supposedly in control are more in debt than those who honestly try to produce. The way it is now, money isn't even an accurate measure of a person's production, let alone their value. It's horrible."

Mendle silently reveled in her words. She was saying exactly what he loved to hear. He told her, "Yeah, artists should plan wealth. Instead they're fooled or manipulated into poverty. Finance should represent value. Creators and philosophers should be leaders. But self-serving tyrants are afraid of them. They might set people free."

"Yes!" Aira exclaimed. "The idea has been introduced that artists shouldn't have wealth. Or that to be creative one must be deranged. Either with drug problems or some other type of aberration. But artists are high-order beings, creators…"

"I was just thinking about that!" Mendle told her, enjoying the coincidence of her communication. "It's partly a scam perpetrated by power-hungry, self-serving walking dead. But also, violations of the soul seem atrocious to artists. They won't adjust, so they seem nuts. But the ones *howling* are sometimes more okay than the smiling oblivious."

"It's portrayed as glamorous for artists to be decadent and irresponsible. I saw one of those pendants saying that creativeness comes out of neurosis. This is financed. And beauty is not."

As Mendle watched her and listened to her passion, the girl's thoughts seemed suddenly incongruous with her demeanor. Dressed in a cotton dress, she looked to him like she should be out hanging wash on a clothes-line in Georgia. He wondered where that thought came from. *Wash on a clothes-line?* It was her appearance, he decided—classic, not outstanding, just fresh. She was so…plain wholesome. He turned back to his painting.

"Artists are more concerned with what they're going to give to the world," Aira mused. "Then there are people who think only about what they are going to take. I guess they've convinced themselves they cannot create anything, so they must take it from someone, or somewhere."

Mendle was loving everything she was saying; that another person thought of these things with such interest was ecstasy. For a moment, it seemed almost too perfect.

"And wars, there's another thing," Aira said, firing up. "They are not fought for principles. Not at all."

He turned around to look at her.

"I just have to do something about this," she blurted out, raising her arms in a grand gesture, then, as quickly as she became enthused, letting them drop to her sides in disappointment. "But I don't know what. I don't even know about me, how can I help the world?"

"You came close," Mendle reminded her of her memory flash.

"I had a glimpse of something. And then there was Onx. That transmutation was weird. I had a surge of some kind of ability, but I don't even know now what I did, or if I did it," she wailed. "It's as though it never happened. Did it happen?"

Mendle nodded. He had seen it with his own eyes when she lifted the vase, yet he had doubts, second thoughts, too, wondering if the thing was really as it appeared, questioning if he really had seen it. "I saw it," he told her quietly, firmly, acknowledging to himself it was telekinesis of some sort. Then there was the interplay with matter the night Onx was hurt. Aira had been glowing. Hadn't she? *True, it was only moments. The light can play tricks upon the eyes.* Yet she did do something extraordinary that night, he couldn't deny it.

She laughed. It seemed strange to her now, and she shook her head. "I said I must not be from here. Do other people feel that way?"

Mendle narrowed his eyes. "Like they're not from Earth?"

She bobbed her head once.

He shrugged. "I guess," he answered. He himself had experienced the feeling. He had read articles about people who claimed to be from other planets, but it never went further than words. Mendle sighed. "I feel as if I've been blind, reading braille with my fingers, and now it's in full sight."

Aira questioned him with a look.

"Something is right in front of me," Mendle said. "Something that has eluded me all my life. I've known it's there, but haven't known what it is." He paused, then insisted, "There's more than these solid walls and the few years we live that's called a life." He shook his head. "Only trouble is now maybe it's so close I can't see it."

Aira looked at the deep blues and violets intertwined in his painting. "I guess I still don't know who I am, either."

Her voice had become suddenly small and insecure. It amazed Mendle when she talked like that, sounding like a little girl, like any girl out of any town, anywhere. Minutes ago he had almost gone to her and put his arms around her. He had been going to kiss her. Now he was certain he couldn't; not with her concerned about herself like this.

Again he thought of telling her about the book he was writing, that he had written about her and about Onx. Shouldn't he at least confess that, on the night she was an emotional mess in the hotel bathroom, he had suggested her name was Aira Flight? And that he was the one who said the dog's name was Onx? He restrained himself again from bringing it up. *She needs to arrive at conclusions and details herself,* he justified, fighting off chastisements and feelings of culpability. *Unless, of course…*

A doubt nagged him, posing the girl under a different light. She was someone unstable, perhaps someone who had suffered a severe trauma and was undergoing a delusion of some sort. The possibility injected by Sandra, that the woman was a science fiction fan putting on a calculated show, surfaced again.

He silenced it. *No. No. It's her, I know. It's Aira Flight.* Then the next logical question suddenly presented itself to him, big as big. If this were indeed the Aira Flight out of his book, how did she get here? How was it that a character from a book he was writing now walked and talked in his living room? *Talk about master artist. First sound, color, clay, words. Then…actual universes, whole entire realities. Whoa! That is the ultimate creation, the ultimate mastery.* Mendle considered, without reservation, that he was potentially a god. He no longer questioned if—only how.

He had heard of quantum realities. The observer actually influenced the experiment. Quantum physics had isolated Thought, the observer, from the particle. *But thought doesn't make particles. Or does it? And how is it I'm writing about her in the first place?* Gone was his self-derision. He no longer questioned his own sanity.

"There's more than what meets the eye," Mendle said to Aira. "We'll see it all eventually. We see what we see, and we'll see more when we see it."

His pragmatism caused her to smile.

Mendle returned to mixing his colors. He continued talking, his back to her, "Like a video game," he referred to her analogy. "Just don't let go of the stick."

Aira's smile blossomed. As she watched Mendle painting, she wanted to go and embrace him. Desire translated itself to her body. She wanted to be physically close, she wanted to touch his lips with hers. She wanted him to hold her, she wanted to give him pleasure. She held the feelings to herself, didn't know why, then realized it was because she was afraid Mendle wouldn't understand, because she herself did not understand. Intense sentiments moved inside her, then a terrible fear of losing him wracked her. It was just one more emotion engulfing her which she could not explain.

I know you, she thought intensely, looking at the back of him as he worked. *Why do I feel I know you?*

chapter

32

It was gloriously civilized at the ballet. In the restaurant of the Dorothy Chandler Pavilion, elaborate crystal chandeliers and candelabra refracted light from their many facets. Along high-ceilinged walls, grand mirrors festooned in gold caught and multiplied reflections of shimmering, subdued lights, casting the room in an aureate glow.

The sonic mood was set by the harpist. From a distance, he appeared to caress the harp he embraced. As he plucked, lilting cascades of ethereal tones poured from his small, elevated, round platform, the nucleus of the room. Conversation murmured; though its circumfluence undulated, the volume never rose above the level of the harp's pacific ripple.

At each table, starched white tablecloths and gleaming place settings boasted of civility, as did the bejeweled, begowned bodies of beings who sat at them.

Around one of the tables, Mendle J. Orion and the woman called Aira Flight dined with Sandra Wilford and Paul Toor. The four had just finished the main course when Mendle excused himself from the table. He wasn't back by the time the waiter brought the dessert. After several minutes of waiting, Sandra decided to start.

"I say let's begin," she announced, picking up her spoon. Dressed in tight, short burgundy crêpe de Chine and faux emeralds, Sandra wasn't aware of many of her own thoughts, nor of the hate in herself. *Three more hours and I'll know who she is.* She focused on that and bided her time until Paul would give her the information.

"Doesn't everyone look beautiful?" Aira effused, taking in the room. She directed her sweeping admiration to Sandra, who sat across from her, and beamed, "It's truly a joy to look at you."

Sandra quickly averted her eyes to the chocolate soufflé in front of her. *Truly a joy—cut the crap.*

"Very sophisticated," Paul said, deeming approval with his tone of voice.

"I guess it's better than wearing white and pretending to be innocence personified," Sandra said before scooping a spoonful of foamy soufflé into her mouth.

Aira was wearing white. The thought that Sandra referred disparagingly to her seemed incredulous.

Paul Toor shifted in his chair. "You look rather lovely yourself," he told Aira. "That necklace is remarkable," he added.

"I'm pleased it delights you to look at it," Aira replied earnestly, her hand touching the fiery diamonds. "It was a gift from Mendle."

Pleased it delights you to look at it? What bull. "A new publishing deal? Or did someone die?" One of Sandra's eyebrows arched as her eyes darted to take a look. *They're huge.* Aira's face, her shimmering eyes aglow with candlelight and the silvery white of the tunic she was wearing, appeared ugly to Sandra.

"It's a celebration gift," Aira told her. "For the licensing of my 'Gain for the Vain' program." Her hand went to the necklace again. "I love it because it's beautiful. When you think about it, diamonds are just stones. Rock. Old coal, actually. Isn't it amazing to think many people would die for them?"

So they're real, Sandra thought, swallowing another spoonful of soufflé. *They are to die for.* "I suppose living with Mendle can be bearable if a girl is getting some…old coal…now and then."

Aira's face riveted into puzzled scrutiny. "What do you mean?" she asked, sensing something, but again finding it incredible that Sandra would mean to be deprecatory.

With childlike fervor, Aira waited for an answer but Sandra hadn't missed observing a moment of ferret-like intensity on the girl's visage. *She's shrewd. That innocence is just a front. She's cracked—escaping a mundane life in Iowa, or running from something.*

Aware of Aira's continuing puzzlement, Sandra made a point out of savoring with leisure the soufflé she had just dished into her mouth. She let the spoon linger behind closed lips, appearing enraptured, though she wasn't even tasting the warm chocolate. She removed the spoon from her mouth, flicked her eyes closed then fluttered them open, rolling them skyward as if to say the dessert was heavenly. She swallowed, then finally looked at Aira as if amazed the girl was still expecting an answer. Nonchalantly she conceded, "Nothing. Just his mood swings. The hostility. Haven't you noticed he's a little, uh, not all megabytes functioning?"

Aira's voice was quiet when she spoke next, yet its sincere, underlying intensity commanded attention. "Is your idea of honesty being critical of others?"

Sandra laughed. "Quaint. Well," she ignored the inquiry, "maybe you bring out the best in him."

"That might be who he really is," Aira offered. "His best."

Sandra fell quiet. *Damn this bitch. She has an answer for everything. And she's quick.* Again biding her time, Sandra smiled. *All I have to do is get through the evening. Then we'll have the facts on this mid-western bleach-head pretending to be Bucketta Rogers.* She drew comfort from the anticipation of seeing Mendle's fantasy crumble.

A stabbing pain shot through Paul Toor's side. *Liver again,* he thought, concealing his discomfort as his hand shot to his side under the table. He had quietly established Sandra's vested interest as having something to do with Mendle. Calmly letting his eyes wander over her features—her shiny, sleek hair, her narrowly bridged nose—he pegged the journalist as being in a rigid state of self-worship. The woman's incapacity to admit her wrongs was among the weaknesses he determined could be manipulated at an appropriate time if needed.

"Mendle and I are old friends," Sandra started up again, covering her tracks. "I adore him. Ask him when he comes back." She tossed her hair and smiled. "Do you always have to be so serious?"

"But what are you being?" Aira asked, more innocently than ever.

"Can't we have some fun? You think you're going to save the world or something? I was just kidding!" Sandra pretended exasperation.

Paul Toor backed up to a point of interest. "Gain for the Vain?" he asked Aira.

"Yes," Aira replied, feeling a little introverted but unable to identify what was wrong. "A manufacturer has licensed the rights to sell a product we hold the patent on."

"May I ask what it is?" Paul asked. *Keep the questions subtle.*

"They're books, printed on special patented plastic. To make it popular and easy to read in the bathtub, in swimming pools, while relaxing in saunas or jacuzzis." *How nice of him to be interested.*

"Clever," Paul commented.

"So you're working now, are you?" Sandra asked pointedly, then, noticing Mendle returning to the table, "Ah! Here he is, he's back," she announced.

Paul Toor bristled with annoyance at the interruptions.

"We just couldn't wait to start dessert!" Sandra greeted Mendle as he resumed his chair.

"Yes, we started dessert without you." Paul conceded a little laugh. *He could be a problem.*

"That's fine. It looks enticing," Mendle said as he eyed the caramel-decorated presentation in front of him. *I wonder what they've been talking about while I was away.*

"And, you see, nothing has happened to your friend, uh, Aira, here," Sandra told him, hastily adding, "You seemed so reluctant to even excuse yourself to the rest room." *As if she's so precious.* She reached for the bottle of Chardonnay angled in an ice bucket. "As you see, none of us have, uhmm, left the stratosphere."

Mendle had been doing well. He was simply observing Sandra. She didn't succeed anymore at creating havoc inside him. He was, however, becoming concerned about the situation, and regretted having allowed himself to be talked into "dinner and a concert." Time passing since seeing her had mellowed the memory of her. Yet, something was awry, it wasn't "just him." *Something, something is not quite right. Things are never as claimed with Sandra.* That, he knew, could be a fast rule.

"Allow me," Sandra gestured, filling Mendle's glass. *Drink yourself to death, you pig.* "Let's celebrate. A toast to your success."

In Sandra's eyes, despite the smile, glinted something cold and hard. *Ironic,* Mendle noted, *she called me a slimy drunk, but how willing she is to pour.*

"None for me," Paul said, placing his hand over his glass. He glanced and smiled at Mendle. *I wonder what his weak link is.*

Purposefully leaving Aira until last as though she were an afterthought, Sandra commented, "Oh, and your glass is still full." She replaced the wine in the bucket, swirling the icy water a little by rotating the bottle as she concentrated on recalling every memorized flaw in Aira's face to make herself feel better. *Her eyes are too big...she has no cheekbones to speak of...her lips are way too full...her chin is not prominent...she is not tall, she's too...formed...too much corn in Iowa.* Sandra smiled smugly to herself. Looking around the room she said pointedly, "Most people are so short."

"What are you working on now?" Paul asked Aira.

"Oh. What I really want to do is crack the speed of time."

The table fell silent, allowing a wash of harp to rise and ebb from their hearing.

Mendle was alarmed. They had made a pact not to discuss amnesia, not to discuss her name, and to avoid any questions about her past by deferring to him, but they had not covered this. In his opinion, it was too close for comfort.

"To solve Death, solve Time," Aira said.

"Solve death?" Paul asked.

Taking the vacuum for interest, Aira was off and talking. "People are being driven into being enslaved to bodies. In the society they are bombarded with things that lead them to be convinced they are matter. It's quite astonishing really. I weep over it frequently."

Sandra rolled her eyes and reached for her wine glass. As she sipped, she glanced over the top at Mendle. *He doesn't look disheveled. The circles are gone from under his eyes.* "You seem tired, Mendle. Are you all right?"

"No," he kept a straight face as he replied jocosely, "not at all." Calmly he kept his satisfaction to himself. *I'm getting good at this,* Mendle thought. *With a little practice I might be able to handle anything slung into my world.*

"Shouldn't we be going soon?" Sandra changed the subject, feeling foiled.

"In a moment. We have time," Paul said.

Sandra shot him a look. *What do you friggin' care about this?* She went on, trying to change the subject. "The food was okay, but what a rip-off. I like to get the best when I pay good money for things."

When Paul redirected his interested look to Aira, she resumed talking eagerly. "All this forced attention on drugs and body parts makes people think they are nothing but sensation devices. Bodies have basic drives. But it isn't this biological organism that creates and loves." She held her arms out at her sides, using her body as demonstration. "How can an *object* create? How can mere *matter* create, love, conceive?"

"Mmhhm," said Paul, adjusting his dark-framed glasses.

"Simply, a person shouldn't confuse their self with whatever the body feels. The person is the person. So the human being should realize there is a duality there."

"You mean like a schizophrenic personality?" Sandra suggested.

"Extra personalities can be made with those subliminal garbage tapes you listen to," Mendle held her in check. "You're just uploading a synthetic phrase-circuitry personality."

"You should try it, Mendle," Sandra said, implying he could use some help. Her eyes were riveted on Aira while she waited for a reply to her question.

In a small gap of silence, Mendle interjected, "I don't want to be programmed. I want to deal with myself, not to cover up what's there."

Aira addressed Sandra. "The duality is material and spiritual." *I wonder if they'll understand.* She explained, "Even when we talk, think about it. There is the sound of the words. And there is the thought. My thought is not the *sound* I make to convey it. The sound may *appear* more tangible, yet the thought actually is. It *exists.*"

"So you contend a distinction, a difference between the material and spiritual in human beings?" Paul Toor asked. *I am nothing.*

Aira continued, "Definitely. I am not this body. Yet I am being it."

Oh, right, Einstein, sounds impressive. "How fascinating," Sandra said.

Aira went on, "Sensations are wonderful, but a huge spectrum of them are neglected because people become fixated only on the body and —television encourages this—on wavelengths of sex and violence. The more numb the human race becomes, the more people need very heavy impacts—like sex, drugs, and pain—to even feel anything."

Yeah. Hurt me, baby. "Why do you lump them all together?" Sandra asked. "Good sex isn't pain and drugs." *You short, stupid idiot. Your thighs are fat. Mine are thin.*

"I don't," Aira replied. "The cultural trend is doing so, destroying sex. I'm saying there are also many more subtle, fabulous sensations— like even beauty, communication, and the accomplishment of goals—to be had in addition to a limited bang. I would say awareness of soul makes better sex."

How does she know about sex? Mendle shifted in his chair.

"The people of earth are being controlled and milked by soul-masters," Aira said.

People of earth! Go, Bucketta. Sandra delicately dabbed her lips with her napkin.

"Viewers of television, for instance, aren't aware of their own physical vulnerabilities. They get used, manipulated by images of depersonalized sex. Their buttons are pushed and they respond like robots. Some of those ads have no faces. It is only body parts. There's no exhilaration of communication, no person-contact, no *soul.*"

"But people are buying it," Sandra said.

"Those who are more aware or in power should exercise responsibility and not just milk people like ants tending aphids," Mendle defended the point of view.

"Compare, let's say, a candy bar and a gourmet delight. The candy is bang, boom, obvious," Aira said.

"And delicious," Sandra said, making the words a sexual innuendo and looking at Aira as though she were crazy.

"But think of the subtle deliciousness of a dish with many aromas and harmonies. Unless the palate is sensitive, one cannot detect a whole feast of possibilities, and just settles for a blast of one-dimensional—bang—taste. Think of what people are missing!"

"Bing, boom, bam," Sandra quipped, and quickly pretended to arrange her napkin, deflecting a sharp glance from Mendle. *She's good at this,* she thought, protesting Aira's euphonious voice and eloquence.

"And how does this relate to…solving death?" Paul asked.

"I say enjoy all you can before it's time to go," Sandra pronounced, pushing her chair back from the table. *What does it matter anyway?* "I prefer life more simple, less complicated, you know. We should enjoy the good things of life while we're here. You take yourself way too seriously." *It's all crap and they're going to suffer with me.* "I mean, come on, what is this material and spiritual stuff?"

"It's about Thought," Aira said. "And bodies."

"Go on," Paul said.

"Survival on planet earth is defined in terms of eating and having shelter. True, but there's more. Yet, the idea is being enforced that people are nothing more than organisms."

"But that is indisputable," Paul Toor agreed. "We do have to eat." A general malaise came over him.

"Precisely. However, there is *another* part to us that *also* has to survive. I'll show you." *Okay, emanate, flow.*

Mendle coughed loudly, then, "I really don't think that's necessary," he said. Sandra caught the cross-flow between Aira and him as he cautioned her with his eyes.

"No, by all means," Paul Toor encouraged.

With his tone of voice, Mendle tried to make the situation mundane. "You're luminous enough already, honey."

Honey? Sandra mentally stabbed his use of the endearment. *And what the hell does he think he's underplaying? You're a regular little glow-worm, right.*

"Death proves the fact that we're biological creatures. People do die," Paul Toor said. "That is pretty final." He felt the sharp pain in his side again.

"Death can present the problem of losing the people you love," Aira said, seeking reassurance from Mendle across the table.

"I would say so!" Sandra exclaimed, her voice oscillating to the shrill side. Regaining her composure, she challenged, "So, you think there's more after death?"

"Only the form dies." *You are a thought-being, life itself.*

"Maybe for some…super-humans," Sandra jibed, managing to keep a conservative tone. "But when this bod goes, hey, that's it. I'm done."

"You don't agree?" Paul Toor asked Aira.

Aira shook her head. "The death process is a waste of time," she said. "Having to be born into a body that defecates and pees uncontrollably, thinking you have to learn to walk, talk, read, write, et cetera, all over again and…"

Mendle felt energy waves tingle up his back. *I don't know.* His hair began to stand on end as he listened to Aira.

"…having to start all over again and losing any progress outweighs the usefulness of death."

Sandra asked, "Usefulness of death?" *She's nuts.*

"Well, death serves acquiring new organisms after these age. It also serves starting all over again," Aira explained. "It appears to serve a purpose."

Sandra arched her eyebrows. "How do you know all this?"

I'm not sure," Aira said, appearing a little confused.

"Go ahead," Paul urged.

Sandra suppressed a smirk, letting enough of it escape to decree judgement.

Aira went on, "When bodies get old and run down, it's an outrage, an insult to the person there—the individual who is nothing like the flesh."

Mendle felt the pain of seeing his parents age.

"Yes, that shouldn't have to happen," Sandra found herself saying, her attention going to her breasts which she noticed were starting to sag.

"Well, wouldn't that be the ultimate cure?" Aira concluded cheerily. "The cure for death?"

Yeah, you and Jesus. Sandra smirked.

Paul Toor blinked. "Have you found one?"

He's too calm, too silent. Creepy. What is up with this? Mendle had fallen deeply silent.

"I'm working on it now," Aira said. The statement seemed somehow ludicrous.

It's been done, babe. Sandra feigned hiding a yawn.

"What is it?" Paul Toor asked.

"Well, Time is particles changing position in space—the sun, moon, and all of them. That's all it is."

"All right."

"The movement of planets, particles, including molecules of the body which wear down, which is what old age is, genetically, is all Time."

Mendle pushed his chair back from the table. What Aira was saying didn't appear to be as shocking to those present as he might have anticipated. In fact, he was mildly surprised that Paul Toor encouraged the conversation with yet another question.

"And how does Time enter in?" Paul asked.

Nonetheless, Mendle's discomfort was escalating. *There's something about him that's dead or something.*

Aira smiled, happy about the interest. "If Time is the change of particles in space, and all particles have different rates of motion, I am convinced it has an overall speed." She paused. "The Speed of Time."

"The Speed of…?"

"Precisely! A uniform speed for which an equation is possible. Such as for light. And cracking that speed will result in finding the very periphery of this universe. Imagine, the edge of the material universe! It also opens the way to new techniques of travel and propulsion. It may provide the ultimate explanation for science's missing link—Thought."

"You mean power of the mind?"

"No. Power of the *soul*. The mind is energy, and uses energy to function. It's a physical thing, too. But when a person knows something, it's done much faster than thinking. Why? Because the person isn't using a mind when they *know*. That's pure thought. I think reality on Earth…"

Why don't you stick to your planet—Iowa? Sandra scoffed, amusing herself with her wit.

"…may be an interface between Thought and Matter."

Reality on Earth, an interface between Thought and Matter! Of course. How is it at times she's so lucid and confident? Mendle wondered. *And other times she sounds like an insecure child?* He rose decidedly from his chair.

"Quite interesting," Paul said.

"Yes," Aira agreed as she stood up. "The sad thing is that, unless there are some changes, I foresee a time when people would want to die and can't."

"Really?" Paul asked, straightening his dinner jacket.

"Because people consider the cure for death is just keeping bodies alive forever." *Instead of being free from matter.* "Medicine may achieve the technology to keep a body going forever. That's fine, but what of the person inside? What keeps the person in good shape? Why did death even come about? People do things they regret. They compromise, instead of understanding, or gaining wisdom. They feel badly when they do wrong. This is what kills them. It's torture. That's why they want to forget." Solemnly, Aira emphasized her point, "Imagine a body that lives forever, remembering and being unable to free one's self from spiritual pain and regret."

Paul held onto the back of his chair as he felt the room shift slightly. Aira continued, "And human beings are so wonderful that even their smallest transgressions haunt them with remorse. Eventually, just from pain alone, many desire to die. It manifests physically, but it starts with the thought-being."

Mendle tried to wrap it up. "If you think about the word 'humane,' it stems from 'humanity.' The natural condition of the human being is not this synthetic, violent, glib, amoral, sex-pumped creature being sold to us as reality."

Short pains ripped through Paul Toor's side again as he listened.

"Oh, Mendle," Sandra chided.

"Human beings can be quite nasty," Paul Toor said. The way he bowed his head when he said it reminded Sandra of a priest she had known.

"The only solution would be to befriend oneself, and to understand," Mendle commented. "The fact that a person even feels bad or would want to forget is evidence that one is essentially good."

"We need to learn to translate experience from pain into wisdom," Aira said. "It's a matter of Love…"

"A difficult emotion," Paul said.

"Love's not an emotion. It's a state of being, an ability," Aira stressed. *To grant life, even to self. Total understanding.*

They were still lingering around the table. When Paul Toor began to cough and reached for his water glass, Mendle used the lull in conversation. "Curtain in twelve minutes," he announced.

"Vast concepts," Paul commented as they headed for the lobby.

"Yes, and concept precedes every discovery. Like the microcosm and macrocosm. It had to be conceived before it could be approached."

Do you ever stop? Sandra grumbled silently. "You are so brilliant, Aira."

"The speed of time," Paul Toor ruminated. "But the technical aspects? Do you have any notes? Any equations?"

"I do," Aira began to say, but she stopped when Mendle gripped her arm.

"Isn't this something, the way these two have just hit it off?" Sandra said. "And it's so nice to see you, um, feeling better, Aira."

Steering away from the subject of memory, Mendle answered for her, "Everything we discussed is based purely on observation."

Momentarily distracted, Sandra glanced at a beautiful woman walk-ing by. "Look at that woman's hair, it just doesn't work with the gown. It's awful," she commented authoritatively. *I can't have them realize she's more beautiful than I.*

"I need to go," Aira said, pointing to the women's bathroom.

"Yes. A mere detail. Bathroom. Well...Lofty ideas or not," Sandra chimed her point, "some things are undeniably *real*, eh?"

Then, with Aira some thirty feet away, Sandra let out a sigh and prat-tled, "How can you stand it? Doesn't it get a little much? Your life doesn't even seem your own anymore. All that sunshine. Doesn't it seem a bit *unreal*? But she is so adorable. I just...love Aira."

Paul excused himself to pick up their tickets at the box office. "I'll meet you by the center doors."

Sandra waited until she saw Paul was at a distance and said, "Mendle, we have to talk. I have information for you. You may not like it, but you have to know." Mendle looked at her guardedly.

"It's about her, this woman you've taken into your house. The amne-sia bit, the space bit...she's from Iowa, Mendle. *Iowa.* I had her checked. I can show you a driver's license. Now tell me she hasn't ever read one of your books. Tell me this isn't a charade."

It was unlike Sandra to be premature in her pacing, but this burned in her to tell him. She saw that her words had an effect on him, then turned and walked away abruptly.

In the ladies' room, Aira was happy to see Sandra.

"I just wanted to put on some lipstick," Sandra told her as she headed toward the mirror in calculated strides.

"I hope I didn't go on too much about things of no interest," Aira said, pulling up her stockings to smooth them.

"No, no," Sandra assured her. *Her hair color looks awful.* "It's fasci-nating. I just feel sorry for you sometimes." She pressed her lips together to blot her lipstick then, after replacing the tube in her evening bag, turned to face Aira. "You're just so deep," she told her, "and men are so beastly." With that, Sandra gave Aira her most sympathetic look. "I ad-mire women who want something out of life!" she told her emphatically.

Aira smiled warmly at her and Sandra allowed herself to really look into the girl's eyes. She felt something trigger inside her. "What do you want, more than anything in the world?" Aira asked her softly.

Taken off guard, Sandra tightened her lips together. She stared at the paper towel dispenser on the wall over Aira's shoulder and thought about it. Decisively, she finally answered, "I want to be somebody."

The answer initially evoked a small smile from Aira; however, there was despair in the reply, and she was saddened to see Sandra was serious. "But you already are somebody," Aira told her warmly.

Sandra suddenly recoiled. It was affection that had triggered, a feeling long thought obsolete. Like a flower sprouting in a toxic climate, the sentiment withered the moment it surfaced in her. Had it been allowed to remain, the solutions which were Sandra's panoply—the hatred, revenge, and destructive intents—would have become obvious and unjustified by comparison. For Sandra, to feel anything at all would mean also to feel what festered in her, and that was too painful.

Shunning the courage necessary to acquire insight, she shut down. "Ha. Women have to fight to be somebody," she said. She was unsuccessful at concealing bitterness as she adjusted her dress and inspected her reflection in the mirror.

"Oh, Sandra. Only the *body* is a reproductive machine. And, for that matter, so is the male body. *Beings* don't have a sex!"

"You've been around Mendle too long," Sandra carped. Aira looked at her quizzically.

"You don't know what I'm talking about?" Sandra acted surprised while, inside, she seethed. *Think about me and Mendle together. We had some hot times, bitch.* Aira shook her head.

"During our last months together he lost his, uh..." Sandra finished her communication by placing her hand down by her pelvis, lifting the index finger straight out, then letting it droop.

Aira's eyes widened. "He doesn't have a problem with that," she said naively. "We do not merge, but I've seen it."

"Hard?" Sandra asked, incredulous. *Do not...merge?*

Aira nodded.

"Well, I'll be," chirped Sandra, hiding her resentment. *Don't "merge"? She doesn't even let up in the bathroom.*

"It's a genetic response," Aira explained earnestly.

"After a while he didn't have that, uh, genetic response with me," Sandra said. *Because the ass couldn't marry me.* "I tried. He has major problems."

"Then it isn't just a genetic drive with him!" Aira said. She started talking very fast. "It seems male bodies are rigged to respond to more stimuli than females. Maybe it's to keep the race going...I've observed some males have a mechanical slavery to sex, having nothing to do with the person and character, just visual stimulus." Sandra stared at her, repulsed and mesmerized.

"But Mendle must be integrated!" Aira exclaimed, her face lighting up in a finale. "His body was expressing how he feels about me!"

When Aira hugged her, Sandra stiffened. Renewed hatred for the enigma of this childish woman wracked her. "Right," she said brusquely, repeating, "It isn't just a genetic drive with him, and I already am somebody."

"Of course. That's just a fact."

The door swung open and Mendle, looking stormy and concerned, filled the entrance. *Iowa? Could that be true? Are people looking for her? What if she has a life? Does she know? What is Sandra up to? Has she told Aira? No, they look happy enough.*

"We were just checking our lipstick. Weren't we?" Sandra said. "Relax, Mendle. You have to learn to relax."

The concert was the dance première of a new composer, pianist Roberto Mastoso, who was himself performing and conducting that evening. By the finale Aira was totally ecstatic. She had been carried through torrents of tragedy and joy. "He's a *god*!" she had whispered at one point in the evening. Completely elevated into a realm of all that was most noble of Man, she was beyond words, and pulsated with such joy and to such heights that she could not contain it. Boundaries shed and she felt as though she were so vast that the sun could have been the nucleus of an atom and the planet its electron.

Had Mendle not been so engrossed in his own thoughts and perceptions of beauty himself, he might have noticed the slight incandescent field which began to emanate around her. Aira felt with such magnitude and intensity that she rose upward and forth, carrying the body, which seemed to her like a grain of sand, over the balcony.

Mendle leaped to his feet, completely aghast. Sandra Wilford and Paul Toor remained adhered to their seats, their thinking processes scrambling to explain what was going on.

Into the air Aira soared, across the large performance hall. Moving to the music, she appeared to hover over the stage while suspended in dance by sheer will. The dancers continued their performance but were looking upward, along with the rest of the house.

"Is that...?" Sandra said, then looked over and confirmed that Aira was no longer in her seat.

When Aira alighted on a platform above the stage, she continued to express and interpret the music which was grand and whole. She skipped and leaped with her head thrown back, her neck and torso arched so that the curve pushed her chest forward, as though she were opening her breast to heaven. Her arms seemed to throw off light as she twirled and clasped them in front of her, then threw them out and up, in longing, as though beckoning the paradise of stars and beyond.

When the last refrain swept through the house with utmost majesty, people rose to their feet and filled the pavilion with an uproar which sounded as loud as multitudes of horses in stampede. Some members of the audience were weeping beyond their logical control while others shouted. The applause was furious.

Roberto Mastoso rose from his piano bench and bowed, then exited with swift strides. His long legs took him backstage where the dancers were preparing to take their bows behind the curtain.

Spotting Aira descending a ladder over by the wing, he stopped in his tracks. When their eyes met, they stared at one another, and he continued over to her.

The curtain began to part. The house was still thundering, and, as the dancers bowed, Roberto Mastoso embraced Aira and they held each other tightly. She was uncertain herself as to what had come over her and what she had done. For those minutes she had been completely unaware of her body.

"Thank you," the girl told the composer fervently, brushing her ringlets back, "for the courage I know it has taken you to remain intact to create this. Such beauty, it is Truth!" She was crying. "And they try to convince us beauty is only a dream."

He leaned back from her, and he was weeping also. "Why? Why did you tell me this?" he asked, as though she had uttered an oracle.

"Because I know. I *know*," was all she could say.

The people clamored for him and Aira gently pushed Roberto Mastoso from the wings. He turned and beckoned to Aira but she would not follow him. So, Roberto Mastoso walked to center stage where he received the public's adulation. The light and admiration of a crowd of people transported out of their limits was intense. In these moments the musician had no regrets that his ruling tyrants had been Music, Beauty, and Art, Principle, Honor, and Ideal. For years to come he would remember what Aira told him, her voice lilting and soft, but fierce, "Through your music, they have found what is true in themselves."

chapter

33

Seeming endless as eternity, the evening passed. Being in Paul Toor's car meant it was mostly over, and Sandra was relieved. Soon she would be rid of them all and have what she wanted. She was beyond hating herself for compromising; doing so had become perfunctory routine to her. Numbly, she was doing it again, pretending to like someone in order to ensure an objective.

"I thought we could have a little nightcap," Paul said, pulling up to the curb.

Not wanting to upset anything, Sandra tacitly agreed. Without waiting for the valet to open her car door, she gingerly got out of Paul's car, concealing her impatience as she waited for him at the steps of the hotel.

When they arrived at the revolving rooftop nightclub, Sandra quelled a desire to turn around. Although these places made her dizzy, she maintained composure, keeping herself perfectly together. "Let's make it a quick one, I still have to do some work on an article deadline," she said.

Waiting to be seated was more drudgery. Though it was only minutes, it felt arduously long before they were finally settled at a table and she could broach the subject.

"So," Sandra put on a self-effacing laugh as she fished. "I told you the person was a little…weird." Paul didn't say anything.

"You probably thought I was crazy at first," she continued, languidly swiveling her chair sideways and crossing her legs for him to view. "I appreciate your tracing her for me."

When Paul seemed unimpressed, Sandra felt compelled to explain. "The extra-terrestrial bit I came to you with was a potential theory. She apparently had some problem with her memory. Actually you won't believe this, but the city detective services first gave me the idea. There was a case some years ago."

It was Paul's turn to volunteer information. Sandra waited for it. Instead of giving her any, he asked, "How long have you known Mr. Orion?"

"Mendle? About two years. He's a little weird himself. I actually tried to get him to see my therapist."

"Oh? Who do you see?" Paul asked.

"Alfred Kaufkiff."

"Do your friends like him, too?"

"Mendle did go, once. Actually I wanted him to bring that woman there, too. Who is she? What did you find?"

"How long have you been seeing Dr. Kaufkiff?"

"Not long." Sandra felt a tug of suspicion. She had been trying to be charming. "I don't see him anymore. Nothing serious. I wanted to get over a relationship." She emanated her most sensible presence.

"How long has Mr. Orion been seeing Miss Flight?"

"That's not her real name, you know…"

"All right."

"In fact, what is it? Let's get that over with, Paul. Then we can relax. You said you found a driver's license?"

"I don't have any of it with me," Paul said, patting his jacket.

"Is there anything you can tell me?"

"Call me at the office. That would be best."

"Don't you remember any specifics?"

He was a wall. "I'd have to look up the file." The tone was final.

When the waitress brought their order, they sipped champagne and looked over the city lights in silence.

"How long has he been seeing her?" Paul repeated his question.

Sandra was annoyed. His persistence surprised her. She didn't turn off her charm; she turned it on all the more, while hardening within. "Almost a year."

"Did you know her before then?"

With a toss of her hair, Sandra purred, "All these questions. Don't tell me you find her attractive, too." She lifted her glass. "Maybe we can talk about it more. After Monday."

"Fine," Paul smiled tersely.

"I'll call you at the office." Sandra smiled. They clinked champagne glasses. When he put his hand on her knee, she didn't say a word.

The constellations twinkled overhead at the Valleyheart house. It was 3:00 a.m. and Mendle still couldn't sleep.

"That friend of Sandra's gave me the creeps," Mendle repeated. "There was something familiar about him. What was his name…Paul Toor? Paul Toor. Where have I heard that?" Mendle searched his memory.

Sensing Mendle's annoyance with her, Aira tried to explain why she leapt off the balcony. "I was just happy. The music was so beautiful. I mean, war is okay. People walk around in an environment that is completely unacceptable, at least in my opinion, and no one says anything. Why should anyone be upset with me just because I expressed joy and love?"

"That's not exactly it, Aira."

"I feel agitated now." She sulked in the white armchair.

"You feel agitated. Let me see. How can I put this? After your gargantuan extravaganza, don't you think someone's going to get curious about you? Wouldn't you like to know who you are before other people do?"

"I'm curious," Aira said, still not sure how she did it. "There was that curtain, it had a cable on it…"

"It looked like you were flying," Mendle yelled.

Aira thought back. She didn't recall anything her body was doing, just a huge ecstasy she seemed to float on.

"Do you know what people would do if they knew about you? That you glow…move objects…heal wounds…in fact…" He trailed off.

"What?"

Mendle mulled over what Sandra had blurted out, about having traced Aira to Iowa. *What did that mean? Was Sandra in fact digging or was it another one of her bluffs, a control tactic?*

Aira was waiting for his reply. Her intention was strong, he actually felt it like suction. "I don't know," he said, suddenly despondent. "Don't you remember anything else?"

"I don't think I was *flying*, Mendle," Aira said.

"I mean about your past."

"I don't. I really don't," she apologized. "And I've read about charisma, telekinesis and faith healing."

"This is crazy." Mendle got up and started pacing. "If you in fact did fly over the balcony, and did not use any cables or ropes or curtains, whatever, to help you down, it confirms whoever you are, you've got something unusual going. If the government knew about you, they'd lock you up."

Aira laughed. "Do you really think so?"

"I know so!" Mendle yelled, his face turning red and scaring Aira. "Look at the news!" he shouted, exasperated. "Rape, senseless murder, those damn carjackings. People buying it as normal, everyday life? Don't you wonder about that?"

"Actually, I have—"

"You know how easy it is to steal a car? So why would people kill their fellows, just blast them to get a car? It isn't necessary. It's because things are getting crazy. People are getting desperate. They go crazy if police get over-anxious. But let's see some riots over nuclear accidents. Let's see some riots over crime, murder, theft! Come on, citizens! Show your damn wrath over drive-by shootings, killing children! Drugs. Political greed. Over people being killed over money. Get out there and riot over that. Grab some criminals and get incensed, dammit. It makes me wild. But no. Crime is being supported. The government hires criminals!" His eyes bulging, his fists clenched, he screamed, "Do you realize where we are?" Some of his rage temporarily spent, Mendle threw himself on the sofa.

"Maybe we can do something."

"Sure." Mendle crossed his arms in front of him. To the tune of the Mighty Mouse cartoon show, he sang, "Here she comes to save the day! Aira Flight is on her way. Here she comes to save mankind! And we say…it's about time…"

Aira started to laugh.

Mendle fell silent and allowed himself to sink into brooding. *If that's even your name.* He decided he would first look at any evidence Sandra offered before mentioning the driver's license.

As Aira watched him, something stirred in her. It was on the periphery of her knowing, just out of reach but distinct, even though she wasn't sure what it was.

"We're only human, but we can try," she heard herself trying to placate him.

If she insists she's human, what does that make me? Sub-human? And the rest of the human race? Tied in a knot, Mendle suddenly sprang to his feet, stomped over to the cabinet, and angrily yanked a bottle of bourbon out of the hutch. "We're up against some pretty big-timers. Pharmaceuticals are big money. It's more than one vested interest manipulating people with drugs, training people into obedient slaves!" Angrily, he twisted off the cap.

Aira's face crumpled into noncomprehension. "Mendle," she said, heartbroken at the sight of the bottle.

Onx had been sleeping in the corner of the room, and was now on her haunches, confused.

"Don't mind me," he hissed. "I'm unlocking my potential!" He started to lift the bottle to his lips.

"Mendle, wait," she stopped him. "When I talk about beautiful things, people just stare at me." She felt huge sorrow pushing up to cry. "I say it's possible to have a true civilization, to cure crime and war...and I'm looked at like I'm saying something insane." He looked down at the floor, and shifted his feet impatiently.

"But that isn't insane," Aira said. "War is. And crime is."

"But it's here. You can talk, talk, talk all you want. You can be Miss Sunshine all you want. That doesn't change it."

"Mendle," she said when she saw his arm tighten to lift the bottle. "Mendle, you...you're my friend. When you drink, you go away."

The simplicity stunned him. "You *are* different," he insisted.

"Do you want me to hold myself back, to make myself look less? So you won't feel bad?"

"No, that's not it."

"Don't be a traitor to yourself, Mendle. We're no different." Aira started to cry as the sorrow broke loose. Realization that had been hovering at the periphery of her awareness flooded her. *I know you. I do know you. I love you. I've loved you forever.* Grappling with the validity of the thought and not wanting to impose it on him, she couldn't voice it. "We're both trapped, Mendle. We both have limits."

"I know!" he howled, elongating the words, his voice ungodly and bestial. He hurled the bottle of bourbon across the room, sending it smashing into the wall where it crashed, shattered, and splattered its contents.

When Mendle looked at Onx, he swore he saw her fur turn a bluish color and smoke sputter from barred fangs. She moved too fast; she was over by Aira in an instant, sitting on her haunches, valiantly flailing her paws.

"It's all right, Onx," Aira said and the animal reassumed her normal Samoyed smile.

Mendle laughed as though he had cracked. *That dog ain't no farm dog from Iowa. Unless I'm seeing things.* He saw himself laughing like a madman and stopped. Amazed at his own behavior, Mendle moaned, "I don't know, I don't know," and, covering his face with his hands, he crumpled to his knees. "God, what am I thinking? What am I doing?"

Aira recalled Sandra's descriptions of Mendle as hostile and moody; the comments had instigated doubts about him. His anguish was real. It did have a reason, even if he didn't know what it was. She went to Mendle and, dropping to the floor next to him, she encircled him in her arms and held him.

"I don't know how I've held on this long." He was sobbing. "I don't know anything. One day I'm a god. The next day I'm shit. It's useless, all of it."

Aira held him, and caressed his head. "I understand," she said.

Mendle wiped his face. "I'm sorry."

"Okay. Whatever it is, there's a reason," she told him calmly.

He laughed abruptly. "That's true," he said. "That's logical. There is a reason." He looked at the smashed liquor bottle and saw how he used it, playing into the very thing he condemned, knowing he would never do so again.

I know you, I know you. I've loved you forever, she found herself thinking. It was intense and real, but she did not understand it completely.

Mendle sat up. "You know, Sandra insinuated that you talk too much and the sunshine bit isn't real. I'm sorry. It affected me."

Aira nodded, perplexed. "But she told me I was deep," she said, confused. "She said things to me, too, about your moods, and that men are bestial."

It shouldn't have surprised him, but it did. "Figures. That's just how wars get started. Divide and conquer. Someone pretends to be a friend to both sides. Tells one side one thing, and the other side something else. It gets each distrustful of, or turned against, the other." Mendle vowed once and for all with no exceptions, Sandra could not be trusted.

"That's true. While pretending to be a friend to both sides, they're actually an enemy, treasonous to both," Aira said. Her eyes narrowed. "It's so incomprehensible. It makes no sense. Cooperation is so much more productive."

"That's why it's insane. It makes no sense," Mendle said.

"My first reaction to something like that is usually 'It can't be' or 'I don't believe it,'" Aira confided, finding her response to evil interesting for that reason.

"Mine, too. Because, I mean, why? We see the symptoms in the society, of sickness, but the cause is almost invisible because no one can believe it—it's so incredible."

"You see, you haven't completely condemned the human race," Aira said.

"Yeah. I have to remember to be specific." It usually was a specific person or two causing the damage, he realized, making it seem like everybody. "What else did she tell you?"

Aira smiled. She playfully lifted her finger, held it straight, then let it droop. She thought Mendle would laugh, but he didn't.

"Yeah, right," he said. "Well, it's true. I'm not much of a man. And I surely wasn't with her."

Aira laughed. "Being a man doesn't rest in your penis," she said. "Nor in your guts. It's a matter of soul. You are a man, and more. You have courage, you do. Because you dare to wonder even if daring to wonder means not having pat, easy answers. You observe and you feel and you dare to communicate it in your work, even if no one agrees with you. You go into areas that would terrify others, yet you're willing to experience even the terror if you must. And loneliness..."

She was exciting him. Her words were enthralling, and, as he listened to her thoughts, he was getting an erection. It had never quite happened that way before.

"...And when you don't travel a paved road, you don't know what's ahead, but you keep walking, because you know it's the right one. That's courage. It takes courage to admit you don't know. To find out. Being willing to experience fear, to do the right thing, no matter what. That's courage. It even takes courage to cry. To admit you don't know. You're a man, Mendle Orion."

She embraced him.

I love you.
I love you.
I've longed for you.
Where have you been?
My love.
It's you.

Mendle and Aira pulled back and looked at one another. Neither of them had been aware of their bodies, or how they came to be holding one another. They almost kissed, but Mendle looked away.

"I have this thing anyway," Aira apologized. "I think I'm looking for someone, for some true love." She shrugged.

He was getting tired. He didn't want to touch the ring of coincidence. "I hope you remember soon. I'll help you however I can," he murmured.

"I'm *me*," she said, her voice lilting upward, almost like a question. To his silence she offered consolation he himself had given her. "The details will come, I'll remember. I almost remembered more tonight."

Mendle shook his head. "You might be...married or something. There might be someone waiting for you somewhere."

He looked at her closely. *She isn't pretending. She isn't lying. She can't be. If she's from Iowa, then she herself doesn't know. It won't explain my book, how I described a character just like her. Then again, I'm not the first man to fall in love with a woman I think I've dreamed of forever.* Mendle shook his head. He was ready for her, body and soul. He got up to shake off the intense desires.

"I just want to make sure you really love me," he explained. "That you know me and love me. When you're completely...fine. You know what I mean?"

Aira nodded, wishing she remembered details of her past and appreciating Mendle's position. Pain seared though her. She felt rejection, even though she hadn't expressed her love to him. *It's only fair I completely know myself before declaring I love him.*

"I sound like a girl," Mendle said, grinning.

"No. What you're talking about has to do with *character*," Aira said softly, not looking at him. "It has no gender."

Feeling understood, Mendle walked back over to Aira, sat next to her on the floor, and channeled his affection into an embrace. As they settled onto pillows on the plush carpet under the skylight, they reminded each other to send a patron's check to Mastoso. They decided to start a "Defense Fund" of their own kind, to champion the 'real minority' and finance the funneling of inspired material into the society. Then, looking up into the night sky, they wandered in thought and drifted, until their bodies fell asleep.

In the corner of the room, Onx could finally relax. She did a final surveillance of the area, mostly through one eye. Then, lazily, she let her lids droop shut and dozed off into the pleasant advantages of being a dog.

chapter

34

Amazing how an entire life can change from one day to the next, thought Paul Toor as he swished mouthwash and avoided his reflection in the bathroom mirror. He snapped his fingers, thinking, *Just like that.* After swirling the mouthwash around a couple times more, he spit it out into the sink, then went to put on his jacket.

The television crackled to life. "…special show for you today. Our guests are the lovely Dr. Midge Wuthers and an unusual inventor—her idea was the 'Bath Books'—Aira Flight."

The television audience was applauding as the host went on with his introduction. "Two lovely ladies. One has very down-to-earth advice, and the other plans to turn bathtubs into libraries! Stay with us!" he announced sensationally before going to commercial.

Mendle was uneasy as he waited in front of the television for the program to return. Sandra Wilford had called him to harp on the driver's license. She said she would give him a photocopy. The girl he called Aira Flight was really Irene Davis from Des Moines. Sandra told him she had fingerprints from a glass traced—all for their own good.

A sense of resignation overwhelmed Mendle. *I have to be prepared to give her up sometime,* he told himself. *What did I expect? That someone I found in a hotel bathroom would stay in my life like that, untouched forever? Living out a role I imposed on her?* He knocked himself for even considering that he had created this person, who was a human being with her own rights, and it amazed him how far out there he had gotten, following that mindset even for a moment.

His eyes slowly traveled to the television broadcast. *Irene Davis. From Des Moines, Iowa. Someone will probably see her, recognize her, report that she's been missing,* he thought. *The fantasy will be over.*

He only hoped that the girl hadn't intentionally fooled him, that the whole thing wasn't some publicity stunt. He was prepared to let her go, but if her amnesia were not legitimate, if she were pretending and the past months had been only a calculated ploy to take advantage of him, if she were to become suddenly somewhat avid and ambitious—he would permanently lose trust in anyone and anything.

✦

"Get on it—and I mean today! You were supposed to have that list to me by Friday. I don't give a damn if it is Saturday. Get it. I'll be here."

The words were ferocious but Sandra kept her calm; as usual, she had it totally together. She set the phone down and silently cursed the new trainee at the newspaper office. Then, settling back into her sofa and, aiming the remote control, she turned the volume back up on the television.

✦

The television talk host was addressing his guest, world-famous clinical psychologist Wuthers, "So, what you're saying is that a girl should invite a man over and offer him fruit before deciding whether or not she should marry him?"

"That's right," Dr. Wuthers said pleasantly, nodding her head, firmly but nicely. "If you want to know what kind of a husband he'll be, you place a bowl in front of him with grapes, bananas, and oranges in it. Now, if he takes the orange, you know he's a very devoted, loyal man, prone to taking very good care of the family. If he reaches for the grapes, watch out. He is fickle."

The host was listening to her very seriously. "And bananas?" he asked solemnly. Dr. Wuthers intentionally tempered her altitude by projecting the image of 'accessible pal' even though mental authority. "You're in luck!"

Careful to exude pleasant warmth and personality, she continued, "Bananas mean he's a real homebody." She concluded assuredly, "Very likeable and home-loving."

From the other guest, there was an outburst of laughter that seemed incongruous to the conversation. The camera picked up Aira and moved in for a close-up.

"You are joking! Aren't you?" she exclaimed. "Are you an actual doctor?" she asked incredulously, shocking everyone.

A panned long shot of the audience showed people exchanging looks and tittering. The host turned to Aira. Careful to restore respect, he emphatically confirmed that Dr. Wuthers was a leading psychologist.

Preceding his statements with "As everyone knows," he referred to some notes listing credentials and famous institutes. Dr. Wuthers punctuated everything he said with bobs of her head and polite, cheery "Uh-huh's," and a "That's right." She was solemnly quiet after the mention of the establishment from which she obtained her Ph.D.

There was a moment of silence in which everyone expected Aira to be duly impressed. The camera came in close.

Instead, Aira said, "You're educated? I'm sorry. That makes what you said especially ludicrous. Yes, really, you're dealing with symbols and significances that have nothing to do with what something actually *is*. Grapes equal fickle?"

Midge Wuthers confidently folded her hands on her lap. "I'd be happy to listen to your theory," she graciously invited.

"What if someone just happens to like grapes?" Aira simply asked. The audience laughed.

Aira turned to them and said, "Is there anyone out there who likes grapes?" There were some yeses and scattered applause.

"Okay," Aira replied. "Does that mean you're fickle? Are you all fickle?" One person shouted "No!" and others followed in unison.

"But I bet she had you wondering about yourself for a minute there! Probably even trying to convince yourselves you must be fickle because you like grapes." The audience laughed again.

Aira asked Dr. Wuthers, "What if someone just didn't feel like peeling an orange in the particular circumstances? What if the man thought it would be messy to peel, or what if he had a hangnail? So he reaches for a grape. Would he then be condemned as fickle? Or maybe some man's potassium deficiency creates a craving, so he chooses a banana. He's a capricious, disloyal individual, but suddenly the banana makes him a homebody?" Midge's face was frozen in a tolerant smile.

Aira was amazed. "Do you call this a science? Seriously?"

"All right, we have to break," the host intervened. "Don't go away, we'll be right back!"

America snackin'. Snack, snack, crunch, munch. Don't lift your armpit unless…Hot, hot, sexy, sexy, sex. Cool fashion at half the price. Fire. Two children—shooting victims. Be noticed. Get close. Women who eat too much. Gangs. Low fat. 25% fewer calories. Earthquake. Murder.

The theme music surged when the show returned, and Dr. Wuthers delivered the statement she had been holding onto during the commercial break: "The human being is a funny animal."

Aira opened her eyes wide in an overly emphatic gesture. "No, doctor, the human being is not an animal."

"Don't you like animals?" Dr. Wuthers deviated.

"Let's remain on the subject," Aira said, and the host lifted his eyebrows to the audience. "The human being is not a stimulus-response machine such as the Pavlov Dog theory would have us think."

"Ah, but we are," Dr. Wuthers said with a smile, trying to infuse her voice with a fun spirit of learning.

Aira shook her head. "Certain responses of the mind or the body can go into play when activated, but people are not animals to be manipulated with psycho-babble. We are not just programmable blood and guts."

"People suffer from many complexes. That is why there are *experts*," Dr. Wuthers stated, placing herself in the position of one who could analyze Aira.

"An impulse is different from a sentiment. Aspects of the body or mind can be activated by stimuli, yes, and this can confuse a person, especially if the *impulse* does not concur with the individual's *sentiments*," Aira explained.

"A person *is* impulses," Dr. Wuthers stated.

"No," Aira told her, "If people understood that their beliefs, sentiments, and ideals do not have to be minimized by any conflicting reactions of their mind or body, they would realize who's home."

"Who's home?"

Aira nodded. "A person can start doing something about it just by knowing the difference," she said fervently, "and people can be liberated from brainwashing that convinced them that they are evil or bad. Don't you see? An individual's ability to observe and reason should be the science of the mind—*freeing* from stimulus-responses, not using weaknesses or buttons further to make people into robots!" Carried away by Aira's enthusiasm, the audience began to applaud.

As the host started to interject, Dr. Wuthers clipped him off. "Very optimistic!" she declared, holding her hand up knowingly, and when the audience settled down, she said to gain their support, "It's healthy to have dreams."

Aira isolated what it was about Dr. Wuther's statement that bothered her and said, "It seems to comfort certain people to think that these are only dreams. Right? Puffywoofy dreams—fine because they can never be realized. So toss the human race its little dreams, but not the big ones that wake and free them. Give them the fragments—a little hope. Give them a few drugs to ease the bleak-pictured reality, the reality that is foisted on us everyday—that we are nothing more than animals, life is hell, and we die?"

"That's a very strong statement," commented Dr. Wuthers without changing her demeanor. She lifted her chin, and her eyes turned suddenly very analytical. The smile was not as wide, but still in place. "You feel very strongly about this."

Benevolently and curiously, Aira gave voice to her realization, "And you appear to have trouble feeling about it."

"Excuse me, where did you say you earned your degree?" Dr. Wuthers inquired.

"I find observation to be my best teacher," Aira answered the question and skirted the issue of her lack of memory.

"Reality is not all that bad," Dr. Wuthers began, talking down to Aira as if to comfort her.

Aira stopped her. "I don't have a problem with reality."

"I'm not saying anything against you," Dr. Wuthers denied pleasantly.

"And I'm not paranoid," Aira rebutted flatly, pointing a finger as she caught the doctor's unspoken implication. The audience exploded into applause.

Aira flushed with pleasure. She was standing up for others, too, she felt. Along with that came a drive that bypassed and left in the dust her introverted concerns about self. Her body was shaking, but she was voicing her convictions, aglow with the feeling that she was doing something for the world.

Raising her voice over the handclapping, she said, "But crime, murder, all manner of aberrant behavior, economic slavery, and fear are not my idea of what to accept as 'reality.' I mean, come on, it's just common sense here. When you look around and have people insisting that disease be allowed free rein but decency and tenderness and values should be quarantined, something is *backwards*!"

Another round of applause went off from the audience. The host was about to say something but Dr. Wuthers raised her hand expertly. "Does the thought of death bother you?"

Aira thought about it. "No. It insults me."

"Quite a bold statement," Dr. Wuthers analyzed.

"Thank you," Aira mused playfully.

The show host, appointing himself referee, parroted the psychiatrist,

"Another strong statement. Are you going to modify it?"

Aira looked at him with mock offense. Then, letting go a big smile, softly said, "No." The audience was hushed.

"But!" Aira sat up straighter, "I will point something out here. We have all witnessed it firsthand. Science of the mind should be a system which gives us understanding and improved mastery of our lives. Yet the practice of these who call themselves experts seems to be…control operations. What kind of music will make you spend money in the stores? What colors make you eat? What drugs make you obedient? And more, I'm sorry to say. How to program assassins. What can make active children inactive? What drugs can break wills and keep people from remembering too much? It's science of pulling strings, pushing buttons, drugging, and enslavement."

Dr. Wuthers held up her hands to show they were empty. "No strings," she said, laughing.

"There's an example," Aira cited conveniently. "Changing the subject, attempting to introvert, using a literal meaning to twist the intended one. Psyche means soul, yet it's denied we are souls! Instead, the agenda seems to be: 'pull strings and keep the human being down into a programmable animal.' It's grotesque frankly. How do I know? I just know. Most of us, if left alone, just want to live, and love. Life could be truly beautiful." Aira stood up in her enthusiasm. The audience went wild with applause and cheering.

Her eyes starting to twinkle, Aira kidded, "Who knows? Maybe I am paranoid. But you know what they say. 'Just because I'm paranoid does not mean they're *not* out to get me!'" The audience laughed, cheers rose, and applause increased.

While the show host had not expected it to be confrontational, he was pleased with the results, from a standpoint of ratings.

"We'll be right back…"

✦

Paul Toor was beginning to burn inside. He turned down the volume as the commercial aired, focusing his attention on a small stack of papers he held.

It won't be long, he was thinking, *before someone becomes curious.*

He thumbed through the papers Sandra had brought him, the final favor he had extracted from her before producing the driver's license she was after. Giving Sandra the impression it was an excuse to see her again, Toor had alluded to, on the additional pretext of mere curiosity, wanting to see any notes that 'Mendle's friend might have' on the subjects discussed over dinner. Sandra, finally getting the point that she'd receive her information more quickly by doing so, volunteered to get any there were to be had. She still had a key to Mendle's. Sandra managed the heist by faxing papers she found at Mendle's house to herself, using his machine when he wasn't home.

Perusing the copies, Toor stopped at a page headed "Speed of Time." Notes were scrawled in longhand, presumably Aira's, about vectors changing between masses as the distance between masses changed. It stated that there was also a constant vector field, and Time was a resultant. The mystery of gravity was somehow a key, as was the fact that the universe was a binary universe, based on terminals of two, positive and negative. Paul Toor's palms were sweating.

✦

Mendle balanced a cup of tea on his way back to the television to see the end of the talk show. He was elated by Aira's conversation; she rang chords in him; he imagined the many viewers getting doses of free life, like vitamins. Despite his turbulent concern with the potential facts about her, Mendle had found himself grinning and on the edge of his seat during the broadcast. Whoever she was, she was right. For thousands of years all manner of men acknowledged the existence of their divinity, until Ivan Pavlov began the movement promoting the theory that love, creation, noble sentiment, and appreciation were mere functions of chemicals.

✦

"She is making a total fool out of herself," Sandra muttered, her attention riveted to the television.

Aira had just announced a plan. The entire world should sing. Every man, woman, child, and living creature capable of opening his or her mouth was to mark a date on the calendar, and, on a given second, stop whatever each of them was doing to unite in song.

"So let's start working on it. Write it down, tell others about it," Aira enthused. "On April 3, 2000, at 3:00 p.m. Eastern Standard Time, every voice will unite in song. Perfectly synchronized, around the entire globe. Sing, shine…and don't be programmed, deprogrammed, or reprogrammed —not any of it!"

Step right up, tell your friends! Sandra sat back and crossed her arms. "A world with no crime is possible. Right," she marveled, staring at the girl's image on the television, then hissed air through her teeth. "And this is the big solution. Just sing."

That's about Mendle's speed. Just the sort of rubbish he thrives on. Thinking about it angered Sandra; all her painstaking effort toward grooving him into being sensible about the real world was being undermined.

"How holistic!" she snapped, getting up off the couch. "Of all the sacchariney, vomitous concepts, this is it." She faced the television and glared. "We'll see how fast you lose your steam, Irene Davis, when your 'mystique' is exposed."

✦

"What about a social security number?" Paul Toor placed the receiver in his left hand as he waited for an answer, and wiped the right palm dry.

He heard Alfred Kaufkiff clear his throat, then say, "Absolutely nothing. The writer, Orion, collects the checks. Deposits are in his name. She has none, no official records."

"None whatsoever?"

Kaufkiff was annoyed at being asked again. "Didn't you also confirm it through the agency?" he asked, irritation like pins in his voice.

All his life, Toor had been second to someone. He was determined now to be first. He was not about to allow even the hint of an attitude to undermine him. "We selected and approached you, doctor, because of your track record. I am sure you can understand our need for double, triple, security in this…sensitive…matter. As well as our need for full co-operation and security."

"Of course."

"What of the writer?" Toor asked, carefully covering all ground. "What if it turns out he does know?"

"Not a credible witness. Records of delusion. Fear of imagining things," Kaufkiff reconfirmed in terse bursts. There was a pause, and he asked, "If you were a citizen, would you believe it?"

Toor hypothesized possible reactions to such a report. *Would it be believed?* He didn't say anything, but Dr. Kaufkiff's subtle roll of a laugh concurred with his thoughts—*absolutely not.* Most people didn't even believe what they saw with their own eyes, let alone wild-sounding claims with no proof.

"How much notice is needed for an isolation area?" Paul Toor finally asked.

"I am completely prepared to be of service on this end. As planned, I'll be on stand by." Assuring Paul Toor of his cooperation filled Kaufkiff with a feeling of importance for having been entrusted.

"Good. Thank you. And good work."

I have to act, Toor justified his actions as he hung up the receiver. He had not expected the talk show booking. Delaying action could lead his superiors to interfere. *That must not happen.* He needed the formulas for himself, for research, he couldn't risk prolonging the process. It was his find; he deserved the credit. He didn't want anyone else involved until he had fully availed himself of the potential for possible discoveries. He needed time, time to study her before anyone else was even aware of what he was doing.

"...I must say this has been an amusing journey into the supernatural," Dr. Wuthers was saying.

"Oh, poo," Aira amicably defused the attempt to discredit her. Her statement threw the audience into uproarious laughter, even the show's host was amused.

"Thank you for being with us," he told his guests. "It certainly has been a pleasure having you on the show." The theme song started up.

"We'll look for your new book, Dr. Wuthers, *How to Choose A Mate.* And, Miss Flight, people with pools and tubs everywhere may be thanking you as they beautify within..."

Credits began to roll for the close.

"...and may the world sing in the year 2000."

The television cut to commercials. Sandra was on her way to the kitchen to make herself a yogurt shake when the phone rang. Snatching up her portable, she barely had it to her ear before saying, "Yes?"

"The information you requested is in, Ms. Wilford. I've modemed it to you by E-mail."

"Good," she said brusquely.

"And, Ms. Wilford..."

"What is it?"

"That was a dead-end. There never was such a number issued by the DMV."

"Of course, of course," Sandra said, not wanting to admit she erred. Feeling affronted by what she took as the trainee's insolence, Sandra vowed to embarrass her in front of the staff on Monday. "I already knew that, I wanted it confirmed," she lied. The trainee hung up, confused that Sandra had her running so hard to get background about the person to whom it was supposedly issued.

"Damn. Damn, damn, damn," Sandra hissed, leaning her weight on the phone.

The yogurt far from her mind, she went for her computer and logged onto the E-mail. There it was in writing. Irene Davis, No such, license number #NC54634 non-existent, never issued by the DMV in Iowa. Neighboring states checked, no result. Irene Davis—there were 3,642 of them.

Sandra let out a long sigh.

Why would Paul Toor give me a false document? She scrambled through her desk, chipping a nail in her mounting fury. Sticking the finger in her mouth, she pulled the copy of the driver's license out and looked at it carefully. In the bottom corner of the picture, barely visible, was the di-amond necklace. *An edge of that white thing. What she wore the night of the concert. The hair looks the same as she had it that night.* The picture on the I.D., Sandra conjectured, must have been taken the night Paul Toor had met them.

The nerve. The lying, treacherous, deceiving scum. It was a disjointed, sketchy scenario, and Sandra struggled to fit pieces of it together. Either they were all in on some scheme together, or Paul had taken that picture clandestinely that night.

But why? And how? she wondered, then, *What do you mean how? Come on, Sandra.* She steadied herself. *You are a worthwhile person. I am a whole woman, deserving self-esteem.* She turned back to pursue her line of reasoning. *If I have a mini-camera and I'm a journalist, what kind of equipment would he have available? The best government can buy. But why? It wasn't me…he was interested in them, in her.*

A television announcement interrupted Sandra's mental quandary. "According to the Roper Organization Survey, four million people have said they have seen UFO's."

Sandra swiftly turned her head and faced the screen.

"December 9, 1965, Kecksburg, Pennsylvania," the narrator contin-ued. "There was a fireball in the sky. Lillian Hays and John A. Hays were witnesses. Some say it was an Ontario meteor. Then why was the Hays' home taken over by two military men, and why were there subsequently 212 military personnel in the Hays' home? This much was obtained by the Freedom of Information Act.

"When we come back, we'll hear about the stars, the circles and dashes found in the field, we'll hear from UFO researcher Stan Gordon, and Clifford E. Stone, a retired military man who personally witnessed aliens."

A commercial was halfway through before Sandra realized she was standing there with her mouth half-open. The agitation was getting to be too much. She hastened to the book shelf, scanned through her tapes, and put the one labeled "Calming Sea and Self Esteem" in the recorder. It was devastating to be betrayed. She lay down on the couch, trying to relax and allow the subliminal suggestions to enter and modify her.

chapter

35

"Another coincidence. My God!" Mendle gasped. He leaned back from his laptop computer on the bed, where he was poring over pages from his novel.

He ran his hands through his hair, grabbing a shock on top and pulling as he looked around the room wide-eyed. It was a Holiday Inn room, matched, arranged, and bolted down much like the hotel room where he had first met Aira—or *whatever her name is.*

Loptoor. He read the character's name from his manuscript on the screen again.

Toor. 'Lop' is 'Pol' backwards. Paul Toor.

Mendle jumped off the bed. *Loptoor.* He had written it months before knowing the man they had just met through Sandra Wilford—Paul Toor. *There has to be something to this. But what?*

He was anxious for Aira to return to the room. Bringing Onx downstairs with her, she had gone to take her overnight bag to the car. The suitcases and video camera were in the car, packed to leave for a vacation directly after Mendle's panel at the science fiction convention. Mendle thought about having her paged, but expected her back momentarily.

Mendle Orion found himself back to his old questions. He had been close to showing her his novel once before to point out the similarities between the character and herself. He never did it because ever since that night in the bathroom when he told the girl her name was Aira Flight, he wanted her to realize anything she needed to by herself. *As if that would be some kind of proof,* he chided himself, realizing that was part of it. He pored over the screen again.

But this—this Paul Toor business—settled it. Mendle needed a friend, someone to talk to about it. He decided to show Aira the manuscript; whatever the outcome, he was confident of one thing—she was a friend.

Mendle got up and shook out his shoulders, reminding himself to relax. *It's time to come to terms with it. The Iowa license. My novel. All of it. I'm going to show it to her,* he resolved, pacing the room. He was going to tell her about the driver's license information, and he was going to show her the chapters of the novel he had been writing just before he met her. It was only fair.

A familiar, foolish feeling nagged him, for having told the girl her name in the first place that night he found her suffering from amnesia. Nevertheless, *something* was going on here. He glanced at the clock. *She should be back any time.* She knew he had to be downstairs for the writer's panel in forty minutes.

He went back over to the bed, to the laptop computer with him, plopped down and began to read, scrolling the screen as he went.

"You're so pretty, Onx," Aira told her.
Onx did not move.
And majestic. Beautiful, actually."
No response.

"And so noble."

Only a dissipated stream of smoke sifted up from behind the miniature dragon's wing.

That's just how she talks to the dog, I've heard her, Mendle reaffirmed.
He read on:

Aira *daoed* her, granting her the right to be as she
was in that moment. She removed her head from beneath
her wing and listened to Aira continue the verse-talk.

"I thought when so dubbed by her, how sure I'd find
my way if I had goodly masters who would not let me stray.
I wished to dub as masters: Love. Truth. Serenity. They'd
feed and house and teach me with total sovereignty."

By the time Aira had finished, Onx was sitting erectly
and proudly. *I am your sensor-mate,* Onx emanated.

"And I depend on you," Aira said. There was that steel
in her soft-tone again.

Mendle opened Chapter Two and read:

Electricity crackled and lights flashed. Bright colors pulsated. Red, red. Yellow, yellow. White. Green, green. White. Blue. Violet, violet. Red. Yellow. Red, red, red. White.

"It isn't wise, Juristac. Not wise for you to be here," whined Loptoor as he limped a few paces behind his co-hort. Ahead stretched a shiny, aseptic corridor.

Loptoor's comment brought a sneer to Juristac's porcine face.

Loptoor. Paul Toor. "What does it mean?" Mendle mumbled. He scanned through the pages where the heroine Aira Flight and her sensor-mate Onx mysteriously lost control of her ship, the Lauryad.

Then he went to Chapter Four:

Loptoor felt his entireness wrenched by a more un-admittable reaction. He dismissed it to himself as false sympathy, the trap, his own trap of deceptive sentimentality, his inability to conceive the Grand Order.

It was Juristac who broke the silence. He spoke. It was more of a gasp, actually, and turned into a low, rasping mutter as the name they both knew stuck in his throat. "Aira Flight."

Mendle reread his words describing Aira Flight in her space craft, the Lauryad, being transported via conveyer toward Z Zone. Aira was looking out the portal and saw people trapped:

From its portal, its commander's attention was temporarily diverted from her plight and directed dolorously to the beings she witnessed.

Amnesiacs. Deluded, dying into solidity. They were living as complete effects, as slaves to programs and outer influences.

Wake up! Aira thought-reached to them. In protest, she came to their defense. "Remember who you are!" she tried to uplift them, but they could not hear her sound-symbols through the glass plates, and they were petrified beyond being even remotely aware of her thought-convey.

Mendle leaned back. It was eerie. *She does talk like that. Has she read this manuscript?* He had to confront her.

He read more:

Some turned to watch the craft's conveyer ascent up the transparent tunnel. They pointed and smiled and waved as though at a celebratory parade.

Suddenly sound piped into the ship's chamber and Aira could hear them. Prepared slogans which were not their own thoughts, none of which matched their eyes, issued from their body-forms. "Howzit going?" "Whazup?" "Yo babe."

Again, Aira tried to expand beyond her form and outside the ship to pervade the area. But again, she could not proceed past a certain stage of exteriorizing without hitting that peculiar sensation, and she was unable to proceed past it. Now it was more intense. *Pain.* Aira cringed back, startled.

The ship continued on the conveyer into a tunnel. Lights suddenly flashed and pulsated, and currents crackled with increasing volume. The atmosphere was zinging and highly charged, and Aira's attention again turned to the urgency of the situation in which she found herself.

Then the announcement, a detached voice, floated into the cabin. WELCOME AND THANK YOU FOR VOLUNTEERING. YOU ARE REACHING Z ZONE.

Mendle heaved a huge sigh, folded down the laptop computer, and closed his eyes.

Downstairs, in the hotel lobby, day two of Cosmotron Con was in full bustle. Aira was waiting for the elevator when she felt a tap on her back. "Hey, aren't you…?" She turned around. It was Rex Benton, the friend of Sandra's who had been there the night she first met Mendle at the science fiction convention in Anaheim.

"I forgot your name," Rex admitted. He leaned forward to smile down at Onx, "Hello, pooch," then straightened up. "I'm Rex Benton. Remember me?" He was dressed like a king, with a purple cape trimmed in white faux fur, and a papier mâché crown.

"Yes. Hello. The roof…"

An elevator came and went with a load of people. Rex grinned. "Are you here with Mendle?"

"Yes. He's upstairs."

"Good, good," Rex nodded, still grinning as he looked her up and down. She was dressed like something out of a mid-century television family show. "I see you've opted for the more…mundane…mode of attire," he commented wryly, "I guess you came as a human." He laughed. "I came as my name."

When Aira looked at him quizzically, he continued, gesturing toward the lobby that looked like a space station landing dock filled with the science fiction crowd in full regalia. "I guess Mendle didn't want anyone *recognizing* you," he alluded. When Aira still didn't get it, he nodded to the surrounding alien attires from outer space, hinting, "Your *pals.*" Then he shook his head. "Never mind. Tell Mendle hello. I've finished my new book."

"Congratulations!" Aira beamed at him.

"Yes. It's called *Viral Rage.* It's exciting," he told her. "But I know Mendle won't like it. Catch your elevator." He pointed to the door opening behind her. As Aira entered it, he prattled after her, "This is a better turnout than the last convention. I'm leaving, just had a one-day pass. Say hello now. I'll have to see Mendle next time. Get the book…" until the doors shut.

It seemed different being there alone without Mendle. When she was his date, Sandra Wilford had been part of it. Even though she scoffed at the seriousness with which science fiction fans lived, she had liked being part of the excitement and the glamor. Now, more critical than ever of everyone and everything she saw, she felt exiled to the periphery.

She was smoothing her hair when she happened to glance through the large, open doors at the other end of the exhibition hall. Doing a fast double-take, she puzzled over what she thought she had seen.

She pulled her yellow linen skirt down to straighten it, then hiked it up more evenly. That always got attention. Her yellow outfit gave a responsible image, conveying the well-adjusted persona she intended to project, but it also had all the right twists to draw sex-attention from men. Sandra knew, the more obviously she displayed her assets while pretending casual indifference about them, the more attention she received from men. Any men. *It used to make Mendle feel he was missing something,* she thought.

Tightening her buttocks in preparation for a walk, she conducted a quick, final mental-check to confirm her appearance was in place. *I couldn't have seen who I thought that was,* she was thinking as she started across the room. *Then again, I could've sworn that was him.*

As she approached the main lobby door, Sandra slowed down then carefully edged to one side of it where she could scan the area from a vantage. She was stunned. She had seen him. *What is Paul Toor doing here?* Sandra's eyes narrowed as she watched him talk to the clerk at the reception desk. Then he turned to two men who had been standing behind him and appeared to have been waiting for him. There was a brief interchange among the three before they parted ways, each in a different direction.

"What the hell?" Sandra fumed under her breath, her mind racing to figure out what they were up to. She had half a mind to confront him on the audacity of giving her a phoney document, but that wasn't her style.

By the time they were out of sight, Sandra had decided to go to the front desk to see what she could find out. She pushed a direct line through the crowded lobby, through the costumed fans, through the whirring of fantasy-winged conversation around her, to the clerk behind the front desk.

"There was a man just here. Black-framed glasses, grey suit, beady eyes, slightly balding," she prompted the clerk who merely stared at her. "Just a second ago," she nudged, "very small eyes, kind of thin face, pallid, sort of ill skin tone—"

"Yeah, yeah. I know who you mean," the reception clerk interrupted.

Well, good, you flea. "What did he want?" *Damn, I'm gonna get you fired this afternoon, you slow dunce. This hotel is a rip-off.*

"He wanted to know if a writer had checked in."

"Mendle?"

"I think that's it."

"Orion?"

"I think so."

"What else?" she pressed impatiently, trying to remain composed. Her heart was starting to beat harder. She felt for her purse and was reassured that she had remembered to bring her motivational tapes for the car ride home.

The clerk thought, then answered, "He wanted to talk to him and didn't know what room he's in."

"Is that all?"

"Yes."

"Is that exactly what he said?"

As the clerk reflected, Sandra huffed with impatience. "Yes," he rolled the word slowly, wanting to be careful about accuracy. "He asked if his girlfriend had checked in."

"And his girlfriend?"

"That's right. He asked for both of 'em."

Sandra twisted on her heel and petulantly scanned the lobby, mentally flitting through alternatives of what to do next.

"It was his agent," the clerk added what he had been told.

"Right."

She began computing her observations. Paul Toor was either on to something, or he wanted to partake in the glory of fame and art. He had a dull enough job; she couldn't blame him, the grey little man. Nonetheless, Sandra felt a desire for revenge, and had to quell gnawings of livid anger in order to think about her next step. She finally decided to venture in the direction she had seen him go.

As she walked, she wondered about the men she had seen talking to him. They weren't entertainment types. They didn't appear very smart, either. She wasn't sure if they were together, or just people from whom he was getting information.

"The car is all packed," Aira told Mendle. "Except for Onx here."

Onx let out a short howl and sulked.

"Oh, Onx," Aira cooed. "I didn't mean to offend you. I love you so much." The dog blinked up at Aira then tucked her nose under her paw.

"You're so pretty, Onx," Aira told her as she set the orange-tagged room key on the bureau. The dog didn't move. Mendle watched them from the bed. The bond between them seemed almost empathic.

"Majestic, actually." Aira smiled lovingly at Onx. "Beautiful. And noble."

Mendle held his breath a second. *Didn't I just read that? The chapter where Aira Flight is in the Lauryad cabin talking to her dragon.*

"Aira," he ventured, for the first time feeling awkward calling her that. "There's something I wanted to talk with you about."

The portrait of willingness, she turned and looked at him. He didn't know what to say. He didn't know how to begin. All he finally managed was, "How is everything?"

"Fine," she smiled, that smile which thanked him for his care and very being.

"I, uh, I thought maybe you'd like to read the new novel I'm working on."

She nodded, and eagerly said, "I would!"

Mendle looked over at the dog. Her head was up and she was panting happily, the Samoyed smile fixed on her face.

"I have it with me," Mendle told Aira. "I don't know what you'll think of it." He stopped himself from going any further when he looked at the clock on the television and realized they had to get going. "Maybe after the panel," he said, getting up from the side of the bed. He dawdled there.

"I'm sure I'll love it," Aira told him as they moved to leave.

"Do you think you might have…read it before and maybe not remembered or something?"

"I doubt it," Aira said. She handed Mendle his stylized fedora hat. "Besides, it isn't published. Is it?"

"No, it isn't," Mendle told her. He put on the hat.

"I would love to read it."

"I don't know, it's pretty strange," Mendle said, watching her for a reaction. There was none, no flinch, not even a quiver of cognizance about his concerns.

"Well, truth is stranger than fiction," she said matter-of-factly.

On the elevator down, sandwiched by people on all sides, Mendle was thinking about Aira's last comment. He had never really thought about it before—not as being actually true—but perhaps it was. He recalled what a friend of his, Mark, said, *'Reality is stranger than fiction because fiction has to be believable.'*

As if to tease Mendle, lest an answer seem impossible and the quest seem too discouraging, another coincidence suddenly glimmered, beckoning him to further ponder coincidence. Rising out of a lively discussion in the back of the elevator, in echo to what Mendle had just thought, someone laughed and said, "Truth is stranger than fiction."

chapter

36

Sandra turned a corner into a large alcove lined with telephones. She froze to a standstill. There was Paul Toor, talking to one of the men she had seen standing behind him at the front desk.

She gripped the convention program brochure harder, clenching her hand into a fist. *I am a whole, deserving woman,* a motivational program responded to the trigger of self-abasement. *I am confident and strong.*

She was deciding what to do when Paul strolled to one of the phones. Since it was a public phone, not the direct line to the rooms, it couldn't be Mendle or Aira he was calling.

Again, Sandra had to stifle emotions that were scrambling her thinking. It was unusually frequent, this distracting feeling that she was losing it. She wondered if her new tapes were as effective as her therapist claimed. Crossing her arms in front of her, she leaned back against the wall.

A costumed fan dressed in a taxidermic wolf head and furry cape walked by across her line of vision. As Sandra watched, an idea flashed. The fan was barely a few feet past her when she acted on it. "Excuse me!" she discreetly called out, stepped forward, kept pace, and charmingly delivered her pitch, including a promise of publicity.

Within seconds, Sandra was donning the wolf head and fur cape. "I'll meet you by the front desk in the lobby," she told him, intentionally shifting her breasts for his attention, now that she saw it was male. Closing the cape around her, she hastened across the alcove.

Once at the telephone adjacent to Paul Toor, Sandra quieted herself and slowed her breathing in order better to hear what he was saying.

He was quiet. *He must be listening. Or waiting on hold.* Pretending to be busy, she picked up the receiver, and opened the convention brochure she had been clutching. Keeping her attention on Paul, she idly glanced at a list of lectures, the sort of bunk that reminded her of life with Mendle. Her vision rested upon: "Flying Saucers Have Landed—UFO's—Encounter the Magic —Extraterrestrial Science."

Paul Toor spoke. "Yes, Kaufkiff please. We were disconnected."

Kaufkiff? My therapist? Sandra felt as though someone had asked her to sit down then pulled the seat out from under her. A memory clicked. *That night at the bar, Paul casually obtained his name from me.* She knew the methods well: pulling strings, following leads, weaving webs. She prided herself on being smarter than the average unsuspecting dummy, but now it was being done to her. *Why?* She listened, steadying her breathing to hear better.

"They're prepared to help me carry her to the car. I wanted to confirm all files have been erased," Paul was saying. "All they know is that A.F. is an absentee patient, homeless from Iowa, who needs solitary treatment..."

A.F., Iowa, A.F., who's...Is he talking about Aira? It was getting stuffy and humid, nevertheless Sandra felt safe in her mask.

"Good, yes, they gave me two. How long after contact with her skin will it take effect?"

Drugging her?

"Good, Alfred. And she'll be out guaranteed fifteen?"

Toor may have already known Alfred Kaufkiff, Sandra speculated. The psychiatrist and the Institute were involved in government programs and crowd control. These types knew each other. *So why wouldn't he have said so?*

The sudden thought that they were not on her side and that, for whatever reason, Paul Toor was going behind her back infuriated Sandra. The rage in her escalated. *I'm going to ruin you, your life will be misery from now on...*

Paul Toor turned and looked directly at her. Sandra was wearing the wolf head; he didn't know it was she behind the mask. Still, she froze for a minute and had to remind herself that he couldn't see her face. She cringed, then was relieved that his gaze did not rest on her long but continued to flit around the room as he listened to what he was being told on the phone. He finally turned and faced his booth again.

"We'll see if he stays sober. I doubt he'll be a problem anyway. I'll go ahead and separate them of course. But have the history ready in case there's a press leak needed. From the S.W. source, either he'll think she's disappeared or will go crazy, no one will believe him."

S.W. source, that's me, Sandra instantly recognized her initials.

As she listened to Paul Toor's stiff, subdued laugh, she remembered when he had casually asked her what Mendle would do if Aira left him.

Suddenly she knew it wasn't just an idle question. In fact, she was certain, not one spontaneous utterance issued from the man. She was revulsed by the memory of Paul's hard lips on hers, of his hand on her knee, of how she had let him rub her thighs, touch her, have her body. She thought she was using him. But now she felt like a disposable object, a piece of trash.

"I saw your new tapes in her living room," Paul was saying. "Is the subliminal self-doubt and incredulity command immediate?"

What? Alfred Kaufkiff programmed my recent tapes with self-doubts? It suddenly made sense to Sandra why she had found herself hesitating, finding everything difficult to believe.

"She mentioned every day. In her car, I think," Paul said.

Sandra felt herself in the grip of a horrible premonition; she was suddenly numb to the floor, indifferent to her surroundings. Floating in the middle of a dream, she was unable to move and unable to escape what it was about to reveal.

Her focus brought the brochure in her hand into view: "UFO's and Military Intervention—Twenty Eight Years of UFO's."

"I am certain you can handle the irascible types," Paul Toor was responding to something. Sandra found herself wondering if Mendle had been right.

Paul cleared his throat. "You should see all the UFO documentation at this place. But it dies out. If he says anything, the story wouldn't be a problem. It might even be camouflage."

He was talking UFO's. The headlines of the brochure congealed into solid black and white that meant something. *Is it possible? Are they real? No. He's government. Sane. Respectable. Dependable. This is science fiction.* Sandra quickly scanned the claims of the literature, staying tuned to Paul Toor's conversation as she read the brochure's information and claims: "Saturday, 5:54, The Ballroom. John Lear Workshop. John Lear, the son of the Lear jet inventor, has over 30 yrs. airline captain experience. He has flown over 160 different types of aircraft in over 50 countries. He holds 17 world speed records in the Lear jet. John became interested in the existence of extraterrestrials after talk with Air Force personnel who had witnessed a UFO landing at Bentwaters AFB. John has extensive knowledge of the government UFO cover-up."

The words she was reading augmented the significance of what she was hearing when Paul Toor spoke next. "All right. We can determine if a biopsy is necessary after we begin the tests. But remember what I showed you on case Z-X 5. A vivisection was required." He listened for a few moments then, with what sounded like a brief grunt, hung up.

Questions jammed into knots of confusion in Sandra's mind. Emotions of fear and regret paralyzed her as the horror of the situation became undeniable. It was Aira they were after.

That driver's license is a phony...Paul Toor had it fabricated. To throw me off the trail. Off the trail of **what**?...*Is she a...a...*Sandra couldn't allow herself to think it. Her blood felt like ice water in her veins.

While eavesdropping, Sandra had been wily enough to invent some idle 'conversation' and pretend to be waiting for information, as though she were actually using the phone. Paul Toor had already walked away and her hands were shaking now as she realized she was still holding the receiver to her ear. She hung up slowly and uncurled her fingers that ached from clasping it so hard.

Damn. There is a story in this for me.

Sandra jolted out of the preposterousness which pinned her. She broke into a run, across the alcove, around the corner and down the hall. When she reached the lobby, she harnessed her gait to long strides.

It wasn't until she was halfway to the elevators that she realized she didn't know what room Mendle was in and had to turn back. On her way to the front desk, she thought to rally some news and media channels. She could warn Mendle and Aira about Paul Toor and look like the good guy to them, then break the story. After that, the enigma of the girl's past would be unearthed by an unrelenting press.

Thinking fast, Sandra made it to a phone. She had worked the hotel before, at a Democratic convention in October. Using her beeper, she contacted the local news channel and the local office of a national magazine for reps to meet her in the International Hall, where Mendle's panel was scheduled in twenty minutes.

She would intervene there with witnesses. She was going to announce the conjecture of government personnel abducting UP's, Unidentified Persons—she liked that—for mental experiments and vivisections. She would sick an investigative team on Paul Toor.

That was safe. It didn't put her own credibility on the line, and still implied "extraterrestrial" or "alien" for attention. As a headline to her story, "UFP" was a good parallel to "UFO." That way she wouldn't compromise her professionalism. She could still cover herself if there were, indeed, a discovery to be made.

Unidentified Flying Person. She liked it. She plotted the outline for her press announcement as she hurried back to the front desk. *This'll teach those scums to try to outdo me.* It was a good feeling to know she commanded the respect she did from her media colleagues.

"What room is Mr. Orion staying in?" Sandra asked when she reached the front desk, her voice seeming strange to her.

"He's popular," the clerk said.

"Mendle. Mendle J. Orion," Sandra rushed him.

"I know. There was someone else looking for him. A man, then a lady. But she didn't ask for the room number—"

"That was me," Sandra told him coldly. When he looked at her with round eyes, she remembered she was wearing the wolf mask over her head. "Just get me the room number!" she snapped, angry with herself for having interrupted him.

"I'm sorry. We're not allowed to give out that information."

Sandra felt as though she were going to burst. "You gave it to the man earlier, didn't you?"

"That was his agent. I can call Mr. Orion and let him know there is someone to see him—"

"Fine. Thank you." *What a liar*, she thought about Toor.

She watched the clerk dial 572. Pushing herself off the desk with her hands, almost losing her balance as she turned, Sandra launched herself back toward the elevators.

Ten seconds of waiting seemed like forever; after fifteen, Sandra opted for the stairs, taking them by two's until she reached the fifth floor.

"Damn, I could've called him," she cursed, steadying her confusions, then slowly opening the door at the landing.

Down the hall, one of the men who had been talking to Paul Toor was knocking on a door. When he looked to his left, he saw a wolf's head peering out of the exit door, some thirty yards down the hall.

On her end of the corridor, Sandra's first impulse was to duck, but, reminding herself of the coverage the wolf-head provided, she forced herself to walk out into the hall and busily pretend to go about her business, avoiding any suspicious behavior.

That must be 572, she thought as she braced herself against the wall and took off a shoe, then rolled her foot around, pretending she was working a cramp out of it.

She could hear the man knock again, but didn't look up. Instead, she proceeded to examine the inside of her shoe, thinking, *He's there to lure Mendle away so Aira will be alone. Paul is probably waiting downstairs until he sees them walk past. No one's answering. They must not be in their room.*

Sandra dropped her shoe to the floor and straightened up. When she saw the man waiting for the elevator, she stalled by feigning difficulty inserting her foot in the shoe, then slowly, making it appear she was checking room numbers, she proceeded down the hall.

Stories of abductions, assassinations, disappearances where people were simply never heard from again, unsolved mysteries, complex plots, and devised schemes swarmed in Sandra's head. The news had always somehow seemed removed—things that happened *inside* the television or appeared on the printed page. This was real time, and the stories she had heard loomed as real now, too.

She didn't feel like Lois Lane anymore as she fathomed the brutality of the real thing. All the stories that had seemed surreal to her converted into hard-core events. She had never before stopped to think of their ramifications, of the actual people, of the stakes to those who played for blood.

Sandra played for prestige and money, and hadn't even planned that to her best advantage. She played to keep others small so no one would get her again. Now she knew that there were those who played for blood.

As soon as she heard the elevator doors shut and saw the man was gone, Sandra turned and ran back to the stairwell. Bitterness permeated her. Intermixed now with terror was the irrevocable sourness of knowing she had wasted her aces and had no more leverage.

I have to reach Mendle and Aira first, she was thinking as she raced down the stairs. Once Aira disappeared there would be nothing else to be done. It might take weeks, months to prove anything, let alone find her. Paul Toor could deny the whole thing. She would have no story, would only be left holding a phony driver's license.

Kaufkiff, she recalled when he handed them to her, had called those tapes 'custom' for her, implying she was special. *They were custom all right, he wasn't lying about that.* She wondered exactly what the subliminal messages were underneath that sound of surf and calming music. Worse, what had his suggestions been when he put her under with hypnosis? Hypnosis motivation, he called it.

As she approached the first floor landing, Sandra thought to have Aira and Mendle paged. She burst open the exit door and hurried toward the lobby.

She was heading for the front desk when the person who had lent her the wolf costume spotted her. "Hey!" he yelled at her when he saw her. Her first reaction was to avoid him and she did so by changing direction and diving into a small thicket of people. This alarmed the fan, who shouted accusatively, even more loudly, "Hey!" and broke into a run after her.

The yell caught Mendle's attention. He was not too far away, making his way to the conference room with Aira and Onx. He heard the noise and turned to see the wolf evading its pursuer. "That reminds me of when I first met you," he told Onx affectionately, remembering how he had chased the dog, sopping wet from the storm, through a lobby full of people.

Sandra was turning a corner when she suddenly stopped. "What am I *doing*?" she cursed aloud under her breath and turned to face the boy who was chasing her. "Here," she told him, yanking the wolf's head off and shoving it at him. She unfastened the fur cape and pushed it into his arms. She didn't know why she had run and tried to have it make sense. "I got carried away."

"Call of the wild, huh?" he remarked with a grin, anticipating some of the charm she had tacitly promised. Before he was able to finish the comment, he was no longer looking at her face, but at her back as she ran away from him.

Sandra's fury was mounting as she checked the time. Her insides were a mishmash of emotions under her efforted cool demeanor. Mendle was due to appear at the panel discussion in five minutes. Maybe they were already there and she could warn them, she decided, and hurried the final distance to the room.

The conference room where Mendle and assorted personalities were conducting a discussion panel also housed a spacecraft model exhibit. It was wall-to-wall people, though none of the panel had taken their seats. Sandra scanned the room and did not see any staff from the media she had called. She kept looking for Mendle and Aira.

Halfway to the front of the room, she stepped onto a small platform for a visual vantage point. When she turned to her left, she saw Mendle and Aira arriving, several yards away. She scrutinized the girl a split second, then hurried down from the platform to head that way.

By the time Sandra reached the corner where she had seen Mendle and Aira, however, they had moved along with the people who tightly surrounded them to some other part of the hall.

Sandra tried jumping so she could see over heads. She called out Mendle's name, then Aira's alternately, feeling like a stranger to herself. *I'm losing it.* Finally, Aira noticed her through a gap in the crowd and waved in greeting.

"I've got to talk to you!" Sandra shouted. Aira held up her hand to gesture it would be a minute. Suddenly, the straightaway between them was obscured by another small group of people dressed as Klingons. Sandra shouted anyway, "I've got to talk to you now!" Her words, however, were lost and had no effect. She stamped her foot in frustration.

It was then that Sandra turned and saw Paul Toor standing a few yards away by the entrance. He saw her too; in fact, he had been looking straight at her. His eyes bored into her as though he knew she knew.

Quickly Sandra turned away and flung herself into the action of the desperate solution which came to her. She had to get away from Paul Toor, yet keep him away from Mendle and Aira. *I'll make an announcement.* The plan she had overheard depended on covertness to be successful; she would make it public knowledge.

Paul Toor wasn't going to take the upper hand away from her. He wasn't going to take away her glory, either. Starting to get frazzled, Sandra edged her way through the gathering, past large cardboard cut-outs and plastic models of larger-than-life space creatures, science fiction characters, and spacecraft.

Arriving at the podium, Sandra frantically looked over her shoulder for Paul Toor but couldn't see him. She stopped, did an about-face and looked again. He wasn't following her. She didn't see him anywhere.

She stepped up on the elevated platform and grabbed a microphone. Smoothing her hair, she closed her eyes and inhaled a mouthful of air, then the words poured from her. "Hello. Hello." The microphone was on, and her amplified voice filled the room. She focused on the crowd. "I have something very urgent to announce. A discovery which may mark the pinnacle of my career in fact. A UFP. I'll explain, but first, there is someone here right now who is in grave danger. She is an alien, though she appears human." The crowd erupted into textures of laughter, cheering, and applause.

"No! No! Please listen to me," Sandra begged. It wasn't how she had planned to say it. She continued. "Please listen!" Her eyes roved the room, taking in the many expressions of merriment turned toward her. "There is a plan to abduct her, to drug her and abduct her, for isolation study—" Another cheer went up as the crowd anticipated some promise of excitement.

"The abduction would give license for such things as mental tests, possibly vivisection. But this person without an identity—" It was a nightmare, the way they were laughing and cheering her on. Wasn't it obvious? Wasn't her despair yet professionalism plain? Wasn't it clear she was telling facts as she had witnessed them?

More and more of the crowd were turning their attention to her, though some were still mingling among themselves. "I'm quite serious," she insisted. "Is the network here, yet?" she attempted to position her credibility, and her eyes finally found one face turned toward her that was not contorted in jest. It was Mendle's.

Their eyes locked. How she hated him at that moment. How small she felt. But she looked at him and kept talking, trying to win her self-esteem. "There is a plan to drug her and take her somewhere to conduct tests, possibly a biopsy. Now, I've notified some members of the media, I would like to ask you to step forward. It's Aira. The parties behind it are P...uh!"

The shot was barely audible and sounded more like a muted zing through the air. Suddenly, a couple of inches below her left shoulder blade, a red blotch spattered on Sandra's blouse. Its diameter increased as the vivid red seeped outward, absorbed by the yellow linen.

While some applauded, the crowd began looking upward for the source of the special effects. They were delighted by the sight of Onx sailing overhead.

She was midway through her transformation—a white dog who appeared to have wings barely beginning to unfurl from her back. Not yet saurian, nor even blue, she was hissing fire nonetheless.

There were three more zings in rapid succession. It was the third one that finally brought her down. Onx fell, her wounds strewing blood on people in the vicinity.

"O-o-o-n-n-n-x!" The scream came from Aira and sounded more like the living howl of a raw wound than a word. She had followed the dog when she first saw her leap an incredible ten feet into the air toward a model rocket.

There was another zing and another and, almost simultaneously, another patch of bright red appeared on Sandra's body, this time just below her neck. The impact threw her backward, snapping her head that way first.

By now someone was screaming, "It's blood, it's real blood!" and the crowd looked like a riptide was passing through it.

Aira managed to get to Onx through the commotion. She had picked the dog's limp body up off the floor and now stood holding her tightly while people bashed and knocked against her in a mounting chaos.

"Aira, come on." It was Mendle. She could feel his grip digging into her arm; he was tugging on her. "Let's go. Let's get out of here."

Although she didn't want to move, she forced herself. She was burying her face against Onx's body, and when she lifted her head, he could tell. She didn't have to say anything. Her expression seared through Mendle like whirling spokes of broken glass.

chapter

37

Onx was dead.

chapter 40 39 38

Aira allowed Mendle to pull her, toward the fire exit behind the podium. Her steps were difficult, the movements made under protest, in a state of unutterable disbelief. The sight of Sandra's crumpled body hit them both.

She looked like a broken puppet that had been thrown away. She was lying on the floor with one arm slung across her belly and the other flung over her head, dangling at an angle from the elbow. Her eyes were open, and her head was twisted to one side with her hair, a shattered pinwheel of midnight, fanned across the floor. As they went to her and crouched beside her, Mendle turned to view the direction from which the shots had come.

In this crowd, he thought as he surveyed the pandemonium, *it'll be difficult to nab the gunman—unless someone's witnessed it.*

Panic had triggered and spread as though the people were gunpowder and fear a match. Some were already leaving the room. He saw nothing but mounting confusion.

Mendle looked over at Aira kneeling beside him with Onx's body across her knees. She had placed her hands on Sandra's wounds.

"Someone went to call an ambulance," somebody said.

"Did anybody see anything?"

"Naw…"

"There's no time, get a doctor…"

"There's a hospital on Torrance," someone else said.

"We can be there in three minutes." Mendle said, taking action.

Someone helped him hoist Sandra carefully into his arms. Another individual helped Aira with her balance as she struggled to her feet, lifting Onx's body. A woman dressed in glittering gold led the way and pushed open the fire escape.

"The car's down here," Mendle directed, recognizing the parking lot. "We're okay, we're okay," he sloughed off a couple of people who attempted to follow them. "Go, go call the hospital, notify them we're enroute!"

Opening the car doors, Aira placed Onx's body in the front seat then hurried to the back. She crawled across the back seat and helped Mendle place Sandra. Aira sat next to her and held her while Mendle closed the door. Mendle ran around the car, closed the back door on Aira's side, jumped in the driver's seat, started the ignition, and they sped out of the lot.

Sandra's voice was small, a mixture of effort and regret. Although she had difficulty, she managed to form the words. "I wanted to be somebody." She closed her eyes, then forced them open again.

"You're going to be okay," Aira said, stripping off her own sleeveless, light blue suit jacket. Pushing the cloth against Sandra's wound to stop the bleeding, Aira permeated the area with life.

With the trace of a smile that seemed to bear the brunt of a joke, there was the hint of a whine in Sandra's voice, "Just trying to…survive…you know?"

"You can make it," Aira encouraged her.

Mendle sped toward the hospital following the blue signs. He blazed around corners and through lights with headlights on and horn blaring. When he glanced in the rearview mirror, he saw Aira leaning over Sandra. Aira was exuding the same translucent luminescence he had seen on that day in the woods when she had healed Onx.

The convention room was still in random motion that resembled a disrupted ant colony. Amidst the commotion, Paul Toor remained motionless, enclosed within the interior of a model space shuttle display. He had secured his gun and now peered through a hole. He had to be fast in timing the moment in the flow of havoc when he could join and blend undetected into the crowd spilling out the door, before the exit was blocked.

He was feeling nothing. He wasn't thinking particularly either, except for the words *stop her, stop her, stop her* playing remotely over and over in his head. He had succeeded in protecting his anonymity, a vital accomplishment.

In the back seat of Mendle's car, Aira was perplexed. Determined not to live, Sandra was fighting her; her eyes had been closed, her face squeezed into a grimace. She opened her eyes again and looked at Aira.

"Survive?" she whispered rhetorically.

Mendle ached for her. He thought of the irony. She had always been so well-adjusted, always so on top of things, or so it seemed.

"I understand," Aira whispered.

"Maybe that's the whole point of morality in the first place," Sandra said weakly. Then, her chest heaved, and she began to cough up blood. She turned her head, lowering her chin to her shoulder, allowing the blood to be soaked up before straightening her body.

Aira wiped Sandra's mouth. "We're almost there," she tried to soothe her, then continued to apply pressure to her neck and chest wounds to stop the flow of blood.

"What's going on?" Sandra whimpered.

Aira felt her go limp under her touch. Quickly, she tried breathing her own breath into Sandra's body. No response. Aira tried again. Nothing. The breath wouldn't take. Sandra slumped over toward the door, her head resting against the window.

She could have been asleep, but she wasn't. She had stopped breathing. Aira stared at the vacant body. As if it couldn't possibly be true, she heard herself saying, "She's dead."

Mendle who had been holding his own breath watching Aira attempt to resuscitate Sandra, exhaled. "Oh God," he said, his thoughts on other dangers as well. He picked up speed.

Transfixed, Aira continued to stare at Sandra's body, then she reached forward, pulling herself up by the back of the front seat. She scooted up enough to peer over and see Onx's body lying limp and devoid of life on the front seat beside Mendle.

The eyes were closed, the mouth was open, and not even a vapor of breath passed through it. Except for the red blood stains on her fur, she looked like a toy, a stuffed toy that had never been alive.

Onx's body had ceased any interaction with the atmosphere. Worse, Aira could not feel her, could not sense any thought from her whatsoever. *I don't understand.*

Aira turned to look at Sandra. The body was propped up against the back door. The face serene and flawless, she looked as though she were sleeping, but she wasn't there.

Just seconds ago she had been there. Seconds ago. *Just seconds ago*, thought Aira, trying to understand.

Aira looked up at Mendle. He had been driving in silence. She wanted to say something to him but could think of nothing.

Thought gyrated, creating the sensation of confusion. In the confusion spun a regret so deep that it threatened implosion. As Aira was experiencing this peculiar agitation, she naturally thought it was her own feelings. Suddenly, she differentiated the gyrations from her own thought; the turbulent agitation was not she; she was perceiving it, not feeling it. The moment she wondered who or what it was, she knew: *Sandra.*

Aira closed her eyes. She could see her. Shrouded with regret, the spirit howled in devastation, not knowing what was happening.

Opening her eyes, Aira saw Sandra's lifeless body there, and, even with her eyes open, could also still see the spirit viewing her body, too, trying to understand it was dead. *Sandra.* The thought-being was dark and mournful. At Aira's thought-reach, the spirit shuddered, suddenly getting an awareness of itself.

Why did you want to die? I could have fixed your body, Aira transmitted. The spirit that was Sandra looked stunned to have been touched by thought-reach. She was confused.

Can you feel yourself? Aira oriented her.

I'm broken, Sandra wailed, lamenting the detachment from the brunette body leaning against the window glass. *I'm so pretty.* Then she realized, she was no longer the discarded flesh she had once called "me."

You can have another one if you want, just as beautiful, Aira told her.

Sandra, the thought-being, did not look as attractive as her body had. Her thought-image was unsymmetrical, vain, hard, and very small, although resembling somewhat its previous physical form.

She hovered around the body, flitting over its nose, its hair, its arms, hands, legs. Distressed and very confused, she was attempting to possess it somehow. She had been very attached to it.

I'm dead, Sandra wailed.

It's dead. Can you feel yourself, who you really are?

Aira pervaded Sandra, trying to orient her to herself. She saw that Sandra's life had been a series of transgressions against herself. The first ones hurt; then she had become immune by numbing herself. This was why she was ugly. Her beautiful body had concealed the reality of her actual condition; without it, she was an obdurate, dull entity, writhing in convulsions of hatred. Sandra's entire life had become an escape from the pain of having betrayed herself.

This is why she wants to die, Aira realized. But Sandra was a soul, and couldn't die.

I want to die, I want to die, Sandra emanated, convulsing as her intentions surfaced.

Aira watched Sandra in a dilemma, unable to part with the body which she essentially had refused to allow to heal. Conflicts raged. She had wanted to die, but now she wanted to keep the body. She had wanted to die because she was hating herself; she was hating herself because she hated life.

Sandra, Aira thought-touched her, *nothing you've done excuses that you condemn yourself. Blame won't fix anything.*

A howl of hate-rage diffused from Sandra. *I am worthless. I did anything to get what I wanted. I wanted to kill as I pretended to give my body. The pay was never enough. Never enough compensation. Look what they did to me! How they made me feel! And you!* She became oriented to herself as a thought-being and perceived Aira. *I hate you! I want to trap you in hell!*

Out of Sandra's contorted ravings, there suddenly emerged a composed image of herself. As Aira watched it, she saw that it was electrical. It was a prefabricated illusion, somewhat resembling the appearance of Sandra's former body. What sounded like stock recorded phrases started running through it. *'I am okay. I am the person I always wanted to be. I am confident. I am calm in front of others. I am a fulfilled, whole woman. I deserve the best. I deserve respect. I deserve wealth.'*

Blending with the phrases were sounds of very low electrical static. Aira also recognized the sound of ocean waves. Wondering about it, she realized that these had been subliminal suggestions, imposed on Sandra through electronic means with motivational tapes.

My doctor, doctor. Sandra relaxed with blind faith.

Strangely, opposite phrases then activated. *'I'm losing it. What am I doing? I can't believe it. Unreal. I better not move. Best to lie down. Lie down, don't think. Don't move.'* It was the same voice, the same hypnotist. Unable to react, ping-ponging in conflict, Sandra's anger increased at sensing betrayal.

Then the positive commands resumed, droning repetitively. *'I am a whole, deserving woman, I am deserving…'*

The phrases quelled the convulsing Sandra, and detached her from her sentiments. Once again, she seemed composed and rational, her real feelings temporarily shut off from her awareness. Though muffled, and though she could not touch them, they still writhed in pipelines through her soul.

Aira would not let go of her. She thought-held Sandra, knowing her essence, not allowing the composed, fabricated valence to take over, even though it was much more pleasant and even prettier. Underneath, she saw the real feelings swarm and swallow Sandra's spirit like quicksand—they would always be there until understood.

Suddenly a jolt of electricity snapped. Sandra's rage overpowered the mental circuitry that had been thinking for her. She thought-attacked Aira. *You! It's you! What are you always so happy about? I hate you.*

Aira purely listened and witnessed her, being there for her. She knew there was something more beneath the hatred, because Sandra was, after all, a thought-being. Holding steadfast against the ugliness, but witnessing it, Aira knew that Sandra needed to meet herself if she were ever going to dig herself out. *What have you done, Sandra?*

Contorted and unbalanced, Sandra howled, *They never knew how I died under my smiles! I was dying under my smiles. No one knows what love is! Only after what they can get. They forced me to hate. And hide. Always hiding. I stole, I lied, I had people lose their jobs. It hurts. I wanted to kill Mendle. I wanted to kill you. I wanted to kill happiness, and decency.* In a final burst of anguish, she screamed, elongated thoughts, *It hurts to care! It hurts so much to care!*

Sandra convulsed. When the convulsions stopped, she looked at what it was that she had been running from—the times she had violated her own feelings. Now they seemed different. Her actions were condemnable, yes, but only from the point of view of change, not punishment. Somehow, there was comfort in knowing what she had done; she did not seem as terrible to herself when facing it as when she had been running from it.

She was not particularly luminous as a thought-being; she was not vast in her concept of responsibility, but the ugliness was gone, and, though dimly, she began to radiate. Sandra expanded in a moment of quiet. The calm amazed her. It had been made safe for her to look, and it hadn't killed her to be honest.

*I hated you because you reminded me of...how I once was...of what I lost...*Sandra cognited, thought-flowing to Aira. After betraying her own life-essence, she had begun to hate Life, targeting reminders of what she betrayed as enemy. So she befriended real enemies and fought Life in a convoluted, confused inversion, an attempt to be right.

The thought-being transformed into a state of self-awareness as a creator, and Aira saw what it was that she had always seen in Sandra: The actual being was a concentration of all that had been good about her. The rest was additives. Without the panoply of thinking devices and other mental brigandine, she was quite simple and unique.

No one did this to me, Sandra thought in amazement. Her image began to shine some. *It was myself I hated. How could I trust anyone, when I felt I could not be trusted and thought all to be like me?*

Another deluge of despair and regret followed as more sequences of her life's memories flashed through her. When Aira made no judgement and understood, every mistake Sandra had made no longer needed to be maintained as right. Viewed in this light, her wrongs restored her right. As Sandra viewed her life without fear, she was purged.

She was alive. There was liberty in knowing she had only to do what felt right. Nothing could ever take herself away unless she agreed, and she knew her integrity was precious. Without it, she was lost.

Sandra felt light, no longer shackled to the need for punishment. The solidity of seriousness dissipated when she realized that her future was hers to create. She was no longer confined to continuing an error just to make it right, or trying to cover up what was wrong by programming herself like a robot.

I'm not afraid to look! Sandra flowed to Aira. She flowed love, and it delighted her. *If something was an error I don't need to continue to do it to make it right. I can view now without fear of punishment. The details don't matter...just that I went against myself!* Sandra's thought-form became more effervescent, more symmetrical, more akin to true beauty.

In the back seat, an outburst from Aira sent a wave of hope through Mendle. He shot a look over his shoulder to see what elicited it. By the time he looked around, however, Aira did not look very merry. Her expression was one of alarm. Sandra was not healed; her flesh was even whiter.

"Are you sure?" Mendle asked, his eyes back on the road. When she did not answer him, he looked again in the rearview mirror.

Aira's eyes were closed and her hands were at either side of her face, palms facing him. She was doing something. What, he did not know, though he knew not to interrupt her. Still grappling with the fear and grief which tore at him, Mendle returned his attention to driving. He urgently wanted to know what was going on to ensure their safety.

Aira was not disconnected from her body in the back seat of Mendle's car, though her primary awareness operated and manifested in other-dimension. Her response to what she was seeing inadvertently had translated to her physical body as a vocal outburst of sound.

As they shared joy and Aira watched Sandra stabilize, she saw something else: an electronic net appeared and encompassed her. As soon as it happened, Sandra ceased flowing thought and rapidly began falling asleep. Then, slowly, she started to change location, but her movement was involuntary, as if she were being pulled somewhere else.

Aira stayed with her. It was most curious. Outside of time and even space, they drifted.

With a jolt, Sandra suddenly popped out of her unconsciousness. *Fatal mistake,* she flowed. *Never accept help from your enemies. It's never help.*

As quickly as she had popped awake, Sandra froze back into unconsciousness. Still, she drifted. Aira's curiosity augmented.

Again, Sandra snapped to, but this time she was less alert. She seemed to be struggling for lucidity. *'I come for relief. Forget it, forget it. Fulfill my bond,'* she flowed somewhat hypnotically, the thought came from her, but was not her own. *'Follow the light, follow the light.'*

She yielded to unconsciousness. Slipping back into unawareness increased the apparent bliss of sleep. When she surged out of it once more, she seemed even more remote. *'Relief, the sweet relief.'* The net around her constricted. It began to hum as some type of current busied itself. Still they drifted, and Aira wondered where.

During the floating, a deep and complete sadness filled Aira, imbued with resignation so acute, it hurt. The sentiment was like the feeling of having to accept a friend's death: nothing could be done. Such utter and total resignation, Aira felt saturated with it, became laden, *death itself,* then realized the feeling was not in her own heart, but in her surroundings.

Sandra still slept and had not generated any more thought. Fascinated, Aira stayed with her as she drifted, watching her and wondering where she would go after physical death. It was strange and beautiful the way she was being pulled; it did not seem to be against her will.

Sounds swelled with the sensation of winds blowing; winds that wailed of loss and promise simultaneously. It was an ancient yet familiar sound, as though it had been sweeping through galaxies, lost and forgotten, for hundreds of millions of years.

Colors began to billow around them—colors which left no distance for perception. First, they seemed to fill Aira from inside as she saw them, then located themselves in the distance away from her, creating space. They were beautiful and intense—violets which thinned to rose, then into veils of pinks which wispily encircled small orbs of luminescence.

Aira felt textures of music; it was sweet, and the atmosphere sticky. Subtle suctions circumscribed her. They were gentle and lulling, and she found herself on the edge of sleep.

They approached a sleek platform and cascades of shimmering crystals began to take form overhead as Aira felt herself relaxing into a sense of the familiar. She felt wonderful and dreamy; even her thoughts were blending into pastels.

Onx was there. She had no form, but Aira recognized her. Having known and loved Onx so, she recognized that thought-being in any form or no form.

It felt thick to think. There were bodies milling around in a hallway. Again there was solidity and distance between forms.

Blissful to have found Onx, Aira was focusing on her. She tried to flow, billowing to her friend, but felt as if she were in a dream and could not move. *Onx!* her thought and love stretched hazily. Then, closer and closer she came to her companion, nearly there, and, just at the moment her thought-reach was about to mingle with her...WHAP!

Stunned, Aira reeled in surprise. In no way at all had she expected that slap as a greeting from Onx. Suddenly, her pastel consciousness became keen, her perceptions acute. Aira looked about her and remembered.

Identity catalogues. Amnesiacs. The Lauryad. Juristac. Beings selecting bodies, identities, entering booths to erase the past. They're coming for the sleep, to forget.

Z ZONE!

All that had transpired started coming back to her; she remembered who she truly was. She knew her past. She knew how it was she had come to Earth-dimension.

Onx, thank you, Aira flowed her love. Yet Onx was gone, and Aira could no longer sense her. She reached and searched in all degrees but could not locate her anywhere.

Never again, she thought, *will I make the same mistake.* For all the power she had possessed before, there had been one thing she lacked— experience. She had been a life-power, but lacked knowledge of rules and conditions of various universes.

Aira thought-scanned for Juristac and did not find him present. As she saw the lost souls around her, she vowed she would not let him get away with trapping life-beings.

Now she had experienced the mechanics of treachery, of force, of agreement and reality, and of physical energy. Pinned in a material universe, she had experienced the vilest and the most sublime. Through all manner of ridicule and opposition sustained, she had not surrendered herself. She had observed and extrapolated knowledge, struggling against succumbing to the idea she was mere matter. From the pain, she derived understanding. She surfaced from what she had undergone, and, because she had remained true to her soul-essence despite most convincing challenges, rose with her innocence intact. She had held onto her dreams literally for her life.

Had she been a painting, Aira's form would have stood nobly strong, her face innocent and open. Her eyes would touch only with love, backed not only with wisdom but also with knowledge which promised she could summon ferocity to defy all that threatened Life. In one hand she would be holding a rose, in the other a sword. Had she been music, she would have been a symphony whose movements welled through divertimenti and sarabandes, then crescendoed. On the triumphant wings of a march would spring the finale of fortitude that inspired victory of the most tender and gentle virtue.

Don't Sandra! Don't! Aira called out with her whole being.

'*I fulfill my bond. I have returned for relief. My errors, the pain,*' emanated Sandra. Stuck to some electronic wavelength like an insect to flypaper, she obediently coasted forward toward the programming chambers.

Aira made the distinction that the phrases were not Sandra's soul-thought, but only slogans to which she had agreed in the past. These slogans had been implanted into her. The life-power of her own agreement held her to them now. Somehow, she had been induced to agree.

...Like what happened to me, Aira realized, recalling when she was bombarded with electronic confusions and forced to make convoluted agreements and decisions. Ironically, it was her own power that trapped her. *Because evil has no power of its own!* Aira rallied fiercely.

Sandra's prior arrangement with Z Zone was being activated out of its dormancy. She was reporting back for the comfort of oblivion.

Unstuck from the electronic nets, liberated in her own ability to maintain a free reality by her power of cognizant agreement, Aira pervaded Sandra with her life force. *Your errors are not reason to forget and forfeit yourself! Your mistakes are not reason to condemn yourself to an eternity of agony. You know this. You saw it.* Sandra did not appear to respond.

If you continue, you will return dormant, becoming ever more solid, a slave. You won't benefit from your experience. This is not truth. Only truth dissolves your shackles and the pain! You saw that! Dear being! The one thing you have that is yours is your choice. You have free will! You have the power of choice! Heed your heart! And choose knowledge, not a lie!

As truth permeated her, Sandra stirred and fought not to succumb to the sweetness of slumber that lapped at her like warm waters. Aira found what was real and alive within the other spirit and continued to flow to her the very nature of life, which was love.

Now others who milled in the distance were beckoning to Sandra to join them. They wailed and whispered; their voices were lament, dirge, and false exaltation, all in one. Voices rose in sound-slogans that droned above them all. "What does it matter? You only live once! Be somebody. Get the identity you always wanted to be. Can't live forever. There's no turning back. Let go. Feel good about yourself. If it feels good, do it. Nothing lasts forever. Let us change the way you feel, let us change the way you feel, let us change the way you feel…" The voices rose and blended back in with the swirling murmurs.

Aira fought not to let go of what was real in Sandra, what was alive, her very self, her life-force. *You agreed to this once. Because you are good, you thought you had to limit yourself when you considered you had harmed. You see? You are life, otherwise it wouldn't have mattered to you to think you violated life. Would it have mattered to you that you wronged yourself or others if you were truly evil? No! You are Life.*

This is a trap. To trap and enslave life. Free your soul from containment. You are a free soul. There is a trillion times the sweetness in being awake, in being the creator of your destiny. With understanding there is not even the need to forgive. You know now. You have the power of choice, to agree or not to agree. Utilize experience to learn. You have the power, you have the power…

Suddenly, there was a monumental snap, as though ropes had been cut. A tension of which Sandra had not even been aware—so long it had been there seeming normal and ever-present—released.

Sandra unfurled into light.

Knowing she was not evil and that knowledge, not ignorance, was bliss, she came home to herself. Guilt peeled from her, as did blame and regret, and she embraced herself as the source, and saw it was she herself who empowered ideas. Mistakes had been staledated solutions. She embraced her power to cause future.

No longer was she contracting. No longer was she anchored to an eternity of ever-condensing deaths.

In a shower of light which had neither speed nor wavelength, she pressed against the final web of a cocoon which pinned her, and released into her own space and time.

Seeing how it was her own agreement that formed certain realities,

Sandra vowed never to agree with anything that made less of her in the ideal.

Aira watched the glow of midnights and opals that was uniquely Sandra vivify into freedom. She was beginning again. She would need to develop, but she was free.

Other beings in the vicinity had been pervaded with the truth in Aira's free thought. That truth, like water meeting itself, knew no barriers. The beings followed, unraveling and unsticking from the electronic webs to which their agreements had adhered them.

Each thought-being was unique, which no prefabricated identity offered, because beings were naturally the very creators of their own identities themselves. Stock Z Zone-issue personalities were tombs of similarities. The pure life of thought-beings made each completely different.

There was awakening and jubilee. Showers of life and purest love released as thought-beings who had been headed for programming re-embraced their integrity, remembering who they were, becoming free to create, free to be sentient as themselves, and free to choose or not choose bodies or forms. Purged by their cognizance, made wise to the mechanism of the trap, they reintegrated with their own universes after eons of slumber. Their power restored, they were the wiser, never again to enter the dimension of Z Zone.

It would have been usual for Onx to be at Aira's side at this moment of ultimate triumph in the freeing of Life, but she wasn't. Aira scanned and called, seeking her to share the sublime victory. Nothing answered. She could not find Onx, either to help her if she were in trouble, or to share the ebullient happiness which cried out to all the stars that there had been a victory for freedom.

Mendle experienced a chill. Though the car windows were rolled up, an eerie wind had blown through it, fanning Aira's hair.

Up ahead, he saw the hospital's emergency room driveway. In the back seat, Aira opened her eyes; tears flowed down her cheeks. Universal comprehension filled her, and she saw again how joy, though ethereal and light, could be even more deep and immense than anguish, and more powerful than force.

So Aira sat, in the dichotomy of victory and defeat. Beside her, a dead body was the discarded evidence of a life shattered and broken by confusions. Sandra Wilford, as everyone knew her, was dead; the being she was, however, had been restored to her intrinsic life, released from the mortal sleep of eons. Though ultimately victorious, in the battle for truth,

Aira was bitterly wounded by the loss of her dearly loved Onx, whose very life had been as important to her as her own.

On the smoggy city street, a car that had been speeding to parallel them caught up alongside Mendle's silver sedan as they slowed for traffic approaching a busy intersection. The driver, who had a penchant for brunettes, had been craning his neck, trying to get Sandra's attention.

"Hey, hot mama!" he screamed and wolf-whistled. As the light turned green, he took off.

Gently, Aira pulled Sandra's discarded vessel away from the window.

chapter
41

"What?" When Aira opened and focused the eyes of her body and saw the road up ahead, she realized she had never really left, yet she felt as though she were returning from another world.

Mendle repeated the question he had asked. "Are you sure?" He prompted her, "You said she's dead."

Aira wondered how much time had elapsed since she had said that, since she had followed Sandra. She must have encompassed other viewpoints and another dimension without leaving her physical location.

"How long ago did I say that?" she asked.

"Just now," Mendle said, rankled by the wolf-whistle from the car that screeched past them.

Sandra's body was beside her, just as it had been left. *Strange,* Aira pondered. It seemed as though at least an hour had passed since she had stared in disbelief at the lifeless body and uttered those words—those amazing, incredible words—"She's dead."

"Maybe thirty seconds ago," Mendle added.

Thirty seconds? So much had happened. Aira looked around the interior of the car in the back seat, and oriented those thirty seconds into their place in time. *The dimension I permeated must have been outside time, or in a relative time.* She conceptualized that within 'relative time' or 'outside time,' hours could occur within the span of a minute. Conversely, fifty years on Earth could go by, and it would've only been an hour *elsewhen.* She speculated relative-time was happening in other dimensions, and it was not synchronous with Earth-rate.

Aira became aware of Mendle's agitated intention. She met his eyes in the rearview mirror and painfully affirmed, "Her body stopped functioning."

"Damn." His lips tightened. "Damn." It was all he could say.

As they turned in the hospital driveway, an ambulance, sirens gearing into a wail, was leaving the facility. When their vehicles passed, Mendle heard fragments of a dispatch about a shooting at the hotel. "I guess they wouldn't have gotten to her any faster," he said bitterly, noting by his watch it was a six-minute response time. He slammed the car to a stop outside the hospital emergency entrance as he said, "Come on, help me."

One on either side, Mendle and Aira managed to hoist and rapidly walk Sandra's body, caped in a blanket, into the emergency room. They lowered the body into a chair and Aira secured it in a leaning position against the wall as Mendle hurried to the admission desk. Positioning his hat to obscure his face, he leaned over and intently informed a nurse, "Someone over there in the corner is dead."

Taking the seat adjacent to Sandra's body, a man lowered himself into the vinyl chair. Settled and comfortable, he turned and addressed the shiny brunette head of hair whose face was turned away from him. "Hello, how you doing?" Not really looking at who, or what, he was talking to, he rambled on, "Grandson's in here for stitches. Playing with my tools, slipped, cut himself. How about you?" He briefly glanced at her again when she didn't say anything. "Got that flu going around?"

The man was taken aback by a sudden flurry of nurses. Among diagnoses and orders for emergency operations around Sandra's body, he heard the word "dead." "Dead?" he muttered, "Why I was just talking to her…"

Mendle and Aira had slipped out of the emergency room and got back in the car. As they drove away and started down Los Angeles streets, Aira held onto Onx's body in the front seat. The white-coated, blood-stained form was empty. Dead. Nothing like Onx had been, just a bizarre shell that now seemed to defy sense or comprehension.

Yet it had been Onx there who helped her when she was following Sandra and found herself in Z Zone. Even though it was already seeming vague, Aira held on to what she knew. Tracing her experience, fitting together more pieces of her past, knowing she had been there before, she said it aloud, partly to make it more real, "Z Zone."

Mendle heard, but his reaction was slow. The phrase took time to arrive through the worries globbing his thoughts, but when it registered, he snapped, "What did you say?"

Aira was about to tell him what had happened, and that Sandra was well now, but when she looked at Mendle, she pulled back into astonished silence, staring at the unexpected and trying to comprehend what she saw. She knew the man, yes, and understood him. Now she recognized him.

When she didn't say anything, "I have so much to tell you," he started pouring out to her. "I want you to read my novel…there are so many co-incidences. Like even what you just said." Aira nodded, then transferred her gaze forward to the road ahead as they drove.

"I don't know what's going on," Mendle said. "But I don't think we should go back to Valleyheart. We're packed for vacation. We should steer clear, until we determine what's going on."

"What do you mean?"

"I mean…" he stumbled over what to say, taking off his hat, running his hand through his hair, gently pulling on it. "We have to find out who shot Sandra. And we need to do it from a safe place." He paused then hesitantly said, part-question and part-statement, "I guess Sandra was talking about you."

Aira thought about it. She recalled some of Sandra's words, and wondered what she knew, how she knew.

Mendle continued, "I mean…I don't know what Sandra was involved in, if we're in danger, if you're really in danger." *'Alien, though she appears human…person without an identity…'* It all seemed unreal to him now, having heard the words spoken by Sandra, of all people. It was as though a rope he had been pulling on suddenly had no resistance on the other end. The thought that he might have actually been right all his life had an effect on him that made his environment seem thin, as though it were evaporating.

As he waited for Aira to comment, the whole thing started to seem preposterous. Orienting himself to something tangible when she didn't say anything, he suggested, "Look, let's get out of town first."

Aira nodded. She swallowed. "Okay," she said.

Stopping at a red light, Mendle looked over at her holding Onx's dead body. There was blood on the front of her camisole, on her arms and hands. It was pitiful. He felt ripped to shreds as he nervously checked the rear-vision mirror.

After they drove in what seemed a long silence, Mendle asked, "Do you know? Do you know anything that can explain why someone would shoot Sandra?"

Aira shook her head, sadly looking down. She softly smoothed the white fur on the body that had once been so alive as Onx. It seemed surreal. *How is it that happy life is just not there anymore? Just **gone***? A dense and unbearable implosion of sadness started Aira crying. The grief was silent, but lachrymal.

Something about dead bodies seems so unreal, Mendle noted, not understanding why; seeing one certainly brought death closer to view. *It happens. To everyone. Permanent. Irreversible.* It seemed outrageous. *It will happen to me.* It seemed impossible; he could not fathom it. *It could happen to her.* He glanced at Aira. *Once the last breath is gone, that's it.* Protest raged in him, similar to what he felt seeing his parents age. His entire being cried out *No*, the cry only magnifying him as feeble and helpless. Oddly enough, it continued to seem unreal; only the evidence was tangible and unrelenting. *Sandra didn't know she was going to die when she woke up this morning.* The thought posed and seemed to mock Mendle.

They had to get as far out of town as possible and make sure they weren't being followed. "We'll stop as soon as we can," he told Aira softly. "We can wash up. We'll bury Onx."

"This isn't Onx," Aira cried, then started to sob. "I don't know where she is. I've lost her. Now I'm alone."

Mendle knew the feeling. "You're not alone. You have me." He breathed deeply, then told Aira, "I love you, I really love you."

Aira wiped tears from her face, streaking it with a thin tint of blood. When Mendle saw the red stain, he abhorrently pulled his shirt sleeve into his palm and, still driving, leaned over to wipe her cheek.

Aira saw Mendle's face was serious with perplexity as he turned his intent back on driving. His words had comforted her, and she was filled with a sense of knowing that he had been true to her. *I know you.* He had valiantly tried to be true to all that was in his heart, despite the world which surrounded him.

Aira sought and pulled up sentiments which she had abandoned as inexplicable. She braved herself to look at the fragments—pieces of a picture that she knew would eventually complete. Though she was afraid of what she did not yet know, it was her courage and belief in the ultimate benevolence of Truth that affirmed her desire to see and strength to look. She sorted through pieces of memory with a faith that the total picture would not hurt, but would free her.

She had seen the sleep zone. *Sleep and unconsciousness of the soul.* Aira groped back, over the memory revealed. *There was someone else there. Someone named Loptoor. He was Juristac's cohort in treason.* She had tried to understand the evil; she literally had not believed, at first, that they would usurp her very cognizance and awareness of herself. *No wonder it seemed incredible,* Aira realized, seeing that to trap and program life-beings was the antithesis of reason and life. *Life would not violate life if it were awake,* she thought, looking through the car window at the city around her.

During the final struggle, Aira remembered, the glimmer of free life in Loptoor had surged from his darkness and tried to reverse what they had begun to enforce on her. She was being programmed to forget. *Toward death, as solid matter.* Loptoor did not succeed in fully stopping it— but he *had* prevented full activation.

Full activation of what? Aira wondered as they drove in silence and she looked out the window. Bodies, bodies, bodies, and faces, faces, faces... *furrowed, and worried, and looking, but not seeing. And the smiles are too few.*

Another segment of memory opened; she saw the fate that would have been hers had Loptoor not stepped forward at the last minute. Had he not interfered, she would not have been able to surge free long enough to avoid it—she would have been zapped into an embryo somewhere, into a baby in a woman's womb to be born as a child. Though not ultimately successful, his influence was helpful. Instead, Aira had surged as herself, still ensnarled in the energy blueprint, but still operating as thought, able to project a body and to manifest physically. *That's how I materialized into this final form. The same happened to Onx, only with a different form.*

Since then, except for glimmers and clues to the contrary, Aira had been thinking she was the form that trapped her. She stared down at her arms and legs, awed by the entirety of what happened as it dawned on her.

She remembered the thunderstorm, the lightning.

The body she had was according to genetic blueprint necessary for the environ—it was organic, sentient, reproductive. She was subject to its demands and limitations. It was completely human—except it had not been born.

Had the Z Zone procedure been *fully* activated, she would not even at that moment be semi-aware in a fully developed female body; if the procedure had not been foiled, she would be an incogitant infant somewhere, grappling to learn body coordination, babbling the beginnings of language, and failing to control waste elimination.

Aira slowly turned to look over at Mendle. She had seen him before, and he had felt familiar, but now she was looking at the actual him.

Battle-scarred, in a human, male body, shaken, but there he is.

Feeling her gaze on him, Mendle ventured, as though hearing her thoughts, "Have you remembered anything? Anything that could help shed light?"

She turned away, the realization crowning everything. *He is the amnesiac. As I have been. Amnesiac, but still himself, the essence I remember.* "I think so," she answered. "There's more coming back to me," she murmured, subdued and expanded by the colossal recognition. *Have you?* she wanted to ask him. *It's you. It's you.* Sleep wearing off, she remembered searching for him, when he had disappeared.

She turned again to look at Mendle. As she watched him, she imagined what his experience had been. So much contested him in this world, yet his courage was still afire, even after being slapped down countless times. Now she more fully understood his pain. There were reasons, reasons he had yet to discover. Aira wondered how this could possibly be and strained to explain the indisputable but astounding actuality she was perceiving.

He was as I was, once—pure thought. Able to manifest appearance in light bodies. Light is the closest physical manifestation of Thought. We could appear however we wished.

Aira remembered how intact and whole Jorian had been. *That used to be his name,* she remembered. His middle initial and last name, 'J. Orion,' were so close to Jorian, Aira smiled. *That coincidence would put him on the moon.*

Her affection for him zoomed into comprehension, its roots spreading back into eternity. *Before Time,* Aira saw, and sighed, feeling released from the somatic of time. She realized eternity was also *After Time. In eternity—outside of Time—'before and after' have happened. Time is part of this world.* The concept of space-time became very real to her, and she felt as though she could actually "go" to the four-dimensional continuum, and precisely locate events in spatial and time coordinates. *I used to be outside of it all.*

Aira admired Mendle as she looked again, reaffirming the amazing. *Jorian.* He had always been principled. *Principio—Beginning.* She studied the face that was now his, his hair, his arms, and knew why she had wanted to love him. Though pummeled, he held true to his heart, valiantly. Despite the insidious reality which circumvented him, and the deceptive elements which opposed him, Mendle would not agree with a world that contradicted the dignity and nobility of the soul.

She remembered the anguish of wondering what happened when he had disappeared from the Home dimension, when she could not sense him anywhere. The unexplained disappearance, the excruciating agony she had felt, then the nothing when she tried to thought-reach him; now she knew—he must have been snared in Z Zone.

Aira imagined what it must have been like for him, a creator, a life being, to be trapped into sleep. He had been living the charade of not communicating, of having to develop and synchronize a mind with data, of not being able to verbalize until he acquired the vocabulary necessary. She thought of Mendle's baby pictures. She thought of him being regarded as a helpless organism, of having diapers changed.

Slowly, over the years, he awoke and reoriented himself…but always around the body and an environment where Matter was lord, threatening pain and death unless complied with.

We used to be able to trans-form at will, and to travel inter-dimensionally. Mendle, when she had known him as his Life-Source, was capable of creating whole environments, of generating space into existence and splashing suns and stars in it, of creating or being universes with thought alone. *How we loved!*

What is this strange place? No wonder his anger, his despair, his frustration. To find himself here, and so. And so many reasons missing from his memory.

How long had it been? He had probably experienced dying also. And droned back to Z Zone, like the others she had seen, to forget, to assume a new body and a new life, to forget the pain. Pain was the only real lie. Dying was an illusion, wasn't it?

She remembered his words once, when he shattered into grief and moaned such awful sounds, sobbing that he didn't know how he had held on so long, that he didn't know what got into him. *Of course, of course, of course,* she empathized.

Many succumbed and agreed completely with the world around them. They might appear adjusted. The true followed their hearts with the courage to hold to principles despite the punishments of a world where only things solid were deemed real.

When Mendle felt Aira looking at him again, he turned. She made the effort of a semi-smile, trying to *dao* him through her unfolding amazement. Her feeling for him was both tender and ruthless love, and she wanted goodness for him with the very power of her life.

Mendle focused through the windshield, directing his attention to the road and traffic as he kept driving. The sight of Onx's body and the memory of Sandra amplified the dull aching in his stomach. Perforated with concern for Aira's safety, his attention was engaged, he scoured alternatives to deliver her from a danger which had not shown its face.

Aira turned away and looked straight ahead at the road as they drove in silence. She wanted to tell him, tell him everything, embrace him, adore him. *It will be of no use to him unless he sees it himself.* He had mentioned something about coincidence between names and words she had spoken and a novel he was writing. As she remembered him, truth came together inside her like tuning dilates to symphony. Once discordant sounds seeking their key and tune congealed to notes; loose notes found their chords, chords their melody, and the melody its bed of time and harmony. So the ring she heeded grew, and she was amazed and awed by her perception, *He's writing out of memory he doesn't recognize.*

Looking down at her hands, Aira remembered the first time she had become aware of them. Standing in the middle of a sidewalk as thunder and lightning crashed in the atmosphere and rain pelted her, she had stood staring at her hands. She had been deceived into believing the appendages were *her.*

"I am not what I see," she had cried, trying to hold onto her sense of self but losing it. She had been engulfed.

As she looked around, she realized something about coincidence. Reality on the material plane was an interface between Thought and Matter. Ultimately, Thought mobilized Matter, whether knowingly or not. *Synchronicity and coincidence are manifestations of that concurrence,* Aira realized, appreciating Mendle's continual fascination with the phenomena. *It's interaction. Life is interactive.*

There were others who knew it. Some knew their own Thought.

Others drifted like frail leaves on the current of Solidity, to which they relinquished their license to create.

Hope surged in Aira as she looked down at Onx's body. Per the intrinsic laws of affinity—its very nature not tolerating distance—a being, even if eventually, decreased and eliminated distances between one's self and those one loved. *That's how Onx and I manifested in the vicinity of one another,* Aira knew. Physical concurrences in life appearing "random" or "coincident" were no accident, but manifestations of this law. That was why she had manifested in Mendle's location, Aira realized. She considered the nature of this, feeling comfort. *Maybe it's impossible, then, to permanently lose those we love. Eventually we...* She stopped.

Eventually. That was the problem. The interim loneliness was painful, and Time, though only an ingredient of one dimension, was something to which she was still stuck, along with the solid body known as "her."

Even though it was only particles and objects that created distance, Matter which only *appeared* solid, now it was physical death making her and Mendle vulnerable to separation. The thought stirred a panicky frenzy in Aira. Thought was the ultimate command force, but the laws of the material world were woven very tightly. *We're in it, now.* She could not bear the thought of losing Mendle in Time again.

Aira looked at him and again wanted to say something to him, something that would make everything all right, something that let him know she knew. She didn't, though. She just slid over in the seat closer to him, leaned her head against his arm and found comfort in the simple physical thereness of him.

All objects are manifestations of something, she realized as she looked about her. Everything she saw, every single thing, began as Thought. *Idea, imagination, generation, concept...from the most mundane, to the beginning principle. Beings did that.*

Here she found herself in a strangely solid world of, for the most part, abandoned creations, in which life-force was being buried, denied, crushed. Nonetheless, all matter was dependent on the 'observer' to exist.

The creation of form initially had been good. Thought-beings, when free, used bodies as vessels, and used them to further Life purposes. Now, many had been duped into thinking they *were* the form and could not create. *I am a creator. A life-being.*

Aira's eyes—large to begin with—widened from the realizations she was having. She sat up and looked at Mendle; her eyes made an impression on him.

"Oh! *Every* thing begins with an idea. There is nothing *but* coincidence.

All Reality is the interface of Thought and Matter!" she gasped.

Mendle nodded; her words gave him satisfaction. This was what he had been saying all along. The company of another who so ardently thought about the things he passionately pondered felt good.

Aira looked out of the window again. *Them, too. If they only knew,* she thought sadly about people she saw driving, shopping, sitting on bus benches. *Thought-beings were once gods. Some mingled with humans, merged with organisms in order to persist and conquer the material universe. Yet even with these solid forms, they would not have degenerated into amnesiacs. It was only the tampering of evil that distorted and inverted, creating the worsening condition. If there was only some way I could tell them.* She wanted to shout from the window, "Wake up!" There was no doubt to her now as she thought about Earth. There was something wrong. *This is why the theme of Good and Evil recurs here on this planet,* she concluded. It was war.

The nature of thought-beings was to reason, to love, to make wishes come true, to further Life. Aira looked around. *Buried as somnambulant slaves being stimulus-response machines, these spiritual beings conceive of themselves as nothing but meat and bones. Yet the meat and bone are only containers.* Aira marveled over people on the street, in cars, seated at outdoor espresso bars, asleep. *In this 'civilization' most beings are living as receipt points of sensation. They're not aware they are affecting the experiment.*

The breakthroughs occurring in quantum physics offered hope. A quantum physicist had isolated thought from matter, and empirically proven that *thought,* the observer, affected the experiment. By a process of elimination of matter to particles to sub-particles, the soul had been uncovered.

Aira had often felt alone, trapped in a strange place. Now, as she looked at the people on sidewalks, at the faces behind steering wheels, along exits, and on roads, all with their somber gazes, their knitted brows, their fears, their smiles, their tears, their scowls, and their desolate vacancies, she knew she was seeing the cocoons of trapped souls. *They're all strangers here. Doing what they think they have to in order to survive; thinking they are free, but all of them under a prison of sky.*

Pervading their desolation, she silently addressed them. *When you get closer to your dreams, you'll know Home isn't far.*

chapter 42

The sun presided over Spring which was out in full regalia. Around Aira and Mendle were mockingbirds and red-breasted robins. Monarchs and other butterflies flirted with rolling fields of blooms.

"It's so animated," Mendle murmured breaking a silence. Aira breathed in deeply and looked out over the Kentucky hills.

"Animated," Mendle said, "*Anima...anima...*" repeating the Latin root. "Soul. Whoever came up with the word '*anima*ted' knew that things move because they have a soul." He admired the hills. "It's so beautiful, all that lush green, those splashes of daffodils...yellows, and the pinks, and the roses, all these colors kissing the sky."

His voice trailed off as he bent his head backward to follow the soaring of two birds across the blue. "Particles," he murmured. "Only particles. But they are *animated.*"

Still squinting from looking up at the sun, he turned to Aira. She was wistfully watching him, hoping he would say something that she wanted to hear.

"This can be such a beautiful place, can't it?" was what he said.

Aira nodded and returned her pensive gaze to the hills. "It really can be," she agreed. "It could be Paradise."

As Mendle squinted to look at her through the bright sunlight, he wondered about the Irene Davis driver's license Sandra had told him about.

"Does the name Irene Davis mean anything to you?" he finally came out with it.

He watched Aira think about it. He was careful to watch her face for an initial reaction, then shot her studied glances as his gaze traveled between her and the hills. After seeming to search her memory, she shook her head.

He knew that he loved her, but he didn't know why she was the girl he often pictured, and, though he knew there was more to Life than the current planetary reality he lived, he didn't know what.

"Why?" Aira asked him.

He shook his head. "Ever been to Iowa?"

She shook her head. "Have you?"

"No."

As she watched Mendle, Aira considered whether to bring up the subject of his origins. She reminded herself that had she been told the truth about her materialization, she might have rejected it. Such a revelation from another would have left her confused. At best, any subsequent discoveries would have been laced with the doubt that they were a result of suggestion, and she would have regarded her conclusions as possibly influenced by outside evaluation.

"Aira." She heard his voice, then she felt his arm around her. Hopeful, she closed her eyes.

In silence Mendle sought words to translate his thoughts. The sound of a word began to form, but he stopped it at the back of his throat, decided it wouldn't do, and replaced it with a soft laugh. He shook his head as he pulled Aira closer to him, then said, "I used to give you a hard time, didn't I?"

"No," Aira replied, not needing the apology in his voice. "I understand."

"All those tirades," he went on, "and, when we first met, my wild overtures to you. But I did fantasize sometimes, just driving along, or going about doing things during the day before I met you. Strange. I felt what seemed like *you*. A presence. Like you were," he paused, then, "kissing me in 360 degrees."

"Maybe I was," Aira said, surprising him. He looked at her.

As their gazes locked, Mendle told her, "I had imagined you just as you are. Well, almost." He looked away. "My imagination, my dreams, the stories I wrote…it was all becoming confused with reality. I'm sorry. There's so much to do, I can't even comprehend how I wasted any time with those fits of anger over nothing."

Aira was disappointed. "Maybe it wasn't over nothing—" she began.

Mendle laughed dryly. The laugh was short and tight, an effort to dispel an irony he was feeling but had not yet defined. "It wasn't over nothing," he repeated sardonically.

He withdrew his arm from Aira's shoulder then idly plucked a blade of grass from the patch of ground between his legs. After a span of brooding, he finally said, "I guess not. I've always felt like a stranger. My entire life I felt like I didn't belong, didn't fit. I'm sure others feel that way, but I don't see them totally losing it, dashing about wildly brandishing their outrage and beliefs..."

"Maybe they should," Aira quipped, and they both grinned over the idea. "Anyway I'm sure there's a reason," she assured Mendle. When he didn't say anything, she continued, "Maybe you're just more sensitive, have higher standards. Some might be more adjusted to the way things are, and maybe it's not so good to be so adjusted to some things. Besides, you didn't totally lose it."

"After what's happened, I should be in fits now. You'd think so anyway." He shook his head. "You'd think, with what we're going through, I'd be flipping out like a pinball machine."

"Maybe the difference is that this situation is an adversary you can see and deal with to some degree. It's the unknown wars that can drive a person mad," Aira proposed, adding, "or the ones leaving you to think the problem rests in you."

Mendle had been clipping little pieces off the grass blade with his thumbnail and now flung away the final remnant. "Yeah," he agreed. "Maybe it's good that I still had it in me to howl, huh?"

"Yes."

Mendle smiled warmly at her.

It was good to stretch after days of driving. The natural world was far more glitteringly beautiful than the condensed, enforced synthetics of the city. In the surroundings radiant with life they both floated in their thoughts.

Mendle's voice became quiet as he said, "I guess I felt really sorry for her. Seeing her like that. Dead and all." He was talking about Sandra. "You know, it has a way of..." He paused to select the words to say best what he was feeling. "Death has a way of...Well, when I saw her there, I suddenly wanted her to be right. About everything," he said.

Aira pulled her knees up, clasping her arms around her legs. As she looked out over the hills, she thought about what Mendle had said. "I guess she looked pretty...wrong...lying there, dead."

"Maybe I felt responsible," Mendle said, seeing the inaccuracy of the feeling but understanding why he felt it. "I kept telling her she was wrong about so many things, but I didn't want her to be *that* wrong."

"She created her own reality."

"I almost wished I had been wrong, if it would have meant saving her."

Another silence, then Aira murmured intently, "It's not just you, or me, who is more than just a body."

There was a steeliness, a resolve in her voice that went through Mendle. The past few days had changed her, he thought, looking over at her. The face was still sweet, almost childlike, but there was a toughness there he hadn't seen before, except perhaps in glimpses.

"You saw her?"

Aira nodded, then said, "There's nothing wrong with you, Mendle." With particular emphasis she then told him, "I think you underestimate yourself." Her voice was still soft and quiet, but the command factor in it felt as though it could forge steel.

"How?"

"Well," Aira thought about it. She wanted to tell him that, as a pure life-being, he was capable of making forms, even universes; however, she decided that might come across as a little too intense. "For one thing, maybe you think you're irresponsible, and that Sandra, for example, was responsible."

It did seem that way, Mendle recalled.

"When in actuality," Aira pointed out, "which of you is actually the more responsible person?"

Mendle thought about it. He thought about the way Sandra relegated even her own feelings to electronic, subliminal commands, the way she never committed herself to specific positions, the way she lied, and didn't value keeping her word.

"That happens frequently," he realized, thinking about many calm types who appeared together, but whose hidden acts were hideously insane.

"Next—you say you're moody, mad, crazy. But what angers you?" Aira asked.

Betrayals, injustices, failures, Mendle thought.

"Right," Aira said, knowing his answer. "Now what's crazy? To get angry about those things? Or not to get angry?"

Mendle nodded, seeing her point. "I could get a little smarter about it, though."

"True," Aira agreed.

He smiled. "Some of Sandra's actions bothered me so much because I saw them in myself." Something rose in Mendle like the dawn. It was his own power he was feeling. He said, "I guess underneath the mechanisms that make humanity similar, each of us is a unique life-source."

Aira watched him hopefully, expectantly, but he didn't take it any further. Instead his thoughts turned to her, to their situation. A fear of losing Aira gripped him. Leaping over hesitation, he told her, "I love you." She closed her eyes and listened. "I won't let anything happen to you."

Aira was about to open her eyes and say something, but did neither when she felt his embrace. Mendle held her, in awe of the difference between how frail her little shoulders were and how vast the power of her heart.

"I avoided the human race," he told her. "I blamed every human foible for my own unhappiness, for the loneliness which gnawed at me. It was like having a piranha for a constant companion." Mendle caressed Aira's curls, pressing her head closer to his shoulder as he did so. He sighed, then said, "I only hated what I felt I could do nothing about." Aira nodded her understanding.

"But most of it was inside me," he said. "It wasn't out there. And the faces I looked at only reminded me that I had decided things could not be as I dreamed they should be. It gnawed at me, eating me alive."

Mendle took Aira's face in his hands and gently tilted it toward him. The sight of her always made him smile, but when he saw her eyes shining with overbrimming tears, he quickly said, "I didn't mean to be depressing! Leave it to me to carry the world on my shoulders instead of a chip!" Aira shook her head.

"There was no piranha in me," Mendle concluded, finding it funny. "It was my own decisions affecting me. Person Discovers They Are Not Aquarium!" he called out the mock headline and laughed. He continued, "Somebody flushed me down the cosmic toilet, and whenever I yelled 'WHY?' they flushed again!...And I started to think that was the answer!" Aira laughed with him.

"I think I'll program myself to like hamburgers," Mendle said, mockingly serious. "Our hamburgers are here." They both laughed at the memory of her being drenched and in shock in the hotel bathroom while hamburger delivery was made the issue.

"What's your beef?"

"It isn't my beef, it's your beef!"

"Oh, sorry. I had a program jam. This beef is becoming a problem, so I'll program myself to stay away from burgers now," Mendle said.

"Then what about the other program to like them?"

"I guess I'm confused. That's depressing," Mendle joked. "I'll have to program myself to handle that."

"But what about your depression over your confusion of the problem of liking and wanting not to like hamburgers?" Aira merrily posed.

"I'll have to program myself to not think about hamburgers ever, and then program myself to be active."

"Oh, can't you just inspect your decisions and do it yourself?" Aira playfully asked.

Mendle mugged a dumb look. "Is that what I'm for? To know, and do, and think?" he asked. "To decide and do?" he spoofed. "You mean I can create things? Wow. I'm actually somebody with my own feelings," he cried. "In fact, maybe the beef is bull, so go away! And quit flushing in my face!"

Mendle and Aira rolled on their backs, their laughter releasing accumulated nervousness. They continued amusing themselves with banter. Each time they thought they were through, one of them would start up again and set the other to laughing.

So, with the feel of the grass against their backs, and the warmth of the sun on their hair, relief came for two tired children seeking paths out of the mysteries that surrounded them. Their laughter slowed to intermittent trickles then finally subsided altogether. Listening to the trilling birds and looking into the blue overhead, Mendle and Aira rested quietly against the earth.

Out of the blue Aira said, "I'm not just a dream girl."

Mendle became very quiet, he almost held his breathing still. After some moments he turned his head. She was facing him, her eyes limpid, open. She whispered, barely uttering the sound, "Kiss me."

Mendle reeled himself quickly in from his dreamy expanse of sky-wandering. Never letting go of one another's eyes, they moved closer, contained in what could have been an eternity, and their lips finally touched. Mendle and Aira kissed.

It wasn't only their lips that came together. The kiss had its own momentum; it was intact, separate. It lived in and of itself and fell out of relative time. The kiss was longer than it was, but shorter than it was.

It was mostly soft and warm. They were aware of each other's warm breath and closeness. They were vulnerable, into one another's sensations, but their lips touching were a bridge to cross into a utopia of sensations the limits of flesh could never know.

When they pulled away, they looked at one another. They gently touched each other's face, caressed the other's hair. They kissed again, deeper in embrace, and pulled away again and looked at one another. Then they just held onto each other very tightly.

They had been on the road for five days. After leaving Sandra's body at the hospital, Mendle and Aira had withdrawn some money at the bank then started driving. They stopped for Onx's burial, then kept on going, taking the fastest route out of California into Arizona.

From Arizona they entered New Mexico, where they thought to stop in Santa Fe to get a postal box from which they could both forward and receive mail under several names. They continued on through Texas, stopping again in Amarillo to acquire another postal box. There was no one in direct pursuit, from what they could tell.

Along the way, they had picked up newspapers, but only one in California had run anything, and it didn't tell them anything they didn't already know. "**Journalist Mysteriously Slain At Convention.**" The story stated that Sandra Wilford was described by an eyewitness as being "hysterical" before the shooting, yet sources believed the incident 'may have been a random, gang-related occurrence.' She had been taken to St. John's hospital where she was pronounced dead upon arrival. A man waiting for treatment there said he had been talking to her for some minutes before he realized she was dead.

"He wasn't waiting for treatment, I heard him say his grandson was there," Aira noted when Mendle was reading the article aloud.

"That's the state of journalism and news," Mendle had commented, not taking his eyes off the paper. "Unbiased? As long as there's blood, crime, and scandal. Facts? A thing of the past. That crap on TV's not news. Think of all the scientific and cultural events, real news, they could be reporting." He curtailed his passion, and went back to reading.

The article further reported that Wilford had been a patient under psychiatric care, and no comments could be made on her personal case history; however, she had been known to suffer from delusions and hallucinations, including the belief that she was in communication with aliens from outer space. Other than this fifth-page mention in the *Los Angeles Daily News*, there was no other coverage, and no further mention of the story.

From Texas, Mendle and Aira drove to Oklahoma, stopping in Oklahoma City for a postal box, then heading for Arkansas. They stayed overnight in a little motel just east of Ozark, near the Ouachita Mountains.

That night they watched some television, a show which interviewed an American teenaged virgin as a rarity, a special phenomenon. She got up and said being a virgin was fine with her, while other girls who had gotten pregnant and left school argued that their lives were just as good.

Then a teenage boy spoke up that he preferred to wait until marriage to "go all the way," to do so as a total, knowing act. The audience booed him. Commercials ran every seven minutes or so, and Mendle made wry comments about some of the close-up shots. "Here come more faceless, wagging butts. Trying to sell me beer and cars."

Mendle and Aira ate popcorn and, opting not to watch a musical extravaganza featuring the heralded rock groups "Split Tongues" and "Kill Yo Mama," went to sleep early.

In the morning they decided to cut south to Louisiana and open a final decoy address in Lafayette. They still didn't know the face of their enemy. They began to wonder if there was one.

Mendle could only surmise that Sandra had become curious, discovered something about Aira and planned to break the story, then someone stopped her. He didn't know which of her claims was a ploy. Had Sandra been lying or up to some manipulative tactic? Then why had someone shot her?

The first couple of days on the road, Aira thought of Sandra frequently, of her unfurling into a being of symmetry, of the difference between that being and the twisted, writhing soul she had first seen. Ironically, Sandra's final choice to do right at the end, though it killed her physically, resulted in saving her immortal destiny.

To Mendle it seemed the news story was being hushed up or smokescreened. Questions revolved like restless vacuums seeking to be filled. *By whom? How many people were involved? For a personal reason, or a national one?* He speculated and worried randomly.

He had shown Aira his novel, and she had seemed impressed. When he asked her if she remembered her real name, because he had suggested 'Aira' the night he found her amnesiac, she lightly shook her head and told him there was a reason he did that.

There was a reason he had been writing the book, too, she told him, and that sent cold chills up his arms and down his back. She had said some cryptic things. She had mentioned that there were things he had to remember. Then she had remarked that 'the plot of a life happened mostly within people.'

He toyed again with the idea of whether he had created this woman into his life out of thin air. He also had finally asked her about the Iowa driver's license that Sandra had mentioned. Aira had shaken her head as if it meant nothing, and, in the silence that followed, the reliability of what he knew of Sandra as source diminished it as a credible possibility.

So much was conjecture. There were tangible tasks at hand and they needed data. Meanwhile, with decoy postal boxes, they could correspond safely, under the appearance of being at those locations, from wherever they ended up.

From Louisiana, Mendle and Aira had headed north, across Mississippi and Tennessee into Kentucky. At Bowling Green, they stopped to wire themselves some money, via a maze of names and postal boxes, from their account in California.

It was then they discovered that a freeze had been put on the account, and they could obtain no information over the phone explaining why. "Only in person," they were told. Somebody wanted them to return to Los Angeles.

Night was pulling its curtain now as Mendle and Aira sat on the outskirts of a cornfield near some hills several miles from Kentucky Lake. They had decided to camp here for the night. They had a little less than five hundred dollars on them.

It was near summer but the night air still had an edge, so they kept a small fire going for comfort. It was more than just physical comfort; it warmed them in other ways.

They were both feeling depressed, oppressed, suppressed, and repressed under the weight of their worries. Adding to those worries, Mendle remembered that in the rush he had not checked out of the hotel at the science fiction convention and fretted about charges to his credit card account.

Aira was thinking about Onx and missing her. It seemed like the first time she had been without her in a billion years. Why she could not even locate her to thought-touch was both a baffling mystery and a horrid concern. Thinking about it led to no answers, only rekindled helplessness, a feeling of total and utter subservience to circumstance.

Mendle spoke, "The main thing is that nobody knows where you are. Until we determine what happened, better to be safe about it. I want to be in the position where I can see them, but they can't see me, for once."

Here she had found Jorian, Aira was thinking, and this was a great relief, but the condition he was in dampened the occasion. He did not remember who he was. Here he was, thinking he was a human being. Furthermore, now that she had finally realized who she was, where she was, and most of how she got there, she was still bound somehow, tied to her physical manifestation.

What a strange place, she thought, looking up at stars twinkling in the night, *this strange dimension in which I find myself.*

It was some comfort that pioneers on the frontiers of science, Bohm and others, were on the brink of breaking barriers: "We are not the discoverers of reality, but participants." Through a process of elimination, quantum physicists had isolated the observer from particles. "All things in physical reality arise from the spiritual," Aira remembered reading, knowing this had to do with clues Mendle had seen yet didn't fully understand.

One way out seemed to be dying. There was always that alternative—simply terminating the body. She wondered what would happen. Without a thought-guide to assist her, she was uncertain she would make it out of the maze. *It's part of me somehow,* Aira thought about her body, realizing that taking its life was a violation against life, and would be wrong. Further, that would only be temporary escape. The only solution was clear. *I have to transcend this through knowledge, or I will never master this trap, and therefore always be liable.* She knew, *My exit from this world can only be through mastering the interface of the material and the unseen.*

Aira turned her head sideways, resting it on her knees which were drawn up as she clasped her hands around her legs. She gazed at Mendle. There was no way she was going to leave Mendle behind in this eternity of repeated death and suffering either.

As a matter of fact, Aira thought, *something must be done about the entire place.*

If people only knew, if they could only see, if they truly considered the consequences of their acts. She grieved at what she had seen in the city. *Most of all—if they only knew themselves.*

It seemed to Aira that she could hear the world's lament, the agony and crying—the tears were of souls who found themselves demoted, suffering, trapped.

"Damn dump," Mendle grumbled, as though reading Aira's mind, about the sorry excuse for a civilization in which they found themselves. "What's the human race going to do when it runs out of orifices to stick something into for a thrill?" Then he fell again into a damp silence.

Neither of them had heard any sign of someone approaching until the twig snapped about five feet behind them. The loud crunch startled them out of their quietude of crackling fire and starlight, and they jumped, at the same time turning their heads.

They had to look up to see the face of the figure looming over them. The stranger stood there, expressionless as the firelight cast glow and shadows on his face. He was holding a pitchfork and keenly transferred his steely gaze from Mendle to Aira.

One of his eyes squeezed a little bit shut. Slowly, he turned one side of his face forward—the side with the eye more open—and he appeared to be looking out of that one eye only as he surveyed Aira.

"I know who you are," he drawled, his head slowly nodding up and down.

chapter 43

"Just a matter of time," he mused, wiping one of his hands on the side of his overalls as he reached for a loaf of bread with the other. In the spacious kitchen of the farmhouse, Mendle and Aira were seated at a wooden table beneath the yellow cast of electric light.

"Yep, I knew it was just a matter of time," the farmer said sagely as he poked a piece of sizzling bacon with his fork. His back was to Aira and Mendle as he stood over the stove, supervising the unruly strips of bacon that popped and threatened to spit hot grease at him from the frying pan.

Mendle and Aira exchanged puzzlement. They both widened their eyes and shrugged to relay that neither one of them had figured out what he was talking about.

Since the farmer's first words to Aira, which he had spoken with the solemnity of an oracle, he had introduced himself as A.J., told them they were on his land, and asked them if they wouldn't like to come in out of the night. He had asked them their names, so it appeared evident he hadn't heard or read of either of them.

It had been wile, not suspicion, with which he had first eyed them, and he had not asked them anything about themselves. He had gone on about himself, saying he was a widower and had lived in the hills all of his life. The man was treating them as if he knew them, with the confidence of familiarity.

He wasn't a tall man, but he had stature. He had a stocky build. His skin was toughened by the sun, and the lines on his face showed that benevolence occupied him more than anything. The gruffness was his grip on honesty, and he appeared to have a sense of humor. At one point he asked them if they ate food—a question to which Mendle replied, "We've been known to do so on occasion," to match what he thought was humor. The rest of the farmer's conversation was casual disclosure about himself, as if they had just been away a while and he was catching them up on all the news.

"Made this myself," he told them, setting a jar of peach jam on the table in front of them. "Not the same as when my Becky used to make it, but I guarantee you won't be complainin' when you try it. Same recipe. Her mama made it that way, and her mama before her. And probably her mama before her."

He stood there a moment, staring at the jar he had just placed on the table. "It's peach. Peach jam. You put it on bread. Here, let me get you the bread," he told them, suddenly remembering he had left it on the counter.

He explained about the jam in that careful tone again, the tone they had taken as humor. It was making Mendle curious. The sound of sizzling bacon presided over the kitchen while none of them said anything and A.J. brought them some pieces of toast.

"You ever had anything like that?" he asked them proudly after they had spread the jam and taken a bite.

"No, never," Mendle paused in his chewing to tell him.

"It's delicious," Aira agreed.

A.J. laughed, eyeing them with that wily look again. "I bet you could say it's out of this world, couldn't you?" he intimated, nodding his head up and down as if coaching them to say yes. He smiled at them as if they were all in on some joke, then turned around to tend to the skillet he had on the fire.

"Was Becky your wife?" Aira asked. She could see the woman's absence, still fresh as if it were yesterday, in A.J.'s eyes when he turned to look at her.

The inquiry seemed to startle him a little, but it also seemed as if the question found him in a place where he had been isolated and invisible, and he welcomed the company. "She went and got sick on me—died," he said it gruffly, then gave way to the wound underneath. "Never goes away," he said about missing her. "It's been close to a quarter century, can you reckon that?" He stared off into his memory. "I sometimes just want to look into those eyes of hers, you know, or hear her say somethin' to me like she used to, anythang, and I ask myself…where are those eyes?" His words finished on a note of incredulity that there was no answer to his question.

A.J. turned back to the stove, only setting to one side the protest he would never throw away. Suddenly he straightened up, as if he just realized he was not alone in the room. "But one day. One of these days," he said, and left it at that.

Mendle began feeling uncomfortable as he pondered some of the comments A.J. had made. He was about to question him when he, holding an egg up in either hand, turned to face them and said, "Now, these are eggs. Chicken eggs. Chicken is a bird. You probably seen some of them. Now. I crack 'em open just like this."

He set one egg down and cracked the other on the rim of the hot skillet. "And then you put the insides in the pan," the farmer narrated. "Just like so. Don't need the shell." He threw it into a nearby bucket on the floor, then continued breaking eggs into the pan. "Use that for compost," he said when he tossed away the last shell.

As Mendle watched the man, he ventured, "You said you knew it was just a matter of time before you met one of us?"

"Sure," A.J. replied without hesitation.

Aira looked at Mendle and smiled at him.

Vigorously scrambling the eggs in the pan before they became too hard, A.J. went back to what he had been saying. "That compost is very important. It nourishes the plants, restores the soil." He rapped the fork deftly on the rim of the pan, shaking off any loose egg, then set it down.

The farmer wiped his hands on the sides of his pants before picking up the platter of bacon. As he brought it to the table, he said "People need a different kind. When you stop growin', you start rottin'."

"That's true," Aira agreed, feeling fonder and fonder of him with everything he said.

A.J. set the platter down and commented, "Figured you would know. Many people on this here planet just walk around absorbin' time and space."

As he returned to the eggs cooking on the fire, he told them, "Many people don't understand about farmin'. All they see is the lettuce and other produce on the supermarket shelves. Guess they don't think about how it got there. That food is the livin' grace of nature. I know about it. I know about the heavens and the earth, and I work hand in hand with that perfection."

"I understand," Aira told him ardently.

"Course not too many people I tell about it." He spooned the eggs into a large blue bowl and brought it over to the table.

"You can hear the music of the spheres," Aira told him.

"Eh?"

"The music of the spheres," Aira repeated. "A music imperceptible to human ears, produced by the movements of the spheres, by heavenly bodies."

"That's right," A.J. said. He chuckled then added, "I hear it with my soul." Another chuckle followed, this time as though he were leaving himself a way out—modifying such statements with a laugh had become a habit with him, Aira noted, to compensate for a lack of those around him who understood.

"I didn't see your vehicle," A.J. said.

"We left it on the road," Mendle replied.

"On the road?" A.J. exclaimed, handing Mendle the bowl and taking a chair. "You think that's a good idea?"

"I didn't think people broke into cars around here, maybe I should—"

"Cars?" A.J. interrupted. "Come on now," he wheedled. "There's no need pretendin'."

Mendle passed the bowl to Aira, straightening the spoon as he did so. The look in her eyes told him she had no idea what the farmer meant either.

"Unless you disguised it, made it look like a car somehow," A.J. said, taking a bite of bread. "Is that what you all are doin' these days? I can see from the looks of you you haven't decided it's safe to tell me, that's okay."

"What is it you would like us to tell you?" Aira asked calmly.

A.J. finished serving himself, set the bowl down, then asked, "What planet ar'ya from?"

Mendle's head craned forward in astonishment. Aira took a sip from a glass of orange juice she hadn't touched yet. The subsequent silence was deep.

By the time Mendle had wiped his mouth with his napkin and was ready to question A.J., the man hastened to explain, "I've been watchin' the landings for some time. I'm well meanin'. But you," he looked right at Aira, "don't you remember me?"

A dream, it's a dream, maybe a bad dream, a dream out of control, Mendle was thinking as the outer reality in his life so solidly coincided with his most inner sanctum.

Aira looked at the farmer a long time before she finally said, her voice very quiet, "I don't think so."

"You were pretty upset all right. And you don't look much different at all."

Mendle took over. "What do you mean?"

The farmer smiled at him. "It's been close to thirty years. No, wait. I was twenty-nine that summer. I'm sixty-two now. Been, let's see, twenty-nine to…" He counted, using fingers for decades. "…thirty-nine, forty-nine, fifty-nine…" Then he finished his calculation quietly and announced the answer, "Thirty-three years. Thirty-three years, and you look the same as you did then." His marveling turned to wonder. "Unless you all look alike?" Aira just stared.

"I figured you brought him to help you," A.J. told her, nodding at Mendle.

"I'm a writer. I'm from Georgia," Mendle found himself saying.

The farmer went on as if nothing was amiss. "I still got it. It's in the barn." He set down his napkin and scooted back his chair. "And I got a piece right here."

Mendle and Aira glued their gazes to him as he crossed the kitchen, mumbling to himself, "Yeah, look at me, boy, my hair's turnin' white and my face do look changed." He went over to a bureau next to a large rocking chair with gingham cushions on it and bent down to open the bottom drawer. While struggling to jar the creaky drawer loose, he grunted and asked, "What d'ya write?"

"Science fiction, poetry, fiction, anything. A friend of mine, Bonta, a writer, actually calls it Quantum Fiction, a new term bringing science up to speed, for when thought meets matter," Mendle found himself babbling on.

"He's a creator," Aira said, wondering when Mendle himself would grasp the full meaning of that.

After rummaging a little, A.J. found what he was looking for and straightened up. Wiping it down as he brought it over to them, he mused idly, "Science fiction, eh?"

The piece of metal he set down on the table was about the length and width of three license plates put together. It was about two inches thick, and one border of it was jagged, as though it had been forcefully ripped from something. It had the look of lead, gray, with a sparse intertexture of fine gold filaments. It was not heavy, though it appeared it would be, and although it looked like metal, its surface temperature to the touch was neither cold nor warm. The sensation of temperature was strangely absent, yet the texture felt porous.

The moment she saw it, Aira's hand shot forward. She caressed the ash-aureate plaque and stared in awe, disbelief, and wonder. Barricades which blocked her memory fell away as melting glaciers drop ice in chunks. When her palm had traversed the entire surface, she slowly traced with her index and middle fingers the symbols that were engraved on it: two hands clasped in a handshake, encircled by two branches of foliage that burgeoned from a star; the hands and wreath were set between two flourishing wings.

"I took care of it," A.J. told them proudly. "I didn't think you'd be this long, though."

Aira looked at the farmer, and his face bloomed in her memory. She remembered.

There had been electrical currents snapping around her, biting at her, filling her with a buzzing confusion. She had been materializing and dematerializing while Loptoor had fought to take the controls in Z Zone, to undo what had begun, to help save her from the one who hated her magnanimous life.

Briefly, during this conflict, she must have been caught, and moved randomly back and forth to different locations. The process must have caused her to materialize then disappear in front of several people before the whole matter was settled. She had never considered it from their points of view.

There had been that astonished woman lying in bed in a room. She had said, "Wow." Aira remembered mistaking that for a form of greeting and repeating it back to her.

For a short period, she had rejoined her ship in the Z Zone disintegration transport. Next, she found herself in the Lauryad crashing through an atmosphere. Although the ship had seemed operational, it was actually breaking apart between molecular integration and disintegration. Then, an impact, as if the ship had established molecular solidity. When Aira was getting out of the craft, she felt torrents towing at her again. She recalled looking around, trying to hang onto something, and using her physical vision to orient herself.

It was a green field. A night sky. There was a man, a younger man, but it was this face, it was those eyes. "It was you," she uttered.

"You said you'd be back, and I kept my promise," A.J. said.

Beside him had been a woman with a kind, strong face and the kindest eyes. "And that was Becky," Aira said, remembering.

"That's right." A.J. nodded. "She was with me." He paused at the memory of his wife then continued speaking, "I'll tell you, though, after you disappeared on me like that, if it weren't for what you left behind I'd a thought I was crazy or dreamin'." Nodding them toward the back door, he said, "Come on."

The promise of morning was but a breath on the horizon. Stars still trembled in the expanse overhead, and the crescent moon lingered in the twilight, becoming more transparent as the halo of day spread. They had not exchanged any words during the bumpy ride across the fields. Now the faded red pickup truck perched on the crest of a hill while A.J. pointed, narrowing his eyes as if he were taking aim down his arm. "There it is," he shouted through the window. His words became vaporous cloudlets as they met the morning air. Aira, who had been semireclining in the back of the pickup, her arms folded across her chest, sat up and looked over Mendle's shoulder.

On the far edge of the basin that sprawled below the hill, a weathered, large barn stood in a fenced patch of its own. Its dusky silhouette was solitary in the distance. Nearby towered a lone tree, the uncontested custodian of the field, with its arms fountaining majestically in mute loyalty.

Their feet made no noise on the damp hay strewn on the dirt around the barn. A.J. eyed the rusty padlock hanging from the slatted wooden door. Then he inspected the worn paint and brushed chips off the wood as he reached into his pocket with his other hand and pulled out a crowded key ring. Barely glancing at it, he isolated a key and inserted it into the lock.

Mendle moved to help him as he pushed and yanked on the massive door. "That's got it," A.J. said, then nodded for Mendle to get the other side of the thick slab of lumber that was barricading the entrance.

From within the barn issued the batting and whooshing of wings in the rafters. "Pigeons and bats," gruffed A.J. as he and Mendle heaved the long bolt onto their shoulders. Aira watched them hoist it off the door. She stood in the morning mist, clasping the etched metal remnant to her chest. Even though she watched the two men raise the log off the door, watched them pitch it to the ground and heard the dull thump when it hit, her thought was between the present and some past that had eluded her because it hovered outside time.

A.J. and Mendle each gripped a large metal ring and, walking backward, swung open the doors. Dank air wafted out, and the flaps and whooshing of wings echoed louder from overhead. Aira adjusted her eyes to the darkness as she walked forward into the barn.

There, marooned on a bed of hay, battered and tarnished, though indisputably sleek and spectacular, was the vessel she knew but had forgotten, and once thought she would never see again.

"Lauryad," she gasped.

Mendle stared, aghast. This was the most amazing thing ever, even though it was straight out of his heart and soul—not to mention his book. He wondered about coincidence, about the whim that had possessed them to stop in these hills, to turn down that particular access road. Was it whim, or something he always knew but couldn't grasp?

chapter 44

On Earth it was day in some places, night in others. Aside from being under the same sun and moon, millions of people across the globe had another thing in common: they sat in front of television sets.

In different regions, clocks throughout the world marked different hours and times while the sun's position varied in the sky, but all of the people were in the same time stream. The same seconds ticked, no matter what number they were assigned between one and sixty.

During about eight of those seconds, millions viewing their TV's experienced program interruption. Their screens blipped to chromatic snow, the sound crackled, then they heard, or thought they heard, "Testing, testing. One, two…Don't you know you are gods?"

The planet continued to rotate and orbit around the sun, casting some of it in light, some of it in darkness.

chapter 45

A breeze meandered in through the window. Lifting the white muslin curtain in billows of respiration, the wavelet took Mendle's attention away from his glass of ice water, and he lifted his face. The morning had been thick and inert. Flies defied the torpidity. Plagued, they blasted about in tight circles of tormented whirring. All else seemed motionless in the tenure of summer heat, and Mendle welcomed the current, even though warm, which stirred the air.

"Damn fools," A.J. cursed as he came in the back door, letting the screen door slam behind him. He wiped the sweat off his forehead. "Been listenin' to the news in the truck," he told Mendle. "'Stead of gas and bombs they should develop a love potion. Planes should fly around and spread it all over the world."

Mendle nodded. "It's in the hands of a few. Their agenda is not what most people would be doing with life," he said. He swallowed a gulp of water. "No man can be sane and discuss nuclear warfare at the same time. I heard they cut back grants for the arts."

"More money for wars," A.J. said. "Fools," he growled, setting his hat on the kitchen counter. "I heard that, too. Said it wasn't the government's responsibility to support art. Who's behind that is worse than fools. They're criminals. What are they sayin' then? The government ain't responsible for creatin'? Just destroyin'?"

"I like the way you get to the bone of the matter," Mendle said.

"Well, I may not be a professor, but—"

"You're more. Sometimes people listen to a guy spout complicated megalamush, and because they don't understand it, they think it must be something deep and great. The fact is he's just said nothing…and that's why he doesn't make sense."

"Gimme an attorney and an IRS agent and they'll make you a business deal you can't understand," A.J. joked as he poured himself a glass of chilled water.

"You're a prince, A.J." Mendle said, admiring him.

"Maybe in a past life."

"I mean it. I really appreciate everything you've done for us. Your hospitality, your belief and support, all the money you've—"

"Aw, now, you know how I feel about that. I knew I was s'posed to help you. Minute I saw you, I knew. I can read faces and eyes. It's my pleasure, it's an honor. You kiddin' me?"

"But we're running into the thousands," Mendle began, concerned.

"Hey," A.J. interrupted him. "I trust you more than some people I got signed paper with. Besides, in all my years on Earth I never seen an armored car following a hearse. Eh? Know what I mean?" The man grinned widely at Mendle, his eyes twinkling with a blend of compassion and defiance for anything that might get in their way.

Mendle's gaze returned the camaraderie. *Country is cosmic. Wisdom and truth live as common sense.*

A.J. laughed his gruff laugh as he walked to the sink. "Boy, it's summer, ain't it?" He twisted the cold water handle, washed his hands well under the running water, then splashed some onto his face.

"Seen Aira?" Mendle asked.

"Not since early," A.J. told him, drying his face with a towel. "She's been in that barn day an' night, that girl." He chuckled, tossed the towel down by the sink and added, "If you can call her that." Thinking about it, he said, "She sure looks like one in those dresses I gave her. 'Bout the same size as Becky was, how 'bout that?"

As A.J. stared out the window, Mendle sensed the man was remembering his wife. She had been gone twenty-six years, yet the years did not seem to distance her presence. He'd talk about her departure as though it were in the past. "Twenty-six years," he'd say, then reach for her in his mind as though she were right there. "It feels like yesterday. And forever."

On the afternoon the farmer had pulled some of his wife's dresses out of the attic for Aira to wear, he was quiet; he was whenever he mentioned Becky, in a conflict of resignation versus protest. He had lifted the cotton frocks out of the trunk so tenderly, his touch lingering on them as he handed them to Aira, telling her Becky would have been thrilled. Then, as he stared off, the same way he was doing now, he had softly murmured, "You know, when I'm like this, I really think I'm with her somehow."

"Maybe you are." Mendle said it before really thinking about it. He knew the feeling. He likened it to times he had felt Aira's presence, before he met her, when he had longed for her even though she appeared to exist only as an idea.

A.J. straightened up suddenly, as if just realizing there was someone else in the room, and turned to Mendle, looking as though he meant to apologize for his lapse of attention. "It isn't fair," Mendle readily commiserated. "But there's more to this picture than meets the eye, there's got to be." He was thinking about the nonsense of death, of Time, how time wasn't linear. Offering hope, he told the farmer, "Aira says we never permanently lose the people we love."

A.J. smiled a wily smile. "Well, come on. I'm goin' into town. I'll ride you to the barn."

"Thanks."

"Still can't get over you all walkin' around like human people," A.J. said, grabbing his hat.

"But A.J.," Mendle protested, never knowing how serious the man was because of the merriment in his tone. They were out the back, letting the screen door slam behind them. "I've tried to tell you."

"Yeah, yeah," A.J. chided. "I know what I know. And somethin' tells me…"

"Tells you what?" Mendle was grinning despite himself as he climbed up into the red pickup.

A.J. shrugged and started up the ignition. "Just a feelin'," he muttered. "But ye ever think of this? You ever wonder why we're always looking up to the stars for answers?"

chapter 46

The sun spiked into the barn through cracks in the wood slats, its rays slashing through the shade creating chiaroscuro. At the far end, Aira was sitting on a wooden crate, illuminated in a shaft of diffused light streaming in from the chute overhead. She was barefoot, wearing a lavender gingham dress limp from the summer heat.

"Hi," she greeted Mendle.

"Hi."

He was smiling at the sight of her as he crossed the distance to her. Taking a seat on a bale of hay near her, Mendle looked around the barn. "I didn't see Sadie," he said, noting that the red Irish setter hadn't met him with her usual custodial barking.

"She was here all morning. I didn't notice she was gone."

Mendle didn't like the idea of Aira being there alone. "Bearwolf's not here, either," he said, looking at the place the red chow usually parked himself as sentinel.

Aira offered Mendle her thermos cup. "How's A.J.?"

"Fine," Mendle said, taking the cup she was holding out to him. He smiled to himself and shook his head. "He still swears I'm an alien."

"Well you say you feel like one," Aira challenged. A sadness shadowed her as she watched Mendle drink from the beige plastic cup.

"Mmmm," he pronounced his verdict of the lemonade.

"I made it myself," Aira told him, pleased. She watched him as he continued to speak, thinking about his mind and how it affected him. It was just energy. It wasn't him, and she saw how an attention flow, when directed to portions of his mind, activated those data banks.

Her data banks functioned the same way; she had initially, upon materializing, drawn functioning information about the environment from them. Now, it was possible for her to know many things without them.

In fact, she found herself needing to think less and less, and capable to know directly, with an instantaneous, fluid ability. Without reference to anything, she could pervade totally an object or area and 'know.'

Mendle was looking at facsimiles of his earlier conversation with A.J. he had stored in his memory. "He still worries about Becky," he was saying. "Said he remembers how she was, then he looks at himself in the mirror, sees how he's changed, and wonders what she would think of him now that he's old."

Aira nodded, thinking that A.J., the person she had seen years ago, though lines altered his face and the hair on his body was turning white, hadn't changed; he was still there. "There's someone at the store he's been talking to," Aira said. "He told me, she's very understanding."

"But he'll always love Becky," Mendle said, almost too defensively.

"Of course," Aira said, comprehending his touchiness. She looked at him. "Do you find all this very strange?" she wanted to know, noticing the way he was looking at the craft.

"Stranger things have happened," Mendle said.

Aira pushed back the wisps of curls that clung to her forehead from sweat. She told Mendle, "I was thinking about what we talked about, that concept 'Too good to be true.'" Mendle nodded, and she went on, "Good is natural, how things should be. The saying should be 'Too bad to be true'!"

Reaching into a brown paper sack, she pulled out a cellophane bag of oatmeal cookies. Mendle watched her undoing the plastic wrap. In the middle of doing so, she threw out another idea. "Affinity doesn't tolerate distance. Do you realize someone wouldn't be your enemy if there wasn't some affinity present?"

"Why would someone who liked me want to be my enemy?" Mendle asked, finding the idea contradictory.

"Maybe because they couldn't be your friend, so they settled for enemy."

Mendle shook his head.

"See, if they didn't care, they wouldn't even be upset. They wouldn't want to play with you in the first place," Aira explained.

As Mendle thought about opponents he'd had, he remembered how, as a child, he had played games of opposing sides with friends. That was the overall condition: there was a game; it was friends, even on the opposing side.

Holding up the bag of cookies and waving them in front of Mendle as she bit one, Aira said, "Feeding and housing bodies can be fun!"

"I guess we're just a couple of happy mammals," Mendle played along, a streak of cynicism souring his tone. An apprehension twinged in him that she was becoming distant.

"Yes," Aira said. "What if we really are a couple of pieces of meat, walking around with all these delusions that we're more?"

"Two Bodies Escape, Say They Are More Than Meat," Mendle did his headline impersonation. His nervousness acted like carbonation, making his laughter a little more effervescent.

"Hey, meat," Aira jested as he took a cookie.

"Okay, cyberpunk."

A couple of bites into a cookie, Mendle remembered, "Hey, I read in the paper that Mastoso has been organizing concerts. Aside from bringing people to their feet, he's being vociferous about building a true civilization."

"That's great." Aira reveled in the thought of the composer's ideas and music reaching others.

"There was some critic who was apparently trying to belittle him, to parallel his work to 'mere theatrics,' and Roberto, in public, told him he was either scum or completely ignorant."

"Then what?"

"The critic lost his composure and snapped, 'How dare you?' and Mastoso replied, 'Truth gives me my courage. And you? How dare you?'"

Aira laughed for joy then voiced something she had noticed. "It's true, celebrities and artists are attacked around here; heroes are not heralded. It's as if the game is to knock down anyone who tries to shine as a beacon."

"He said graffiti gangs should be captured with nets and given mandatory, even if abbreviated, courses on the Renaissance to teach them how to really leave a mark on the world." Mendle laughed. "And he said any woman who inspired his daughter to wear her underwear on the outside of her clothing should be made to wear tampons on her ears and look at herself in the mirror until she realized something." Mendle was laughing hard again.

When Aira finished drinking some lemonade, she said, "It was so sad, earlier I was watching a movie on the television about the man who created a cure for syphilis." Mendle fell silent, wondering what that had to do with anything.

"I cried, actually," Aira said, coming to the point. "Why is it that every great man in the history of this planet has been fought and slandered? Voltaire, Galileo, Dante..."

"Gutenberg, Mozart," Mendle continued, seeing her point and listing others who were persecuted during their lives, only to be later heralded for the genius of their contributions to civilization. " 'Great spirits have always encountered violent opposition from mediocre minds,' " he spoke Einstein's quote as he thought of it. "He must've gotten it, too. The list goes on."

"It's horrible, think of what they suffered. Trying to serve humanity. The world maligns them, then feeds off their work for centuries. Why?"

"Makes you wonder what people see when they look," Mendle said in wonderment. "Some even worship the image of a god who spoke of love and immortal life nailed to a cross. Figure that one."

"Why not worship the image of him rising from the dead?" Aira asked.

"You'd think it'd be a reminder to the human race not to make a similar mistake. I mean, can't they tell when the person is alive? Crucify first. Venerate later." A thought loomed. "What's chilling, actually, is that maybe they *can* tell when the person is alive. Maybe it's only safe to venerate true genius and artists when they're dead. But while they're alive, they're thought to be dangerous. Because they're awake. Thinking, and communicating, disturbing the comfort zone of oblivion." Mendle was on the brink of knowing something.

Aira nodded. She sighed and said, sadly, "And maybe it's partly that they're just…invisible…to most. When their bodies are gone, then people truly see them by the work they leave behind." She took these things to heart. It was comforting to both her and Mendle that they each cared. Dropping her head, Aira said, "I can't accept it or become immune. It's not normal. I can't rest, Mendle."

"It isn't the whole world," Mendle consoled. It pleased her to hear him saying it.

"It isn't even 'people,' not as a whole," he said. "It's only a few who make it look like it's everywhere and everyone. And the 'masses' get lulled into false comfort, or think they can't do anything, or doze in their servitudes. The War on Drugs? It's being waged on us. It's really the War of Drugs, to keep people controlled and ignorant."

"I guess the greatest philosopher would be the one who teaches people to observe. That's the technology that's needed, one of the soul, of life itself."

Mendle thought about it and agreed.

"Mozart's music feeds souls," Aira said, thinking about it. "To think he ever suffered hunger is an outrage."

Mendle agreed, "There's already enough suffering for artists in retaining the courage to remain sensitive, to feel in the most tender manner and depths, to interpret life. Being sensitive in this society is a sensory overload." After a pause, he continued, "Why not market art and quality with the same vigor with which gossip is pandered?"

Aira brightened, "Maybe partly because things truly great and beautiful are a little ahead of current reality. Seeing what others don't yet."

"And partly because the no-talents don't want the comparison, so they market the garbage. It's a monopoly. Editors seeking sensationalistic slime-gossip. Television producers seeking the same. Music executives fixated with genitalia. These people are impostors, not 'gate-keepers'!"

"And people don't demand quality."

"Or else mediocrity feels safe…"

"But it's actually dangerous. It robs people of their own individuality and opinions. They just blend in."

"The good guys need to get organized," Mendle said decidedly, "even though they're the very ones who don't particularly aspire to conquest. It's a matter of duty now."

Yes, Aira cheered him silently. Their thoughts and the rapidity with which they exchanged them was increasing velocity.

"And the degraded!" Mendle said. "Like these films that promote continual killing and maiming of human bodies. They address subjects pertinent to social ills, but never, never solve them."

Mendle was on his feet now. "That's the work of frauds, lepers using art to contaminate others," he decried. "Art uplifts, offers solutions, understanding, axiomatic arrival. Art and genius is work of the soul. It doesn't just regurgitate random social disease and enforce it on people as reality."

When Mendle fell silent, it felt as if the ideas he had just expressed blossomed and continued outward, moving and affecting atmosphere. With the fervor of a vow, he spoke out of the quiet, "Something can be done about it all."

"Great souls don't *agree* with degradation and limits," Aira insisted. "Their visions are more real."

"The majority of people don't want trash," Mendle defended the human race, "even if they feel impulses or fascinations or sensations and think it's their true feelings. They watch in fear, thinking they had better watch so they'll be up-to-date and know how to handle it. But it's all a created reality that's being foisted on them! The rot they've been fed doesn't give them a handle, just smears mess around."

"I won't agree people are bad," Aira chimed her support.

"Ah, but people aren't supposed to be gods. They're fallen and must continue to punish themselves," Mendle pronounced sardonically.

Aira slapped her palm against the hay emphatically. "When that's believed, people become enemies to themselves."

"But there are criminals around," Mendle conceded the fact.

"The problem with criminals is maybe they're punished into oblivion, into not caring or feeling their worth anymore. They should be penalized and educated, not punished. Penalties and education give a way to regain honor." She stopped, then whispered, "We are *life*-beings."

Perturbed, Aira fell quiet and thought a moment, then asked Mendle, "You know what you said about it being just a few people creating havoc?" He nodded and she went on, "It's true. The fact that others follow and compromise themselves is the resulting sickness. Look at the news— a race driven mad and howling, while the ones busy making it so remain hidden."

"It's true with wars. Covert tactics, slander and the perpetuation of erosive ideas are part of the means used," Mendle said. He declared a line from a poem, " 'The news is disease in disguise, pretending to be information!' "

"It's so incomprehensible, maybe that's why it's difficult to see. 'Political correctness' is just cowardice," Aira said.

"Religious teachings paint the picture that man is evil and an animal," Mendle said, thinking, *This is one of the best damn conversations I've ever had.*

"Religious teachings do that?" Aira asked, appalled.

"Political powers took over religion. What we see is other factions taking advantage of that corruption. Rather than correcting it, they use the failings toward their own end, to incite people to revolt against what's called religion; they promote perversion and lack of spiritual value and ethics under the guise of freedom for people's 'rights' to do what they please."

"Someone must have altered an interpretation. I don't think a religion would have started out claiming a human being is evil."

Mendle beamed a little. "I could never understand why any God would want people to remain in ignorance."

"Right," Aira said. "Someone has given God a bad reputation."

The thought amused Mendle. "Yeah. God is Life. God has been slandered, too! Insidiously."

"That's why Gutenberg was attacked for inventing the printing press, which facilitated making knowledge available to all people. Political interests used their concoction of 'God' as a pretense, to crush everyone,"

Aira realized, "claiming that the Deity said knowledge was evil."

The way Aira was looking at him, fervor burning in her eyes, comforted Mendle. He told her, "I'm glad I'm not the only one who doesn't think the current condition of life on the planet is normal. I mean, this is not 'The Way It Is'…as some would like to have us think."

"It's important to know who your friends are," Aira said with determination, "so we don't get sabotaged trying to help the rest."

"True," Mendle said, remembering when he had first tried to tell her that.

"I'm sure there are others who have seen this."

"Truth makes sense," Mendle said. "You're right, religion has been altered and poisoned to the point of getting people to reject spiritual pursuit. The political maneuvers to discredit religion manipulate people into thinking it's fraud. But the corruption and short-comings they hold up as evidence, isn't religion. All religion means is 'a binding of beliefs.' It should be the recognition and practice of divinity in life. It's been around since the ages. The pursuit of survival of the spirit, Thought, Life…and Beauty, Truth. *That* is the soul. Religion has been around since forever. And now it's not cool to think of divinity."

"Yes," Aira said, "I am a soul. And you. And each being…"

Mendle was looking at her strangely, wondering what she was saying. Again, she had likened herself to him, and to other human beings.

"Are you wearing your microcassette?" she asked him suddenly.

"Yes. Why?"

"Is it on voice-activated?"

Mendle checked his pocket. "Oh, yeah. Thanks." He clicked it off.

That wasn't why Aira asked, she had hoped it was on, but when Mendle started to talk to her, she didn't interrupt. "When I left Sandra," he started to say, "I was broke. Had no money at all. There were all sorts of reasons why I should stay with her. It made survival sense according to my physical needs."

"Why did you leave her? If it was survival to stay?"

Mendle pushed a small, silent laugh through his nose. "Because I was dying. Shutting off myself. At first it didn't seem so bad. Food on the table. Roof over my head. I wrote. But what she wanted from me, well, I didn't love her. Not the way she wanted me to, anyway."

He stopped talking and Aira sensed he wasn't telling her something he was thinking. "What?" she nudged kindly.

"At the risk of not sounding very macho-stud according to the news, I'll say it," Mendle prefaced. "I didn't want to marry her, so I couldn't stay with her."

"I understand," Aira said. He was looking at her expectantly. She smiled, excited by his integrity, and interjected playfully, "You're much more exciting than beef."

Mendle smiled. "After a while, when that feeling of what was right for me wouldn't be quiet, I couldn't do it anymore. Even though I had nothing to go to, even though part of me told me I was a fool, I left."

"Did you pretend to her?"

"No, she knew," Mendle was quick to say. "Hey, she knew, but she didn't care. Said it's how the world went round. Come to think of it, I think what gave her some sort of twisted pleasure was to know I was compromising." He thought about it, not very proud of it, but he'd never seen that part of the twist before, and it put everything in fuller perspective. "I *was* giving her what she wanted!" he realized. "I did fall into a warped interchange. I was trading myself off…and I knew if I continued there'd be nothing left. Nothing left of *me*. Even though my stomach was sated."

Mendle aligned the experience to a new point. It was a revelation into just how great his victory had been. Even though the reasons for his decision had not been supportable by tangible, solid evidence, he had not let go of his sense of right. *The threat that I would **not** survive if I acted per my sense of right was the illusion. There **is** always a **why** that supports being true, even if I don't know what it is at the time, even if solid things roar I had better give in.* He saw the gain; it was the very stuff of *him*, immeasurable by pounds or inches—his essential fabric.

"So the moment I befriended myself again, the *moment* I did that, it was like Life Force itself came to my rescue. Things started happening that defied odds and physical reality, in my favor. It seemed miraculous, but I understand the mechanics now. I was liberating me, what I really am—soul, kin to Life Force. Thought. It's a very tangible thing. Then my book was published." *It's as if I, as soul, have biceps, muscles, triceps, and the right decisions pump them.*

Mendle turned and looked at Aira. "And then I met you," he said, and he still hadn't figured that one out completely.

As he looked at her, Mendle realized his feelings about Aira were different now than when they first met. When with her, he felt much as he had in childhood—possessed with quietude, unhampered by others' translations of the world. Even the desire to have her physically did not encumber him anymore.

And why should it, he thought, *when sex is not a measure of love, nor just a triggered response.* He couldn't understand the right to abortion being called 'Pro-choice.' In most cases women *did* have a choice; it wasn't as if they were usually forced to become pregnant.

As the periphery to his view of life widened, Mendle realized that sex had a purpose, and was something done with decision. *You find someone you love. First. Some 'one' is not just some 'body.' Then you express creation and admiration through sex. It has a purpose. The passing on of legacies, through children or other ways, in this dimension.* The idea of family filled him, and felt sacred.

More and more, sheer life blossomed, became a tangible for Mendle to touch. He could put his finger on it. What was invisible to many became more real to him every day. It was as beautiful as magnolias blooming out of thin air—the candescence of animating spirit outshining all that appeared solid.

Aira's thoughts had wandered, and she asked Mendle, "What do you hear from Los Angeles?" Fondness from their previous topics brimmed over in her voice.

"Nothing concrete. They still think we're vacationing. We were wanted for questioning, but for some reason things have totally died down. The case was closed as a random accident. I don't understand it. I guess we just keep taking one step at a time."

Mendle looked over at the Lauryad, the sleek front end resembling an Aerostar van. *Pretty soon none of it might make any difference to Aira at all anyway,* he told himself, trying to prepare himself and not dwell on his own personal interests only. He reproached himself for the hopes he could ever start a family with her.

"How's it going?" he asked.

"I still haven't cracked the full debrief code on transport operation. Actually, I like your idea of turning the front end into a car."

Mendle laughed. "I was kidding."

"No, we can always keep working on the operations chamber. If I get it to fly, then it can easily reinstate."

"So, no progress on getting it spaceborne?"

Aira shook her head in the negative. "But I did get it to give me some information. I calculated how long ago it was when I first was ensnared and lost control of the ship. I was in limbo-suspension forty years before materializing."

"Forty years before materializing?"

Aira nodded. "Earth-time. But to me, in my dimension, it was only minutes."

"So you materialized…"

"In the field here," Aira confirmed.

"That was thirty-three years ago," Mendle recalled A.J. having said it. "Then you disappeared?"

"Dematerialized. To the other dimension," Aira nodded.

"And… "

She just smiled and looked at him, then explained, "Actually, after that, I didn't permanently solidify in this plane until about a year ago." She smiled, making light of it.

"You're one year old?" Mendle smiled.

"*I'm* eternal," Aira said, and returned his smile. They held one another's gaze for some moments. Then Aira told him what happened. "During the struggle, I was in the limbo phase, I managed to reconnect with the Lauryad briefly. That was about thirty-three years ago. The craft remained molecularly condensed in this space-time, on A.J.'s field that day. When A.J. saw me, I dematerialized, becoming reabsorbed in the adjacent dimension. The ship stayed here in the field, I went back into my own space-time. In the conflict, it seemed like moments to me, but I was suspended interdimensionally for thirty-two years. I finally condensed permanently that day in Anaheim last year."

So, Time is happening somewhere else very, very fast, Mendle thought.

"And other places very, very slow, much slower than here," she answered his thought, and, from his surprised expression, decided not to do that anymore.

The talk was shaking Mendle a little. She was growing more distant by the day, talking about her time, her plane, her dimension. It was fascinating that, during what to her had seemed like minutes in her dimension, decades had occurred on Earth. Her body, even though it had only become moleculary stable the night in Anaheim, first materialized thirty-three years ago. Full grown. He wondered if she aged.

Yes, she was about to answer, but didn't; she had told him, many times, she was human, just like he.

"Did you hit a storm?" Mendle asked, remembering the thunder and lightning the day he met her.

Aira hesitated. "I guess you could call Z Zone that," she said. "But, more importantly, I made some decisions that enpowered resulting events in my materialization," she said. *Like wanting to be with you, wherever you were.*

Z Zone. A figment of my novel. And here she is talking about it. How can this be? Mendle grappled to know.

"Anyway," Aira resumed, "part of the control panel is missing. There's been major damage."

Mendle felt relief and guilt at the same time, for wishing she would not leave.

She was thinking the problem through aloud. "I'm wondering if the craft's operating basis is dependent on some other atmospheric condition that doesn't exist here."

"Why me?" Mendle decided to ask. "Why the bathroom in Anaheim?"

Aira looked at him. She let out her breath with a puff of air. "Maybe …by the sheer physics of affinity. It decreases distances."

"You mean…you *liked* me? That's the reason?" Mendle gawked incredulously. It seemed a little too simple.

"Decisions dictate mechanics—sooner or later." She could feel the questions swirl and burn in him. The answers were what he had to know himself.

She turned her attention to the Lauryad, still thinking aloud. "It seems to me I remember the craft was not propelled as a mass through space and time. That's why it didn't burn. Rather than moving as a whole, it traveled through a process of disassemblage and reassemblage of structure, possibly moving space to *it*, aligning vectors with nuclei."

Aira took the lemonade from Mendle.

"About how far are you, from, uh, leaving?" Mendle asked. He suddenly felt as though he were in some self-scribed ludicrous scenario, and began to laugh, high and hard.

Aira looked up from pouring lemonade, straightening the thermos and propping it on her thigh.

Despite his glee, he quieted down to look at her. Aira's momentary silence, coupled with the sadness he interpreted on her face, sent panic through him. "Would I be able to go?" he asked, trying to contain himself.

"I don't want to leave you behind," Aira told him gently, then cast her eyes downward, hesitating for lack of words. She finally looked back over at him. "But the journey, the main one isn't going to be in that," she said, shooting a look at the Lauryad. "It's going to be on the inside." She fervently hoped Mendle would understand.

Aira welcomed him as he searched her. She felt that he knew something, and he felt it, too.

"Kind of like 'place' is…largely…a state of mind?" Mendle tried to describe what had been at ineffable depths. "Is that what you mean when you said there was more than one way to fly?"

Aira nodded. "Something like that." She decided to show him. "Would you really like to see me?" she asked.

Mendle regarded her with a look blending quizzicalness, hesitancy, and interest. She hadn't returned his merriment, and it oriented him to a focused concentration.

Aira was looking down, picking at a straw of hay. "Will you love me if you see me as I really am?"

Mendle stuttered silently over words he could say, then blurted, "Of course." All manner of possibilities rostered through his imagination—bodies from creature-movies to his wildest dreams. "Except if you're green," he forewarned jocosely, offsetting apprehension.

"You know when we said most of the plot in a person's life happens on the inside?" Aira asked him.

"Yeah. That's why I see so many old people staring at that little invisible box in front of them at the end I guess." He looked worried. "That little box contains the plot of their life, their development."

Aira smiled at him reassuringly.

"But I do see you? Don't I?" he asked.

"More than most," she said. "But I've just recently seen myself."

"I know you're light, you glow..."

Aira shook her head.

Over by the Lauryad, a dish towel by the step ladder rose into the air, as if picked up by invisible hands. "That's me," the blonde, blue-eyed body told him, nodding over in that direction.

Next, a bucket across the barn lifted about three feet from the ground and smoothly traveled several yards. "That was me, too," the blonde, blue-eyed body he had known as Aira said.

"What?" Mendle gasped.

"That's right." She let that settle. "I'm invisible," she told him. "Invisible," she repeated. "The closest thing to me is light. But I'm not even light." With that, her body illuminated with an aureate glow. The glow, then, retaining the resemblance to her physical image, separated from the body, disappeared and reappeared on the far side of the barn.

Mendle's glance ping-ponged between the light body and the meat body sitting on the bale of hay beside him. "But...but..."

"I'm not here and there. I am simultaneously where I extend a viewpoint," she told him, using the body to speak.

Mendle grasped it. "So astral projection isn't going somewhere else, in space and time, but *encompassing* something else...right from where you are. And you can be in more than one place at once...?"

He looked over at the shimmering image across the barn then at the body next to him. It smiled at him. He looked back across the barn. The light faded. But a voice issued from over there. "I'm still here, Mendle. You can't see me with physical eyes, though. And I'm right next to you, too."

It's not that she glows, Mendle thought, remembering the night he saw her body become incandescent when they rescued Onx in the woods. *She isn't the light, she is…no thing,* Mendle gasped inwardly.

Yes, yes. It's me, remember?

I do see you. I feel you. I know you.

Yes, yes.

The body next to him reached out an arm and touched his leg. Mendle jumped a little.

"This is amazing," he uttered.

His heart was racing. *She loves me. I can feel her. It's you.* He negated his senses. *What am I thinking? No.*

"Try it," she said.

"Huh?"

"Look at the roof, outside the barn."

Whoa. I did it. Mendle was agog, having sworn he saw the top of the roof. *That's what you mean by viewpoint. Like a damn periscope. I can put it anywhere…?*

Aira nodded. She described her arrival to him, "I was running in the street during the thunderstorm…"

Mendle recalled the unusual, raging storm that day. He also remembered the chapter from his book.

"I was repeating to myself, over and over, that I wasn't what I felt, and I wasn't what I saw. I was just about to remember what I had just forgotten. I was trying hard to hold on to what I knew, but it all slipped away." *But I cried for you, I cried out for help, for someone who loved me.*

"Okay."

"I'm not what I see, I'm not what I feel," Aira relayed to him what she had kept repeating. "I am who sees, I am who feels. I am who decides and wills." She looked at him expectantly when she finished. "There's a difference," she said. "Do you understand?"

Mendle thought about it. "Seeing is receiving the effect of outer stimuli," he said. "On the other hand, being 'the one who sees' is being the creator, projecting, influencing. The first is only receipt point. The latter is generative, causation point."

"Right."

Yes! Aira silently cheered him again.

Mendle focused on a bale of hay, let it fill his senses, conscious his eyes were registering the image with photons. Next, he looked around and let the objects he saw—the walls, the ceiling rafters, floor—dictate his location. He could see how he might feel he was all these things, interconnected with everything he saw around him. The illusion was that they assigned him a location.

Then he took another point of view. *He* was looking and perceiving —distinct from anything around him. "Whoa," he mumbled, liking the difference. *I am the source point.*

I am! "Could it be I'm invisible, too?" Mendle gasped.

Aira was ecstatic to hear him say that. *I see you.*

"Oh my God," Mendle said, his voice pushing a lot of air through the words.

chapter 47

Aira rubbed her hands together and brushed some crumbs off her dress. "Well, I have some good news for you," she beamed.

Washed in the cool spray of her smile, Mendle guessed, just by the expression on her face. "You cracked the communication code?"

The look on Aira's face was his answer, and Mendle jumped to his feet. "You cracked it?" he exclaimed. "Come on! Show me!" He literally jumped for joy. "You cracked it!"

Aira hopped off the crate she'd been sitting on. "Yes," she cooed in baby talk. "I'm an intelligent mammal."

Heading for the larger communications control chamber of the Lauryad, Mendle climbed the ladder and Aira followed. "Oh, I'm proud to be a mammal," Mendle sang on the way, "a mammal, yes, I am!" Aira joined in.

Inside the chamber, "You compare yourself to me, to other humans," Mendle pointed out, curious. "We're different, and yet…" His words fell silent, and he felt drawn into the expanse of Aira's soul as he sought her eyes.

She said, "We're basically the same." Then, in the manner he had adapted tracking with, she threw out another idea, "The dolphin is the only natural enemy of the shark."

Yes, one needs to know what to look for, he thought, *to recognize signals. Childlike joy does not equal weakness, and is often a sign of power and genius —more so than assertive, grounded, pontificating seriousness. Is this, my own human form, deceptive?*

Aira directed their attention to the notes. "We have a field, right?"

"Right." Mendle defined the term, "The region of space in which specified physical effects exist."

"Okay. Now, fields can be created and set up. As is the case with current broadcast techniques being used by the media."

Mendle acknowledged with a bob of the head.

"Well, what you told me about 'action at a distance' started me thinking. Usually, fields are defined as such because they can be detected. But, in the case of isolated bodies, such as the Earth and its sun, there is no detectable means of contact. Not detectable, but each has its own field, which in turn affects the other."

"Right," Mendle said. "We know that a magnetic field always surrounds a current-carrying conductor."

Aira nodded. "Right."

"So, how do you tap into the network frequencies to consistently broadcast what you want to broadcast over them?" Mendle asked.

"The problem was not so much what frequencies as much as power. How to generate enough power. Next, how do we keep the power source anonymous? So we can't be traced."

"How?"

"Quasars." Aira said it as an unveiling. "If electric charges can be made to vibrate back and forth, there are varying magnetic and electric fields about the conductor. The variations of these electric and magnetic field intensities are propagated through space as waves. The vibration is not mechanical, since it travels through a vacuum."

"Quasars emit radio waves," Mendle said.

"Right. Now radio waves here are created with electronic and electrical equipment. But, let's back up a minute. Black holes absorb. Quasars emit."

Mendle nodded, following so far.

"Okay. The way I can take an object out of its space and time is by seeing it as it is. Exactly. Part of that entails seeing its radiation, and the radiation of all objects interacting with it."

"Like even a piece of holographic film contains the image of the whole thing?"

"Yes," Aira clipped the end of his last word, not wanting to go into that aspect of it.

"But those aren't black holes?"

"No. They were...spirit holes. *Nothing* holes. Another universe, another dimension. It's beyond location. Back to back with the air all around us, so to speak. It's beyond location...because *location* is defined by relative position of objects."

"Go on," Mendle said. It was difficult to conceive of nothing, but he saw the glimpse of Life, as potential, without location, outside of time, outside of space, outside of mass. *The nothing which made something.* He felt parts of his own self stir; the ideas were water to dormant seed.

"All right," Aira murmured. "So. Quasars emit. Black holes absorb. They are the basic activators of this universe, current-carrying conductors. This universe is 'kept active' by them. A magnet is a smaller manifestation of the principle. Positive. Negative. Currents. Energy flows.

"Okay. So, there are givens. Rules of the field. To win the game, you have to play it, and to play it, one knows the rules. Otherwise, one isn't a player but gets stuck and crushed. Let's get back to the larger electromagnetic fields." Aira stepped down to the control board.

"We have all this based on particles. Positive-Negative. Matter is neutral, but everything is potential. Viscosity is an electrical flow. The more viscous..."

"Wait. I forgot what that word..."

"Viscous? Sticky. The more viscous a thing is, is a result of its electrical charge. More charge, more sticky. Making for different densities. Some aggregates form dense solids. Other aggregates form gases. Others energy, or currents."

There was something bizarre about everything. He had written about the very control room they were standing in.

She looked like a barefoot country girl in her checked gingham dress, the summer humidity clinging languidly to her curls. He watched her beckoning him to the control board with the wondrous excitement of a child.

"Flows between terminals," she recapitulated, holding one fist out, then the other, "positive-negative." She pointed to something on the control board, "This is a Circumference Scanner. It plots points in space."

I know, I wrote about it, I described it.

"…It sends out sensors in every conceivable degree and direction. By the use of vectors."

Mendle nodded.

"You know how on a sphere, if you pick a point on it, there's the exact opposite point on the other side?"

"Yeah." He concentrated to keep track with her.

"Okay." Aira held up a piece of paper. "Let's say this is a television screen. One side emits. That's what we see, the emission of an image. On the other side of that, directly on the other side, is its opposite. Absorption. One side inflows. The other, outflows."

"Are you saying that for every quasar there's a black hole?"

Aira nodded.

"Directly on the other side?"

"In this case, yes. I've locked into a power quasar. On the Scanner I've plotted the exact location of its black hole, in the interface dimension. By vectors. Now, with this black hole…anything I teleport to its radius is instantly absorbed. It absorbs all energy incident on it, with no reflection at all. Instantaneously, it is spewed out, through the other side. And our quasar is our broadcast station." Aira finished and sat back expectantly to see if she had been clear. "Another incidental detail, by the way," she threw out, "is that one is cold, the other hot. To emit, the temperature is hotter than the surroundings."

"How do you get an image or sound up there to be broadcast on the radio waves of the quasar?"

"This," Aira said, indicating another instrument on the panel. "A Particlization Device. It construes the negative atomic image of an object, or designated space and all masses contained within, wavelengths, whatever. The negative design is called Blueprint Concept. Everything we see, with our eyes is the positive. And it has a negative. This calculates the speed of bombardment, arrival, the projection necessary for an image to resemble a positive. Something like a photograph. If you look at a picture of a woman, let's say, you see the positive, and the negative also exists. Well, on this, you can even *design* the negative. Or reproduce negatives.

When activated, particles attach to the blueprint concept and make a positive."

"As you were describing everything, this world suddenly didn't seem so solid at all," Mendle marveled, awed.

"It's not," Aira stated matter-of-factly.

"So we won't even need the video camera," Mendle said.

"No." Aira replied, "That's why I was asking about your microcassette earlier. Our conversation is taped. Maybe we can test that on the air?"

Mendle nodded. He loved the mischievous smile that beamed from her like sunlight thrown off water. She was like diamonds, he was thinking. "The first cosmic talk-show," he said.

Mendle looked down at his hand. He was seeing it in positive. As he contemplated that, he saw the negative, saw the electrical blueprint to which particles and sub-particles adhered. Particles accumulated, like ridges on a holographic grid.

That's how I materialized, Aira wanted to tell him, but decided to hold off. "The process also bypasses the atmospheric mechanics of a wave. The entire process is instantaneous, bypassing distance," Aira said.

"The way light can travel through a vacuum," Mendle ruminated.

With finality, Aira said, "It's operational. Ready to go."

"You're brilliant," Mendle said. *And most would not know it, looking at her,* he thought. "We can transmit on any TV and radio station?" he asked.

She nodded. "On *all....*"

From two souls in the barn, to the stars and back, it began:

Wake up. The Great Slumber has gone on too long. No matter what you've done or feel, believe in your dignity. We must begin to build a true civilization. Knock off the drugs. They keep you from seeing. They provide temporary illusions of relief, then encumber you by additions to the mental maze and trappings. They interfere with time-space perception. Your clarity of observation is vital if you want to be free. Seeing is your greatest gift, your greatest weapon.

I hereby declare war on the destruction of human dignity. War and crime should not be tolerated. Don't tolerate them. Take responsibility for your region and area. It begins with you, extend it to your family and those close to you. All of you. Each

and every single one of you. On April 3, in the year 2000, the world will sing.

See the garbage and bad news pumped at you for what it is. Insist the news broadcasts not be biased toward the minority of murders and vile occurrences. These should be quarantined. Insist on being provided with real news. Science. Education. Discovery. Art. The rest is in the minority.

The only way to freedom is through knowledge, not ignorance. You can do, you can be what you want. You are alive. You have yourselves. The only way you can be destroyed is by selling yourself, by agreeing to do so. And, if you've already done so, just look at it. You don't have to keep doing it to be right. So go out and feel good! There is nothing more brilliant than when the heart surges to overcome that moment of fear.

Aren't you tired of symbols and symbolism? I mean, what IS simply IS…a banana is nothing more…than a banana.

Hello. Embrace knowledge. Embrace colors. Embrace language, true music, art, poetry, elevated dance of the soul. If you love and know words, they will free you. To open a word and know its meaning is like opening a door. Words are the bridges we have to one another, to life.

How did that come across?"

"It transmitted perfectly. I flipped to 7, 5, and 2. It was on all of them!" Mendle laughed. "Better than *Romper Room, Mr. Rogers, Captain Kangaroo!*"

"Mendle…"

"I'm not teasing. I like it." Reading her thoughts, he emphatically told her, "No. It is not too simplistic. You yourself said the dolphin is the only natural enemy of the shark. Are you kidding? This is great. Compared to the rest of the rot that's on the air?" He was out of his body with exhilaration.

As Mendle scanned the Particlization settings, he informed Aira, "It's only negatizing the immediate proximity. There's no real image, just a ghost-like silhouette. Those stars behind you were sometimes there, sometimes not. There's some time-lapse delay, but the audio is right on."

"Okay. Do you like the stars?"

Mendle checked the cut-out sparkle set they had constructed.

"Yes." He smiled. "Another?"

Aira smiled back.

"Hey, this is like that movie *Babes on Broadway* you liked so much," Mendle told her. "Just like Mickey Rooney and Judy Garland. Hey! Let's put on a show!"

Aira picked up a newspaper from the floor of the cabin.

"Ready when you are."

"I'll just do a commentary…"

"Righto." Mendle made eye contact with her, "Knock 'em alive."

Hi. Sorry to interrupt your program but I have something more important to say to you. It's quite urgent. Let's take a look at today's newspaper. All right. Let's stop calling our bums 'The Homeless.' What they are is the apathetic. Their spirits are broken. I can't blame them. This is just one of our many social diseases and can be remedied. Same with crime.

Now, the current trend is that good people are the victims. Criminals don't care about the human heart. In fact, they prey on it. They count on you to care, while they have the supposed advantage of being numb. How did they get that way? By going against themselves. They were not always so. They did something harmful, couldn't tell anyone about it, ostracized themselves, shut down their hearts, and it went from there until they had to stop feeling.

Now, honest, productive people can get angry and start saying that if someone doesn't care about them, why should they care? This gives them a reason to commit acts they wouldn't ordinarily do. Then they feel bad about themselves, and so become ineffective. Don't take the bait. Many of the truly insane can pretend to start acting good. The good guys can start seeming wild and bad because they've been driven to do things they don't like. Be smart. Learn ethics. Get organized and intelligent! Support the family and family units. Loyalty, honesty, honor, love, help.

Don't you know you are gods? You ever wonder why parables here say the kingdom of heaven is within? That means you. On

April 3, sing, sing, sing! The words will be forthcoming. Write them down.

As for the political intrigue—all vested interests involved in the current skirmishes and wars will be exposed if they do not come clean and quit perpetrating the violent insanity. Reason can be applied on the majority. Force is needed for the few individuals who perpetrate random chaos for vested interests.

And, as a final note to this transmission, support and nourish the Arts. It is in your power to be creative. You don't need permission. It is your right to observe and create. Leonardo da Vinci did not have a Ph.D.

"Let's do one, really short."
"But we'll be interrupting soap operas…then the slime sensational show."

Hello. Most people say "Times are changing" or "That's the way it is," or "That's life," when the saying should go, "That's Death."

"Okay, ready. And…go…."

Hello. A beautiful woman or handsome man used to be the image of someone's face. More and more, the TV hurls images of headless, faceless torsos, butts and bulging biceps. It's drugs and looks, instead of character and personality. A big gun does not replace strength of character. When psychiatrists ask for gut feeling, they ask for genetic response. Well…good morning! You are not your bodies.

Hi. There are two ways you can live forever. Trapped as matter, thinking you are matter, or free to create. There is a parable here on Earth about selling your soul to the devil. The devil represents those things which drive you into disability as a spirit. Hell is misery. If you go against yourself, you die. You are souls. The spirit is not maudlin, passé, not an intangible. It is you. And you have the power to create. Align with Life. There is a hero inside each and every one of you. The hero is the real you. Just as a hero lives inside me. The hero is the one who takes the next step when the road seems too long.

Either way, you do live forever. Do you want Paradise or Inferno? You are not bodies. Thought does not come from the brain, but uses it.

"Could you get me a cup of water?"
"Sure."
"Do you think we should polish this up a little before broadcasting?" Aira asked.

"What?" Mendle exclaimed. "If we aired Chopsticks it would be better than most of what's airing out there!"

She flipped the control. "We're on the air."

Mendle, feeling gratitude for the reins of his power to serve, began to recite the poetry he felt was the cream of the Earth.

...Our birth is but a sleep and a forgetting,
The soul that rises with us, our life's star,
Hath had elsewhere its setting
and cometh from afar;
Not in entire forgetfulness,
and not in utter nakedness,
But trailing clouds of glory do we come
From God, who is our home.

William Wordsworth, "Ode to Immortality"

Hello. I declare war. I declare war on the destruction of human dignity and the spirit. I love this country. I love this planet. I love its people. People want to live. They want to love. Most of us, anyway. Please, Mr. President, lead us in the singing...all leaders! You know, it isn't "getting worse." Someone is making it that way. That's right. It's not "the government" or some group. Groups are made of individuals. Hold individuals responsible.

There is always a "who," a someone. Public officials can hide behind the group, especially since they can't be sued or held responsible as individuals. The few, hiding behind their chaos and generalities, make misery. But, if you see things getting worse, find the right who. And remember, things don't just get worse. Someone is making them that way.

Life, left to its own thrust, flourishes! And, as for the color of body skin—to say, "I did this even though I'm black, or pink, or yellow, or white" is conceding a self-assigned inferiority which doesn't even exist. Same with anything…women, men, children. There are no limits imposed by physical substance, be it gender, race, color. Limits stem first from decisions and ideas. Let's stand for Mankind…'Man' as in Human.

I will be transmitting words to our anthem, the words of our song, as humans. An anthem for gods, trapped, who can be free. Don't settle for anything less than your true power and nature. Befriend yourselves, no matter what. Let's begin The Age of Reason and Thought. Take the quantum leap to your true selves. Declare an Amnesty! A day in which we can tell one another our transgressions without fear of punishment. To understand is to forgive. Let's discipline ourselves to move onward. And…let's start having some fun around here.

You are as good and beautiful as you know your self to be.

To car radios and television stations…the thoughts went out. Some were culled from the purest and most elevated creators that had passed through the world, others, unpolished but sincere, were winged off the cuff—naive, uncensored, unglossed, unpoliticalized, uneconomized, falling upon the globe, permeating and stirring the hearts of Men.

Don't be de-spiritualized.
Don't be de-spiritualized.

And the broadcasts continued.

48
chapter

The late afternoon sky over the hills was suffused with rosiness, and golden light diffused the end of day. Inside the barn by the lone tree in the back fields, a different symphony was occurring. Up in the hayloft, Mendle and Aira were in each other's arms. They had been enraptured in a crescendo of kisses and caresses and now held one another, feeling their hearts beat through one another's bodies. The physical responses to the physical expression of their love escalated naturally, just as they had projected their bodies would respond. Before they were stuck to human bodies, the different ways they had loved were many, the potential was infinite. The rules were different now in this universe of quantities, limits, and givens.

"Remember when you told me your body works, but it was *me* you wanted?" Aira asked Mendle.

Mendle nodded and, though she couldn't see his face since his head was pressed against her shoulder, she could feel him smile.

It was love that made his touches sweet and powerful. Aira had always found sex curious; as an energy, it did seem to have a thrust of its own. "I understand why it's good to first determine the person and decide about sex, rather than let it decide you," she said.

"Powerful stuff, isn't it?" Mendle semi-joked as he held her.

She smiled. "It has a punch to it."

"I guess bodies are not just limiting traps," Mendle said.

"They don't backfire as long as the beings who possess them don't forget who they are."

"I know what you mean."

"Actually, this whole material universe is a good game," Aira said, "and would be, if not for the forces of evil that use it to entrap and enslave. Look at how much beauty there is when life is left to flourish."

Mendle felt the dampness under Aira's hair against her neck. The days were still hot, the heat lasting into evening. He brushed her ringlets up and blew on her neck. He pulled her closer to him and they embraced and nestled, pressing each body tightly against the other, feeling the pulsing sensations; they were enveloped by a totality of love.

She felt sweeter to him than any woman he had ever known. Not because she was "good," "hot," and "sexy," as the current magazines advertised desirable women. Just the opposite. She was unrehearsed. The intensity of pure, uncontrived expression coursed through her. Her touches tingled with a living care and desire that danced throughout and kindled all of him.

"This is the best sex I've ever had, and we're still wearing clothes," Mendle said, and they both collapsed into laughing.

Then they kissed more, and looked at each other, and kissed more, giving and receiving the sensations to brinks of height.

Mendle pulled away, and rolled over on his back, taking a deep breath and exhaling it hard.

"I guess the sensation of the body is rigged to ensure the procreative act will occur, love or no love, on a biological level," Aira said.

"Yeah." Mendle reached out and took her hand.

"And I guess between life-beings it's a language to express love, or so other bodies will be available for the future," she went on.

"Do you know anyone who needs one?" Mendle asked.

"Maybe someone who would like to come help us," Aira mused.

After some silence, Mendle said, "I'm not being hypothetical."

Aira didn't say anything. After about a minute, Mendle murmured, "Marriage is forming a team, to keep the life force inviolate and powerful." He rolled back over to her and, propped up on his elbow as he gazed at her, caressed Aira's hair. "It's called making love because life is born, life is given to a vessel." He paused, then, "It's a sacred, very holy thing."

Even though they had not consummated the sex act, she understood more fully why Mendle called it "making love."

"And souls are Love..." she finished for him, smiling.

Creation of forms, for life and mutual protection, is what childbearing was all about. Sex is holy. They both met in thought.

Will you marry me? "Will you marry me?"

When Mendle asked Aira the question, she did not have to consider it long. She already had.

She poured forth *yes* with every part of her being, and whispered, "Yes," with a whisper that filled his being like the glorious wind, a sail.

They embraced one another, both in the tides of joy that poured from them.

Suddenly, there was a loud snap. It jolted them and, alarmed, Mendle and Aira sat up in immediate attention. There, his head poking up through the trap door to the loft, was Paul Toor. He was trying to keep climbing and simultaneously regain his balance from the ladder rung that had snapped under his foot.

"Oh, it's you," Aira said.

Mendle was assimilating the situation. When Paul Toor leveled a .357 magnum automatic at them, the atmosphere could have imploded into the dead silence that followed.

Aira could feel Mendle's arm tense up at the sight of the gun, and she feared for his life, worried that he was going to do something that would trigger Toor.

"You," Aira uttered. "It was you who shot Sandra...and Onx, wasn't it?" She stared into him and what she saw was becoming ever clearer. She felt amazed she hadn't seen it when they had first met.

"Come on," Paul ordered, managing himself all the way into the loft and waving the gun for them to start down the ladder. "Slowly. Slowly."

Mendle's sizzling annoyance boiled over into raging fury just as he was rising to his knees. Suddenly he lunged and whirled, his arms extended like spokes, and bashed the gun out of Paul Toor's hand. Then, springing forward, he ploughed his head into Toor's stomach, pushing him over the edge of the loft. Still in perpetual motion, Mendle scrambled to his feet.

"Nerd!" Mendle complained. "Grab it, Aira," he told her, pointing, expecting her to levitate the gun off the barn floor from a distance, the way she had demonstrated with a bucket days earlier. He stood at the edge of the loft, staring disgustedly at Paul Toor recovering his glasses from his sprawl on the ground below.

Toor looked up. Their glances locked in stalemate. Mendle confident —Toor, unsure what was next, part of his attention on the gun about fifteen feet away.

He read the situation. Mendle glanced at Aira. Worry flickered on his face as he watched her intently staring at the gun. She was obviously failing to do something. Her face was totally legible. She was disappointed, worried.

When Mendle saw Paul scrabble on his knees toward the gun, he jumped off the loft, directly down toward it. He had the magnum in his hand within seconds of thumping to the ground. Toor now scuttled to his feet, turned and headed for the door.

Blam!

The blast and rattle of the bullet Mendle fired into a nearby bucket quickfroze his attempted exit. When the bucket stopped clattering, Toor held his hands out and slowly turned to face Mendle.

"Just hold it," Mendle warned. "I don't want to play shoot 'em up but I will if I have to," he promised, holding Toor in his sights.

Aira crouched at the edge of the loft.

As Mendle sauntered toward him, he spotted a nearby rope and started heading for it. Toor knew he'd have to act. He waited for Mendle to approach, then cried, "Aooww, my side." Feigning a pain from his memory, he dropped to his knees, clutching the ground in front of him.

When Mendle got within a couple of feet from him, Paul Toor hurled dirt and sand at his eyes and struck a blow to Mendle's gun hand, knocking the magnum into a pile of hay. Simultaneously, he went for the .380 Back Up II double action in his jacket, whipping it into aim. Just as he extended it into level aim…

Crack! Something stung Toor's pistol out of his grip, and he dropped to his knees, clasping the right hand with his left. Next, *Whack!* His eyeglasses were ripped off his face and dashed to the ground several feet way.

He looked up. A slightly out-of-focus image of Aira was above him. Nothing in her hands. Some kind of energy was fulminating from her fingertips.

"You know how much I hate to use force, Loptoor," Aira said, apology lacing the steely tone of her voice as she talked to him from overhead.

Toor lunged for his gun on the barn floor again, rolled a couple of sideways somersaults, then tumbled one backward. Just as Mendle had cleared his vision and located the magnum automatic on the hay, Toor was on his feet, grabbed him and held the Back Up double action to his head.

"You hurt me, I hurt him," Toor flatly told Aira.

Aira held her breath. He was nearly dead inside, if there even was any life-being there at all. *He feels nothing.* **Nothing.** *It's frightening, it's why he would do just about anything.* Then she located him, barely any thought there at all, mostly enmeshed in material, synthetic complexities.

She looked at Mendle. *Do something, do your stuff,* he seemed to be pleading her.

"Let him go, Loptoor."

"Loptoor?" Mendle asked.

"You're around forty-five years old. That's about right," Aira went on, braving her voice.

"Do it, Aira," Mendle said, guiding her with his eyes to what was just behind Toor.

There was a tire iron right there, begging to be leveled on Toor's head from behind to knock him out.

Aira tried to extend herself but couldn't. She was stuck to her body. She could not manage the interface and cursed the inconsistency of her ability.

Panic pulsed through her as she focused on the gun pointed at Mendle's head. Her heart was racing. She could not budge a vapor puff three inches away, let alone perform any feat from behind Paul Toor that would salvage Mendle.

Since Mendle shouted "Do it," Toor tried to anticipate the scope of possibilities that meant.

Aira kept talking. "Except you were *born*, Loptoor. You were a baby. It took me twelve years Earth-time to even first materialize thirty-three years ago. I went back and forth in my dimension, but you...you must have been offered 'the courtesy' right after me. You've had a few more years here than I have. Born directly. Remember *before*...?" Toor fought not to look at the things which started to clamor in his mind.

She had to do something. "Look!" she suddenly shouted, pointing when she yelled. Toor jerked his head over his shoulder to see what was there. Amazed it worked, Aira sprang from the hayloft.

Toor saw her leap in his peripheral vision. He turned back, lifted the gun from Mendle's head, and went to fire right up at her.

"No!" Mendle yelled, and bashed the man's wrist.

Blam!

The next second Aira landed on Toor. Mendle broke free and scrambled for the magnum, this time securing the cold metal in his hand. "Hold it, hold it, hold it, you stupid maggot," he screamed at Toor as Aira struggled with him. She was doubled over, gripping Toor's wrist with both hands, fighting to keep the Back Up in his hand pointed away from her.

Blam! Toor squeezed out a random shot.

"Damn it!" Mendle shouted, enraged. He moved in close and pressed the magnum into Toor's back, whacking the pressure in and out to make sure he felt it. "I've got it on you, you cretin, drop it, drop it." He aimed in the air, fired a shot, then jammed the muzzle to Toor's back hard, and roared, "Drop it!"

Toor did. Aira let go of his arm and, somewhat feebly got up. She leaned over to pick up the gun, staggering a little off balance. Mendle was relieved only when she straightened up, stood there and brushed herself off. No red blotches. She hadn't been shot. He had thrown the aim off.

"Sorry about that. Not very original, but…" Aira said.

In the brief glance between Mendle and Aira, gratefulness traveled between them. Mendle let himself breath more freely. He began to feel nausea, but braced against it. It was the incomprehensible, he realized as he held the gun on Paul Toor.

Mendle's whole being was still cocked and ready to fire. "Who else knows about this?" he demanded, breathing hard.

"No one," Toor replied.

"We'll ask you once more. Who else, Toor?"

"If you kill me, you'll never know." He was chillingly calm, perfectly composed and even-keeled.

"It does not destroy a person to admit they were wrong. Look at it. The way to be right is to see where you're wrong," Aira said matter-of-factly, despite her highly pumped condition. She carefully stooped to pick up his eyeglasses.

"Yeah, that's right," Mendle agreed. It wasn't something he would have selected to say in this occasion, but he backed her up.

'Stop her, stop her, stop her.' The circuit played over and over in Toor's head; now he was becoming aware of it.

"Killing is not my style," Aira said, positioning herself in a firing stance, point-blank range. "You'd only show up somewhere else, worse off than you are now."

Paul Toor started to rise to his feet.

"Slowly," Mendle warned.

Toor complied, and stood up, still exuding pretended composure. Suddenly, he made a break.

"Stop!"

Clutching his side, where his throbbing pain was acting up for real, he ran toward daylight. Aira and Mendle bolted after him. Heaving himself against it, Toor pushed open one of the massive barn doors, and slipped through the opening.

As soon as Mendle and Aira reached the outside, they slowed down, amazed by what they saw. The barn was completely encircled by animals. Cows, bulls, sheep, pigs, horses, dogs, all of them united in a chain of determination to prevent Toor's escape.

Aira thought of Onx, her dear Onx, and she wondered if perhaps she was behind this summons of life. She had the impression of thought-touching with her, a glimpse of Onx's intelligent vivid eyes and alert little face. Aira eagerly scanned the rows of animals. She saw Sadie, and Bearwolf, and many whom she recognized. But no Onx, and, when she could not even sense her, the hope that had surged dropped to a hollow ache.

Paul Toor turned back to face them when it was clear he would not find an opening.

"This is what happens when you align with Life," Mendle said to him. "Life becomes your friend. It's a wonderful fabric."

Mendle leaned up against the side of the barn and watched Toor make one more attempt, trying to fake out the animals in the direction he was going to take. But they covered him steadfastly, holding the circle unbroken. A bull charged forward a few steps, intimidating Toor back away from the circle. Defeated, but still calculating, Toor stood in the hot dust and raised his hands in surrender.

Coolly, Mendle said, "You know, there is nothing more brilliant than when the heart surges to overcome that moment of fear. All manner of wonder awaits."

"You got that right," Aira said, thinking about her leap off the hayloft. "Take the leap, Loptoor," she coaxed him.

"You can try honesty," Mendle said. "You can always go back if you don't like it."

Aira ferreted Paul Toor with her vision for some moments. He stood, solidly, not even heeding the pain ripping at his side.

"There isn't anyone else!" Aira suddenly exclaimed. "Remember how we were wondering who was behind it, and my well-being was in danger of government seizure, and we imagined all manner of things?"

"Yeah," Mendle replied curiously.

"It's him. This weasel and Dr. Kaufkiff. That's all. An example of the few who make it look like everybody. Isn't that right, Loptoor?"

Paul Toor's eyes flickered to the left and right. Mendle wondered why Aira kept calling him Loptoor, puzzled how she might have seen the coincidence in Paul Toor's and the character's names. *This is one I'm going to solve.*

Some cows mooed restlessly. The animals were focused, each contributing their particular skill.

Aira handed Toor his glasses. "You need to see as much as possible," she told him, pervading him deeper. She scanned him for some moments, then announced to Mendle, "And now, he's even excluded Dr. Kaufkiff from his little schemes."

"She's right," Toor said, still composed but feeling something unraveling from the inside. He was confused by the lack of solid cover, by her ability just to read him. "I didn't want anyone to know. I wanted it for myself," he admitted.

"What did I ever do to you?" Aira asked him.

Toor began to crack up inside. He was slowly becoming sentient, and saw he had no real reasons which truly justified the destruction and harm he had caused. "It's just me," he admitted, his beady eyes still beady despite their opening wider when he saw Aira begin to glow.

She was good. Beautiful. He had no excuse to harm her.

Electricity began to snap and pop in the atmosphere surrounding Paul Toor's body. Aira knew what he was looking at. When she thought-touched Mendle, she saw he, too, was remembering.

"Aaowaah," whimpered Toor, suddenly crumpling to the dirt. He writhed in pain, clenching his fingers into the earth and clumps of hay. "I was going to do it again," he moaned. "Going to let Kaufkiff do the same thing to you. But I tried to stop it in Z Zone. I tried, I tried, I tried. But I failed. Failed..." he rolled over on his back, grasping his side. "Aaaaoowwhaaaagre."

The howling of his anguish was excruciating, even dampened as it was by the wide air of the fields. Aira stood still, understanding as he viewed his hell. She didn't avoid the confrontation of any of it, nor of him.

It slowly began to make sense to Mendle, why he had written the book, why he dreamed of Aira, why Loptoor, why many things. It was his own memory. "This is amazing," Mendle uttered, staring into his own revelations. *I've been being born onto Earth for ages. This is her first time.*

He had known her. He had known her before Time. It was he who had also been amnesiac. Before she materialized into the time stream, they had thought-touched across dimensions, she *had* been in actual danger while he was writing the book. He *had* felt her kissing him, looking for him.

He had known Z Zone. Nevertheless, his soul, his origins, his very self could never die. Torture, agony, regret, but souls could never die.

"Don't kill me. Don't. They all want to kill me," screamed Toor. "That's why I hated life. I feared what moved and thought for itself. You can't be free, or you'd kill me if you knew me! Aaaoooaaahh." What had always been underlying his synthetic calm was now evident. Then, as abruptly as the outbursts had begun, they subsided.

Aira glanced at Mendle, and she knew that he had remembered. They looked at each other as they hadn't done for eons—each knowing the other knew. Mendle's luminosity was Aira's joy and victory.

"My liver," said Toor as he sat up. "The pain is gone." He covered his face with his hands, and his ribs began to heave. But when the sound came out, it was laughter. Tense, highly-strung, nervous laughter that could have easily modulated into crying grief.

"It's where I was kicked in the side! I was unconscious, I tried to help you, right before I was sent through Z Zone!" he babbled. "I was sent on vacation, and was supposed to stop you at every turn, I, uh, this is, the pain is gone." He collapsed again into a sputtering release of laugh-crying.

"That's very good you looked at all that," Aira told him.

"Aira," gasped Toor, uncovering his face and looking up at her. He looked considerably less pressured. "Don't make me go back. Let me stay here. I can make it up. Let me make it up," he pleaded.

"You know I don't trust you," Aira said.

"I know. Keep me locked up until I'm well. I trust you, Flight. I know you can get us out of this. Lock me up. I'll do anything you say until I earn the privilege of trust. I don't know where I've been. It's like a dream, a nightmare. I'm confused," he whimpered. "I tried to help you once," he said. "I've been, I don't know where I've been. I feel like I'm just waking up, I..."

Mendle began laughing hysterically. "I'm not laughing at you," he shrieked. "It's me!" he howled, feeling more alive than he had in ages.

But even the idea of a very long time seemed strange now, as he saw that there was only now, that time was but the change of location of particles around now, and that he had never really gone anywhere nor been anywhere except right where he, himself, was.

As he looked at Paul Toor, Mendle saw how the man had taken on the personality of those who had crushed him. *Just like the bully on the block,* Mendle remembered one from his childhood, and how some of the kids the boy beat up began to talk like him.

There was hope, he knew, and he saw with his entirety how people were woven in a net of stupidities: some having taken on the personalities of those who crushed them, some ingrained with artificially enforced synthetic thoughts, others making dim decisions in an attempt to solve problems physical survival posed.

Mendle had often asked himself, "Could there be this much stupidity in the world?" The answer was *Yes,* and he found it funny to realize how much of that stupidity had been his, and to know again what he had always known.

The completely dead were few. The natural thrust of Life was to thrive, to heal, to grow. Hope surged that recovery of the civilization might be more rapid than anticipated, once those who were actively destroying it were isolated.

They're not obvious—only the symptoms are—but they can be located, Mendle resolved. As he viewed evil, he knew that it had no power of its own, only the capacity to upset and spread fear in the living. Evil was a parasite, Honesty, its enemy, Life its host. When viewed directly, evil could not stand in the light. It depended on fear and darkness. *Only Life has power.*

"Little bit of trouble here, eh?" It was A.J., making his way through the ring of animals.

"A.J.!" Mendle greeted him.

"This gentleman giving you trouble?" he asked, scrutinizing Toor.

"Little bit," Mendle replied.

A.J. looked Toor over. "Now, now," he said. "What do you want to be troublin' these good people for? If you can't be an asset to someone, then don't be a detriment. Just go and find somethin' else to do."

"I think we've reached an understanding," Aira said. "Trouble is, we don't know if we can trust him to keep it."

"Well, it's not how one picks up a fork that makes a gentleman, that's for sure," A.J. commented, noting the irony of how shiny Toor's shoes were.

"He knows it and we know it. He wants to stay, be locked up until he proves himself," Mendle said.

"I think I can arrange that," A.J. said. "Got a dungeon in the cellar." He turned to Toor. "You sure about this?" he asked him.

"I trust her," Toor replied.

"Okay. How far do we take this?" A.J. asked Aira.

"He may try to use this against us, press charges," Mendle said.

"I'll make a statement, I'll do anything," Toor pleaded. "Do you have some rope in the truck?"

"Chains," A.J. replied.

"Fix it so he doesn't run away," Aira ordered somberly. "We'll take him to the cellar, give him some food, and I'll be talking to him."

"Thank you, thank you," Toor said.

Mendle approached Aira, zinging with amazement. "I went through convincing myself I must have created you out of sheer thought...to thinking I was mad, deluded, commander of the universe....Now it's plain. It was before Time." *I know you.* Aira nodded. "Then I sensed you in your Home dimension." *Our dimension. It's you.*

I love you.

What took you so long?

Aira smiled. "Did you ever think of your name?" she asked.

Mendle looked blankly at her.

"J. Orion?" she prompted.

"J. Orion," he repeated. "J. Orion. J...." It hit him. "Jorian."

"Another coincidence," Aira smiled.

"You knew?"

"Yes." When Mendle was about to comment she defended, "Well, you knew about me, too..."

A.J. walked by. Mendle was in a state of exhilaration as he followed him to the truck.

"You know, I thought there was someone following me when I went on that last mail run," he told the farmer as he moved to help him get some things from the truck. "In fact, at one point, it was around the postal place in Lafayette, I thought I saw him, but told myself it couldn't be."

His words brought an ironical smile to Aira's lips. "Sounds familiar," she murmured, keeping watch on Paul Toor, the .357 and .380 both pointed at him. "It can't be," she repeated the most oft-used phrase about evil, remembering that was one of the ways she had first gotten into this mess.

"Oh yeah. I'm the more wise to that one now," A.J. was telling Mendle. "Besides, you know that even science doesn't talk about possibilities, but probabilities. Nothing is impossible."

"That's right," Mendle said.

"You know it," A.J. reaffirmed. "People like Ross Perot know about benevolent wisdom. You got to be a loving tyrant if you want to survive in this world," he said. "You got to stay awake, look around, see what's in front of you. Looks can be deceivin' now, but you got to know what to look for." He stopped, lifted his hand to the back of his neck, and told Mendle, "Ya know, I could a jus' sworn you was glowin'," then went about finishing espousing views.

The two men were just reapproaching Aira and Toor when, in the middle of looking grateful at being able to stay, Paul Toor suddenly screamed, "No! No! Aira, help me. They're taking me back."

Suddenly, he fizzled in a flash of light. He literally exploded into a fluorescent light puff that smelled acrid, somewhat like phosphorous. Within moments, there was nothing but a pile of dust where he had been.

"Reckon that," A.J. marveled, a little subdued by what he'd just seen. "I've read about it but I'll be darned if I ever thought I'd see it." Mendle looked at him. "Spontaneous combustion," he drawled.

Aira had quickly gone to her knees. The air was still and quiet as they all stared at the spot where Toor had just had been.

They barely heard her whisper, "I forgive you." Then Aira slowly looked up, as if suddenly coming back from somewhere else. She stood up. To questioning looks, she explained, "Just making sure I booted someone out of the way of danger."

The animals began to meander on about their daily living. Just like that. And Life continued.

"You know, it'd be a shame if y'all didn't think about the swimmin' hole," A.J. said, throwing his jacket in the front seat of the truck. "Look at that beautiful sky." When he looked up and saw Mendle was just standing there, he waited.

"About the preacher, A.J.," Mendle began. "I think we already are. We'd like to make it a social ceremony."

"Local custom," A.J. said affectionately. The farmer's eyes actually twinkled. "Get in," he said, hopping into the truck and slamming his door. "You'll like this man, he means well."

As they drove off toward the farmhouse, Aira looked back at the barn. Now she knew the mechanics of evil. Even though she could not grasp it because it made no sense, she felt she could recognize it. Partly by that very fact: it made no sense. Yet it wasn't a powerful, snarling monster, though it had to be conquered. It was the dense, impotent parasite of good.

It had taken the parson only an hour to get there. By the white porch swing, A.J. stood, ready to play one of his favorite records on an old phonograph system. Under the umbrella of the fragrantly blooming lilac tree, Mendle and Aira pledged love and fidelity, and were pronounced man and wife.

A.J. ceremoniously set down the needle on the phonograph, and the music *As Time Goes By* played.

As Mendle and Aira walked off toward the swimming hole, they heard A.J. thanking the preacher. In his manner which layered truth in with levity, he was telling the man, "Nice to see young people loving each other, isn't it? They say in these parts, when two people love each other, they pledge fidelity and create family units, see there."

"You getting enough nutrition?" the preacher asked him.

"Oh, yeah, plenty, thank you."

"You know, A.J. if someone told me you died, I wouldn't believe it."

"Thank you Reverend. You better not."
The sound of the men laughing tapered into the distance.

The sun unfurled orange and pink banners across the sky, and soon night fell.

The waters of the swimming hole were very warm, still sated with the day's heat. A full moon cast its blue-silver on the pond, sheerly veiling treetops and fields with its shimmer. Fireflies softly pulsated their glows into the dark.

All was quiet within Mendle, and he felt a vast stillness…a calm which he knew to be himself. He reaffirmed his vows to Truth, knowing it would never harm him.

Humanity became his humanity, and admiration filled him to think of the battle-scarred lot. Individuals were special, trying valiantly to survive. As a father, he would know what to protect and foster in his children —the values of their ancestry, their heritage, of who they truly were.

Feeling Aira's back in the water slide underneath his palms and fingertips, Mendle held her body close to his.

If I were a forest, "If I were a forest," she whispered to him, *you would greet me as the rain, leaving no foliage untouched, nor moss unmisted by your dewy kiss. You would become the breeze, to fill me with your love's whisperings,* "you would greet me as the rain, leaving no foliage untouched, nor moss unmisted by your dewy kiss. You would become the breeze, to fill me with your love's whisperings."

The life of another is as important as one's own, Mendle thought. "If you were the sky," he murmured to Aira, *I would unfurl myself in you, as a rainbow…of colors yet unseen. I would become oceans of stars in your night,* "I would unfurl myself in you, as a rainbow…of colors yet unseen. I would become oceans of stars in your night."

Between kisses, Aira told him, "You see? You were right all along."

"Right. The details always come later."

"Jorian, by any other name, is as sweet…" Aira said.

"It was right there in front of me all the time," Mendle said.

"Can you finish the book now?"

He thought about it, "I may do it under a pen name," he said. "Or give it to another writer."

"I had an idea for tomorrow's broadcast," Aira said enthusiastically.

"What?"

"Create your life."

Mendle loved it. He loved her. He loved life.

Knowing all he had been through, Aira witnessed his total joys and his sufferings as she loved him.

"I would effuse in you as sunset and sunrise, to blend in you the rose and golden Eden of my love," she whispered.

"I love you many times, forever…" he told her.

Times forever… "Times forever…"

Times forever. "Times forever."

And so, body and soul, Aira and Mendle made love. They had always enjoyed Beauty together. Its creation began between them, to delight one another. They had everything within themselves and in each other.

It was Love they worshipped, the service of Life. They knew that acts of creation were born of it. It was they, after all, who *daoed* Beauty, and all they saw.

The planet grew smaller and smaller, until it could have been the iris in an eye. Perhaps smaller still…a speck of magic, something they dreamed in the very act of Life: Love.

It was a perfect summer night.
So good, it was true.

chapter 49 - 60

All great things come of love's labor. They are first conceived; then, tenderly and ruthlessly, the birth is seen to. Then they exist.

The blood is the serum, the essence of the source. The sweat is a result of exertion. The strive and strain against obstacles. The pull and tug of commanding the counter-efforts of given elements in a universe of energy and force, made crazy by the resignation of creators.

It had been simpler for Mendle and Aira once before Time…when creations had not been abandoned for trillenia. Now, in a world where creators denied their own makings, where they had succumbed to being the effect instead of cause, where they had dubbed the environ God, there were agreements and the subsequent substance of ages to be dealt with.

The year became years, which became months, which became weeks, then days as the given change of particle location continued and perimetered Time.

And they persisted in their dream, because they knew what they knew. It was this, and only this, that gave them strength.

Despite all that contradicted them, including their own inner wounds and fear which threw doubt and negation at them, they endured, relentlessly protecting and forwarding their thought into existence.

And so, the idea traveled: The world could sing.

There were many things in existence which screamed it could never be. But the heart surges in response to things it knows are true. It surges to embrace them, without repulsion, and, in doing so, becomes linked with the vastness that is its true nature.

The word had spread and there was much communication between people.

And the day came.

When the hours passed into the hour, and it became minutes, there was a quietude which began to seep through the globe. It was night in some parts, day in others, Spring in some parts, Fall in others, and, in the final minutes of the designated time, uncertainty and fear reared their heads.

Then it began.

Wherever they were, whatever they were doing, people stepped onto the streets, into their yards, onto the decks of their boat, stood in the aisles of their planes, trains, buses, on sidewalks, in fields, buildings.

Some were uncertain, hesitant, and feared they would be the only ones.

But it did not matter, for it was their song, in their hearts, and they knew it was one that must be sung. It was this, and only this, that gave them their strength.

Buildings around the world began to empty into the streets. People looked around, and they saw they were not alone.

As the moment approached in Kentucky, Mendle and Aira walked to the crest of a hill, and soon, they saw A.J.'s red pickup making dust across a field.

When he stopped at the bottom of the hill, they saw he was not alone. He glanced at his watch, as he got out of the truck, and waved to them, then helped a woman out of the front seat. Someone else jumped out of the back of the pickup, a woman with red hair, and the three began climbing the hill.

A.J. called out to Mendle and Aira midst the final steps of ascent toward them. "This is Beth, the gal from the store I been tellin' you about."

She looked at him with a depth of certain devotion, a quiet sunniness, like the glows that collect in tranquil woodland pools. The woman was younger than A.J., her body was that is, about half the age of his. She was radiant with patience, as though she had seen things beyond her years.

"Just like my Becky used to," he had described the way she looked at him. "Sometimes when I look at her, it's that same comfort, like I've known her all my life," he mused to Aira and Mendle once, then shrugged, saying something he often said, "Well, I guess there's more to life than meets the eye." With that, he'd twinkle at them with his wily smile.

As they stood atop of the hill, when Mendle and Aira greeted the woman, they recognized what A.J. had described. Her face was strong and kind. And, recognizing what was looking at her through those eyes —*those kind eyes*—Aira remembered. Becky had died some near thirty years ago. This woman was about that age; the life-being had been born about that long ago. Maybe just after Becky "died"? Aira smiled to herself. As Mendle would say, the details always come later.

When Aira turned her focus on the redhead, A.J. made the introduction. "This is Ona," Aira heard as she stared into those greenest of
eyes, so alert and intelligent. "We were headin' back from the store, she
was hitchhikin'. Said she knew about the singin' and had to get here."

Tears overbrimmed in Aira's eyes.

"Well, I'll be," A.J. said as he watched them embrace.

"Love is a stronger cohesive than agreement," Mendle narrated to
A.J. Perhaps it was the three-inch fiery nails, or her blouse's blue-green
turquoise which had a peculiar resemblance to dragon scales that tipped
him off.

"Thought it was about time I became more responsible," Ona murmured to Aira. The woman's voice was a little rough, just how Aira imagined Onx's would be if she could talk. "I thought it was about time, you
know? To speak up," she said, her voice sonorous with emotion that
throbbed against the boundary of words.

"Ona? Ona, is it?"

Ona nodded a little shyly. Her eyes began to well up.

"You're beautiful," Aira told her, noting the marine green eyes, se-
quined blouse, and the graceful nails threatening to be claws. When Aira
looked up from admiring her manifestation, she swore she saw flickers of
pleasure come out of Ona's nose.

"Nice to meet you," Aira played along the meeting-in-Time game.

"We'll go on," Ona said, with fiery determination.

"You know how it is with some people, you just feel like you've known
them forever?" Mendle commented.

A.J. knew exactly what he meant and squeezed Beth's hand.

Aira closed her eyes in gratitude for Life. Her smile was a prayer, and
tears flowed down her cheeks. As small and frail and mortal as she found
herself, all limits gave way to a vastness her body could not begin to
contain.

Standing on the hillside, they all held hands.

Ten.

Nine.

Eight.

Seven.

Six.

Five.

Four.

Three.

Two.

One.

A tone rose to the heavens. Its wings were the power of the human voice. Its heartbeat, the will of the human spirit.

The voice came from individuals, each and every one unique. It began in a soul, and passed the throat to turn into sound.

The sound of some was timid, the sound of some was small. Yet each sound vibrated the air, and was essential. For the tone would not have been the same had it lacked any of them.

As the tone grew, so did the power of each voice.

Leaders in all realms and activities of life knew that the power they had come to hold existed because they were responsible to serve the many, thus power was a position of service. And those who had entrusted their leaders knew it was for a purpose, and the purpose should be maintained.

Responsibility became a matter of preference, a matter of how much one wanted to cause and be responsible for, and the sphere could encompass their own body, their family, their associates, the animal kingdom and plant life…and continue past all of humanity, into the influence over molecules and particles, and even beyond the material universe.

But it was a matter of choice.

Slavery was only self-assigned. And the conflict of master and slave vanished and became, instead, a harmony of interaction and mutual dependency…For the masters were servants, and the servants masters of their own chosen realms.

Each and every voice was vital.

In all the planet, there were but a handful who could not sing. And they feared the glow because they were in terror of being killed by anything that moved. But as Life became free, its power was not of death.

And so the tone rose, and swelled, because many had heard the rumor that suffering did not have to be eternal, and they considered the idea that they were good.

The sound issued.

And, what had begun as a quavering human voice…became divine.

The tone lingered. It was eerie and ethereal. It was huge. It became an immense exhalation into the planet's atmosphere…a breath…an exhalation of life.

Then the song began.

Some had learned the words, others read them from a page, and, though the sound-symbols were different from each tongue, the melody was the same.

The people knew what had made them human. It was not their short-comings, but their hearts.

> We have known suffering,
> But dare to wonder why.
> A breath of light expands,
> and hearts flourish to fly.
>
> Truth can never die,
> for it is Life itself,
> and Life is the victor,
> the soul the only wealth.
>
> So we release our Beauty
> and shine it to the light,
> to shed all forms of slavery
> As gods we now take flight.

There was a sigh in the vastness.

EPILOGUE

Aira and Mendle send you their love from the hills of Kentucky. Even though the location may have been changed, for reasons I am sure you understand, they have promised to keep me informed of their adventures in progress so that we can soon take you from *Flight* to *Beyond The Speed of Time*.

In writing the final chapter, I took the liberty of having the world sing. Aira and Mendle said that, since every reality begins with an idea, this was fine.

As a result, I've received some questions about it affecting authenticity. I've also received a flurry of protest (from just a few, mind you) regarding this being an utter impossibility, considering all the bad news (every night on TV), and in view of reality.

I did consult with Aira about this. Her response was this. She asked me to tell them, "Sorry. I just couldn't agree."

Perhaps you will be surprised at just how powerful you are, and what a difference you can make.

Dear makers of reality, we look forward to singing with you.

—The Author

GLOSSARY

aberree – one who wanders from his inherent nature; in the Supreme Tribunal jurisdiction, aberees are those who insist on being matter and only recipients of effect, and have forfeited their creative natures.

Archaic Condition Prevention – a series of training regimen that enabled life-beings to find and apply general axioms of truth to in situations never before encountered. The truer the axiom, the more problems it solved and the greater the sphere of its application. Such ability prevented decaying conditions resulting from incorrectly applied solutions in new universes, thus preventing the basic mechanic of how evil came about and began contaminating universes.

ash-aureate – substance of spaceships, grey in color with gold filaments; does not bind molecularly with surrounding atoms. Maintains blueprint concept (see definition) during fission-regroup process.

Blueprint Concept – the commanding idea around which matter and form aligns. It can be actively postulated and generated by thought, or made to mechanically persist.

concept-flow – to project the essence of a thought to another thought-being, bypassing the need for sound; instantaneous communication as it bypasses distance.

congruate (con'-groo-ate) *verb* – to make congruent, to inter-relate events and data so the entirety makes sense.

Conquest, The – A period when parasitical forces of evil entangled life of the Galactron sector and overruled its intelligence, thus perpetrating the Dark Regime, a period which lasted 4 spirals.

cosmic smile – a coincidence seeming miraculous, evidence of alignment and allegiance with Life.

contour-image – a theory developed by psychiatrist Alfred Kaufkiff which is meaningless and has never helped anyone; founded in his attempt to classify wishful thinking as a sickness.

dao – to bestow with love or a sense of well-being by surrounding safety that promotes unique and natural being. To love so much it gives life.

Dark Regime – An era in which life-beings were trapped by a race that considered it could not create; souls were captured and enslaved, used as commodities.

E-motion – wavelengths that have frequencies which can be experienced and read, and by which the benefit or detriment of a situation can be gauged; also entertaining as sensation. E-motion can be artificial or can be genuine judgement-response.

eternal nature principle – there is no birth or death with thought and life; only time and matter and energy have form, only form has beginning and end.

Euphorisiac – liquid or electronic wavelength which can be ingested or topically received by a life-form; vibrates a form's blueprint-system, the stimulation simulating the frequency of euphoria.

fission-regroup process – spaceship travel, technical term; a mode of travel in which molecular structure is disintegrated (fission) then reintegrated (regroup) along a designated vector-path, or to charted space-time. Faster than propelling mass through space and time.

form senses – biological relay points that read environment.

fractors – a time measurement, miniscule increment; on earth, a fractor is less than a millisecond.

Identity Program Booth – cubicles in Z Zone where thought-beings can acquire personalities and identities, including gender, planet, race, role, likes, dislikes, to let these do the walking while they snooze. Random Scramble is available for those who do not even care to choose.

jeté – a leap, a dance move.

Lauryad – a type 4X shuttle craft equipped with communications instruments and arts which travels by manipulating space fabric.

Liberverus Loriad – a travel "handle" of Aira Flight's in the Lauryad; literally: truth-freedom transport.

linking nuclei – part of the procedure of fission-regroup; vectors are calibrated in a direction or charted location, then a "trade-off" of electron, positron, and neutrons is done around adjacent nuclei molecularly shifting masses from place to place.

life-being – a thought-being who has engaged in a set of shared circumstances (i.e. a universe) with other thought-beings for inter-change of creation and communication.

life-form – physical manifestation

M/D-barkation panels – Space station entry ports for extended stay periods where craft needs housing; arrival courtesy platform with hangar service; in Z Zone, design used to trap crafts for occupant extraction.

micro-buzz – an agitation of quanta, most closely approximating thought's non-wavelength; the fine and nearly imperceptible motion of micro-buzz makes it viscous.

moolah – money, a form of currency used and sometimes worshipped on earth.

morathene – substance used for flooring made of moroleum, a hard surface which also absorbs shock, easy maintenance for hygiene and ultra-gloss aesthetics.

Normal-mode relocation – spaceship travel, technical term; molecular intactness and propulsion through space and time

Particlization Device – An instrument which construes the negative atomic image of an object, or of a designated space and all masses contained within it, via wavelengths. The device reads negatives, designs negative, or reproduces negatives, then, when activated, particles adhere to it and it creates a molecular "positive", or object. The negative is called Blueprint Concept. All objects are the positive image or manifestation of their blueprint concept.

poly-view – many views; ability to take, see, reconstruct, understand, or track more than one point of view. When used to describe "tracking", it means the ability to project memories in holographic accuracy, state-of the-art projection, not limited to one point of view.

prevedent – fore-sightful, *pre*-before, *vedere*-to see

Quanta – a category of sub-atomic phenomena, always somehow both, a particle and a wave.

Random Scramble – (see Identity Program Booth)

Raze – an x-ray-type scanning device which reads thought and life presence through matter, counting life-beings as well as material forms.

Reality Screen – projected configurations that emanate misleading environmental conditions.

sensor-mate – a companion with exceptional skills in sensing danger and changes in the environment.

spiral – time units

Sound accelerator – device which speeds sound waves up into corresponding light displays, used primarily for entertainment.

sound-symbols – noises with agreed-upon meanings, used to relay concepts; used instead of or with thought-reach.

space-time – a four-dimensional continuum within which any event may be precisely located; consists of three spatial coordinates and one coordinate of time.

Supreme Tribunal – Sonrial, Rilia, Tolara, Rheson, Flozal, Juristac, Maytra, Bilzia, Aira; nine members each with their own Home dimension, united in the purpose of bringing beauty and communication among universes and restoring knowledge and aesthetics to sectors entrapped by the Dark Regime.

talk-show – a forum popular on earth in the late twentieth century in which aberrant or sensationalistic social conditions are platformed and discussions conducted under the supervision of a "host."

The Course – Tribunals united purpose for Life to gain experience: maintaining freedom of individuals as experience is gained, without violating the principles and nature of Life.

thought-being – soul perceiving and, knowingly or not, creating life.

thought-reach – to touch with thought; done by decision; to directly relay concept without use of symbols.

Tracked, Tracking – running memory facsimile strips of experiences and adventures, and projecting them so they are visible to others; done primarily for entertainment.

Truth Bearers – Those dedicated to freeing thought-beings with knowledge and beauty kindred to their true natures. Some were members of various Tribunals under the Supreme Tribunal, others were not members but aligned in desire for safe and restored life. Missions included delivering arts and cultures of various civilizations and Home dimensions to various zones.

22-18-A – twenty-two, eighteen A; one of Aira's favorite music selections in the Lauryad; winds and movements of the spheres with sound of stars, and imported foreign instruments.

Understanding Catalyst – high ability possesed by vast thought-beings, to mediate sides by ability to see the right of varied points of view.

vector-path – a straight line postulated relative to surrounding atomic structure.

verse-talk – speaking in rhyme.

vortex – a spinning condition.

Z Zone – sleep zone; the zone entered to avoid pain and regret; when done voluntarily, an alternative to understanding; a zone enforced on thought-beings posing a threat; storage of souls.

Speed of Time - Definitions

Force — Strength, impetus, intensity of effect.
Physics: an impetus influence which produces or tends to produce motion or change of motion.
Binding power — as of agreement

Velocity —
Physics -
a Time rate of change of displacement.
Mech.
1. a Time rate of change of position.
2. a rate of motion in which direction as well as speed is considered.

Resultant —
① resulting from combination of 2 or more agents.
a force, velocity, etc. equal in result or effect to 2 or more such forces, velocities./
② That which results

Vector

XA, XB Vectors
XP, Resultant

Math
a complex quantity possessing BoTh magnitude and direction and represented by any of a system of equal + parallell (and similarly directed) line segments.

Biology an insect or other organism transmitting germs or other agents of disease.

The SPEED OF TIME ①

Time: is The change of location of particles in space. Masses moving (changing location) in space.

To find The speed of Time

force - an influence which causes motion. Does a force have to do with it.

The uniform equation which measures The rate of change for The physical universe.

Or is force a resultant of 2 or more masses with space Between Them, Therefore energy or flow is possible.

or is Time a Resultant?

Speed of Time

(2)

what is The **constant** ?

velocity = space ÷ time ?

for any equation, There is a constant, even if
hypothetical:

$\frac{Time}{}$ = ▬▬

Vector

Velocity =

mass

(of masses changing location)

Vectors change –
vector **field** remains The same –
encompasses physical univ. including Time.

is The vector field The constant?

matter = condensed motion of particles.
so is it condensed Time?

VANNA BONTA writes for page and screen. Her credits encompass more than fifty published articles, three poetry collections, short fiction, journalism, and screenplays, including a story for television's *Star Trek: The Next Generation*. Since her first published poetry book at age eleven, her work has been translated into Japanese and Italian. Her poetry has won international acclaim, including a gold medal from the city of Florence, Italy, and also appears in *The American Poetry Association Anthology* in libraries at Yale, Harvard, Oxford, Cambridge, Le Sorbonne and Tokyo Universities. Two of her songs won awards in the Billboard Song Competition and the American Song Festival. As an actress, she has made several film and television appearances, including a cameo as Zed's Queen in *The Beastmaster*, and voice-overs for many films, among them Disney's *Beauty and the Beast*, *Hocus Pocus*, and *The War*. She was recently directed by Mel Brooks in *The Visitors*. Vanna Bonta is currently residing on planet Earth.

Ordering Information

☎ **Telephone orders:** Call Toll Free   1-800-879-4214.
Have your Amex, Discover, Visa, or MasterCard ready

✉ **Postal Orders:**   BookCrafters Distribution
615 E. Industrial Dr.
Chelsea, Michigan 48118-0370 USA
Check or M.O. payable to: BookCrafters Distribution Center

FLIGHT by Vanna Bonta
Hardcover $23.95
ISBN 0-912339-10-1

Sales Tax: Please add 8.25% for books shipped to California address
Shipping & Handling: $3.95

Inquiries and information:
MERIDIAN HOUSE
6755 Mira Mesa Blvd.
Dept. 123-224
San Diego, CA 92121-4311